The Wrong Sister

FIONA PALMER

The Wrong Sister

hachette
AUSTRALIA

Published in Australia and New Zealand in 2022
by Hachette Australia
(an imprint of Hachette Australia Pty Limited)
Gadigal Country, Level 17, 207 Kent Street, Sydney, NSW 2000
www.hachette.com.au

Hachette Australia acknowledges and pays our respects to the past, present and future Traditional Owners and Custodians of Country throughout Australia and recognises the continuation of cultural, spiritual and educational practices of Aboriginal and Torres Strait Islander peoples. Our head office is located on the lands of the Gadigal people of the Eora Nation.

A catalogue record for this book is available from the National Library of Australia

ISBN: 978 0 7336 4622 5 (paperback)

Cover design by Christabella Designs
Cover photographs courtesy of Trevillion and Alamy
Author photo courtesy of Craig Peihopa
Typeset in 12/18 pt Sabon LT Pro by Bookhouse, Sydney
Printed and bound in Australia by McPherson's Printing Group

The paper this book is printed on is certified against the Forest Stewardship Council® Standards. McPherson's Printing Group holds FSC® chain of custody certification SA-COC-005379. FSC® promotes environmentally responsible, socially beneficial and economically viable management of the world's forests.

To friends, new and old, from all walks of life. Some we call family, some we see only once in a blue moon. But forever in our hearts.

Debbie Dowden, *one amazing lady.* **Fiona Hall,** *avid reader, and speedway geek (just like me!)*
My mum, Sue, *simply the best.* **Jacinta Holmes,** *my awesome talented friend.*
Julene Cronin *(my sister from another mother).*

1

Ellen

ELLEN SUTTON SQUINTED UP AT THE CRYSTAL-CLEAR SKY, the sun shooting shards of light like a polished chandelier. Above, the thrum of Ashley's small aeroplane echoed across the empty horizon but she struggled to spot it in the endless pale blue. She craned her head out the open window of the little red bull buggy just as she hit a crab hole, smacking her skull into the doorframe. 'Bastard,' she grunted through gritted teeth, wishing she could rub her head, but both hands were needed on the steering wheel. It would have been worse if her messy blonde bun hadn't acted as padding.

A twiggy shrub appeared, one too big to drive over. Ellen gave a split-second jerk on the wheel and then another as she cut a path through the scrub like a pinball on the Indiana Jones machine she used to play at the Bowling Arcade as a kid. She never could beat her older brother's score. A flash hit her eyes, light reflecting off metal as Ashley flew low over the treetops hunting for more beasts to her right. The loud rumble of his plane gave her goosebumps. She wondered what it would be like to swoop low looking for cattle. Was it just work for Ashley or was it exhilarating? Ellen needed excitement and hard work to keep her mind from wandering down the dark path she'd been trying to avoid. *Unsuccessfully.* At least the flies kept her busy. With a wave she shooed the buzzing mass gathering at the corners of her mouth, chasing moisture in the bone-dry air.

It wasn't the gazillion flies or the intense heat. It wasn't the red dirt, crimson as if blood had soaked the soil, nor was it the sparse bushes – the only visible green until you came upon a small pocket of grass where the cattle liked to graze. It wasn't any of these things that made her feel so far from home.

It was the isolation. She had gone from Albany – crammed full of retirees and tourists – to this mammoth cattle station just out from Mount Magnet in Western Australia, with less people than she could count on both hands. And yet when she'd left Albany, she'd felt alone, trapped in her own internal prison. Her family and friends were pushing in the walls on her cell with each passing day, not that they realised nor understood. Even though the isolation made Albany feel like a world away, it was that same isolation which felt like freedom.

Escaping to Challa Station felt like a move to Mars. Disconnection was what she'd been seeking, and she'd certainly found it. About 600 kilometres north-east of Perth and 206,000 hectares in total size, Challa was truly remote. And yet Ellen wasn't alone here. Especially with the mustering crew Ashley and Debbie had on now, plus there were over a thousand head of Santa Gertrudis-Droughtmaster cattle, with hides the colour of burnt caramel and cute faces she just wanted to smoosh with kisses. More so the gorgeous calves, so full of life and antics. They reminded her of her own cow, Carla, the most awesome pet a kid could have, and seeing these guys made her heart ache for a much simpler time in her life.

And just when she felt like she was starting to find some sort of calm and peace to work through her feelings, this impending family trip to Karijini was about to ruin it all. *Why couldn't they just all stay in Albany?*

'I need you to get here as quick as you can,' Ashley radioed. 'There's a mob of about twenty here. Watch the plane . . . under my left wing . . . right now.'

Like a big-eared Santa Gertrudis flicking away flies, Ellen tried hard to shake away her thoughts and planted her foot, her adrenaline notching up as she felt more like a rally driver than a cow herder. Branches slapped the old Suzuki, its body groaning as it rolled and twisted over dormant water courses, the little engine singing its heart out. Thank God her dad had taught her how to four-wheel drive growing up. She clenched her jaw, grinding her teeth together so she didn't accidentally bite her tongue with all the jolting.

'El, Gazza, I need you over here now,' called Ashley.

'On my way, boss,' she muttered, driving as fast as she possibly dared through the minefield that was station country. A blur of white appeared on her right; Scott was flogging along in his tiny bull buggy heading for the same location. The rest of the crew were dotted about, managing mobs in other places.

Ahead the ground unexpectedly vanished. Ellen jammed on the brakes just as her front wheels tipped over the edge of the sharp embankment of a dry riverbed. Like a pen seesawing on the edge of a desk, she felt the buggy rock precariously.

Bloody hell, she was driving like she belonged in a *Fast and Furious* movie. Shoving it into reverse, she made ochre plumes as the wheels spun sending her back to safe flat land.

That was a lucky save.

She rested her head on the steering wheel and sucked in deep hot breaths, but she was still smiling. Adrenaline was as good as any drug.

She glanced around, hoping no one had witnessed her near demise. Lord knew she didn't need to rack up any more points today, especially after Joel caught her bogged in some sand earlier. That probably got her ten points.

Ellen navigated a better route over the riverbed, selecting a less extreme decline, and that's when she spotted old Gazza in the light blue buggy, its nose speared into the bottom of the bed like an old fence post.

Snatching up the radio, she gave him a call. 'You alright, Gazza?' Her nursing instinct kicked in, imagining the trauma he may have sustained and the steps she'd take to help him.

'Yeah, I'm fine, El. I managed to stop me head from smacking the steering wheel.' A deep dry laugh followed. 'Damn, I was hoping no one would see me.'

'That looks like fifty points coming your way,' she teased. 'Maybe more if you need help getting out.'

Ellen sat idling a hundred metres away, torn between helping Gaz and getting to the cattle. She liked ol' Gazza. She liked the whole crew. Especially because they didn't dig into her past; most kept to themselves and just shared a joke every now and then.

'I'm coming, Gazza, hold tight,' the radio blared.

Scott's white rocket shot right across her path, kicking up dust like a passing willy willy, causing her to jump.

'I've got a tow strap. El, you head on to the cattle,' Scott added.

'Rogie,' she replied before putting the buggy into gear and heading to where Ashley had last indicated with his wing tip.

'Get some photos, Scott – we need proof for tonight,' Ellen called.

The reward for getting the most points for the day was a lovely satin pink nightie to be worn the next day by the winner ... or in this case the biggest loser. Yesterday it was Joel who collected the most by forgetting to take his radio – thirty points; cutting off a mob – ten points and then his tyre rolling past his buggy while he was driving along – forty points. Today Joel had the pink nightie wrapped around his Akubra hat. It didn't have to literally be worn, just on you at all times. Getting bogged today would have guaranteed her points, but Gazza having to be pulled out of his vertical descent, well, that might just be enough to take the pink nightie.

Three hours later, she'd slowed from the previous fast and furious adrenaline to meander behind a group of cattle. Thinking time. It was the hardest part of mustering for Ellen. Sure, the scenery was nice, cows' butts excepted, but the sluggish crawl seemed to highlight the heat, flies *and* the voices in her head.

Voices of her sister, her brother, their partners, her parents, and worst of all, herself. It was almost laughable that she'd come all this way to escape them only to find out that it was herself she needed to escape. If only that was possible.

The rumble of the buggy and the moos of the cattle had a rhythmic warmth that lured her mind into the murky history she was trying to forget and the imminent future that goosepimpled her skin, even in this heat. It made her feel stuck in this moment, afraid to look back and too scared to go forward. How was she supposed to sort her life out in limbo? She couldn't hide from her family forever, as much as that seemed like the easiest option.

She'd never run from anything in her life before. Oh, there were times she'd wanted to, but she'd stuck it out like a true steadfast Sutton. She'd been accused of spreading herself too thin and being obsessed with making things the very best they could be (just ask her sister). Carrie liked to call it 'analism' – perfectionism at its worst. What was wrong with wanting to do something to the best of your abilities? So, she may have rearranged her bedroom countless times until she had it just right, but once she did, it had stayed that way.

'You look deep in thought, El?'

The voice had come from the radio, but she glanced around, realising the buggies had grouped closer together as a few mobs of cattle had joined up and were keeping a now bigger herd contained as they moved them to the designated collection point. Nearby, a small Suzuki idled along, a handsome silver fox smiling at her. His tanned face was like a map of the ground with worn creases and marks, the years having taken their toll, and yet he was nonetheless stunning. Mick was twelve years her senior, not that it was an issue when a man looked that good. And he had kept her warm on more than one occasion (like the nights weren't hot enough already) but they both knew what this was. He was here until mustering was over, and Ellen . . . well, she was selfishly using him to forget.

Her heart may as well be the red sand beneath the hundreds of hooves, trampled to dust. It felt like there was nothing left of it; the fact it still kept her alive was almost a miracle.

'You been thinking about me?' Mick yelled out as he drove closer, one eye still on the cattle out front.

'Always, Mick,' she replied with a smile. Ellen played his game – after all, Mick was the Panadol for her headache. In those moments with him, her mind was silent. And silence was golden.

They stopped their buggies, giving the cattle room to move along. Mick waited until she glanced at him before pointing his finger at her, then to himself and to his watch with a suggestive wink.

Ellen nodded her reply. One last roll in the hay tonight before she left. *Why not?* After all, she was a single 28-year-old with no ties, no commitments . . . *no life*!

It's funny the change time can make. A year ago, Ellen's life looked much different. Cool days, hospital shifts, coffee down the main street and family catch-ups; the hope of an exciting future. Now it was heat, flies, working herself to distraction, taking every day, every minute and every step as it came. Uncertainty was the new normal.

Coloured blurs of more buggies appeared around her as they collected together like flies over a dead carcass, directing the cattle into the yards set up to hold them.

Time moved quicker from here, the meandering thoughts pushed aside as they penned and drafted the cattle before

loading them onto the nearby truck. By this time Ashley had
landed his plane on the nearby strip and joined them.

A few jokes were thrown about as they worked, but they
kept the main banter for the shed after they were done. The
sooner they were out of the flies, heat and dust, the better.

The first beer to hit the throat was like heavy rains after a
drought, pooling into scorched earth. Ellen had gained quite
a taste for beer since coming to work on the station. No gin
and tonic or wine, just a crisp cold beer earned through sweat,
which made it all the more sweeter.

'I'm not looking forward to this,' said Gazza, cracking open
his beer and dropping down onto one of the many plastic chairs
in a wonky circle in the workshop.

'Well, I for one, am super glad you took a nosedive, Gaz.'

His bushy possum-tail eyebrows shot up. 'You're mean, El!'

'Haha, for good reason, Gaz.' Joel sat in the chair beside
her, causing it to squeak. 'About an hour before your circus
act, El got bogged. I thought the nightie would be hers for
sure, until you didn't watch where you were going.'

Gazza dropped his head. 'Ah shit. Glad I could help, El,'
he said unenthusiastically. 'I can't believe you've managed to
miss out on the pink slip all mustering. Damn.'

'El flies under the radar,' said Mick with a grin. He plucked
his trucker hat off, wiped his brow with his sleeve and tucked
his hat back on his head before taking a seat.

El sat quietly, a smile tugging at her lips as she listened to
their banter.

'Surely she has to beat mine.' Gazza's deep rumble, like it
was coming from the bottom of a gravel pit, boomed around

the shed. 'Getting bogged, rookie mistake.' His rotund belly shook with another round of laughter.

'No, I got out by myself,' El protested proudly.

Joel laughed. 'She was rocking the buggy like crazy. Funniest thing I've ever seen.'

Ashley was near the whiteboard tallying up points as the crew called them out. 'Paul, you get ten points for upsetting the cook. Pulling the cucumber out of the salad and throwing it away is wasteful.'

'It's spewcumber,' he grumbled. 'Not fit for human consumption.'

El chuckled. It wasn't often she could laugh for real these days.

They continued to banter back and forth, mentioning more points to allocate, taking digs at each other and discussing the breakdowns.

Feet aching, she crossed her legs. The heavy, steel-capped boots, red with dust and wafting of cow poo, were nothing like her hospital trainers. Ellen didn't know if she could go back to nursing just yet. Hopefully the saying was true and time healed all wounds. Seemed a funny sentiment for a nurse – shouldn't she be the one healing the wounds?

'El?'

'Huh?' She glanced up and realised Joel was speaking to her.

'I said are you all set to leave tomorrow?'

She nodded because her mouth refused to lie for her.

If Joel detected the uncertainty in her expression, he didn't mention it, but his eyes crinkled as he studied her warily. Poor kid had been nothing but nice, the whole crew had, and yet Ellen had remained quite reserved throughout her time at the station.

Joel suddenly grinned. 'You'll love Karijini. Magic spot.'

'So I hear.' It was only for a few days and yet Ellen felt like she was about to drive off the edge of the earth. The eight hundred odd kilometres there didn't worry her – she'd done over nine hundred to get to Challa from Albany. But it was what awaited her that felt like a big black hole. And that blackness had her churning with a queasy feeling that needed more than Mylanta to cure.

Think of the positives!

Scrunching her fists, she focused. The silver lining would be seeing her brother propose to Ingrid, who she loved like a sister. This whole trip was his idea. Bodhi wanted his sisters' help in making his proposal magical, and who was she to deny him that request?

Bodhi and Ingrid deserved their fairy tale and Ellen would make sure it went off without a hitch. This was not something she could leave up to her sister. Even Bodhi had admitted that.

'El, I need you. Carrie lacks attention to the small details, actually any details, and I need this day to be perfect. *Please*!'

Ellen had reluctantly called her sister and planned it down to the colour of the confetti, leaving strict instructions on what to bring.

'God, you're not even here and you're still bossy,' Carrie had said. 'I promise I won't forget a thing. I'll have Fin remind me. Probably a good thing you're not here, you'd probably spill the beans to Ingi.'

'I would not.'

'You've always been too honest, sis,' she'd said and laughed. 'You and Bodhi are terrible.'

Was that the real reason Ellen had moved to Challa Station? Maybe Carrie was right, and she couldn't trust herself. Honesty had always been part of her moral compass; now that it was broken, she felt lost in the wilderness. Or should that be lost in the lower Murchison region?

Ellen gave Joel a half-hearted smile. 'I'm sure I'll love it, I'm just not sure I'm ready for the family reunion.'

2

Carrie

HER ARSE WAS NUMB. SHE LITERALLY COULDN'T FEEL IT. Carrie Sutton lifted her feet onto the dash, her toes pressed up against the glass.

'You know how dangerous that is, right?'

Carrie groaned. 'You sound like my sister. It's fine, I trust you won't crash. You're the most conscientious driver I know. Besides, it's not like this poxy campervan can do dangerous speeds. Hell, it can't even get to a hundred.' This trip was bloody long enough let alone crawling along at snail speed. Her numb butt was protesting as much as her bored brain.

'It's not me I'm worried about. What if someone else runs into us? You've seen how many accidents there are along this road. You might want to have babies one day so having your femur smashed through your uterus won't help.'

Carrie grimaced, not from the picture he painted but the word 'babies'.

Fin held onto the steering wheel with two hands, ever so safety conscious. How that managed to irritate her, she wasn't sure. Couldn't he look just a little more relaxed, like rest his elbow on the open window? Oh yeah, because the aircon didn't work over eighty, they had to travel with the windows down just to avoid being boiled like prawns. So her ears hurt, her hair was a mess, and they had to almost shout at each other to be heard. But she'd rather have no aircon than make this trip any slower. *I'll have fucking grey hair by the time we get there!*

'I'm not that fussed on babies. No great loss. I'll just get a dog.'

Fin risked a quick glance away from the road. He was living on the edge.

'You don't mean that?' he asked.

How could a man look so damn sexy and yet be so vanilla on the inside? Don't speed, don't be reckless, don't colour outside the lines . . . Living with Fin wasn't the roller-coaster ride his image would suggest. He'd attracted her with his cool hipster vibe, the styled short back and sides with that long straight top that flopped over in a delicious way. He usually sported a beard but had trimmed it knowing the heat they were heading into. But the short stubble worked for him. *Hell, everything worked for him.* From the little black circle earrings he wore, to the beanies and fedora hats, everything suited him. Carrie couldn't wear a hat without looking mother-of-the-bride horrible. And what was the point of styling your hair if you were just going to jam a hat on your head?

'I do! I can't see myself having kids anytime soon. I'm far too young,' she scoffed.

Fin snorted. 'Babe, you're twenty-seven. My mum had a seven-year-old by that age.'

Carrie rolled her eyes. 'That was way back then. Now mid-thirties is the norm.' She certainly wasn't going to consider it for at least five years. Maybe then she'd feel differently about screaming newborns.

Her dark chocolate waves cascaded over her chest, making her black singlet feel like a jumper. She'd kill for an icy pole. She didn't want to put her hair up considering it had taken fifteen minutes to do this morning at that caravan park with its dodgy bathroom lights. It probably looked like a rat's nest now, thanks to having the windows down. God, why did she bother.

'What about marriage?'

The question took her by surprise. 'Marriage?' *Why the hell would he bring up that?* The word made her feel suddenly carsick.

'Yeah. With your brother about to pop the question, have you ever thought about it?'

'Shit, Fin, we've only been going out eight months.'

'I'm not saying we get married now, I'm just asking if that's where you see us heading.'

He said it casually, but Carrie could tell by the tight strands of muscle at his neck that he was deeply invested in her answer. Staring ahead, she watched the massive blue tub on the truck in front being escorted by a team of pilot vehicles. It didn't matter; they'd never pass it, they could barely keep up with the oversized vehicle.

'Carrie?'

With a big sigh she turned to him. 'I don't know. I can't say I've given it much thought. I prefer to live day by day. You know that. Why bring it up now?'

Sweat oozed from her pores and she felt queasy. *God, was he going to propose?* Carrie rubbed at her eyes and then instantly regretted it; half her make-up was on her fingers and she'd probably smeared the rest. Damn heat.

'I just thought maybe we should discuss our relationship,' he said. 'Lately, I feel like we just glide along because it's comfortable, not because we want a future together.'

'What are you saying, Fin?' Her voice rose an octave or two. By the look on his face, it was the latter.

'I don't know. Maybe we should . . . break up?'

Her eyebrows twisted out of shape. 'Are you saying if we're not going to get married, you want to break up?'

Fin seemed cool and calm. Had he been thinking about this a bit? Did he really not want to be with her? But worse was her own confusion over what scared her more – a break-up or marriage?

'I just don't want to invest in a relationship that won't end in marriage and kids,' he said. 'You know how I feel about starting a family – you said once you want those things too?'

His intense eyes held her gaze for a split second before returning to the road.

'Yeah, maybe. But like . . . way, way into the future.' Carrie realised then that she was not ready for that step, that level of commitment, not with Fin, maybe not with anyone. Or did that just mean Fin wasn't the one for her? 'I'm not ready yet, Fin. I'm busy with work and don't have time for a child.' He opened his mouth, but she cut in quickly. 'And before you ask, I can't give you a time or date either. I just don't know. Can you be happy with that?'

To give up her scissors and make-up brushes for nappies and bottles? *Not yet, thank you very much!*

Damn her brother for deciding to get married. It was his fault she was going through this squeamish conversation with Fin.

And damn Bodhi for becoming great mates with Fin. Of course Fin would be feeling left out, a little jealous even. Hopefully when they got back home and everything returned to normal, he'd be fine with how things were for a bit longer.

Fin stared ahead, focused, while the soft skin on the side of his head pulsed. Was he weighing it all up? Should they break up? Carrie wasn't sure what she wanted.

'So that's a no to breaking up?' he finally muttered.

Carrie crawled across to the driver's side and kissed him, and before he could protest she moved her lips to his ear and down along his neck. 'It's a no,' she murmured between kisses. Then she pressed her hand between his legs, gently rubbing.

'Um, Carrie . . . what . . . um . . . whoo . . . oh.'

His words faded away as she undid the button and zipper of his denim shorts.

'I'm bored,' she said before wetting her lips.

'Jesus,' Fin puffed. 'I'm relieved this old campervan can't go any faster.'

'Do not pull over,' she demanded. 'I'm not making this trip any longer.'

'I know what you're doing,' he said between moans.

He pulled the van over, ever cautious, but it only made Carrie work quicker.

'You can't always use sex to get what you want.'

But that was the last thing he said on the matter because in truth, Carrie had been using it to get her way for a while. She cared about Fin, he made her feel safe and protected. He loved her like no other man had and he turned her on, always. But was that enough to stay with someone? Was she too scared to shake up her life because if you took away Fin and the salon . . . what did she have left? Who was she really?

'Oh, bloody hell,' she exclaimed afterwards. 'That only chewed up five minutes. How much longer?' She pouted. 'This place better be worth it. Why couldn't Bodhi have proposed at the beach or a nice restaurant back in Albany like anyone else?'

Fin shook his head. 'You are the least romantic in your family. Even I've heard Ingi banging on about her dream to travel north to see the gorges. You know she was meant to take that trip with her brother. I think Bodhi has planned it perfectly. You could take a page out of his book.'

Carrie pulled out her phone and prayed for a signal, choosing to ignore Fin's comment. 'God, not even a bar?' She threw it down and rifled in her bag for her nail file and started on them with gusto.

A sign flashed by; they were coming into Mount Magnet.

'Maybe we should go and surprise Ellen?' After all, Carrie was curious to see what had been keeping her so far away. Were all the mustering guys super-hot? It had to be – what else was there up here beside red dirt and flies and skin cancer?

'I thought she didn't want us to stop in. Isn't she meeting us up there?'

Carrie turned in her seat to face him. 'Why is that, do you think? Is she hiding some boyfriend we don't know about? I still don't understand why she came here. She had a perfectly good nursing job that I know she adored, only to throw it in to chase cattle in the dust.' It wasn't much of a tourist destination. No beaches, no restaurants with fresh seafood, no pretty streets and stunning views. Was there even a hairdresser?

'Maybe she just needed a break?'

'Midlife crisis, more like it,' she huffed.

'Besides, this place has its own natural charm, and it's still a new experience,' said Fin. 'El might be enjoying the change of scenery.'

'Yeah, but it's no white sands and stunning ocean blues, is it?'

'You need to get out of Albany more. I just hope you appreciate these sights. Folks dream of coming up here.'

He sighed like the disgruntled parent of a teenager. Fin sometimes had a way of making her feel infantile and her opinions insignificant. Maybe they were. She didn't know why she was so flippant. Was it because she didn't feel deeply about anything these days? No passion? Is that why she clung on to Fin? He was so grounded and sure. Her lighthouse in rough seas.

'Why don't you want to go see her? I thought checking out a station would be right up your alley?'

'Carrie,' he said with a sigh tacked on the end, 'I just want to keep the peace. If she doesn't want us there, then I'm not about to make things awkward. Who knows, maybe it has more to do with the owners not wanting all sorts of visitors while they're busy with mustering.'

She shrugged, maybe he was right. 'Argh, I'm going to try and sleep.' She pulled the lever and fell backwards as her chair reclined at breakneck speed. She giggled and reached for the packet of lolly snakes. 'Where do you think Bodhi and Ingi are now?'

'That's not sleeping,' Fin teased.

She shot him a glare. 'I'm sure you'd prefer it if I was asleep.'

'There'd be less whining about the heat, your sore butt and, as you like to put it, "the slow-arse turtle bus".' Fin grinned.

Carrie couldn't help but return his smile. 'She is a turtle. I'm sure you picked the slowest one.'

'Hey, it was you who wanted to do the whole "let's be backpackers" experience. I bet you're glad I talked you out of the Wicked Camper with all the bright artwork.'

'You mean the spray-painted collection of dicks?'

They laughed. If the shoe was on the other foot, Carrie wouldn't have let him forget it. He was a good man – kind, forgiving, gentle, thoughtful. All the things Carrie forgot to be because she was so busy with life. She thought about doing nice stuff, like buying her mum flowers for her birthday, and then would leave them behind in the salon, or double-booking when she said she'd drop in for a cuppa. It's not like she did it on purpose. She loved her mum and her friends. Maybe she should invest in some books on how to improve your memory? Or as Fin had once suggested, 'Why don't you just slow down?'

She glanced out the window at the wide open plains crawling past in slowmo, and smiled. Wasn't she doing that now?

3

Ellen

THE VIEW FROM THE COTTAGE WAS LIKE NO OTHER. RED dirt, dotted with a few scraggly trees and small green shrubs no higher than her knees, stretched out until it blended with the light cornflower-blue sky. Golden sunrays streaked over the horizon, bringing with them the hum of flies and fading the early morning freshness. Bare patches of earth were patterned with animal and insect prints, along with Ellen's boot marks, telling stories, showing life. Including Mick's prints from his late-night visit. He didn't stay, spooning and sharing morning breath wasn't a part of his plan. Much to her relief.

It was nearly six thirty, time to hit the road. She moved away from the window and rinsed out her cup in the old-fashioned sink. It was funny how this little home felt so comfortable. Rustic like her nana's wheatbelt farm before they sold up. It had a toilet outside on the veranda in the laundry, much like this place. The cement laundry sink was exactly the same and Ellen had vague memories of being bathed in it by her nana.

A chook-wire fence ran the perimeter of the cottage, which was once the main home on the station, generations before; now it spent its later years as the workers' quarters or for overnight stays for mining personnel. There was a faint narrow track that led to Ashley's sheds and Debbie's home. Ellen was always on the lookout for the weed equivalent to LEGO, aka calthrop. Especially when one had gone through her thong on her second day here. She'd rather be jabbed by a needle than stand on those bloody prickles.

Closing up the cottage, she picked up her swag from the veranda, along with her clothes bag and headed to the gate. From the outside the cottage looked like an old abandoned home, its garden gone, its shell weathered. A Hills Hoist stood silent on the opposite side of the fence, neglected and still like the statue of a soldier long forgotten, looking out of place on the ochre sands. A shed covered in brushing filled up the back corner of the yard.

Ellen threw her swag into the back of her Hilux dual-cab ute. Not the usual car one would expect a midwife to own but it came in handy to move furniture about, or her mum's sculptures, or even just to get to some of the beaches on the weekend. And it had a roof rack so she could strap on her surfboard, or Bodhi's. Bodhi had taught her to surf when she was twelve. For the company or for shark bait, she wasn't sure. But they had bonded over many surf trips together. Not Carrie – she wasn't a fan of getting smashed in the waves, she preferred the calm waters of Emu Point to glide along in her little bikinis. Ellen, on the other hand, had been dunked, churned up and spit out by the ocean so often that 'drowned rat' was her sexy beach look. She wasn't a bad surfer, but when she mastered something, she liked to push herself and step up to the next trick or bigger wave, usually with spectacular wipe-outs. Persistent, her dad had called her, like when she'd tried for the millionth time to build a house out of cards. Stubborn was what her mother called her when she refused to give up trying to make her pottery clay look like her nana's favourite teapot. And Bodhi and Carrie just called her a try-hard.

Always have to be the best at everything, Carrie would say while hugging the life out of her. It was said without malice, but Ellen wondered if deep down there was a sore spot that sometimes festered into sibling rivalry. It probably didn't help that their mum had often said, *Carrie, why can't you be better behaved like your sister?* every time she got herself into mischief.

Right now, Ellen was none of these things. She hadn't persisted. She hadn't tried her hardest. Instead she'd run away to Challa Station like a coward. There was no 'dust yourself off and try again'. For the first time in her life she'd reached a point she never thought she'd get to.

Adrift. Lost. Empty. Life seemed to float in limbo with no forward movement, no direction, no purpose, no dreams. Just day by day.

A wave of sadness rippled through her body at leaving the comfort and safety she'd found here. But this wasn't goodbye, she'd be back after the few days with her family.

Ellen took a deep centring breath and then drove towards the sheds. She slowed down and saw Ashley already moving about, doing repairs to the leaky radiator on the blue buggy.

Honk. Honk.

Ash stood up and gave her a wave which she returned before continuing past the house and workers' quarters. Might be a few sore heads in those quarters this morning, she'd wager. With a chuckle she squinted down to the horse yards, knowing Deb would be down there with her beautiful Morgan horses. One had not long ago birthed a foal, which Ellen was spewing she'd missed.

'I could have used a midwife,' Deb had joked when she'd first arrived.

Not that she would have been much help. A vet she wasn't. Yet as a child growing up with pet cows and sheep, cats and dogs, chickens and ducks, there had been plenty of births and new life. All those magical moments had directed her to becoming a midwife. Although animals could also die through birthing complications; real life was no different. At the mature age of ten, she'd cried for two solid days when the lamb she'd helped pull out died a day later. But it wasn't just Buttercup she'd cried over, every pet they'd lost had been mourned – most buried by her own hands, the family made to stand around the grave with flowers and say something nice about the deceased. Bodhi would always say something like, *Buttercup, your life was short, but you lived it to the fullest.* And Carrie would decorate the box to help them over the rainbow. Ellen would usually be the only one crying, but at least they all were there for her in those moments. If only they could have been there for ALL the moments.

Their menagerie was probably why Carrie went into hair-dressing and beauty – she was always brushing their coats, trying to plait their tails or put tiaras or tutus on them so she could take photos with their mum's old camera. Ellen would never forget the time their dad came home and was staring out the window before saying, 'Does Carla have a hot date tonight?' Carrie had bedazzled their cow with her glittery stick-on earrings and a scarf tied around its neck.

Even though they lived in Albany they were lucky to be on some land, the city having grown out to them. Her mum and dad still lived there, while Bodhi and Ingi lived in a home they'd bought together last year, and Carrie was living with Fin. Ellen had her own place, a little house on the hillside where she could see Middleton Beach. It had a big yard, and heaps of room for animals and kids. Only now it was being rented by a single guy who worked at the Port.

Ellen didn't stop when she saw Debbie in the yards, standing next to her handsome gold-coated gelding whose white mane and tail were stained an apricot colour from the dust; instead she gave another toot and headed over the cattle grid and down the gravel road that Ashley had recently graded. She had a long drive ahead. Carrie would be a few hours in front after staying the night at Meekatharra. But at six thirty, she doubted Carrie would be out of bed yet.

And her brother was still a day away. Just like they'd planned.

The scent of eucalyptus and other green leaves filled the cab of her ute, thanks to the two plastic bin bags full of love-heart punched-leaf confetti. In true Ellen style she wanted to make sure she had more than enough. Even now she was thinking of stopping and collecting more leaves to punch tonight. Besides, that gave her an excuse to escape socialising with Carrie and Fin. Could she fake a headache and head off to bed early? God, how was she going to handle seeing them all again? The prickling of anxiety was spreading across her neck at the thought. It was uncomfortable and suffocating. Gritting her teeth, she forced the fear to the back. 'Just take one minute at a time,' she muttered. 'You can do this.'

Ellen drove to Mount Magnet, over cattle grids in the road that would rattle her bones each time. The landscape was mostly flat; sometimes there'd be random plateaus with their gravel tops and breakaway edges. Fascinating countryside. Even once she hit the Great Northern Highway, the view just seemed to go on for miles, but the traffic was almost chaotic. The lifeline north – trucks delivering supplies to towns and mines – plus heaps of tourists heading for warmth.

Bang!

The steering wheel jerked in her hands before she could comprehend what was happening. Heart pounding, she eased on the brakes and pulled off the road as best she could while the whole ute shuddered.

Shit!

Ellen rested her head on the steering wheel as she sucked in steadying breaths. This was the last thing she needed – a busy road, close to forty-degree heat and a tyre to change.

She hoped this wasn't a prelude for the whole weekend! *Suck it up, Ellen, it's no different than changing the buggy tyres.*

At least she was safely away from the road and on flat ground. Jamming on her straw hat, she got out and removed the jack from behind the back seat, all the while muttering under her breath. She didn't dare open her mouth wide for fear the flies would congregate inside.

She managed to get the jack in the right spot, her spare out from under the tray, and was trying to undo the first few wheel nuts but was out of luck. She tried another one, grunting with effort on the wheel brace. The dust must have set them rock hard. She wasn't even making them budge.

She grabbed hold of the ute tray and lifted her foot up onto the spanner then pushed on it with all her weight. The wheel spanner slipped off the nut and sent her cartwheeling into the gravel.

Ellen lay face down, taking a moment to adjust to this new-found position and the humiliation she felt. Gravel dug into her skin and her shin hurt from where the metal had connected. It hadn't helped that she was in thongs and not her work boots. *Rookie mistake*, Gazza would have told her.

She was so busy lying there feeling sorry for herself that she didn't realise a car had stopped until she heard a voice.

'Are you okay?'

She detected an accent. Swiss? German? Both? Ellen lifted her head and peered through the loose strands of her hair to see a man leaning over her. A very cute man. *Oh shit.*

She scrambled to get up, adjusting her hat. The man offered his hand but she ignored it as she righted herself, cheeks burning. Was that even possible when it was already so hot?

'I'm fine. Just feel silly,' she admitted as she finally clocked her do-gooder. He was tall and lean with golden skin and sun-bleached hair tied up in a loose bun on top of his head. A vision of Debbie's horse flashed before her eyes. El hadn't been a fan of long hair on men . . . until now.

'Can I give you a hand?'

She was momentarily confused; she'd already got up . . . but then she realised he meant with the tyre. 'Oh, please. The nuts are hard.' Her mouth dropped open as he smirked at her words. *Why am I such an idiot!* 'I was trying to use my weight when I slipped. You don't have a bit of pipe, do you?'

She'd seen her dad use pipe as a lever but as she took in the stranger's car, she knew she was out of luck. A handy mine ute it was not. Parked about a car length behind her was a stained white minivan, its windows lined with a collage of faded stickers. Now his slight accent made more sense.

The man had picked up her wheel brace and was squeaking the nuts loose with his long lean arms.

'Shit, you're not wrong. These are tight.'

He did exactly as she'd done, standing on the spanner to get the next two undone. Except he didn't faceplant the dirt like she had. Her shin was starting to throb, but she resisted the urge to rub it.

'Thank you for stopping,' she said as another car whizzed past, bringing a slight breeze. She wiped her brow and noticed the sweat at the base of his hair and down his neck. 'It's too hot to be outside for long.'

As he got the last nut free, Ellen started pumping the jack while he lifted the tyre off and put the spare on.

'Thank you. I've got it from here if you want to get on your way.' She felt bad. He was getting all hot and sweaty. Though he wore it well. His eyes were a vibrant blue, so iridescent it was hard to look at anything else.

'I'm nearly done.' He shot her a wink.

She had a speech prepared about not being a helpless female and that she'd changed plenty of tyres over the years, but she was still grateful that he'd stopped and so bit back her words. It was nice to be offered help and Ellen wanted to be better at taking it.

'Can I offer you a cold drink? I've got a Coke?'

He smiled and nodded as he tightened the last few nuts. El quickly fished two Cokes from her small fridge on the back seat. She handed one over as he handed back the wheel brace.

'Thank you.'

He put the can against his neck first. Beads of sweat rolled down his skin. It was like she was watching a Coke ad. She'd certainly have what he was having.

'No – *thank you*,' she replied.

'Hans.'

'Pardon?'

He held out his hand. 'My name is Hans. And you are?'

They shook sweaty hands. 'Ellen. Nice to meet you, Hans.'

He opened his Coke and sculled half of it. El had forgotten she was even holding one.

'Let's get out of the sun.' She could feel it burning into her arms already. That would teach her for wearing a sleeveless top, plus her denim shorts didn't cover much of her legs either. Hans wasn't any different in shorts and a tank top, but he was wearing black Converse sneakers on his feet. She should have gone with better foot protection too – but after six months in boots her toes had been enjoying some freedom.

'Catch ya later,' he said, heading to his van.

He spoke like an Aussie, and yet the hint of his homeland was there. As she climbed back into her ute she wished she'd asked him how long he'd been in Australia, or where he was going or where he was from. But the side of the Great Northern Highway in searing heat with flies and snakes and freight trucks rumbling past kicking up stones wasn't the place for a conversation.

Reluctantly she pulled back out onto the road and watched the minivan grow further and further away in her rear-vision mirror. She wondered if they might meet up again at the next roadhouse or two.

Ellen cranked the music and the aircon and thought that maybe going to wherever Hans was off to was better than meeting up with her family.

You can't keep running, El!

Oh how she wished her mind would be quiet.

Desperate for distraction, she turned up the radio only to hear John Butler Trio playing, and before she could shut it down, memory lane came calling.

4

Ellen

Last year

THERE WAS A BUZZ IN THE AIR. IT WASN'T SUMMER FLIES but the sounds of spring – bees humming, birds chirping, wildflowers and grasses whispering in the soft breeze – combined with the exciting build-up to a concert. The same anticipation before a big storm as you watch the dark clouds roll in and the sky is filled with thunderous booms and flashes of light and the hairs on your skin stand on end, waiting for the drops to fall, waiting for the heavens to unload in a massive climax. And then the smell of the rain, the reward for the wait. In this case it would be seeing one of her favourite singer/songwriters. If only she had someone to share it with.

People walked beside her, voices upbeat and laughing among friends. Ellen smiled. Even though she was alone she didn't feel lonely. Sure, it would have been better if Anne's gorgeous two-year-old hadn't started spewing this afternoon, causing her to cancel. Anne had been in tears from the frustration of missing the concert after months of anticipation mixed with the worry of having a sick little girl. Ellen had listened to the symptoms, reassuring Anne she would be fine, to keep up the fluids and get some rest.

Anne had laughed then. 'Me or Isla?' She again apologised for standing Ellen up and thanked her for the free nursing advice.

Finding a last-minute replacement had been hard when Tanya was doing Ellen's night shift at the hospital and her mum was attending an art dinner at the Shire's expense. 'How could I possibly give that up? After all these years of paying rates, about time I got something in return.' It was probably a good thing as her mum would have ended up near the stage close to the speaker, giving Peter Garrett a run for his money. How she ended up with their dad, who had only ever danced at their wedding and would rather watch the footy with a beer and a pie, she'd never know. Opposites attract?

Her dad was out too. 'I've got . . . ah, invoices to catch up on,' he'd stammered down the phone. 'But if you don't want to go alone, honey, I can come. Paperwork can wait.' And that was her dad – prepared to endure hours of something he didn't like just to keep her happy. Mind you, he'd been doing just that his whole married life. He was so pliable, easygoing, and had a big heart.

Carrie, her darling little sister . . . well, there was no point even trying. Carrie preferred current pop hits and was probably out at some party with her friends anyway. And Bodhi was down south on a wiring job and Ingi was working at the restaurant.

Ellen wondered if she needed more friends? Carrie seemed to know half the town while Ellen moved around with blinkers on, so focused on her work. But it didn't matter, it was just bad timing, bad luck, or maybe good luck, whichever way you wanted to take it. Ellen was a big believer in putting out good vibes and the universe would take care of you. Yeah, some of that may have rubbed off from her mum.

So, Ellen was going solo. But she'd been to Wignalls Winery before, it was a beautiful spot to listen to music. Who needed company when you had John Butler Trio and The Waifs? She adjusted the picnic blanket on her arm the best she could, while carrying a bag full of food in the other.

Ingrid had dropped her off before she went to work and said she'd also pick her up after. 'That way you can have some drinks. You might even find a hot single bloke there,' Ingi had said optimistically.

That was the last thing Ellen felt like. She was still touchy after breaking up with Josh nine months ago. She thought he was her 'ever after' man. The 'marry me and have my babies' type, but instead he was the 'pretend I love you but get my ex pregnant' sort. It had been a spectacular crash and burn and quite frankly, she just didn't trust herself to pick the right man at the moment.

She *was* over Josh, without a doubt, but she'd seen them in the hospital with the new baby just last week and the hurt, jealousy, anger and betrayal had bubbled up all over again. Thank God she hadn't been on duty. Awkward. It was bad enough having to walk past their room and trying to hide so she didn't have to put on fake niceties. What ate her up the most was that she'd been wearing those stupid blinkers again and hadn't even noticed, had not even had an inkling of Josh's deceit and lies. She was just a gullible woman and that hurt. How does one learn to trust again after having your heart not only ripped out but paraded around on a stick like some victory flag? Josh didn't even seem that remorseful, he was so busy with the excitement of becoming a dad. *Fuck you, Josh.*

'Oh, hi, Ellen,' said a man walking beside her. 'Nice dress.'

He was watching the folds of teal flare out as she walked and the three sets of ripples at the bottom move like a gentle waterfall. She'd teamed it with her denim jacket and tan ankle boots, dangly earrings and lots of bracelets.

'Thanks, Ted. It's nice to get dressed up after being in nursing scrubs all week.'

'And without the hospital hair!' he added.

She self-consciously touched her loose golden waves and wondered if she should change up her standard work ponytail from time to time. 'Ah, thanks, Ted,' she said hesitantly. 'You look different too,' she replied. She'd nearly said without a dinner trolley in his hands but thought better of it. They weren't great mates, just work acquaintances, and she was relieved when he strode off with his group of friends.

Wignalls Winery was situated on the outskirts of Albany. Its green paddocks had been opened up for parking and the concert area was set up near the buildings. At the gate, Ellen showed her ticket and her food bag and then walked on into the crowd that was growing by the minute. A large stage was off to her left and the bar to the right. People had already claimed spots by the stage and she had to walk a bit to find an area to lay down her rug. Outside vendors had been brought in – a coffee van, a pizza van, and a few others were dotted around the back as well as numerous portaloos.

Happy with her spot – close enough to see Mr Butler on stage but not too close to have her ears blasted by speakers – she placed down her bag of goodies and attempted to open out the rug.

'Oh, here, can I help?'

Her eyes lifted past a denim button-up dress shirt, the sleeves rolled halfway up his forearms where swirls of ink marked his skin, to his kind chocolate eyes. After a beat or two, she dropped her eyes, having stared for longer than appropriate. Fitted black jeans and tan pointy boots. Yeah, he was rocking this look.

He didn't seem to notice as he reached for a corner of the rug and helped her shake it out and place it down on the ground.

'Thanks,' she said with a smile then kneeled and began to unload a small chopping board, cheeses, salamis, boxes of crackers, olives and dips.

'Oh wow, you came prepared,' said the man.

Ellen glanced up, surprised to see him still standing there, drooling over her snacks.

'Have you got a group of friends turning up? I can move over further if you like?' he asked politely.

'Oh no, this is just for me.' She grinned, totally smug with her smorgasbord. 'I actually had a friend coming but she had to cancel last-minute. Sick kid.'

'So, you're solo with *all* that food?' His chiselled jaw dropped and she could see his mind ticking over. 'That's a travesty.'

Ellen laughed. 'You're welcome to share.'

He smiled. 'Could I . . . um . . . propose an arrangement?' He touched his lips with a finger, waiting for her reply.

El squinted up at him warily (he could be a drug your drink kinda guy) but also curiously (how harmful can someone who smiles with his eyes be?). 'What is it you propose?' she asked, wondering if she was going to regret it. But in the back of her mind, she heard Ingi's voice. *Go, enjoy, and don't think so hard. Just have fun.*

'Well, I was wondering how you were going to protect all this,' he said gesturing to the rug, 'when you need to get drinks or go to the bathroom. And so, I was going to propose that for a small corner of the rug and maybe a few bites, I could fetch your drinks and be a rug guard.' He wet his lips with his tongue as his eyes glided over the assortment of food.

'You haven't eaten dinner yet, have you?' she asked with a smile.

His eyebrows shot up. 'That obvious?'

They laughed. He seemed harmless, and so far, polite and not creepy. Oh, and did she say hot? He also smelled amazing – not of the usual Lynx deodorant or some fancy cologne, but freshly showered, maybe with a lemon myrtle soap. He was gobsmackingly handsome but his open easy demeanour made her at ease in his presence.

'Sure, why not.' She had been hoping she'd run into someone she knew who could buy her a drink or two, but this deal was way better. Maybe the universe had provided?

'I have brought enough food for an army.'

'I noticed.' He chuckled, deep and rich like a good wine. 'Do you always over-prepare?'

'Um, I prefer to call it being well organised.' El's lips curved. 'Please take a seat. I'm Ellen.' She held out her hand.

He sat down, legs out in front of him and turned to slip his hand in hers. 'I'm Murray. Nice to meet you, Ellen. Actually, it's awesome to meet you and I'm so glad you're well organised. You're like Mary Poppins with a bag full of everything.' He grinned, his clean-shaven face shining in the setting sun.

'Oh my God, I so wanted to be her growing up. Refined, able to sing, and just perfect in every way.'

'Who says you're not?' he teased.

'Ha, I do.'

'Stop setting the bar so high.'

He said it as a joke but he had a point. She knew she was her own worst critic.

Murray people-watched for a moment, as others set up chairs and blankets, talking excitedly as friends rocked up. Then he sighed and turned to her. He didn't seem fazed that she'd been studying him.

'I thought I'd be the only person here to come alone.'

'You and me both. Not many of my mates appreciate good music, and those who do couldn't come.'

'Damn, sounds like we have the same problem. My mates weren't interested, they prefer heavy metal or hard rock, and the one person who would kill to be here is in Perth.'

Typical, he probably had a girlfriend. Oh well, easier to enjoy the night then. 'Well, it's their loss. Although I am glad I can share this with someone who appreciates it. It's more fun with company, you know?'

'Yep. Awesome things should be shared,' he agreed. 'So, what would you like to drink? I might head to the bar while it's not too crowded.'

'Good plan. I'll have a red wine, please.' Ellen fished into her bag for her purse, but Murray waved her away.

'On me.'

For a nanosecond her earlier drugging drinks thought popped up and she vowed to be vigilant.

Wrangling his limbs, he stood up and wandered off towards the bar. Ellen leaned back on her hands and took in the late afternoon atmosphere. These concerts were so much fun, like a Sunday barbecue with the family.

Murray was a nice surprise – it sure beat sitting and eating alone. Tall and eye-catching, he navigated the path back to her, drinks secure in those large hands. Maybe he was a dick like Josh, a player, a ladies' man, but Ellen wasn't here to find out. This was just one night of company, not the start of a relationship. Is that why she felt so relaxed beside him – no strings, no pressures, no hopes to be dashed?

'That bar is crazy,' said Murray, holding two plastic glasses of red wine.

He held one out, but Ellen reached for the other, figuring they both couldn't be spiked. Murray seemed unfazed.

'You like red wine too? I figured you for more a beer man.'

Murray managed to sit down without spilling a drop and then took a sip. 'Judgy,' he said with a smirk. 'I do drink beer,' he added. 'One day I'd even like to make my own.'

'Like home brew?'

'No, like for a boutique brewery, my own label, locally sourced.'

'Oh, nice. Well, I wouldn't mind a winery. I could see myself swanning about the place, running taste-test tours and selling handmade chocolates.'

'Who wouldn't like the sound of that? Have you been out to the Boston Brewery in Denmark?'

'Hello, who hasn't? That place got me addicted to ginger beer,' she said with a chuckle. 'Will you have a ginger beer option in your brewery? 'Cos if you don't, I won't visit.'

'Oh harsh.' His eyes sparkled. 'I'm sure I could whip up an Ellen's Ginger Beer.'

'That's got a nice ring to it. I approve.'

Grinning, he lifted his cup, forearm flexing, tattoos moving as if coming alive on his skin. She was fascinated by them, intricate in design and drawn so lifelike by someone clearly talented.

He caught her staring. 'The shading is amazing!' she said.

'My cousin did these,' he offered. 'He owns York Ink down the main street.' He smiled. 'I get a family discount.'

'No way! My brother just booked in with him to get a piece done on the back of his leg.' Ellen touched the butterfly on his arm. 'What do they mean to you?' she asked then took a sip of her wine. 'Oh, please, help yourself to the food. If I'm going to interrogate you, you may as well have a full stomach.'

He chuckled and went for a cracker and some dip. Ellen followed suit.

'I told Chris the ones I wanted, and he mashed them together. They all mean something to me. There's a whale because I've seen a few now from Marine Drive Lookout, the *Amity* ship, a rose for my mum, butterfly for my sister, clock with my birth date . . . you get the drift.'

She took his wrist and rolled his arm over. 'Is that the pine trees at Middleton Beach?'

'Yep. Many summers spent there with my sister having Mr Whippy ice-creams.'

'Oh, us too. Maybe we were in the same line once? It's a very Albany experience, isn't it?'

He nodded knowingly, a mutual childhood memory that was shared with most locals.

'You know, I can see them from my kitchen window every morning. There's just something about those pine trees that grounds me, makes me feel like I belong.'

'It's a sense of place. Landmarks to our memories.'

His words echoed deep. Ellen had never thought of it like that, but it was true.

'Do you have any?' he asked. 'Tattoos?'

She held out her hand and spread her fingers, and tried to ignore the warmth in his touch as he brought her hand closer to inspect it.

'Is that a bee?'

'Yeah. A bee stung me there between my fingers when I was in the garden, pruning without gloves. Little did I know I'm quite allergic. It's kind of a memento.'

'Oh wow. Are you like deathly allergic? He's very cute though.'

'Yeah, cute bee nearly killed me,' she replied, deadpan.

'Who needs murderers when there are cute bees.'

Her lips spread wide, she couldn't help it. She liked this man. Talking with him was so easy and fun. 'Indeed.'

'Here's to living life,' Murray said, lifting his cup.

They clinked plastic and sipped while The Waifs started a quick sound check and then began to play. Ellen moved her shoulders to the music while making a dent in the food. Murray helped, as promised, and still there was lots left. They shared smiles and managed a few words between songs.

At some point Murray disappeared, returning with another drink.

'Thanks, I'm paying for the next one,' she said, grabbing his lean forearm and giving it a gentle squeeze. Lightning may have danced across the black sky or maybe it was just sparks from the touch, but the way Murray was looking at her now, she knew he'd felt it too. Was it the wine? The good company? Or the music? All three mixed, making her feel ridiculously lost in his eyes. She could feel the vibe he was giving off. Heart racing, she took a sip of her drink, but still couldn't look away. Her body was humming like live wires and every time she got close to him, the hair on her arms rose as if from a build-up of static electricity.

'I have to admit, I'm glad we found the same spot tonight,' she yelled over the music.

'Me too. I don't mind going solo but it is nice to share good music with like-minded people, you know?'

'Totally,' she agreed. 'I've seen John three times now. He's amazing every time. Just so good live.'

Murray stared at her. 'Three times, no way. This is my first. I missed him when he was here last time, I had to work.'

'Sucks to be you,' she teased. 'I also saw him at the Big Day Out in Claremont.'

'Was that the one Birds of Tokyo were at?'

She nodded and rattled off the names of a few other bands.

'No way. I don't think we can be friends anymore, I'm too jealous.'

Friends? Ellen tried to take a sip while laughing and it didn't go down well. She coughed and Murray patted her on the back. Even that touch was enough to make her skin hyper aware.

'You okay?'

'I'll survive.'

They sat in easy silence for a while as John Butler Trio played one of the songs from their latest album. Quite a few people were standing and dancing now.

'This is so cool. I should come to these things more often,' he said as the song finished. 'I've been overdue a decent break.'

'You should. Nights like these are magical.'

El felt euphoric – everything from the night sky, the music, and the attention of a handsome man had her feeling alive and special. It had been a long time since she'd felt this good. Especially after Josh left her feeling like a gullible idiot and made her question so much about herself. To think she'd believed him to be the one, had imagined a future with him, and he'd been laughing behind her back the whole time. It still made her sick, made her feel worthless. Tonight was helping to fight those feelings. Seeing the way Murray looked at her, that raw powerful attraction, the wine buzzing through her body, all collided into a wash of confidence and bravado that had long been missing. His dark eyes drank her in, causing her abdomen to pulse with desire and setting her cheeks on fire.

'So, I take it you live in Albany?' she asked, wanting to know more and needing to move to the safety of conversation.

'Yep. My whole life. I work at the family business, and I know my dad wants me to take it on,' he said with an eye roll.

'But you don't?'

He shook his head. 'No.' Then laughed as he leaned closer. 'Don't tell anyone. I've never actually shared that out loud before.'

Ellen lifted her hand and raised two fingers. 'Scout's honour, it will die with me.' She frowned and looked at her fingers. 'At least I think it's something like that.' She shrugged as Murray's eyes danced with laughter.

He sobered slightly, looking wistful. 'I really want to start my own boutique brewery. A bit like this place where people can come for live music, see how we make our beer, have tastings and a meal. My mate owns a farm and we've talked about using his barley. But it's just a pipedream. I haven't even told Clementine yet. Clem's my sister,' he added quickly.

'Well, it's not a pipedream if you really want to do it. I think it sounds awesome. Great for the tourists.'

'Especially if we sell fancy chocolates,' he said, nudging her shoulder.

'And don't forget the Ellen's Ginger Beer,' she added.

'What about you? Are you following your dreams?' he asked.

He leaned towards her, their shoulders just touching and their lips closer so they could hear each other.

'I am. I'm a nurse, I help deliver babies and hopefully one day I'll have a few of my own.' She wondered if that would shoot fear into his eyes but they remained adoringly fixed on her.

'Me too. A family would complete my life,' he said.

'Not many guys seem that keen, or would admit to wanting that,' she said.

'Maybe you haven't met the right guy yet.'

'Ha, you hit the nail on the head there. Finding the right guy *is* my issue.' She grimaced. 'But I love being a nurse,' she said quickly, hoping to change the direction of the conversation.

'That makes sense. I'm picking up a super-caring, nurturing vibe. And I doubt you'd have any trouble finding a guy,' he said, leaning into her.

El closed her eyes, drinking in the feeling of him and his words, desperately wanting to believe him. When she opened them the world around her faded to the background and he was watching her as if she was the most amazing creature he'd ever seen. She'd never felt so wanted, her body tingling with anticipation and desire. If she didn't do something soon she'd internally combust.

The band started the next song, the crowd cheering at the choice. El tore herself away from Murray to dance and take a moment to douse some flames.

An upbeat song came on and El held out her hand. 'Come dance?' He didn't hesitate, rising and taking her hand. El felt the earth tilt when his large hand linked with hers, its tingly warmth making her wonder what it would feel like if he touched other parts of her body.

He danced beside her, not once letting her hand go as they laughed and moved around on the rug, trampling leftover crackers and empty dip containers. Between songs they stood side by side, discussing music. She could feel his breath caress her ear as he spoke.

'I knew we'd have similar tastes. Except I've never heard of The Jezabels,' said Murray.

'You must – great Aussie indie rock band,' she said. They were standing so close that they were always touching some part, shoulders, elbows, arms, fingers. And what didn't touch seemed to arc out like static reaching across the void. All her senses were heightened. This sweet, polite, sexy man was making her feel so uninhibited.

You have broken man-picker, remember? Her mind threw out a weak warning but El ignored it. It's not as though she wanted to marry this man, this was just one night of having fun. No demands, no preconceived notions about their future . . . It all just came down to this very moment. No past. No future. Just this.

'Oh, I love this one.' She started swaying to the melody of 'What You Want'.

'From the 2004 album,' Murray dipped his head, his lips brushed her ear. 'Care to dance?' He held out his hand.

The wine was making her feel warm and fuzzy and the stars twinkled above like a million fairy lights. Night had long ago settled and the crisp air felt refreshing against her flushed skin. Ingi's words echoed through her mind. *Enjoy yourself.*

Taking her advice, Ellen slipped her hand into his and Murray pulled her gently to him as they swayed together. The sexual tension was so thick she could have scooped it into a cone and licked it. With a contented sigh she nuzzled into his neck as her hand headed south to his lower back. Sometimes it was nice just to be held by a handsome man and believe in the dream again. Murray's hand also migrated south while their other hands stayed joined as if to prove they were still trying to dance. But dancing was just an excuse. The sky fell around them like a dark snow globe filled with sparkling stars and they were the centrepiece.

Ellen smiled, tilting her face to look up at him, but he was already watching her. Her eyes dropped to his sensuous lips.

He cleared his throat and spoke in a low sexy tone. 'I really want to kiss you.'

5

Ellen

ELLEN HAD BEEN WISHING THE SAME THING. THE STARS AND the music were like the setting of a romantic movie – it didn't feel real. But damn how she wanted it to last, to live in this moment for the rest of her life.

In the past she would often replay the best parts in her favourite movies over and over again, riding the high. Mr Darcy holding Lizzy's hand as she stepped off the carriage, Noah telling Allie 'It still isn't over' and snogging her in the rain, or in *Sweet Home Alabama* when Melanie delivers that line, 'So I can kiss you anytime I want'. For years Ellen had relived those moments, dreaming, wishing, and tonight it felt like it was her time.

'I wouldn't say no to a kiss,' she whispered as she pressed in closer to him, her need like a drug, almost a desperation to keep this sensation alive and never let it end.

He dipped his head, soft warm lips pressed against her cheek. Her breath caught in her throat; seconds stretched out. Blood rushed to the spot where his lips touched then rushed along to her lips as they finally kissed. A tentative kiss. A quick kiss that left her content and yet aching for more. All too soon the cool night air replaced the scorch marks.

She let go of his hand and he stiffened for a moment, until she moved her hand around his back, hugging him and tucking herself against his lean body. Murray relaxed and reciprocated, melting into her warmth. She felt the press of his lips against the top of her head. He inhaled deeply as if taking a last breath before diving to the bottom of the ocean, sending shivers through her body, delicious shivers.

Side by side, arm in arm, they watched the last few songs play out, no words spoken, just a shared contentment.

'I wish they could keep playing all night,' he said as the last encore ended.

The band wished them a good night and the crowd clapped and cheered. Reluctantly Ellen pulled away from Murray and joined in the applause.

'Maybe we might find ourselves back here at their next concert,' she said hopefully.

'That's a deal.' He glanced around as if cementing it to memory. 'I'll be disappointed if you don't turn up.'

She laughed. 'You might be happily married by then and never give this another thought.'

'So might you.' Murray smiled sadly.

Ellen was overcome with the feeling that life was about to revert back to normal and this dream would vanish like a tiny bubble on a breeze.

'I can't see me forgetting this night anytime soon.' His voice was heavy, laced with desire.

Me too. But Ellen couldn't find the words to reply; he had mesmerised her brain and body.

'Let me help you pack up,' he said with a sigh.

A nervous flutter began to build, edged with desperation that the night was ending so soon. She was not yet ready to give up this high.

Around them people folded chairs and rugs before flowing towards the car park, singing and wobbling along.

'Have you got a ride?' he asked.

'Um, yeah, my friend is coming to pick me up after her shift.' Ellen hadn't even looked at her phone all night. Not once. There were no messages, just a notification from Facebook asking if she would like to reactivate her profile. This year's resolution had been to cancel all social media and try and live life more in the moment. Sure, it could have been due to changing her profile to single and then dealing with the baby bump photos of the ex which Josh had posted excitedly. Why have that rubbed in her face? Letting go of her socials had been a freedom she didn't realise she'd needed.

'I'll just send her a quick message,' she told Murray, then let Ingi know the concert was over but she was in no hurry.

'Done.' She waved her phone. 'Come on, we need a photo.'

Murray stepped close behind her, crouching slightly so his head was closer to hers as she held her phone out for a selfie.

El laughed. 'I hope you're not doing bunny ears?' she said while she took the photo.

'Never.' His chest pressed against her as he chuckled. 'No bunny ears, but how about this?'

El was still posing when her hair was brushed back from her shoulder and Murray's lips were pressed against her neck, then again closer to her ear. So caught up in the tingles she forgot to take any more photos and all too soon he'd stopped.

Had that even happened? Was she so drunk she'd imagined it?

'Come on, I'll wait with you until your friend shows up.'

He carried her empty food bag while she put the rug over one arm and her handbag on her shoulder. Murray tucked her free arm into his and together they walked with the crowd out to the car park. They idled along, not wanting to rush their departure.

Beams of light cut paths across the dark landscape as cars poured into the winery to pick up people, who were like schools of fish flowing into the grassy paddock car park. Happy drunk people, some singing at the top of their lungs.

'I didn't hear you singing much,' Murray said.

'Oh, for good reason. You would have found another picnic rug to share otherwise,' she said with a chuckle. 'My brother says I'm worse than nails on a chalk board.'

'No way, I don't believe it,' he scoffed. 'But if it's any consolation, I got asked to leave the church choir when I was young.'

She snapped her head up. 'You're a churchgoer?'

'No, my mum was with the church and would take me along. I think she dreamed of me being a singer, but I guess He had other plans. She still has her faith, but the rest of the family don't really believe. Well, we all just have our own ideas.'

'I'm sorry you can't sing, and ruined your mum's hopes and dreams,' she teased. 'My mum is quite disappointed that I didn't end up with her artistic talent, so I'm also a dream killer.'

He squeezed her hand and laughed. 'No doubt we'll put the same hopes onto our own kids as well. Let's wait by the trees so we don't get run over.'

Ellen followed him to the back of the paddock, along the edge where big pine trees and shrubs made a dense bushland. Car lights continued to flash around like hundreds of kids playing spotlight. Her empty hand brushed against his as they walked, sizzling sparks up her arm. Her little finger splayed out, catching his, then one by one, all their digits intertwined.

'How are you getting home?' she asked.

'I'll message my sister later.'

His words hung in the air like thick smoke, hinting at something more, waiting.

'I don't want to leave,' she confessed.

The heat in his gaze was illuminated by a passing car, so smouldering hot that she couldn't breathe, could only hear the pulsing of her heart like a loud echo from a million bouncing ping pong balls. Ellen tugged his hand, pulling him into the dense trees until they were hidden behind a thick trunk. She could still hear the cars and merry voices but also their rapid breaths as if they'd climbed a mountain together. She dropped her things. She knew she would regret not ending this night right. She was feeling reckless, all her inhibitions had taken a hike.

'Murray.' His name was a thin whisper on her hot breath. Standing on her tiptoes she pressed her hands to his chest and nuzzled his ear, letting her lips brush against his skin in the same way he'd done to her.

His body went taut under her fingers. Concerned she'd been too brazen she stepped back only to be held fast, his grip gentle on her arms.

'Don't . . .' He swallowed slowly, as if words were stuck in his throat.

Don't what? Don't leave? Before she could analyse further his hand came up to caress her cheek, his thumb brushing along her jawline and close to her bottom lip.

'Don't stop,' he begged.

And then she realised he was fighting to control himself. His hands were trembling, his breaths rapid. Was he trying to be the perfect gentleman? But that all vanished as soon as he dipped his head and brushed his lips across hers. Every hair on her body stood up as the sounds around them faded to just a loud echo of her want.

Shaking hands cupped her face and he claimed her lips. Soft and sensual. Slow.

It wasn't enough. She needed more, as if he was oxygen and she was all out.

He paused, severing the touch but still close enough she could feel his breath on her lips. 'I need you to tell me to stop,' he implored.

His body was trembling. She could tell he was on the brink of no return but there was no way she was going to tell him to stop. She'd lost that battle long ago. For once she was only thinking about what she wanted. Reaching up, she threaded her fingers into the hair at the nape of his neck and drew him down. The moment their lips met she made sure it was hot, wet and deep. Rapid breaths and groans escaped past their melding tongues. He tasted so good.

Murray propped her against the tree trunk and pressed into her as his hands busied themselves in her hair, over her breasts and backside. Her tongue lashed against his, turning her legs to jelly. Want sent her hand to his waist, ripping his shirt out from his pants before splaying her hand across warm taut skin. There were no thoughts of stopping, no thoughts of repercussions. She wanted all of him NOW.

Below, his pants were straining, so tight the zipper's days must be numbered. Ellen worked his belt free and released him, palming his length. Murray gasped against her mouth before he pushed into her palm, making her heady with passion. She didn't want to give him a chance to think, to get hold of his control, to even think about shutting this down.

Gathering up her skirt, she guided his hand to her sodden folds, needing him to quell the ache.

He trembled. 'Oh my God.'

With his deft touch he made fireworks explode before her eyes as she tried to hold on, hold back, make it last. She managed to rifle through her bag, to her special pocket for her emergency condom, which she'd never needed. Until now. Keeping Murray distracted with her mouth and rocking against his hand she covered his length before she guided him to her.

Murray removed his hand, and she bit her lip in frustration before he lifted her onto him and settled her back against the tree, she wrapped her legs around him and tilted her hips, sending him deeper.

Her lips crushed against his, mashing with each thrust. Ellen had never been so turned on before, so ready to teeter over the edge . . . and suddenly she was there. She clung to him, moaning against his mouth to stop herself crying out as she shuddered.

'Oh, sweet Jesus,' he muttered before releasing his own climactic groan.

Ellen hung on, enjoying each wave and knowing her release had done him in, felt alive on that knowledge as if it was a superpower.

Against the trunk they rested, still connected, breathing hard. 'I . . .'

Ellen pressed a finger to his lips, not wanting to spoil this moment.

Her phone rang seconds later – as if life was out to prove it didn't stop for any private moment. Righting themselves she quickly found her phone and answered it.

'Hi, Ingi, you're here?' she said, walking out from the bushes to find a near-deserted car park. 'Awesome, thanks. We're at the bottom end of the car park.'

Hanging up she quickly brushed a hand over her dress and hair before turning to Murray, who had tucked in his shirt and picked up her rug and bag.

'Your lift, I presume,' he asked.

'Yeah.'

Her reply seemed small and insignificant after what they'd just done.

Murray opened his arms and she fell into them without hesitation. He kissed her head while they hugged, heartbeats racing against each other. Ellen breathed him in, memorising his scent, and the feel of his strong muscled body and the way she fitted perfectly under his chin, and other . . . things. Car headlights aimed for them like a spotlight. Ellen stepped out of his embrace as Ingi pulled up.

Window down, she leaned out. 'Someone call for an Uber? Oh *hello*,' she said, glancing at Murray.

Ellen opened the back door and put her things on the seat.

'Ingi, this is Murray. He's been keeping me company until you got here.'

Her eyebrow shot up, and Ellen knew she was analysing just what 'keeping me company' meant.

'Aren't you lovely? Thanks for looking out for my mate.'

'Any time,' he replied.

Ellen knew Ingi would interrogate her on the way home.

'Are you sure we can't give you a ride?' El asked as Murray walked her to the passenger side.

He opened the door for her. 'I'll be fine, thank you.'

This was the end of their night. She hadn't been expecting anything like this, but it had certainly given Ellen the belief that she was desirable, and filled her with hope and confidence.

'Thank you.' She kissed him goodbye. It was more than a peck but nothing of the heat they'd had moments ago. She gazed at those wonderful brown eyes and wondered if he really understood how much he'd given her. 'Bye,' she whispered.

She went to move but he didn't let go of her hands. Their magic was about to dissolve. The clock was turning twelve and her coach had arrived.

Lifting her hand to his lips, he kissed her knuckles and finally let her go. Ellen climbed in the car and waved, watching him until she couldn't see him anymore.

'Okay, spill. Who was that delicious man?'

Ellen smiled into the dark interior of Ingi's car. 'Murray.'

'Murray who?'

'I actually don't know. We didn't get to that.'

'What do you mean?'

'I don't know. It didn't seem important. I think we both knew the night was just there to be enjoyed, with no expectations. Does that make sense?'

'Yeah, I guess. So you didn't even get his number?'

Ellen stared ahead, not really seeing, basking in the warmth still flooding her body.

'Earth to Ellen – hey, did you get his number?'

She blinked, focused on Ingi and sighed. Pulling out her phone she brought up the photo they'd taken together. 'All I have is this.'

And the memories.

6

Ellen

Now

THE ROAD BLURRED BEFORE HER AS IF SHE WAS DRIVING IN heavy rain. Tears rolled down her cheeks and dripped from her chin. *I should have turned the damn radio off!*

For fear of crashing, Ellen pulled off the road. She'd already dropped her speed, dawdling along at eighty kilometres as she'd become lost in her memories. A few cars sped past, happy to have her out of the way.

Dropping her head to the steering wheel she let the tears flow, hoping they'd take some of her pain with them. Being at Challa had given her a distraction, a reason to keep everything bottled up. But this trip, that song . . . it was all too much. Life had turned to shit after that concert. That night was the last real happiness she'd felt before everything started to take a nosedive. She'd somehow held it all in because letting it explode . . . well, that would be too messy. And Ellen didn't do messy.

Knock, knock, knock!

She jerked her head up to see someone standing by her window. Wiping her face, she tried to make her bleary eyes focus while grappling to wind down the window.

'Are you okay?'

After a few blinks, she realised it was Hans, the backpacker . . . again. *Oh my God, how embarrassing. He must think I'm a fricken looney.*

She had no words, she couldn't believe she was in this predicament . . . again.

'I recognised your ute and pulled over, just in case the nuts had worked loose,' he said softly.

Her wheel nuts were fine, but as for the nuts in her head . . . they were rolling around and rattling her teeth.

'I'm sorry. I'm just having one of those days,' she said, voice husky from crying. 'I heard a sad song and I ended up like this. I couldn't see the road, so I pulled over. Car's fine. I'm not.' She reached over and grabbed a tissue from the glovebox and wiped her face. 'But thank you for coming to my rescue again.'

'Wait here,' he said before disappearing.

Ellen finished drying her face, relived that it was just tears and not snot. She glanced in the mirror quickly and groaned at the swollen panda eyes blinking back at her. *Just great.*

'Here, I find sugar helps with sadness,' he said, his teeth bright white against his tan skin. 'And there's nothing better than Sour Worms.' He opened the packet and handed it to her.

'I swear I'm not normally like this. I've . . . I've been through a trauma which I'm trying to overcome.' Ellen felt a moment of self-pity and pushed it away. She plastered on a fake smile. 'I actually love these, thank you, Hans.' She bit the end off the lolly. 'Do you do this on a regular basis? Help crazy ladies in distress?'

He tucked a strand of hair behind his ear and chuckled. 'Not usually. But I'm in no rush so I like to stop and help if I can. Gives me time to soak up this amazing country. A life well lived is one full of moments.'

'I like your philosophy. Hopefully, next time it can be me stopping to help you.'

He grinned. 'Sure, I'd like that.' His smile disappeared as concern returned. 'Are you sure you'll be alright?'

Ellen held up the packet of lollies. 'You've helped me immensely. It's okay, you can go. I'll be fine. I promise.'

He studied her for a moment before nodding and slapping the top of her ute with his hand. 'Take care, Ellen. I hope I see you around again.'

Hopefully not like this!

'Me too, Hans. I owe you.' And with that she popped the rest of the sour worm into her mouth and waved him goodbye.

She ate another two in quick succession and had to admit she did feel better. The sour hit matched the bitter edge that clung to her skin like the red dust. And the sugar, or Hans, or a combination of both, she wasn't sure, had given her a distraction and she was ready to continue north. How lucky she'd been to have him stop both times, a handsome young backpacker. Could have been much worse.

At Newman she stopped and stocked up on some fresh supplies, as there wasn't much from here to Karijini. She didn't have to worry about cooking equipment as the others had that in their vans, but she got a few things to put in her small fridge – cheeses, dips, leafy salad mix, and some more bags of lollies for good measure. Ingi was bringing the meat as they had the biggest fridge. Bodhi had splurged and hired a fancy Maui campervan. Ellen had a swag, and if the flies or mozzies got too bad, she could sleep in her ute at a pinch.

From Newman onwards she noticed a change in the scenery. Red rocky hills began to appear, along with plateaus and outcrops covered with tall ghost gums, green shrubs and grasses. Massive mountains and escarpments rising out of the flat valleys. Large dark red termite mounds scattered throughout hummock grasslands like works of art. Some would be nearly as tall as her, Ellen mused. Such iconic landscape. Made you appreciate all Western Australia had to offer in one state. A straightish line would take you from a cool coastal Albany at the bottom to a warm rusty Karratha just a measly one thousand and nine hundred–odd kilometres north, and that wasn't going to the very tip near Kununurra. That would set you back well over three thousand kilometres navigating all sorts of roads.

Turning off the Great Northern Highway, she headed along Karijini Drive and goosebumps covered her arms knowing the gorges were so close. Karijini was one of those places everyone talked about visiting, a place lucky tourists and grey nomads had on their bucket lists, that backpackers wanted to Instagram, a place that had seemed so far out of reach for Ellen, until now.

As much as she couldn't wait to see the sister she loved, part of her dreaded it. And it would get worse tomorrow when Bodhi and Ingi turned up. What they'd see was a Mona Lisa, calm and serene, while if they just scratched off that oil veneer they'd see the truth, that she was closer to a Jackson Pollock painting.

The Karijini sign appeared. Then the National Park sign-in area, which she continued through because her pass included the park fee with her campsite at Dale's Gorge. Another right onto Dale's Road, and it felt like she'd been driving for ages before finally coming to the camping area. Digging out her paperwork, Ellen followed the narrow, one-way road with speed humps every hundred metres or so, keeping an eye out for Bungarra Loop. Knee-high wood markers with reflective tape and numbers indicated individual campsites, and on the other side was the natural bushland – green grasses, spinifex, acacia shrubs, mulgas and eucalyptus trees.

At number 35, Ellen stopped and parked her ute. The ground was literally hard as rock, and it wasn't so much red as a deep mahogany. Thank God she didn't have a tent as there was no way pegs were going in that ground unless she had a drill. Bodhi was sharing this site with her, so for tonight she had the spot to herself. Carrie was next door and sure enough, there was a campervan parked. Her insides involuntarily twisted like a month's worth of cramps. Dragging her lower lip across her teeth she stared out the window in their direction.

How long had they been here? Had they gone straight to the gorge for a look? *How many minutes do I have before I need to put my mask in place, find that happy voice and pretend like I haven't changed?*

Luckily the campsites weren't on top of each other, so she couldn't really see the neighbours, meaning her sister, but she could see the toilets. Ellen knew she had to leave the ute at some point, and besides, she'd been busting since turning into Karijini.

The toilets were two long-drops side by side with a little veranda out the front. They were spacious and clean with a fresh bucket of blue water and brush at the ready. There was a faint scent, not overpowering, but she bet at some point the heat of the day would warm the earth up enough for it to permeate. Tonight's visit might not be as nice. Exiting the toilet, she checked her watch. It was about four o'clock and it was still too hot to think.

Ellen headed back to her campsite and startled, almost skidding in the dirt. Carrie was standing by her ute.

'El!' she squealed.

Carrie ran into her arms, her chocolate waves billowing out behind her. Only her sister would have her hair down in this heat. It was a sweaty, clingy hug, like a koala clinging to its mother. Waves of black coffee and white flowers hung like heavy mist from Carrie's favourite Black Opium perfume. It was a scent that grounded Ellen, her anxiety dissolving away as love flooded her heart.

'Hey, Carrie. I missed you too,' she said, hugging her baby sister. It's funny how the love for your family trumps all. For the moment at least.

'You look amazing. Must be all the sun you get up here,' Carrie said, holding her at arm's length. 'God, I've missed you.'

Anyone would think Carrie used to hang out heaps with her big sister; Ellen didn't even think Carrie would notice her absence. Then again, Ellen used to drop by her salon with coffee and a chat, but it never worked the other way.

Carrie's make-up was usually on point but today it looked like cake icing on a hot day – she was surprised Carrie hadn't noticed it yet.

'So, did you remember all the bits for the proposal?' Ellen dropped her sunglasses down as the glare off anything shiny, including the rocky ground, was almost too bright.

'Yes, bossy britches. All work and no fun you are.'

Carrie still looked happy to see her, bossy britches or not. Suddenly Carrie stood taller and smiled as Ellen heard the crunching of footsteps behind her.

'Well, hello stranger!'

A smile came to her lips. Ellen didn't have to turn around; she was all too familiar with that slight accent. 'Hans?'

He put his hands up in the air. 'I'm not following you, I swear. How weird is this?'

His hair had been retied at the top of his head. Sunlight caught the golden honey colour.

'So crazy. I didn't even think to ask where you were headed,' she said.

Carrie looked as though she was at a tennis match, head turning back and forth between them. 'How do you two know each other?' she asked, plastering on the sweetness.

Ellen put her hand on her sister's shoulder. 'Hans, this is my sister Carrie. Hans was my rescuer today when I had a flat tyre.'

'More than once,' he added with a smirk.

Ellen squinted. 'I'm not sure Sour Worms count?'

'In my book they do,' he said beaming.

Carrie thrust out her hand. 'Nice to meet you, Hans. Are you staying here too?'

'Yes, I'm right over there,' he said pointing back past the toilet block.

Ellen could just make out his van.

'I saw you walking this way and I just had to check it really was you. I think the universe is conspiring to put us together.'

A brilliant idea hit her. 'Maybe it is. Maybe it's so I can thank you properly with a beer later?' If Hans joined them, then the talk would be focused on him and his life. No one would go digging through hers. Holding her breath, Ellen waited for his reply.

'Oh yes, do come and chill with us if you have nothing else to do,' said Carrie. 'Maybe he could help us with the set-up?'

'What set-up?'

'Oh, a secret proposal. That's why we're all here. My brother is going to propose to his girlfriend,' said Carrie. 'You should totally join . . .'

Ellen put her hand up to slow down Carrie. 'No pressure. But you're welcome anytime you want some company.' *Please let that be all the time!* She was well aware he was travelling alone. 'How many nights are you booked in for?' She hoped that didn't sound too forward or stalkerish.

'Two nights. And thank you, I do enjoy company, but I don't want to impose.'

Carrie shook her head. 'Ellen will be the odd one out, so you'll help even things up.'

Thanks, Carrie, like I need pointing out I'm going to be the lonely single lady.

'See what I have to put up with?' She laughed awkwardly.

'Well, you know where I am too, so if you're feeling like the odd one out you're always welcome,' he said, pointing back to his van. 'I need to finish setting up and then I'm going to head down to the gorge for a quick swim.'

'I think I will be too,' said Ellen. 'And we have a few things to cart down there ready for tomorrow.'

'I'll stop in on my way past and see if I can be of service.'

He dipped his head and headed back to his campsite.

As she expected, Carrie wheeled around on her and whispered, 'Who was he?' She took her arm and dragged her back towards her van, demanding details. 'Come on, come and see Fin and then tell me EVERYTHING that happened today.'

Ellen's gut churned. Hans was a nice distraction but everything she was holding deep down inside her was even harder to hide now that her family was converging.

She just hoped she could survive the weekend and get back to Challa Station in one piece, because at the moment she felt like a porcelain vase on the highest shelf just before an earthquake.

Just breathe, Ellen. Just breathe.

7

Ingrid

THE SUN WAS SETTING AT KARALUNDI CARAVAN PARK, JUST
north of Meekatharra, throwing handfuls of pinks, yellows,
oranges and golds across the sky like one of those fundraising
Colour Runs. The heat was brewing up clouds which reflected
these awesome colours. Ingrid Byrne had seen amazing sunsets
back home, but here felt different. It was still, quiet and steamy
as if the air breathed around her, licking her skin, dampening
her hair. Birds warbled and insects clicked and buzzed and
yet there was that quietness that made her want to speak in
a whisper.

Ellen came to mind. There was so much left unsaid. That
baggage was like a backpack full of stones. Ingi wanted, no
needed, to know that she was okay. Face to face was the only
way she would truly know. Ellen wouldn't be able to brush
her off and hang up now.

Ingrid turned away from the setting sun to look upon Bodhi.
Bathed in light, like a golden statue glistening in the rays.

Sweat clung to the edges of his short dark hair at the nape of his neck and made the longer top bits curl in the damp heat.

'Want to go for a walk back up the driveway and see if we can find the cattle?'

'Just because we saw them on the way in doesn't mean I need a closer look.' Bodhi pouted like a two-year-old. Ingrid squeezed her eyes shut and he grinned, knowing she'd been swayed.

'Okay, you win.' She frowned. 'Will they try to charge me?'

Bodhi chuckled. 'It's me you should be more worried about,' he warned as he pulled her closer using the belt loops on her denim shorts.

'What were you thinking about just now?' he asked as he pressed a kiss to the top of her forehead.

Ingrid ran her hands along his muscled arms and shoulders and threaded her fingers together behind his neck. 'This heat, those colours . . . you,' she added and loved how he smiled and the gold tones in his hazel eyes swirled like the waves he loved to surf.

'And?'

And he knew her so well.

'And Ellen.'

'I know something has happened between you two. I don't know what it is but I hope you can sort it out while we're up here.'

Ingi nodded but kept her mouth shut in case she gave too much away. She hated lying to Bodhi – well, not lying exactly but lying through omission. Same, same wasn't it?

'Are you regretting bringing me here now, with no waves to surf?' she asked, hoping to change the subject.

He rolled his eyes. 'Never. The caravan park people said I could put the sprinkler on. It'll have to do.'

He wrapped her up in his arms and kissed her before letting her go. It was too hot to be swaddled together.

'Besides, this trip isn't about me. It's all about you and my sisters. I'm just here for the ride.' He groaned at his own pun. 'A wave-less ride but still one worth every minute.'

He took her hand and together they set off along the grass towards the Karalundi Caravan Park entry road, Bodhi in his thongs and Ingi wearing her canvas Converse shoes – she wasn't taking any chances on a place she was unfamiliar with. Ants, trampling cattle, bugs, snakes . . . there could be any number of things up here she didn't know about.

'Are you enjoying it so far?' Bodhi asked.

'Totally! I've only ever left Albany to drive to Perth for doctor appointments. This . . . this is a whole other world. It amazes me how things are green and survive in this heat and that dirt. It looks so unfertile compared to some of the black soils we get back home.'

He stared at her as if she'd done something cute. She reached up and checked her glasses weren't crooked.

'What?' She pushed against his chest.

'Nothing. It's just, I love watching you experience things for the first time. I love the awe on your face. Like the time you caught your first wave. I can't wait for you to finally see Karijini.'

'Oh my God, me too.' She swung their arms as they walked to circulate some air. 'This is already the best birthday present I've ever had. And you've given me some good ones over the years.'

Like the expensive knife set he'd ordered in especially for her. Or the time he rocked up at work in an old GT Ford Falcon he'd borrowed and they drove to Denmark for a meal at the Boston Brewery before he gave her the most beautiful necklace. Reaching up, she touched the simple gold chain with the love heart and the word 'Mikey' inscribed on it. Her nose prickled and she had to clamp her lips together to stop them wobbling. Mike would have loved this trip. In a way it was because of him that she had Karijini at the top of her bucket list.

Gee, don't cry now, you silly woman. She'd done enough of that when Bodhi surprised her with this trip. Cried so hard that he'd started to stress that he'd done the wrong thing. 'I'm just so happy,' she'd managed to blurt out and the fear on his face had faded to relief.

There were days when she wondered if Mikey had a hand in them being together. Actually, she was pretty sure he did. It was hard to explain but she felt his presence sometimes.

'Are you worrying about your uncle?' Bodhi asked. 'He will be okay at the restaurant. You remember what he said?'

She laughed. 'Yeah, that I may nearly run the place but he's not dead yet and he's quite capable without me for a week.'

'Good. Remember that. I want you to completely relax and soak up every second of this trip. Besides, it's a bloody long way to come back and do it again.'

The bushes beside them moved and Indi jumped and squeaked. 'What the hell!'

Bodhi gently tucked her safely behind him then leaned to take a better look. 'Oh, it's a baby calf.'

Ingi looked around him, holding his waist tightly. 'That's a baby! It's the size of a pony.' The chocolate-brown calf was nestled in the bushes with its big ears and pink tongue lashing over its wet nose.

'Think of all those steaks, babe.'

She slapped his back and pulled away. 'Shh, it will hear you.' She took a step and paused. 'Do you think there might be more . . . like a big scary mummy cow? Or one with horns?'

Bodhi didn't laugh at her concern, nor did he even smirk. He squeezed her hand. 'Wanna go back?'

Ingi nodded rapidly. 'Yeah, it's much safer back there. Besides, it was nice under that gum tree on the lawn. So nice to see lawn.'

'Totally agree. Although the ocean would be nice if I could see it.'

As he spoke, she was lulled by his soothing voice. It made her think again about seeing Ellen and Carrie, but more so Ellen. They'd become as close as sisters after she started dating Bodhi and gained a whole new family. She'd missed Ellen dearly when she'd run off up north. Of course, Ingi knew why, but she couldn't say, couldn't even tell Bodhi, which she hated. She loved him with all her heart, but Ellen had made her promise, and she also loved Ellen. Why did life have to be so complicated? You couldn't protect someone without hurting someone else.

As much as this trip was about her and Mikey, as well as her and Bodhi, it was also about Ellen.

The Suttons were a close bunch, enjoying family lunches and birthday parties, but none of these had been the same without Ellen. At their last family barbecue Carrie had lamented how dull it was without Ellen organising all the little details and making sure it was a great night. She was the one who always remembered Mikey's birthday and would arrive with flowers or chocolates, or they'd just go to the beach together. No one's birthday passed without Ellen making it memorable for them.

She used to be the spark in the room, not the life of the party – that was Carrie – but El was like warm fairy lights, constant and uplifting. She made you feel special. Bodhi and El shared a unique bond, probably from all those hours surfing together, but they seemed to understand each other without words. Ingi didn't have any siblings left and never had a sister. Meeting Bodhi and being welcomed into his family meant more than any of them would probably understand.

The first time she'd seen Bodhi had been at a beach – Mutton Bird Island beach to be exact, where surfers liked to go. Ingi would sit on the beach and watch the waves and the surfers. He'd parked his ute not far from hers one day and she saw him run off towards the water, surf, and then return. Each time after that, their eyes would meet and he'd offer a warm smile. He had caught her eye for some reason – maybe it was the way he'd help other surfers, offering up his wax or leg rope, or even his board when one of them broke theirs. Months passed until one morning she arrived and he was already there, the only one in the water. It was a shitty day, overcast, cold and drizzly. But Ingi persisted because the cold and rain made her feel alive, and she never left until the last minute as if squeezing every drop from the view.

This day, instead of the usual warm smile, he put his board down on the sand, peeled the top half of his wetsuit down, threw on his towel hoodie and approached her. She remembered watching him, unashamed to take in his every move.

'Good morning,' he'd said, water dripping from the bottom of his wetsuit.

'Hi,' she'd replied.

'I've noticed you come here just about as much as I do. You don't surf?'

She'd shaken her head.

'You okay, though?' he'd asked, his voice full of concern.

'I'm not contemplating suicide if that's what you're worried about.' She remembered the shock on his face. And the fact that she knew there was some truth to her words.

'I really thought you were just a hot chick and I wanted to get to know your name,' he'd said, sitting down beside her. 'Actually, it was more that some days you seemed so sad. It worried me. Today I thought I'd do something about it.'

She'd been moved by his honest openness. 'Thanks for checking in. It's nice to know people take notice.'

Neither of them seemed to know what to say after that and so they sat, watching the waves and the clouds. Ingi had felt relief that he hadn't run off. Having someone sit beside her, where Mikey usually sat, was comforting. His company had been more soothing than his words.

'So you really don't surf at all?' he'd asked eventually.

'No.'

'Then why come here? Only surfers usually come this far out of Albany.'

'I used to come here a lot with my brother. He loved to watch the surfers.' Ingi had no idea why she was sharing all this with a random stranger. Yet, even though they hadn't talked before, he didn't seem like someone scary, in fact he had that calmness like Mikey. She'd turned to him. 'He died a few years ago. I only recently started coming again to feel closer to him.

He loved the wipe-outs. Watching your boards fly up in the air or you guys getting pounded always put a grin on his face.'

They'd shared a sad smile.

'Well, if you ever want to learn I'd be more than happy to show you. Then your brother can watch you stack it. I'm sure he's got the best view in the house.'

Ingi's throat swelled up now, as it did back then. That had been the moment she knew this guy was worth knowing.

'I might take you up on that one day. I'm Ingrid, by the way. Friends call me Ingi.'

She'd held out her hand, her short nails painted blue to match her glasses, and slid it into his larger frozen hand.

'Ingi, beautiful name. I'm Bodhi.'

She'd burst out laughing then and struggled to get her words out. 'Bodhi? A surfer named Bodhi. *Point Break* was one of my brother's favourite movies,' she'd spluttered. 'But I must say, you're more like Keanu than Patrick.'

'Well, my mum was a massive Patrick Swayze fan and so when I was born, I got the name from that exact movie.'

'No way!'

'Yes, way.'

It had been a morning that changed her life. So many connections to Mikey, how could she not think that he'd brought them together somehow?

They'd talked for a bit longer until she realised she'd be late for work.

'My uncle's gonna kill me,' she'd said.

'Will I see you again?' Bodhi had asked hopefully.

There was no way she could have resisted seeing him again. Since Mikey's death she'd been in a limbo state – work, sleep, repeat. Coming to the beach had been her first step in finding something to live for, something to take away the monotony and feeling of being lost. Bodhi had sparked something deep inside her, a yearning to be whole again, to feel alive and be worthy of life. She had to find a way to live for her brother too.

'For sure. You're going to teach me to surf,' she'd added with a grin.

Bodhi nudged her shoulder now, breaking her reminiscence. 'What are you thinking about? You've got that loved-up smile.'

'I was actually thinking about the time we met. When you came over and spoke to me that morning.' She stopped walking to face him. 'I don't know if you realise the impact you made on my life then. I wasn't suicidal but I wasn't happy. I wasn't living.' How could she explain it? 'I felt dead inside, like I was drifting untethered in the ocean.'

Bodhi brushed strands of her straight hair back behind her ear. 'I'm so glad I plucked up the courage to talk to you.'

'Courage?' she asked.

'Yeah, you were this gorgeous petite girl, torn jeans and dark hoodie, cute glasses with the saddest eyes. I think I fell in love with you there and then.'

'And now?' she asked.

'Now, you are fused onto my soul. I love you more than you'll ever know.'

Bodhi tipped up her chin and kissed her.

'I love you too, Mr Swayze.'

8

Ellen

Back then

ELLEN PLACED THE FLOWER ARRANGEMENT SHE'D MADE ON the table while Ingi was heating up the food she'd brought for the lunch. Light filtered through the large windows from the backyard, making the house feel warm and welcoming. But it had always felt like that here, especially with some of their childhood artworks still on display and lots of Lorraine's own art pieces around the house, from her collection of chicken feathers arranged into wreaths to pottery wares next to mosaic mirrors. And her paintings, inspired by the Albany landscapes.

'You two shouldn't have gone to all this trouble,' said her mum, swanning around the kitchen with a glass of champagne in her hand.

Ellen and Ingi shared a secret smile. Lorraine Sutton loved 'all this trouble' and would be disappointed if her children didn't lavish love on their wedding anniversary. Or birthdays for that matter.

Lorraine looked like one of her bright attempts at oil painting in white cotton pants with a bright orange, rusty red and yellow striped overshirt, and if that wasn't enough colour she'd thrown on lots of necklaces and bangles. Colour was life for her mum, even her long curly hair had been painted with copper highlights. She was the colourful mixes on a paint tray against the plain blank canvas. Ellen preferred unity, everything to match, calm colours and neutral tones. *Stop playing it safe*, her mother liked to say.

'Mum, it's not every day your parents celebrate thirty years of marriage.'

Ellen had brought some flower petals and scattered them across the large table set for seven. A bouquet of lilies sat in the middle of the table; Ellen brought them every year as they were her mum's bridal flowers. Bodhi preferred to leave the girly stuff up to them; he would man the barbecue or pick up flowers or cakes but that was it, and Carrie would put in for the joint present. Sometimes she'd offer ideas on what to get them. The rest was left to Ellen – organising food, flowers, the gift, and coordinating everyone else.

'Why do I always end up doing all the work?' she'd complained one year.

'Because you're good at this stuff, sis,' came their replies.

Well, she couldn't argue with that. Just picturing how this day would go if it was left up to Carrie made her shudder.

'My God that smells divine, Ingi. I'm so glad my Bodhi found someone who could cook. We are so spoilt.'

'I can cook, Mum,' Ellen stated.

Lorraine hugged Ingi and kissed her cheek while Ingi held a spatula she'd been using to stir the pasta sauce. 'Yes, but not like this girl. She's a real chef.'

'I can tell who the favourite is,' Ellen muttered.

Ingi laughed and then noticed a drop of sauce on her grey t-shirt that said 'Adventure, then Pizza'.

'Oh drats.' She pushed up her black glasses with pale blue edges that highlighted her blue-tipped hair.

'You must be the messiest chef I know and the only one who wears Converse,' said Lorraine. 'But I love that about you. Cooking is like art, it's expression, it's passion. You're not immersed properly if you're not at least wearing some of it.'

'I love that, Lorraine. Next time I make a mess, I'll remember that.' Ingi beamed.

Lorraine studied Ingi for a moment and smiled. 'I don't know how my Bodhi ended up finding such a wonderful woman. You're always cooking for us – don't you get sick of it?'

'Never, especially when it's appreciated by those I love. It makes my heart sing.'

Lorraine looked like she was about to cry. She brushed Ingi's cheek with her finger. 'Love you too, kiddo.'

Ellen felt a shift in the air around them, a change in energy as her mum spun towards her. *Oh no!*

'With Carrie in a real relationship,' she glanced towards Ingi, 'now all I need is my oldesr daughter to find a perfect man and we'll all be happy.'

'Mum,' Ellen groaned.

'You should have seen the guy she hooked up with at the John Butler concert,' Ingi said.

'Ingi!' Ellen stared at her friend before checking her dad and Bodhi were still outside talking work.

'He was so hot and he was drooling over Ellen.'

She shot daggers at Ingi. 'I think you are abusing your standing in this family,' she retorted.

Ingi poked her tongue out, gleefully aware she'd dumped Ellen in a steaming hot pot of water.

'Oh, do tell. What am I missing, Ingi?' Lorraine pulled up a stool by the kitchen breakfast bar and settled in for the story.

'It's nothing, Mum.' Ellen tried to shut her down, but as usual she was having none of it.

'Ellen, honey, I can ask again when everyone is sitting around the table, or you can tell me now while it's just us three.'

She knew she was beat. 'It's nothing really.'

'Ingi thinks he was something.'

'Urgh. It was just a man at the concert.' It was hard not to think about Murray. She'd already worn her phone out looking at the photo she'd taken of them both. She didn't regret anything from that night, except maybe not getting his phone number. It wasn't until later she wondered if he could have been worth hanging onto. She'd been hoping he'd remember she was a nurse and come looking for her at the hospital. In her dreams she might have fantasised such, but in reality, it was just a bloody awesome one-night stand.

'More, please?' Lorraine demanded.

'There's not much to tell. It was a great night. We left it at that.'

Lorraine frowned. 'What a shame. That's the risk with one-night stands, Ellen. For all you know he could have been the one and you let him go. But then again, they can also make someone appear better than they are. He could have been a dick once you really got to know him.'

Gee, since when has Mum been an expert on one-night stands? Ellen shook her head, not wanting an insight into her mother's youth.

'I think he would have been worth a shot,' said Ingi. 'He was handsome, Lorraine, like a sexy lumberjack. And he was so sweet to Ellen, had old school manners . . .'

'You saw him?' Lorraine spun on her seat to pump Ingi for details.

Ellen walked over to the breakfast bar and sat beside her mum – she might have more luck keeping her contained being closer. But realistically she knew there was no containing Lorraine Sutton. She was the kind of woman that if you told her to get back into her box she'd likely smash her way out and come at you harder.

Ingi sighed. 'He was keeping her company until I picked her up. It was so romantic.'

'Sounds lovely.' Lorraine reached out to hold Ellen's hand, her bangles rattling against the benchtop. 'You know I just want you to be happy after . . . well, I won't mention that idiot's name, but I must admit you seemed much happier after the concert. Did this man have something to do with that?' Her eyebrows wiggled.

'No doubt. He was so good for my self-confidence.' Her skin still tingled as she thought about him.

'Go on, show your mum the photo,' Ingi said.

Ellen shot Ingi a look to say that was borderline betrayal, but she couldn't get too mad. It was nice to be centre of attention for a good reason. She pulled out her phone to show her mum the photo when the front door burst open.

'We're here!'

Foghorn Carrie. Ellen smiled.

'Finally,' Lorraine called out. 'Can always count on Carrie to be last to the party. I was hoping Fin might help fix that issue.'

Ellen laughed and got up as her mum rushed to greet her younger daughter. Hopefully the excitement at greeting Fin, Carrie's boyfriend, would make her mum forget about her one-night stand. For now at least.

Carrie bringing a man to a family celebration was big news. It was a first. Bodhi sometimes joked that she was a horse on a carousel ride, some blokes never made it a full circle. Their mum and dad had already met Fin and when Ellen had asked why she was the last to find out about him, her mum had explained that Carrie didn't want to rub it in her face when Josh was strutting around with his ex and new son. 'Bodhi and Ingi haven't met him yet either, so don't get your knickers in a knot,' she'd added. 'I think she's serious about this one as she's keeping him all to herself.'

'What have I missed?' said Carrie as she bounded in and threw her bag down as if she still lived here.

Actually, she still had half her crap in her old room which Lorraine had tried to convert into a studio.

'Hey, sis, you look fabulous. Cute top,' said Carrie as she threw her arms around her.

'Ellen was just telling us about this hot one-night stand she had,' said Ingi as she turned to greet them.

Ellen frowned. 'Ingi!'

But Ingi's face had paled and her mouth dropped open. For a moment Ellen thought she was worried she'd upset her, but Ingi wasn't even looking her way.

'I want to hear everything about him, El, but first let me introduce you all to Fin. Fin, honey, this is my sister Ellen and my brother's girlfriend Ingi.' Carrie was beaming. Beside her was a man, his eyes wide in shock.

Ellen felt faint, as if an artery had been sliced open and her blood was pumping out at a rapid rate; her body wanted to sag to the ground like an empty sack. It was an eerie out-of-body experience.

It was Murray. Handsome Murray she'd spent a night with. Had sex with. Here, standing beside her sister. Her brain was struggling to understand. It was definitely him – she'd remember those eyes, those tattoos, those lips, anywhere.

'So lovely you could come, Fin,' said Lorraine. 'Carrie hasn't brought any boyfriends to our celebrations before. I'm sure you know how special that makes you.'

Lorraine gave him a hug, which he reciprocated but his eyes remained on Ellen. Yeah, he remembered her too.

Lorraine was oblivious to the sudden temperature drop and the shocked expressions on three people's faces.

'I know, he's pretty special.' Carrie winked before kissing his cheek.

Ingi regained composure first. 'Hi, *Fin*,' she said, exaggerating his name. 'Nice to meet you.'

Ellen was confused. Had he lied that night? Did he regularly seduce solo girls at events, giving false names? Was he a player? Had she been conned, again? Was he now conning her sister?

But she quashed those theories when she saw the way *Fin* was looking at her. There was shock in his eyes but also something else. His face started to flush and she knew he was thinking of their bush escapade. Images of that night became clearer than ever. Turning her back to them, Ellen reached for her glass and took a gulp while sending Ingi a 'What the hell' look.

If she thought it was an illusion, the sound of his voice soon confirmed it wasn't. She'd know those husky tones anywhere. The way he'd murmured her name against her ear as he'd pumped into her. *Jesus fucking Christ!*

'You too, Ingi,' he stuttered.' And my name is actually Murray. Murray Finlay.'

Tremors ran through her body. *Murray.*

'But Murray is so old-fashioned,' Carrie cut in. 'Fin suits him so much better.'

'Fin is what everyone usually calls me, except my family,' he added.

'Oh, that explains it . . . um, I mean, thanks for explaining that,' muttered Ingi, shoving her glasses further up her nose before turning around. 'Oops, can't burn lunch.'

'Nice to meet you, Fin. I'll go get Dad and Bodhi,' Ellen said as she jumped up and headed outside, trying to keep her eyes away from Murray aka Fin. Her steps felt wonky, like she was drunk or walking under water as her brain still tried to process this. Murray was Fin, Fin was dating Carrie. *I've slept with Carrie's boyfriend. Shit.*

Once she got outside, she collapsed back against the door. How was she going to get through this dinner? All the moments Carrie had mentioned her new boyfriend Fin started to play back in her mind as if she could somehow have guessed or known. Yet she'd let most of the comments go, as Carrie did prattle on a bit. *Fin is so cool. He's the most considerate boyfriend I've ever had. I think he could be the one.*

That last comment had occurred in last week's phone call when they'd been planning the anniversary lunch and she said she was going to bring Fin to finally meet everyone – because *I think he could be the one.* Just how long had they been dating? Before or after the concert? Ellen tried hard to remember when she first found out that Carrie had a new man.

'Ellen, you okay, honey?'

Colin Sutton stood before her, the sunbeams behind him like he was an apparition from God, his Brut aftershave filling the air as if he had to make up for all the times he never used it.

'I'm fine, getting a headache,' she said truthfully. *More like a migraine.* 'Carrie has arrived.'

'That explains the headache,' muttered Bodhi under his breath. 'The new boyfriend is here. Time to play the tough brother,' he said with a chuckle.

'Bodhi, don't scare him off. He's the first one she's brought home. He's done okay if he's lasted this long,' said Colin.

Her dad was a large man, heavy-set but not overweight as his electrician business kept him busy. Colin was the big cuddly teddy bear you went to for hugs when you fell over and hurt yourself because you knew he'd scoop you up and carry you to the house and dry your tears. Only now she was too old to be cradled, but she still craved her dad's safe embrace.

Ellen moved away from the door. 'I might just sit out here for a bit. Fresh air might help,' she added as they headed inside.

Bodhi gave her a weird look.

'I'm fine, go inside,' she ordered.

She didn't hear the door shut behind them as she sank into the chair on the back patio. Her mind went back to Carrie and Fin. Carrie in a fitted black dress more suited for an evening dinner with high heels and full face and blow-waved hair. Fin was in denim jeans and a black dress shirt like Bodhi – Carrie no doubt having mentioned that it was a dress-up lunch. His tattoos were on display and he still wore those black earrings. He had quite a bit of stubble across his jaw but she'd know those lips anywhere. Closing her eyes, she swallowed hard and tried to push him from her mind. That night. Those feelings. His scent.

The door cracked opened and suddenly that scent was all too real. Too close.

Her eyes shot open and there he was. Fin looked at her with as much discomfort as she felt.

'Hi, um, your brother said you had a headache, so Ingi gave me these and told me to bring them out. I think they wanted time to talk about me, and Ingi knew we needed . . . a moment.'

'More than a moment, I'd say.' There was way too much to sort and analyse. Her headache made a real appearance, and her thoughts kept tumbling together like a long string of Christmas lights.

He put the water and packet of Panadol on the table beside her chair.

'Look, Ellen, I'm so sorry. I don't want you to think I'd normally cheat on your sister or on anyone. I've never done that before I swear,' he said, his voice trembling. 'We'd only been casually seeing each other for a week or two before the concert.'

Ellen put her hand up. 'I wish you'd told me.'

The one time she was self-indulgent . . . she knew it would come back to bite her on the arse. It hurt to look at him, but she couldn't look away. That magnetic pull was as strong as it was that night. It only made her head hurt more. She pressed her fingers against her temple. 'She's only ever called you Fin.'

His chest rose and fell for a few seconds. 'Carrie hates Murray.'

Tiny papercuts lanced her skin upon hearing him speak her sister's name. 'This is so awkward.'

Fin shifted from foot to foot, his hands in his pockets one second then hanging by his side the next. He raked one through his hair. 'Yeah, so crazy. Who would have thought . . .'

Seconds ticked by.

He cleared his throat. 'After the concert I told Carrie I'd been with someone.'

Ellen cringed at his words. She was that 'someone'.

'That's when she asked if we could be exclusive. So we started dating officially,' he whispered in a rush.

'So she doesn't know it was me?' Ellen squeaked.

The shake of his head was minute, as if wary about drawing attention to himself. 'I didn't mention names, I just confessed what I'd done.'

No wonder he never came looking for her. Disappointment flashed through her but it was fleeting. He was with Carrie. He. Was. With. Carrie. *Oh my fucking God*. This shit could only happen to her. And here she thought Josh was a once-off bad – okay, ridiculously bad scenario . . . and yet here she was, taking it up another notch.

He rubbed at his beard. 'What do we do? Do you want me to tell her?'

Ellen buried her head in her hands. 'Hell no.' She couldn't hurt Carrie. She glanced at the door, half-expecting someone to come out any second. 'We carry on as if we've never met.' The lump in her throat was hard to swallow. She couldn't tell what he was thinking and they didn't have the time to really talk this through. 'Look, let's just forget it ever happened. She doesn't need to know it was me.'

Ellen didn't really know what she was saying, she just blurted out words she thought he wanted to hear and that would not hurt her sister. Besides, who would want to come clean to his partner about sleeping with her sister?

'Yeah, I guess,' he replied.

He didn't sound very enthusiastic, but she had to try and see it from his perspective. He'd just found out he'd cheated on his girlfriend with her sister. Even though they hadn't been 'officially' dating, it still would have hurt Carrie to find out he'd had a one-night stand. Acid churned in her stomach. She didn't like lying to her sister either. But life was full of white lies, used to protect those we love. *No, you don't look fat in those jeans, dear. Yes, dinner was lovely. Oh, thank you for the wonderful gift.*

'I don't cheat,' he said rubbing his hands over his face. 'Well, I didn't. Shit, I feel so bad. This is karma biting me. I totally deserve this.'

'Murray, don't . . .' Her words faded away at the intensity of his eyes when she mentioned his name. *Mental note – call him Fin from now on.*

The door opened and they both jumped.

'Lunch is ready,' said Bodhi.

Fin gave her a strained smile and headed to the door.

Ellen opened the packet of Panadol and took two with the water. Then she stood up and took five deep breaths.

You can do this, Ellen!

Her pep talk didn't work. With dread she headed for the door.

9

Ellen

INSIDE, EVERYONE WAS TAKING A SEAT AROUND THE decorated table. More champagne was being poured as Lorraine moved about, playing hostess.

'Honey, Dad said you have a headache. Are you okay?'

'I'm fine, Mum,' she said, showing her the Panadol packet in her hand. 'You sit, I'll help Ingi serve up.'

Her mum looked about to protest so she got in first. 'You're the stars of the day. Go sit with Dad and enjoy,' she ordered.

Lorraine blew her a kiss and joined Colin at the table, where he was explaining the family electrician business he ran with Bodhi to Fin.

Ellen went to stand next to Ingi. 'Thanks for that,' she said.

'Did it help? Did you sort something out?' she whispered while throwing glances over her shoulder as they huddled together over the stove.

'Yep, pretend it never happened,' she said with a shrug.

Ingi frowned, ladle frozen mid-air. 'Are you sure that's wise?'

'Honestly, I don't know, Ingi. I'm still in shock.' Ellen picked up a plate so Ingi could serve up her famous saffron pasta with Foriana sauce. 'But I don't want to hurt Carrie. Is it really important that she knows? She's had plenty of one-night stands, and they weren't dating.'

Yet she still felt shitty.

'I'm sorry,' Ingi said, her blue eyes full of concern.

Ellen had no reply. Were there any words to describe how she was feeling and what was happening here today?

Together they finished serving and carried the full plates to the table. Ingi served Fin and Carrie, much to Ellen's relief. Distance was key today. Her thoughts were confusing, having spent the last month fantasising about him only to have to now try to forget him. He'd become the guy she pictured while wearing out the batteries in her vibrator. In her mind, they'd had many thrilling liaisons that he wasn't even aware of, so it was no surprise Ellen had trouble disassociating.

'This looks amazing as usual, Ingi. My favourite,' said Colin as he picked up his fork.

Lorraine rolled her eyes. 'We know, dear, you say that every time.'

'Don't worry, Lorraine, we made your favourite dessert,' said Ingi as she took her seat beside Bodhi.

Lorraine picked up her champagne glass. 'I've got mine right here,' she said with a wink.

Ellen was sitting beside Ingi, which was opposite Fin. It could have been worse, she could have been next to him. But this meant that every time she looked up she risked catching his eye. How were you supposed to look at someone you'd spent intimate time with? They'd orgasmed together and yet, in reality, they were complete strangers. Carrie knew him intimately. Ellen shuddered at the thought. They'd always had different tastes in men. Until now.

Carrie nodded as she finished her mouthful. 'This is so good, Ingi. See, I told you she was an amazing cook,' she said, turning to Fin.

Then Carrie set her eyes on Ellen and Ellen felt the blood drain to her toes.

'So, who was this hot bloke you were talking about? Must be good to catch your eye, El – he'd have to be perfect. Spill!'

Ingi began choking on her water, Bodhi started patting her back, meanwhile Fin looked right at her, and she knew her face was turning pink. *Just kill me now!*

She jumped up and got Ingi a napkin.

'Thanks, I think it has bones,' Ingi said, her voice hoarse from coughing. After patting her mouth with the napkin, she turned to the guest. 'So, you know a bit about us, Fin, but we don't know anything about you? Where do you work?'

Ellen squeezed her leg under the table, a hidden thank you for changing the subject.

He began to open his mouth when Carrie cut in.

'Fin works at the White Pearl Hotel. Not only that but his family own it,' she said grinning. 'I get discount drinks.' Carrie patted his hand. 'One day, it will be Fin's. He practically runs it now, don't you, babe?'

Ellen saw his eye twitch and she remembered their conversation about his dream. Had he not told Carrie about it yet?

'Um, yeah, you're all welcome to come down for dinner at the Pearl any time. Hey, Ingi, this is the best pasta I've ever had.' Fin was staring at the pasta on his fork. 'Did you make this from scratch?'

When she nodded, his mouth opened in surprise. 'Wow, it's so good. We could use a good chef . . .'

Bodhi put his hand up. 'Whoa, hold your horses there, chef-pincher. She already has a good job.'

That raised Fin's eyebrows even more.

Ingi put her fork down. 'I work at L'antica Osteria.'

'Oh, wow, that explains a lot. The Italian food there is to die for,' said Fin. 'How did that come about?'

Ingi glanced at Ellen, as if seeking approval to be nice to this man, all things considered. She gave her a smile – right now she could kiss Ingi's feet for being centre of attention and keeping the spotlight off herself.

'Well, it's actually my uncle's business. When he was a young chef, Uncle Pete went to Italy with a friend who owned a little townhouse in Montone. Of course, he ended up working in a restaurant there called L'antica Osteria, which means the ancient tavern or local place of food. Something like that,' she said waving her hand. 'Anyway, Uncle Pete fell in love with the local medieval village and the food. He learned as much as he could and then opened his own L'antica Osteria here. He goes back often to pick up any new dishes. They treat him like family.' She laughed. 'Anyway, Uncle Pete has taught me everything he knows and one day I hope to travel to Montone and see the village for myself. Uncle Pete says the food always tastes better there.'

'Must be the local ingredients,' Fin said. 'That's a very cool story. I never knew that. I assumed some Italian immigrant had started L'antica Osteria because the dishes are so authentic.'

'Thanks. Next time you stop in, let me know and I'll make you some of my favourites.'

'Oh that would be awesome. I've only ever ordered takeaway because what with work, I don't have a life,' he said with a chuckle.

'I know that feeling all too well,' she replied. 'It feels like a second home, but I do love it.'

'Well, you're very lucky then. Not many can say that about their job,' said Fin.

Carrie's fork paused in mid-air. A line formed between her eyes and then it was gone and she was back shovelling food into her mouth. Ellen wondered if her sister was thinking about herself or Fin?

'I love my job,' said Ellen.

'We know,' chorused Carrie and Bodhi before laughing.

'What's so funny?' asked Fin.

Ellen could feel his eyes on her and politely smiled back.

'Oh Fin, growing up she was always going to be a midwife,' said Carrie. 'She used to mother all our pregnant pets.'

'Remember that time she tricked Mum into buying a girl rabbit to go with Bruce and make lots of babies,' said Bodhi. 'Mum had been so strict, only boy rabbits.' Bodhi was laughing and couldn't finish.

'Ellen was my good child, until she really wanted something, like babies. Then she'd figure out a way to get what she wanted,' said Lorraine, pointing her fork at her elder daughter.

'What? I swear that the pet shop guy said it was a male rabbit. To this day I still believe he had no idea if he was selling me a rabbit or a hamster,' quipped Ellen.

Carrie was laughing and grabbed Fin's arm. 'She used to play nurses. She'd put a sheet over my legs and pretend to pull out her baby doll. So we all knew she'd be a midwife. She'd carry that baby doll everywhere; it had a car seat and everything.'

'I used to worry she'd be pregnant at seventeen,' said Lorraine.

Fin gave her a frank look. 'So, no kids yet?'

Ellen was about to reply, but was still getting over this family display of so-called love.

'Ellen believes in love and marriage so she's still waiting for the right bloke. Aren't ya, sis?'

'There's nothing wrong with that, princess,' said Colin. 'Don't rush in and end up with a drongo. You take as long as you need.'

'Thanks, Dad.' At least he was in her corner. She flicked her gaze to Fin. 'It's not wrong to want what my parents have, is it?'

'No,' he agreed. 'In fact, I think most of us would love to have what our parents do.'

'So, yours are still together then?' asked Bodhi.

Fin put his fork down and used a finger to get the last of the sauce from his plate. Ingi was watching him, grinning from ear to ear. Ellen filled with pride on Ingi's behalf and loved that he wasn't putting on any airs and graces for their benefit.

'Amazingly, yes,' he said proudly.

'And on that note, Dad, I think it's time?' said Ellen.

'Already? Lucky I came prepared today,' he said with a chuckle.

'Oh yay,' said Carrie, clapping. She turned to Fin. 'My parents do this at every anniversary. We make them tell a story from their years together. But it has to be something we've never heard before.'

'That's cool,' he replied, picking up a napkin.

Ellen tried not to notice how he ran his tongue across his lips as he wiped his mouth.

'Prepared? You didn't mention this one,' Lorraine said. She reached for his hand, bangles jangling.

Colin grinned. 'I like to keep some surprises up my sleeve. Can't have you getting sick of me.'

'Never,' she said and they shared a quick kiss.

Colin took a deep breath and sat up straight, holding the table captive. 'It was before I'd asked your mum out. We were both down at the Kalgan River for this ski day and I'd been roped in by my mates to drive the boat. Anyway, your mum was having her first go on the tube . . .'

'Oh my God.' Lorraine covered her face with her hand. 'Not that story, we have guests.'

'Don't stop now, Dad. This must be good,' pushed Bodhi.

'So, I'm giving her the ride of her life . . .'

'Oh Dad,' Carrie groaned. 'Bad choice of words.'

Ellen snuck a glance at Murray . . . argh, Fin. He seemed to be enjoying himself; his big shoulders looked relaxed and at ease.

Colin continued unperturbed. 'Next thing, Lorraine's legs are in the air and she'd stacked it. I wheel the boat around to see if she's okay.'

Lorraine groaned, reaching for her glass and downing a large mouthful.

'Her beautiful hair was all wet and she's frothing around in the water in a panic. Here I am thinking she can't swim. "It's okay," I tell her, "you have a life vest on." But she's still bobbing around churning up the water. Then she looks at me with these wide eyes. "I've lost my bather bottoms," she says.'

'Oh no, Mum.' Ellen was trying not to smile. A foot brushed against hers and she went rigid. She stared at her dad, not allowing herself to glance at Fin.

'What did you do?' said Ingi.

'I was so embarrassed,' said Lorraine. 'Not just that, but the cutest guy I'd ever seen was the only one who could help me.'

'I told her you can't stay in the water forever. I did offer to try and find her bottoms.'

'But I knew we'd never find them.' Lorraine tilted her head and smiled at her husband. 'You know what this gorgeous man did? He took off his own shorts, standing there in the boat in his undies, and gave them to me to put on in the water. Then he helped me into the boat and took me back to shore.'

'Ah Dad, that's so sweet.' Ellen wanted a love like her parents. They'd set the standards so bloody high though, it was a tough act to follow.

'I fell in love with him that day,' said Lorraine, as she gazed at the loved ones around her table. 'It's all we want for our children. To find that right person who makes life worth living.'

'Carrie, um . . . how did you two meet?' Ellen spluttered out. She'd been wondering about it so much that the words had bubbled up and overflowed. If only there was a way she could stuff them all back in her mouth.

'Well, it's not as romantic as Mum and Dad's story,' said Carrie, putting her hand on Fin's arm. 'I came out of the salon with my arms full and a roll of tape bounced and rolled down the street. Fin ran after it for me. I thought he was so sweet and handsome. Then that weekend I'm in the White Pearl, and who should serve me? Mr Handsome. So I asked him out before anyone else could.'

Ellen inwardly groaned. Of course she did. Carrie always went after what she wanted and usually got it.

'Fin says he has a rule that he doesn't date girls he meets at work but because we technically met earlier in the street, he let it slide. And so he took me to lunch the following week and it progressed from there.'

Carrie smiled at Fin and her shoulders lifted like she was Grace Kelly who'd married her prince. The sound of her words oozing affection made Ellen feel sick.

'Must be going okay to progress to a special anniversary lunch,' said Bodhi. 'Have to be pretty serious to get these invites.'

'Should I be concerned I'm the first guy she's brought over?' asked Fin.

'Not at all,' Lorraine said. 'Carrie was just waiting to bring the right one home. I think she's found him.'

She might as well have just swallowed a mouthful of sour lollies, because right now it was taking everything in her power not to pull a face. It was still so weird looking at Fin and knowing both sisters had slept with him. It was doing her head in.

Lorraine's eyes stopped on Ellen. 'Maybe you could bring that man you like around next time. I want all my kids to be happy.'

Ellen held her champagne glass tight and stared at the bubbles, as if she was counting them all. 'That won't happen, Mum. I won't be seeing him again.'

'How do you know if you don't try!' she scoffed.

End this conversation now, Ellen.

She plucked up the courage and faced her mum. 'I know because he already has a girlfriend.' She shrugged.

'Oh honey. You've had shit luck when it comes to men. I don't know why, you have the biggest heart.'

'That's why, Mum,' said Bodhi picking up his bottle of beer. 'They all take advantage of our El. The best girls always get treated badly. If I see that Josh about town, I'll let him know what I think of him.'

'Bodhi, no,' she sighed. That's all she needed. Why had this dinner suddenly become about her love life? She didn't want Fin to hear all about the Josh saga. What would he think of her? That she was weak? Naive? Stupid?

Bodhi leaned forward to see past Ingi. 'Why not, sis? He didn't just cheat on you, he knocked her up.'

Before he said any more, Ingi leaned over and whispered in his ear. 'Not now, Bodhi.'

'That Josh was a prick,' said Carrie. 'You'll find the right guy, sis. One who deserves you.'

'Enough about my sad life, please,' Ellen begged.

'Sorry, sis.' Bodhi stood up and collected an envelope from the kitchen table. 'Here, Mum and Dad, open the present we all got you.'

Once again order was restored, the spotlight gone, so Ellen could blend in with the others.

'Oh wow, a weekend in Denmark with a special dinner at Pepper and Salt,' said Colin.

'Silas will take good care of you,' said Ingi. 'He is the king of spices.'

Colin and Lorraine kissed and then smiled at each other.

'Happy anniversary, you two. Time for cake!' yelled Carrie.

'How did we get so lucky?' Colin said to his wife. 'We've got these great kids, a great life.'

'It's all down to your great wife,' she replied with a chuckle.

Ingi nudged Ellen. 'Help me with dessert?'

Ellen didn't need asking twice. She sprang up, desperate for some space, and quickly collected everyone's plates. She tried to take Fin's without looking at him, but he wouldn't let go until she did.

'Thank you,' he said.

He offered her a smile, and it was sincere. Maybe they would get past these confusing times and she'd feel comfortable around him.

After all, he was the first guy Carrie had brought home to meet the family. They were getting serious.

10

Carrie

Now

'THIS IS SO EXCITING. I CAN'T BELIEVE OUR BIG BROTHER IS getting married,' said Carrie, throwing an arm around her sister.

Ellen grinned. 'I know, crazy, isn't it? It seems like yesterday he was ripping our dolls' heads off and trying to put sand down our bathers.'

'Or beating up the boys who looked sideways at us at school,' Carrie added.

As brothers went, he was pretty good. Even though Carrie knew Ellen was his favourite – those two spent lots of time together. Carrie was just that bit younger and not interested in the things he wanted to do but Ellen would play his games of backyard wars or LEGO. She even learned to surf. If Bodhi wasn't into surfing she wondered if Ellen would have even tried it. What did Ellen do for herself when she wasn't trying to please everyone else? Besides her hospital work, of course.

Being a midwife had always been her thing. Carrie liked the idea of getting to dress babies and toddlers in cute outfits but that was about as close to thinking about kids as it got. The sleepless nights, baby spew and poo bit didn't appeal at all. She preferred them older, like the chatty ones who would tell her about their cool tricks on skateboards or bikes while getting their hair cut.

'Do you think Bodhi and Ingi will have babies right away?' she asked. Carrie wasn't sure Ingi was ready for babies either. At twenty-six she was still quite young and had a great job, but she had mothering tendencies like Ellen. Carrie had seen her interact with babies at the restaurant, having conversations with them or helping to distract kids to bring some peace to the table.

'I think so.' Ellen's features scrunched into her thinking face. 'So we have about four hours until they're here. Bodhi was going to text when they got to Newman and then the countdown is on.'

Carrie should've known. Straight into the set-up. 'I'm going to put my bathers on and go for a swim while we're there. We have plenty of time to set up.'

'All depends on how many trips we have to make. I've heard it's quite a trek down and back.'

'We'll rope your new friend into helping – that should cut out a trip.'

Any excuse to spend time with Hans. His hint of an accent was delicious and there was a gentle ease about him, which probably came from being a backpacker. Time wasn't important, experiencing life was. Carrie loved the idea of that. There were days she wished she could just pack up and wander. Maybe then she'd be able to find out what her life was missing. She had everything and yet felt empty – maybe not empty, as her life was full-on, but something wasn't right. She should be happier. Why was her smile only skin deep? There were even days she didn't want to get out of bed, days when anxiety about life and the pressures of being herself felt so hard. Did everyone feel like this or was she just not as strong?

'We'll go over all the things we need to carry down there and decide before we hassle him. Hans has been my rescuer too much already,' Ellen groaned.

Carrie steered her sister towards their camp. No doubt she'd want to make sure Carrie had brought everything she'd requested. As they stepped around the campervan, Ellen's body went tense and she let her arm drop from around Carrie's waist.

'Hey!'

Fin was sitting in a camp chair, a straw Panama hat perched on his head and a cold drink in his hand. He seemed excited to see El but also apprehensive. Carrie wished her sister would get over her jealousy. Although she had to admit deep down there was a part of her that loved having something her sister didn't. Their mum fussed over Carrie now, so happy with Fin, which made Ellen 'poor Ellen', 'still single Ellen'. And since she had run off to Challa Station her parents were even more upset with their elder daughter. For once Carrie's short-lived boyfriends and drunken escapades weren't the popular topic.

'Hi, Fin,' Ellen replied politely. 'Good trip up?'

'Yeah, it was good,' he said.

'Except for the limiting speed of the campervan,' added Carrie. 'Oh and the dodgy aircon.' Carrie opened up the van and pulled out all the stuff that was packed on the bed.

'Are you going to go and set up now?' Fin asked.

Ellen nodded. 'At least get it all down there, check out the best place for it and then maybe cool off.'

'I vote for that!' said Carrie. She stepped into the van, door open, and changed into her bathers.

'Well, I'll go change and grab the rest of the things and see if we can manage it all.'

Ellen left and Fin joined Carrie in the squishy van to grab a towel and change to swimming shorts.

'See, she was friendly,' Carrie whispered. 'Maybe the break at Challa is doing her some good.'

They'd discussed reasons why Ellen would make such a drastic move when she first disappeared with a rushed 'I need a change'. Fin seemed to think work had got too much for her at the hospital and she needed something completely different for a while.

Which made sense, as Carrie knew that the hospital took its toll on her. The emergencies, the sickness, the heartache. She wasn't only a midwife – it was very hard to work full-time as a midwife in the smaller regional hospitals, so she had to do general nursing also.

As a kid, Ellen would cry herself to sleep after their pets died. She felt so much, took on so much pain. In a way she'd taught Carrie to bury her tears because she never wanted to be that person crying in front of anyone, to be the person everyone stared at, to have her feelings exposed. Sure, it probably made her look like a cold-hearted bitch at times but that didn't mean Carrie didn't cry herself to sleep some days. She just preferred to do her grieving in private.

Thirty minutes later they had loaded up El's ute and driven down to the car park near the gorge. Fin was carrying pickets, PVC pipe and a hammer, Ellen had black garbage bags full of confetti, flowers and decorations. Carrie had bags of water, towels, lengths of white silk, proteas and more foliage.

Fin reached out to take one of El's bags but she gave him a look that would cut glass and moved away from him.

'You can take one of mine,' Carrie said sweetly. She offered up one of her bags to him before starting on the path.

At first they couldn't even see the gorge as the red gravel, grasses and ghost gums appeared to continue into the hilly distance. But from the edge of a rustic metal viewing platform, the sides stepped down like jagged brickwork into the deep gorge. At the bottom, large trees made a lush green canopy of leaves and below them a sliver of greeny-blue water was just visible.

'Maybe we should go down and check it out first?' Carrie said as they walked onto the platform.

'Um, you want to make an extra trip up and down that?' El asked, pointing to the rusty coloured steps.

'Over there, look, a waterfall.' Fin gestured to the right.

Carrie saw how far away it was, realising just how long this staircase walk was going to be. 'Oh.'

'Yeah. Let's get down there and out of this heat,' said El, heading to the stairs and starting the descent.

'I want to take photos, but my hands are too full,' Carrie said. It was as if a builder had placed slab after red slab on top of each other to create this massive steep rock wall. 'It's amazing.' The stairs had ended for the moment and a walkway hugged around the edge of the gorge. There were seats at different intervals and little viewing stops, but her favourite areas were when the gorge wall became one side of the walkway. In some sections you could see where huge rock chunks had broken away, or bits that looked like they might collapse one day soon.

'We can take photos tomorrow morning when we come down with Bodhi,' said Ellen, who had paused and was soaking up the view of the cliff face.

Carrie wished she had her good camera, the one her mum had got her when she was doing photography at school. There was so much texture and light she wanted to capture.

Soon they came to the bottom of the gorge and her legs felt a little like jelly. 'I'm glad we brought all this now,' she said, leaning against the railing. 'Going up must be a killer on the thighs. I hope Hans is available for hire.'

'Who is Hans?' Fin asked.

'Just some hot backpacker that El found. He's camping not far from us. You'll meet him soon.'

Fin's forehead creased. 'Right.'

'It's okay, babe. He's not a serial killer. He helped El twice today. If he was going to chop her up into bits, he would have done it by now.'

Ellen was facing away from them, but Fin still spoke to her. 'What happened?'

'Nothing serious,' she muttered.

'She had a flat tyre. What was the second time for, sis?' Carrie turned to Fin when she didn't reply. 'I don't know, they were sharing some inside joke about Sour Worms. I'm sure you had to be there.' She turned back to the view. 'So, this one is Fortescue Falls, yeah?'

'Yep.' Ellen stepped from the walkway onto the rocks at the bottom of the gorge. 'How cool are all those sheets of rock? It looks like Ingi's tiramisu. Imagine when it's flooding and water is rushing over them.'

They got off the walkway and stood on rock – layers of light and dark from under their feet and up the sides of the gorge walls. The lips of the rocks were rounded, polished smooth by rushing water over the years. Carrie dropped her things, bent down and felt the texture.

'No wonder the warning signs say get out if it starts to rain,' said Fin.

'Let's swim,' Carrie said eagerly, after spotting a couple in the pool beside them. They were over in the far corner by the waterfall. It kind of reminded her of the flooding staircase at school when the roof collapsed in a heavy rain.

'How about we get to Fern Pool first and drop all this stuff off,' said Ellen. 'You can have a swim there, and then here on our way back?'

'Sounds like a plan,' said Fin. 'Looks like we keep going this way.'

Carrie groaned. For people who didn't get on, Fin and El always seemed to agree on everything.

El paused, letting Carrie go behind Fin. Before long she felt the need to complain. 'God, how far away was it?' Her feet were starting to ache along with her arms.

'This walk is the best bit,' said El.

'Yeah, it is, but these bags weigh a ton.'

Bats clicked and screeched nearby in a patch of tall trees and there was a faint scent, probably all their droppings. They scampered over rocks and past exposed tree roots that were so crammed together they looked like hair. When the path returned to dirt, the edges were thick with grass, some that came up as high as her shoulders.

'This is perfect,' said Ellen, making Carrie look up.

Her sister was right – Fern Pool was a tropical oasis. A body of water edged by the gorge, ferns and grasses. At the far end, a rock ledge jutted out above the pool, and water rushed over it creating a waterfall. A young couple sat on the rocks underneath, the cascade making it picture perfect.

'I wanna do that!' Carrie dumped her bags on the ground while El continued past to the little wooden pontoon by the water's edge. It sat nestled between two massive tree trunks and was the entry point to the water.

'Is that where we're going to set up the arch?' asked Fin.

El moved on, her lips pinched in thought. 'I think over there off to the side, out of the way of any traffic. And the waterfall makes a good backdrop for photos.'

'The pegs will go in the dirt better there too. Good plan,' Fin agreed.

El frowned.

Fin sighed.

Carrie rolled her eyes. Agreeing again and hating each other for it.

Carrie hoped Fin didn't take offence. He was too sensitive when it came to El. It was like he couldn't handle someone not liking him – he had to be everyone's friend. Even the homeless bloke he let camp by the back door of the pub during rainy weather.

'I'm going in.' Carrie didn't care about helping set up, not yet. She was too hot and that waterfall looked so inviting. 'Come on, Fin.'

He glanced at El. 'Did you want a hand first?'

'No, you go,' she said and turned her back, busying herself with her bags.

'I'll leave these here?' he asked but she didn't reply.

Carrie waved for him to just drop it all. 'She'll sort it.' Then she stripped off her clothes and shoes as Fin took off his shirt and shoes. He kept glancing at El who was fussing over the bags still, her back to them.

When they reached the little pontoon, Carrie took his hand and squeezed it. 'It's not you, babe,' she whispered. 'El's just preoccupied. She's got no one here to share this with and Bodhi's about to propose.'

His lips tightened.

The couple who'd been under the waterfall had since swum back to the pontoon and the woman glanced up at Fin with hungry eyes. Carrie couldn't blame her – Fin was fit, with his six-pack and muscled arms. Tattoos adorned one arm while the rest of him was flawless skin with just a scattering of hair between his pecks and at the top of his shorts. Even Ellen snuck looks at him on occasion.

'Don't stand still too long in here or the fish come nibbling,' said the girl, before yelping and rushing up the little ladder to the top of the pontoon.

'Ugh,' Carrie groaned, glancing at Fin.

'You won't notice them. Come on.' He dived in and popped up. 'It's so good. Ellen, come on in!' he shouted.

'Come on, sis. Finish that after you've cooled off.'

Ellen sighed and pulled off her shirt then shrugged out of her shorts.

'Is that your underwear?' Carrie asked as Ellen joined her.

She was wearing black cotton undies and a black crop-top, which could have passed as bathers to anyone not paying close attention. Carrie doubted they'd get past Ellen's petite curvy body. It was a shame she didn't use it to her full advantage. Carrie had tried to spice her wardrobe up over the years but her sister had no dress sense when it came to enhancing her best features. El always went the softer, safer approach. Cutesy, never sexy. Cotton over leather. Flats over heels. Practical.

'I didn't think I'd need bathers at a station,' Ellen grumbled. 'You can't tell, can you?'

'No one will notice,' she said. But she noticed Fin watching.

Carrie took her hand. 'It's just like old times,' she said. 'Remember at Middleton off the pontoon?'

Ellen smiled, and for a moment Carrie felt like she had her sister back. History and the present merging together, strengthening bonds. Carrie's chest squeezed. It had been a long time since she'd seen Ellen's real smile. Or her own, for that matter.

Yet it didn't occur to Carrie to figure out why her sister didn't seem happy. Maybe it was hard to get personal with El because Carrie didn't feel able to help her. She couldn't help herself, so what use was she?

11

Ellen

Back then

'COME ON, EL, LET'S GO IN. YOU KNOW THEY MAKE THE BEST cocktails,' begged Tanya as she stumbled to the door.

El thought that Tanya probably didn't need another drink but she was the support person this time and so she followed her inside the White Pearl.

Her breath caught in her throat as Tanya led her inside, across dark wood floors and over to the bar where she pulled up a stool and sat. El stood awkwardly. Why did she feel so on edge? Of course her mind tried to tell her it was because she hadn't been out for drinks in ages, hadn't been to the White Pearl in even longer, but her gut knew it was all lies. It was Murray, being here in his place of work without the buffer of family. The last time they'd been alone was at the concert. Enough said!

'Right here?' Ellen asked, eyeing off a booth with brown leather seats in the far corner. The place had had a makeover in the last year and now had a warm glow from the industrial-style lights that dropped down from the high ceiling and bounced shadows over the cream walls. In corners and on the walls were green leafy plants in dark pots. For a front bar it felt super trendy and relaxing. A shame Fin's family owned it. She could have easily made this her regular.

Pifft, as if you would ever go to a pub on a regular basis.

'Yep. Closest spot to the grog,' Tanya said with a wink. 'God, we haven't been here for years. Place looks great.' Tanya squinted at Ellen. 'Why haven't we come here sooner?'

She shrugged and took a seat beside her and was relieved when a woman came to serve them. Ellen could have hugged her. Would Fin really be working behind the bar though? She pictured him in an office or in a storage room ordering more wine, overseeing kitchen staff and the like.

'What can I get you ladies?' asked the barmaid.

She was around their age and pretty. One side of her head was shaved undercut style and her long dark hair was tied up so you could see small tattoos behind her ear. Trendy and with spunk, a lot like Ingi. Maybe that's why El felt herself at ease with her instantly.

'I'd love a Painkiller please,' Tanya requested as she leaned over the bar.

'Make that two, please,' Ellen said with a smile, holding out her card as she tried to focus on the music playing in the background. 'Is that The Jezabels?' Damn, this pub was totally her type.

Before the woman could lift the EFTPOS machine, it was being pushed away by none other than Mr I'm So Hot with My Beard and Tattoos and Smouldering Eyes.

'It's okay, Clem,' said Murray. 'I've got this.'

Oh damn. Tanya, you owe me big. Ellen swallowed. Yeah, it was still awkward being around Murray. *Fin, call him Fin!*

Clem's eyes narrowed as she glanced between them. 'Sure,' she dragged the word out slowly. If she was waiting for an explanation, she didn't get one. She shrugged and went to serve another couple at the end of the bar.

'Is that your sister? Clementine?' Ellen said.

He beamed. 'Yes, that's Clem. You remembered?'

'Of course.' She remembered everything from that night. Which was as helpful as a splinter festering away in your foot.

'And yes, that is The Jezabels. I'm glad you told me about them. I also found The Preatures – have you listened to them?'

Heat rose in her cheeks. Talking music with him seemed intimate, or was she still having flashbacks to that night?

Ellen nodded. 'Yeah, they have some great songs.'

'What about San Cisco? They're a WA band.'

Argh! She wanted to keep talking with Fin, but the less conversation she engaged in the better. It was so easy. Like breathing. He breathed out she breathed in, that's how their conversation had flowed at the concert. Not once had she needed to think up things to say or pretend to be interested.

A few days ago they'd all gone out for dinner, just the five of them – Bodhi, Ingi, Carrie and Fin. Ellen without a date of course. It was hard not to notice the way he was with people, making sure everyone's glass was full or passing napkins before they realised they needed one. Maybe that came from working in hospitality or maybe he really was a thoughtful bloke. He could read a room, know what you needed before you did yourself. Moved between conversations with ease.

Bodhi and Fin had talked flat out – surfing, work, you name it. Anyone would think they'd been lifelong mates! His laughter was genuine and infectious, a deep rumble that came from his heart and always finished in his eyes. Fin would let people finish their story before he'd talk and he'd listen completely. Maybe that was Carrie's attraction to him? When the rest of them zoned out over Carrie's longwinded stories, Fin was still invested. Ellen didn't want to like him, but it was hard not to. Which made being around him hard. If she wasn't careful she could really like him lots. Or maybe they could just be super awesome friends. *Could you do that with someone you'd secretly had sex with? Someone you still found yourself accidentally fantasising about? Jesus, El, you're asking a lot.*

And she knew it, knew that line was there, but with each dinner or coffee catch-up Carrie brought him to, the more she got to know him, and that line was fading, like chalk marks in the rain.

Tanya was watching them with a very drunk ogling expression, which only made Ellen feel more uncomfortable.

She realised she hadn't replied to his San Cisco comment. 'I'll, um, check them out. Thanks.'

'Great, let me know when you do.'

He stroked his beard as he spoke, and probably didn't realise he was doing it.

'Don't move. I'll make these drinks and be right back.' He paused, shooting her a smile. 'I'm so glad you stopped in.'

Tanya hardly let him walk away before pointing at her and him. 'You know the hot barman?' Again, more drunk ogling.

'Shh,' she warned. 'Yes, that's Fin, who Carrie's dating.'

Tanya grimaced. 'Oh, what! That can't be. He seems too good for her.'

'How can you tell after half a second?'

Tanya clumsily touched her nose – on the second attempt. 'I have a nose for these things. I warned you about Josh, didn't I?'

'Touché.' Ellen played with the tassel on her purse. 'Thanks for not rubbing that in, by the way,' she said with a frown.

'What are work mates for?' Tanya smiled, her mascara smudged from a bout of tears earlier.

'Here you go, two Painkillers.' Fin deposited both drinks in front of them.

Tanya pounced on the glass and inhaled it. 'You, my good man, are a hero.'

Before Ellen could try to wave her card at Fin again, he said, 'On the house.'

She was ready to fight it when Tanya gripped his hand in hers.

'Oh, thank you,' she purred, fluttering her eyelids at him. 'So delicious.'

They all knew she wasn't talking about her drink.

For a 36-year-old single woman who was well respected at work, Tanya could behave like a sexed-up cougar on the juice. Quite entertaining at times. Other times, not so much.

Fin's ears went red.

'Murray, um, Fin,' Ellen corrected herself. She noticed how his eyes lit up when she said his real name. For that reason alone she was going to strike it from her memory. 'This is my friend Tanya. We work together.'

'At the hospital?' Fin held out his hand and shook Tanya's. 'Lovely to meet you, Tanya.' He went to pull away but she wouldn't let him.

'How did you end up with Carrie?' she interrogated.

He swallowed and glanced at Ellen.

'Ignore her, she's very merry,' Ellen managed to say.

Tanya let his hand go and waved Ellen's comment off. 'Hardly.'

'If you must know I met Carrie first outside her salon, then again right here, as a matter of fact.'

'Oh romantic,' Tanya said a little too sarcastically. She reached over and had a sip of Ellen's cocktail. 'This is sooooo good. I think I'm going to need a painkiller for my Painkiller.'

She started laughing at her own joke. Fin cracked a smile.

'Shall I bring you some food?' he offered.

Ellen felt herself sag with relief. 'Oh, yes please.'

'Hang on. I need the ladies' room first,' Tanya said. Manoeuvring herself off the stool, like a two-year-old with short legs, she righted herself and headed off.

'It's on the left, Tanya, behind the door,' Fin directed.

Tanya waved her thanks as she staggered around to her left.

'I'll get her some water.'

'Thank you!'

Moments later, he placed two water bottles on the bar along with some hot chips. Ellen was impressed with his attention.

Oh Fin. Stop making me like you.

His arm lay across the bar not far from hers. She wanted to tuck her hands away from temptation. After their meal the other night he'd scooped her up for a hug goodbye. Nothing out of the ordinary – he'd done the same to Ingi – but there was something about the contact that didn't feel platonic. His warmth, scent and beating heart against her chest had knocked her for six. It had reawakened memories and fantasies and screwed her up so tight she'd almost jittered mechanically all the way home like a wind-up toy.

That was the moment El realised she was losing the battle to keep Fin in the 'just friends' zone. From now on, she needed to put up a wall, to stop engaging with him. You couldn't fall for a man if you hardly spoke to him, right?

He leaned over the bar now, his words soft. 'Will Tanya be okay? She seems sad.'

'She'll be okay. I'm keeping an eye on her,' said Ellen. 'This is what we do, I guess. Tanya had an awful day at work . . . she lost a patient.'

Concern swirled in his big dark eyes, almost the colour of his beard but minus the reddish copper tinges.

Ellen hurried on to explain. 'An older man she'd been caring for over the last year or more. He had a wicked sense of humour and she'd taken quite a shine to him.'

'Oh, I'm sorry. Looks like you took a shine to him too?'

She sighed, realising her eyes had gone all watery. 'Yeah, I had a few shifts with him. Sweet old guy who lost his wife six years ago. At least they're together again now. He'd talk about his wife all the time. A timeless love.' And who wouldn't want a love like that?

'I thought you were a midwife?'

'I am, but in regional areas there are no full-time midwife positions, so you need to be an all-rounder. Majority of my work is midwifery, but I fill in for other shifts too.'

'I'm guessing you love the midwifery more. There'd be less heartbreak and death, more happy moments,' he said.

'Most definitely. I see beautiful babies being born, the tears of joy on the parents' faces – especially the ones who've been trying IVF for years and finally have their baby.'

El was playing with the condensation on the outside of the water bottles, tracing patterns with her finger. 'But it also has its share of heartbreak too. Some babies don't make it. Some are born with disabilities or have complications – but luckily those cases are rare. Seeing off an elderly patient is different to saying goodbye to a newborn who hasn't even lived.' Ellen couldn't help the tears that welled in her eyes. She tried to blink them away before they ran down her face. 'I've only ever witnessed that once, and it still stays with me as if it happened yesterday. Every job has its hardships, but nursing . . .'

Fin had somehow moved his hand on top of hers.

'That's awful, Ellen. I don't know how you get through it. I have hard days, but I don't have to deal with death and sickness. I really admire nurses. It takes a special person to care for the dying.'

She shrugged, finding the compliment hard to accept, or was it just his hand on hers? Regretfully she withdrew her hand from under his on the pretence of adjusting herself on the stool. He was being so sweet and compassionate. *Why couldn't you be an arsehole? It would make this so much easier.*

'Luckily it doesn't happen that often. But when it does, we tend to blow off steam.'

'I totally understand that.' He paused, his brows drawing together.

'What?' she asked, needing to know what thought had just popped into his mind.

He shrugged. 'It's just that your job makes me feel bad for how I feel about this place and wanting to do my brewery. Seems so silly to get worked up over a pipedream when you're out there saving lives.'

'Don't do that,' she said, suddenly annoyed. 'Don't make light of your dreams. You should fight for them, big or small. We all should.' Ellen reached for the hot chips, needing some other distraction for her hands and mouth. 'If you want to start your own brewery then bloody do it.'

His lips curled in a warm smile, his eyes watching her so closely as if he was reading her soul. She shoved more chips into her mouth, wishing he'd stop looking at her like that. It made the hairs on her arm stand up.

'I hear you, Ellen. We only have one life.'

'Exactly. If we don't do what we desire, we'll just live with regret.'

An awkward silence fell between them and El wished she could take back her last words. Especially that one – 'desire' ... it just made her mind spin back to his lips all over her as he pressed against her ...

Stop it, stop it. She squeezed her eyes tightly shut, not caring if she looked like a twit. Was he thinking of the same moment? El desperately wanted to look but was too scared in case he could see the sex scene playing out on her eyes like a massive drive-in movie screen.

The door opened nearby. El had never been so relieved to see her friend. Fin leaned back and reached for a towel and began wiping down the bar.

'Right, I think I'm ready for another Painkiller,' said Tanya. It took her two goes to sit on the bar stool properly.

'Drink this water first and have some chips.'

'Oh chips.' She pounced on the basket like a lioness onto a deer.

'Then I'm going to take you home,' Ellen said.

Tanya tried to slurp the dregs of her cocktail then glanced at Ellen's, which was also empty. 'Oh, I guess all good things must come to an end,' she said, jutting out her bottom lip.

Ellen managed to grab a few more chips, and as she licked the salt from her fingers, she felt her face flush when she saw Fin watching. She'd love to know what he was thinking – erotic thoughts or that she ate like a two-year-old? Did it ever cross his mind? That night? Did he have random flashes of sex with her? Had he ever fantasised about her or had he pushed it into oblivion the moment he decided to be with Carrie?

'Let me help you out,' Fin offered as he walked out from behind the bar.

His jeans hugged his legs and the top two buttons undone on his black work shirt revealed too much skin for Ellen's liking.

'Are you trying to make my life harder,' she huffed and then froze when she realised she'd said it out loud.

'Pardon?'

'Nothing,' she said quickly, waving him off like she was shooing a fly and not weeks of pent-up frustration.

Fin put his arm around Tanya and helped her out to the front of the hotel. The night air was like stepping into a coolroom. It ticked over to eleven thirty while they waited on the damp pavement for a taxi.

'We'll be alright here if you have to get back inside,' Ellen said.

'It's fine. Clem has the last few under control,' he said with a smile.

'El, my feet hurt,' said Tanya. 'Oh, our taxi.'

Fin opened the door for her and helped Tanya inside.

'Ever the gentleman.' Then she shuffled across to the other side of the car.

'Thank you, Fin.' Ellen made a point of no body contact. She'd hate to be the fly that got stuck in the honey, so she gave him a quick smile and turned ready to bolt into the car.

Fin reached for her arm, pulling her back to face him.

'Wait, Ellen, are we . . . are we ever going to talk about . . . you know . . . *that* properly?'

She glanced back at him, heart heavy. 'What is there to say? We can't change it.'

He frowned. 'I want us to . . . I don't know. We can't undo what happened, but we haven't really talked about . . . like, how are you? How are you handling this?'

'I'm handling it fine.' *Liar.* 'You and Carrie are serious. You made your choice, and she's happy so I'm happy. You and I are friends.'

It all felt a little forced. El wasn't sure she believed it herself but what else could she say? She needed to distance herself from him until she could get a grip on her stupid head and heart. Both were trying to make her life harder than it had to be.

'I better get Tanya home. Night.'

She was climbing into the car when he replied, ever so softly, to the point Ellen would wonder if she'd imagined his words or quite possibly made her own version of his reply.

'*What if . . .*'

'Let's go,' Tanya said to the driver.

Ellen shut the door, the cold glass of the window pressing against her brow as she stared out at Fin.

Her mind whirled. *What if I picked the wrong sister? What if I want you instead? Oh God, Ellen,* as if he'd been about to say that.

She was only deluding herself. This fantasy had to stop! She couldn't ruin her sister's happiness for her own stupid heart and then find out Fin didn't even feel that way about her. Anyway, could that even work? Jumping from one sister to another? Not without a lot of hurt and anger that would tear her family apart. Ostracise herself from her sister and parents, all because of a man?

Even though Ellen knew all this, her mind kept reeling and repeating his words.

What if . . .

That night she sent Ingi a message.

It started with the exploding head emoji and ended with, *I need help!* She didn't expect a reply – hell, it was midnight, most normal people were asleep, and yet her phone buzzed. Knowing Ingi, she'd probably not long got to bed after a late night at the restaurant and was still trying to wind down, no doubt playing Candy Crush on her phone. Which was what Ellen should be doing, not lying in bed stressing.

Concerned face emoji. *What's up, El? Everything okay?'*

No. Crying face emoji.

Ingi didn't reply, just waited.

I saw Fin at the White Pearl tonight.

Oh. And?

My head's fucked. I thought I could be okay with this! That I'd get over him . . . but the hug he gave me that night after dinner . . .

Ellen didn't know how to finish that message. Her thoughts were jumbled together like a drawer full of useless utensils.

Yeah, I saw that.

What do you mean?

Ellen jiggled further under the blankets as if they could buffer her from the world as her phone light cut through the darkness of her room. Type faster, Ingi.

Well, I don't know, maybe I was reading more into it, but I felt like it was a very 'familiar' hug. Sorry, it's hard to explain. And don't worry, I don't think anyone noticed it went longer than a usual hug goodbye.

Oh my God. I hope not. It was just that I got swept away and completely forgot where I was. He probably thought I was a cling on!

I doubt that. He didn't seem to mind one bit.

Ellen wasn't sure if that was reassuring or not. Had she been totally embarrassing? Obvious? What had Fin thought about it?

Seeing him tonight, I realised I'm not coping. I thought it was just about the sex but I actually think I really, really like him. Every time I see him, it gets worse. I keep hoping he'll be a dick, just so I have an excuse to hate him.

No such luck, I'm afraid. He's the real deal.

Trust me to have a one-night stand with the best bloke I've met in years, maybe forever.

Life's a bitch. What can I do to help?

IDK. I'm so bloody confused.

Let's catch up tomorrow for a chat. This needs more than my fingers can text.'

Thanks, Ingi. You're the best. Love you.

Love you too, El.

El flopped her phone down onto her chest. Talking it out with Ingi would help. Someone on the outside but with insider knowledge. She felt a bit better for getting that much off her chest.

One thing was for sure, she couldn't spend any more alone time with Fin. Not unless he decided to become a real prick sometime soon.

12

Ingi

Now

'SETTLE GRETEL,' SAID BODHI. 'WAIT UNTIL I COME TO A complete stop, please.'

Ingi was practically bouncing on her seat. Sure, she was excited about finally being in Karijini but they'd also pulled in beside Ellen's ute. Ellen! Finally she'd get to see her best friend.

'I didn't realise just how much I missed her until now,' she said, gripping the door handle.

Ellen was waving like she was guiding a plane into dock, it even had Bodhi smiling like an idiot.

Ingi was out the door the moment Bodhi had applied the brakes; she could hear him cursing behind her. Ignoring him, she ran around the Maui van. Ellen had her arms open and they both screamed as they collided into a firm hug.

'Oh my God, I've missed you so much,' said Ingi.

'Me too,' said Ellen, her voice raspy.

It all became too much – the silence, the secrets, the heart-ache, and Ingi suddenly found herself crying and felt her best friend's body also shaking with sobs.

'I've been so worried about you,' Ingi whispered. 'And I've missed you like crazy.'

'I've missed you too. And your cooking.'

Ingi chuckled and pulled back. They stared at each other, tears rolling down their cheeks as a silent understanding passed between them. With the tears were smiles.

'Gee, I hope I get that kind of reception,' said Bodhi. He'd climbed out of the van and was waiting his turn. 'She's not going anywhere for a few days, Ingi,' he said.

Reluctantly she let go of Ellen and wiped her face as Bodhi hugged his sister.

If he was curious about their emotional reunion he didn't say. Ingi hoped he didn't bring it up later, she didn't like lying to him. Or 'withholding information' as Ellen referred to it.

'Missed you, big bro.'

'Right back at ya, sis. I miss our surfs together. Instead, you'd rather be chasing cows.' He held her arms and studied her. 'You do look different – leaner, tanner, fitter?'

Ellen laughed. 'Maybe. There is less access to all those fancy cheeses and wines but I've become a bit of a beer drinker.'

'No way,' he scoffed. 'Not the bush chook?'

'Yep, red Emu cans all the way.' Ellen beamed.

Ingi pulled a face. She couldn't think of anything worse than that beer.

They prattled on, teasing each other and catching up while Ingi opened the van and got out the three camp chairs they'd brought.

'Where's Fin and Carrie?' Bodhi asked.

Ellen pointed down the track. 'They're in the next bay.'

'Shall we go say hi?'

Ellen shook her head. 'I'm gonna stay here and help Ingi sort dinner. I hope you brought some pasta,' she said hopefully.

'Of course.' Ingi beamed at Ellen's delight. 'You go, Bodhi. Us girls need a catch-up anyway.'

'Roger that,' he said before hugging Ellen once more. 'God, it's felt like years, sis.'

It had been about five weeks, but who was counting?

He grabbed two beers from the campervan fridge and went over to see Fin.

'Those two still thick as thieves?' Ellen asked.

Ingi nodded, passing over a cold beer before joining her in the camp chairs.

'Fifty Lashes, nice.'

The late afternoon was warm, the sun setting and taking with it the intense heat. Mozzies and flies went about their business but left them alone for the most part.

After her first sip, she replied to Ellen's question in full. 'Yeah, they're still best mates. Always hanging out, which is annoying as I've been trying to avoid Fin. It just saves a lot of discomfort, you know?'

Which had been bloody hard with Bodhi and him insep- arable. Ingi had to keep making up excuses not to join Bodhi when he went to Fin's place, or when he invited them over, she pretended to rush off to help at the restaurant, inventing sick workers and shift changes. There were times when there was no escaping it and she tried hard to be occupied in other rooms of their home. If Fin noticed, he never said. Bodhi had commented a few times, but she made up some excuse about giving him 'man' time. Ingi sometimes wondered if Fin stayed with Carrie because of Bodhi. He fitted into the Sutton family so well. And in her opinion, he was more suited to Ellen. Damn Carrie for meeting him first.

'I'm sorry you have to be in that position, Ingi. You know I'd change it if I could.'

'Don't,' Ingi said, reaching for her hand. She almost burst into tears again seeing the pain beyond the depths of Ellen's hazel green eyes. She was still hurting. Running away hadn't healed anything, not yet. Her nose wiggled with the effort to halt her tears. 'I'm glad I can be here for you. It kills me to think of you battling this alone. I wish you had others to confide in – could you talk to your mum, let someone else in?'

The defiant fire in Ellen's eyes made it clear she wasn't sharing anything.

'Enough about me. Are you excited to be finally here? Your brother would be so proud.'

Hell, the water works threatened to overflow again. All Ingi could do was nod and sip her beer. The metal on her necklace was warm with her body heat as she fingered the inscription.

I wish we could have taken this trip together, Mikey.

That night the dingoes' howls kept her awake. She felt safe in the van, but she feared for Ellen outside. At one point Bodhi realised she wasn't sleeping and when she told him why, he laughed but then explained she'd be fine. 'No one has ever been attacked by a dingo up here and there are hundreds of tourists coming through all the time.' He made a valid point.

The next time she woke up it was early, the sun peeking through the slit in the curtain. Today was waterfall day! Ingi bounced out of bed as Bodhi grumbled and rolled over, so she started on breakfast. Once the first rasher of bacon hit the pan and began to sizzle, he was up like a shot.

'I'll make the coffee,' he offered. He opened the van door. 'Sis,' he said loudly. 'Sis, you awake?'

'I am now with all your hollering,' came Ellen's reply.

Ingi grinned. God, how she'd missed the dynamic of these siblings. Like her and Mikey. He'd tell her off for dawdling when pushing his wheelchair and she'd tell him to get out and walk if it was faster. He loved that she didn't tiptoe around him. He got enough of that every day and she knew he craved to be treated like everyone else, even if just for that moment.

'You want a coffee?' Bodhi asked.

'You asking me or the whole park?' she teased.

Ellen was sitting up on the back of her ute, hair knotted and her eyes sleepy. Her nose twitched as she sniffed at the air.

'Is that bacon?'

Bodhi rolled his eyes. 'Geez, don't tell everyone, will you.'

'Brekky?' Ingi asked in a quiet voice, unlike the other two.

'Oh, yes please.'

The air was crisp with the fading night and Ingi couldn't wait to go exploring. But first, feed the gang. The bacon must have stirred Fin, who popped over as they were dishing up.

'Carrie's still dead to the world, I'll eat hers,' he said with a wink as he raked a hand through his long fringe, setting it back.

Ingi involuntarily smiled at Fin. Some days his charm took her by surprise. He was a great guy, Ingi just couldn't face him without feeling like she was betraying her friend.

Half an hour later they had assembled – Carrie half-asleep but still eager – to walk to the gorge from their campsite. Being early, they didn't have to worry about the heat so much and the walk would be nice.

'So did you guys get down here last night?' Ingi asked as they reached the viewing platform.

'Yeah, just for a quick swim. We didn't get to Fern Pool though,' said Ellen. 'We didn't want to see too much without you guys.'

'Aw, cool. Well, let's go.' Ingi led the way down the stairs but stopped for photos and realised the others were doing the same. There was no phone signal but phones were still handy cameras. 'It's like walking down into a sunken garden!'

At the bottom she stood stunned at the beauty of the rocks and the cool green water. No one else was here. The scenery gave her goosebumps. Bodhi came up behind her and put his arms around her waist.

'It's beautiful, hey?'

She could only nod. Bodhi turned her to face him and pressed a kiss to her lips.

'I really want to do that Dale's Gorge walk,' said Ellen. 'They say it takes about three hours return.' She glanced towards the back edge of the Fortescue Falls where the pool turned into a small running creek and the path for the walk started.

'I want to check out the Handrail one,' said Ingi as she took Bodhi's hand and carefully stepped up and down the little rock ledges to get closer to the falls. It wasn't a fast flowing waterfall, instead it was gentle and peaceful.

'Careful, the rocks are really slippery, especially in the water,' said Carrie.

The rocks were dark, almost black where the water flowed, yet alongside, the dry red tiers had creamy stains that ran from the top to the bottom like a ghost waterfall, somehow bleaching the rocks from previous flooding.

'Some of the rock layers look like stripy zebras – alternating light and dark shades,' said Fin. 'It's hard to imagine how many years it took to create this layering, and the wearing away to make this gorge so deep.'

'So philosophical.' Bodhi grinned. 'Come on, let's see the other one.' Bodhi took Ingi's hand and guided her up the steep rocks from the pool. His hand was very sweaty. 'Sorry.' He wiped it down his shorts and gave her a funny smile.

As they made their way along the track to Fern Pool, Bodhi didn't say much but she could understand why. It felt like a place of God. A place where you wanted to absorb every sight, sound, touch – but not so much scent when they passed some noisy bats. Ingi glanced around, mouth open, eyes wide. Massive boulders as high as a two-storey house had green creepers growing from crevices, their long bare roots dangling almost to the ground. There were even fig trees, at least Ingi assumed they were from a similar family, their roots twisting over rocks like big albino pythons. Lush green ferns grew from the damp cracks at the bottom of the rocks. *We must be getting close*, she thought.

'Oh wow. It's so different from the last one but just as pretty.'

Ingi walked straight up to the pontoon and stood mesmerised by the waterfall tinkling away in the background. Bodhi stood behind her, his hands on her shoulders gently massaging them.

'Hey, you guys, come check this out. There must have been a wedding here yesterday.'

Ingi headed over with Bodhi, the ground opening up into a small clearing overlooking the water with a sheer rock wall behind it. A beautiful arch structure had been erected by the water's edge, draped with white silk and adorned with stunning native flowers down one side.

'You two go stand in it, I'll get a photo,' said Ellen, gesturing. 'Then Fin and Carrie next.'

'Oh, it's gorgeous!' said Ingi. 'Look at the ground – it's covered with green love hearts.' She bent to scoop up a handful and realised from the smell that they were made from eucalyptus leaves. 'That's so cool.'

'Ingi, smile!' Ellen ordered.

'If only you were wearing a white dress,' Carrie teased.

Ingi stuck her tongue out but had a weird feeling when Carrie just beamed back at her. Even Fin was smiling like an idiot. She turned to Bodhi, half-expecting him to be making bunny ears for the camera and instead found him kneeling on the ground.

'Ingrid Byrne, you are the love of my life,' he said, staring up at her.

For a moment she thought he was having a lend of her because of the wedding set-up. But then she noticed he was holding something in his hand and her heart thumped against her chest.

'You're the one I want to spend the rest of my life with and I'm pretty sure your brother would approve. Your dad does too.'

A golden glow from the morning light filtered through the canopy of trees, giving Bodhi an angelic radiance. His eyes swirled like honey and reflected the love she felt for him. Tears welled, making his perfect features blur but she knew every freckle, every line, every part of him by heart. The scar above his ear from a surfboard fin, the lump near his ankle where he chipped a bone trying to skateboard, and the little crease between his eyes that appeared whenever he was deep in thought.

Bodhi knelt before her, his face expectant. 'Will you marry me?'

He held up the ring, waiting for her reply as tears fell down her face and over her goofy grin.

'Yes, absolutely!' she replied and laughed at the relief on his face.

He slipped the stunning diamond ring on her finger then scooped her up into his arms. His lips were warm and now wet from her tears, but it was perfect.

'I can't wait to marry you, to have you with me for the rest of my life and to start our own family,' he said as he tucked his head into her neck and hugged her tightly.

Ingi went rigid at that last word. She realised just how much she'd been swept up in the moment.

Oh no. This was not going to end well. Only she couldn't say anything right now – he was so happy, and the others were crying tears of joy and taking photos.

'Bodhi, wait.' But he didn't stop nuzzling her neck and covering her in kisses. 'Bodhi, please. We need to talk first.'

She slipped the sparkly ring from her finger and pressed it into his hand.

His smile died slowly as he cocked his head and stared at her in confusion.

'Ingi?'

13

Ellen

'CONGRATULATIONS!'

Ellen clapped and dabbed at her eyes before glancing down the pathway. Hopefully Hans was not far off with the champagne. Last night she'd asked if he would mind bringing down the chilled champagne about ten minutes after they left. He'd excitedly agreed, and this morning had been sneaking around camp as they headed off. He must be nearly here.

Ingi and Bodhi were still holding each other, and Ellen couldn't resist a few more shots from different angles. She couldn't wait to go through the photos later and find the perfect one to get printed on canvas or framed for them.

Suddenly Bodhi's body went stiff and there was tension in the air. Her eyes clocked the ring being returned to her brother's hand. Had anyone else noticed?

'I love you and I do want to marry you, but I can't. Not yet. We need to talk first.'

Ingi shook her hand at him until he took the ring back.

'I don't understand,' he muttered.

'Doesn't it fit?' asked Carrie.

Ellen shot her a look and silently begged her to shut up. But Carrie had never been very good at picking up on cues.

'Somebody order champagne?'

'Yes!' cheered Carrie and ran over to Hans as he appeared, forgetting the train crash that was happening before them.

Ellen went to meet Hans and give her brother some space. Fin stepped in beside her. 'What's going on?' he whispered.

'I don't know,' she mouthed back.

He nodded and she knew without saying anything else that he'd attempt to keep Hans and Carrie busy, buying alone time for Bodhi and Ingi. Fin was always on the same wavelength as Ellen, unlike Carrie, who was usually so many levels up she was in space. She was already searching for the plastic cups in the bag Hans brought.

'It went off perfectly. Good job,' said Fin, giving her a wobbly smile. 'The rest of it is out of our hands.'

There was a tingle in the air, a spark of the past. Ellen wondered if she'd ever stop thinking about that night at the concert. 'I know. I just wish I knew what was going on.'

'Same,' he whispered.

Hans and Carrie were chatting away about their favourite champagnes while they tried to pop the cork. Meanwhile, Ellen thought about the way Fin and Carrie had acted during the proposal – happy and excited, but no warm and fuzzies between each other. Not that Ellen expected them to be close to marriage, but usually dating couples would be affected by the romance. She didn't think Carrie wanted marriage yet, but then again . . . what did she know? Maybe Fin was her one? Maybe Carrie would say yes if he asked her?

The thought of that was too much for Ellen to handle.

Shaking it from her mind she smiled at Hans. 'Thanks, Hans.'

'How did it go?' he asked uncertainly as he glanced past her to the couple.

'Um, good, I think. We're just giving them some time.' What else could she say?

Ellen helped Carrie fill the plastic flutes with champagne and jam strawberries on the rims.

'Waste not want not,' said Carrie and took a big sip before yelling over her shoulder. 'Do you guys want some champagne?'

Ingi and Bodhi slowly walked over to join them, Ingi smiling but Bodhi looking like a lost little boy. Ellen noticed the ring missing from Ingi's finger. Did this mean they weren't getting married?

'Did you guys know Bodhi was going to do this?' Ingi asked as she stared at the champagne in wonder.

Carrie opened her arms. 'Why do you think we're all here? Bodhi planned this whole thing for you.'

Ingi turned to him. 'Really?'

He nodded. There was a half-attempt at a smile. Ingi was holding his hand, which just made everything more confusing. Did she not want to get married? Maybe she didn't believe in the piece of paper? Even though she clearly loved Bodhi.

'We were here last night setting up. This is all for you!' said Carrie.

Ingi pointed towards the archway. 'Ellen, did you do all that?' she said. 'Of course you did. It has your name all over it.'

Ellen stepped towards them with two glasses, but Ingi hugged her instead of taking them.

'Thank you. It was perfect.'

'Thanks, sis,' said Bodhi, taking a glass.

'Gosh, it wasn't just me. We all pitched in,' she said.

Though Bodhi looked like a man confused at why they were celebrating, he didn't look too dejected, so that was a good thing at least.

He swung Ingi's hand in his, grinning down at her. 'I knew you wanted to see Ellen, and I know you've been wanting to come to Karijini, and I've been wanting to . . . propose . . . so, well, it kinda sorted itself out. And when I told Ellen and Carrie, of course they wanted to help.' He put his arm around Ingi and they clinked their plastic flutes. 'Here's to you.'

'To Ingi,' everyone replied.

'I'm still trying to process all this. That you kept this secret,' said Ingi, pointing at them.

'It was even better having Hans to bring down the champagne because it would have been a bit suss us carrying that down,' said Ellen.

'See, it pays to have a breakdown,' Hans said with a wink. 'Or two,' he added.

'You're never going to let me forget that, are you?' Ellen wished he would.

'I might be persuaded,' he said. He turned to Bodhi and Ingi. 'Hello, Ellen's family.'

'Oh shit, sorry. You guys haven't met,' said Ellen. 'This is my brother Bodhi and Ingi.' She'd been about to say fiancée but that would mean a ring on a finger. Yet they'd all heard Ingi say yes. So what had changed her mind?

'Hans, hey, nice to meet you, mate. Cheers for the breakfast,' said Bodhi, taking another sip.

'Hi.' Ingi waved at Hans before turning her question-filled smile to Ellen.

Sadly, there was nothing to tell in that department. Although Fin's reaction to Hans had been a little amusing. Ellen was sure he seemed put out by the handsome newcomer. Nothing obvious, just a vibe she was picking up. Fin was remaining quite reserved when he was normally open and friendly with everyone. Of course, though she'd like to think it was because of her, realistically it was probably because Hans was encroaching on their 'family' trip.

Fin cleared his throat. 'I propose a toast to . . .' He glanced nervously at Ellen.

She scrunched up her face. *Don't look at me, I don't have any answers.*

'Friends, family and Karijini,' Fin finished, raising his plastic flute.

Carrie was chatting away and topping up people's glasses. She did that when she was nervous or unsure – filled awkward silences with chatter.

Fin stood beside Bodhi, watching him carefully. Bodhi and Fin shared a silent exchange as only two guys who knew each other really well could.

Ellen could see the bond between the two men had become stronger. It was quite upsetting. Fin was more immersed in her family than ever, which just made her life so much harder. It meant she couldn't go home any time soon. She knew being this close to Fin again would be a test, and she was failing it. Badly. She could sense where he was at all times as if she had an infrared sensor tuned into his body heat. And her stupid heart would race when he'd smile or look at her, or even just walk past leaving a hot heady scent. Yep, she'd need two years hiding out at Challa Station at this rate. How do you stop loving someone? If she could cut herself open, find that cord attached to Fin and sever it in two, she would. Then life could go back to normal.

Stupid body, stupid heart. Why couldn't her mind be tougher!

They mingled by the water's edge for a while, until the bottle was empty. Then they had a swim, and by the time they got out, a family carrying coloured pool noodles had arrived.

'I wish this could stay up forever, it suits the spot,' said Ingi, glancing back at the arch.

Ellen was glad she liked it. It felt good to be making people happy again. 'We'd better get it down before the ranger comes. It's easy to pack up. And those flowers are for you to take back to the van.'

They had the arch packed away in no time and headed back to camp.

'We have a night booked at the Eco Retreat,' said Bodhi. He was still holding Ingi's hand but his shoulders were tense, and his usual enthusiasm missing. Preoccupied with Ingi returning his ring, no doubt. 'I thought it'd be nice to try some fancy food at the restaurant, that way you all don't have to eat my omelettes.'

'God, bro, are you still making your omelette surprises?' El scoffed. Bodhi was famous for his throw-together omelettes, usually comprised of leftovers, cold meats, potato salad or chips, et cetera – it all went in.

'Yes, yes he is,' Ingi replied. 'But he sure knows how to make them tasty.'

'While we'll be dining on kangaroo and barramundi, what will you guys do?' asked Bodhi.

'I want to drive to Kalamina Gorge for a look and then get back to do this walk when it's a bit cooler.' Ellen had hoped to escape for some quiet time to herself.

'Oh, that sounds good,' said Carrie. 'Can we come with you, sis? You have the ute for it, and we don't have room in our van for more than two,' she pleaded.

Ellen counted to five, hoping that by not replying straight away her sister might get the hint.

'It'll be fun, you can play tour guide,' Carrie added.

Ellen did the only thing she could think of to survive the day. 'Hans, would you like to come too? I've heard that road is rough as guts. My ute might be more suited.'

Carrie grinned. 'Yes, Hans, do come!'

Fin craned his head around to look at Ellen, his expression unreadable except for the tiny frown line between his eyes. She'd love to know what he was thinking. She'd made a point of staying behind him, always putting someone else between them. In reality, it was like using a wire fence to stop a flood.

'I would like that, thank you, El,' said Hans. 'Although I fear you're just asking me in case you need to change a tyre.'

He grinned at his own joke. Ellen returned his smile, relieved he was coming. It was nice how he'd automatically started calling her by her nickname. Was that a backpacker thing? So at ease with meeting new people and going with the flow?

Back at camp they got ready. Ellen fussed around, emptying the back seat of her clothes and water bottles and putting the Engel fridge on the back tray.

'Here, Carrie said you don't have bathers. I have a spare set. I think you need them more than me,' said Ingi, shoving them into her hand.

'Oooh, yes, thanks. I'll go put them on now.' Before Ingi could leave, she quickly asked, 'Hey, are you okay?'

Ingi smiled. 'Hopefully. We just need to work some things out.'

Ellen wanted to ask more questions, but she could tell it wasn't the time or the place. Ingi had said all she was going to say on the matter. 'As long as you're both okay?'

'Of course.'

'Thanks for the bathers. Enjoy your night.'

Ingi got in the van and Bodhi drove them out of the campsite.

Ingi had given her a nice red one-piece. There was a reason Ellen hadn't asked Carrie, even though she'd bet her left leg that she'd packed four pairs – all tiny bikinis with thong bottoms, close enough to dental floss. Ellen thought G-strings were for underwear, not for the beach with kids and seedy people around. Maybe it had to do with her mum's exercise phase when she used to wear this coloured leotard that disappeared into her butt. As a seven-year-old, Ellen had been quite the prude, or maybe that leotard had made her one?

Hans walked up wearing an Akubra hat and climbed in the front of the ute.

'You like?'

'I do. It suits you,' she said, shutting her door.

'Thanks for the invite. I'm enjoying your company. Your family are great.'

'They are indeed,' she replied.

'Sorry,' said Fin, climbing in the back. The peak of his grey cap framed his brown eyes perfectly. 'I hate keeping people waiting. Carrie is still fussing,' he said with a sigh.

Ellen glanced in the rear-view mirror as he rested his head back against the window, eyes closed. 'Carrie can irritate even the most patient of people,' she said with a grin, then regretted it when his eyelids fluttered open and he returned her smile.

'I'll get the aircon happening,' she said, giving her whole attention to the process of starting the ute and setting the air.

'So where have you come from?' asked Hans.

'We're all from Albany.' Ellen was going to explain where that was but Hans' face lit up.

'Oh wow, at the other end of the state,' he said. 'I intend to tour the great south. I've seen the beaches at Esperance. Sand so white.'

'It's like that around Albany too. You're welcome to stay with us if you ever get down there.'

'That's if Ellen ever comes home,' added Fin. 'She's not living in Albany at the moment.'

She was trying to process the tone behind his words when Carrie threw herself into the ute.

'Let's go.'

Ellen ended up catching up to Bodhi on the same road because the gravel was so rough, like the roughest road she'd ever been on. Her ute was protesting so she could only imagine how bad it was in the Maui van.

'I hope they shut all their cupboard doors properly!' she said, gritting her teeth.

'So where are you now, if not living in Albany?' Hans asked curiously as he gripped the door handle.

Somehow through the bouncing she managed to explain that she was working on a station.

'Hello? Is anyone going to talk about what happened back there?' Carrie interrupted. When no one said anything, she elaborated. 'Ingi said yes and then it all got a bit weird. She's not wearing the ring. What's going on?'

'I don't know but I could tell Bodhi is just as confused as us, I think,' said Fin.

'Ingi told me they need to discuss some things first,' said Ellen.

'Like what?' asked Carrie, leaning forward in the seat. 'Whose name she uses? Who's going to look after her parents when they're old? How many kids they'll have? What could be so serious to give a ring back? Clearly, they're in love.'

'Maybe she's got certain religious views,' added Hans. 'Or had an affair she needs to discuss and clear the air first? The whole "don't get married with secrets" thing.'

Ellen bit her lip. Was it her secret that was holding Ingi back? Could Hans be right? *Shit*. Or it could be something entirely different, even worse. El knew about Ingi's family history, and her brother's death. Maybe it had something to do with that?

Carrie laughed at Hans. 'Not likely. Ingi is devoted to Bodhi. Maybe she's really rich and wants a prenup?'

By the time they reached their destination they were none the wiser and so shook up from the road that they fell out of the ute in relief.

'I was starting to get carsick,' said Carrie, holding her head. 'I haven't felt like that since Bodhi got his L-plates and Dad let him drive us to Bluff Knoll.'

Carrie walked ahead with Hans while Fin hung back with El. 'You have a theory, don't you?' Fin asked her under his breath. Ellen opened her mouth but he cut in.

'Don't pretend you haven't. You've got that look.'

Ellen frowned. She didn't have a look ... did she? But he was right. 'I wonder if it has something to do with her brother's disease, Duchenne muscular dystrophy. That kind of thing takes a toll on people, especially when Ingi was so close to him.'

'You think she has the disease too?'

Ellen shrugged. 'I think it's best we wait and see before jumping to any scary conclusions,' she said and quickened her steps to catch up to Carrie and Hans.

A small ghost gum marked the edge of the path, just after a sign warning 'Cliff Risk Area'. They soon found out why.

'Oh shit, Fin, don't get too close.' Carrie was reaching out to him.

There was no safety rail, no steel lookout. Just a cliff edge where you could see the water below, if you were game enough.

'Can everyone step away from the edge, you're making me nervous.'

'Let's head down. It's too hot up here!' Ellen found the way down. No metal staircase, just a natural rocky one. 'This way.'

They made their way down in single file, the temperature dropping slightly with each step.

'Oh, it's as pretty as Fern Pool,' said Carrie, the first one down.

She wasted no time stripping off and getting in, arms raised and making 'ahh' noises as she submerged further into the water. Fin stripped off his shirt and followed her in while Hans sat in the shade. Ellen joined him so she didn't have to share the water with a half-naked Fin.

'It's beautiful, no? I just want to soak some of it up before I swim.'

This gorge was nowhere near as deep as Dale's Gorge. This one was just a baby in comparison.

The others swam around quietly, enjoying the tranquillity. There was only one other couple there and a few they'd seen walk off down the gorge trek. Ellen found herself watching Fin from behind her sunglasses, because, well, he was something to behold when he was shirtless with water dripping from his pecs. It was tauntingly painful, but like a road crash, she couldn't look away. Her sunglasses were starting to fog up but they hid her secret spying. Yet she noticed he glanced their way a lot. Or was that just wishful thinking?

Plop. A small rock fell into the water with a splash. Everyone looked up, squinting against the midmorning sun.

'Is it deep down there?' a voice boomed.

'Pretty deep,' Carrie yelled back.

'Can I jump?'

'Hell no,' Fin shouted.

He was sitting on a submerged rock near the edge, basking in the sun like a model, head strained skywards to where the voice had originated.

'Surely no one would . . .'

Ellen didn't even get to finish her thought when a black shadow streaked across the gorge wall, followed by an almighty slap against water. It sounded almost like breaking glass.

It took a moment before anyone moved, still too stunned to understand what had just happened, then Fin broke out in freestyle to get to the man.

Ellen and Hans stood and rushed to the water's edge, trying to see.

'Shit, is he alive?' said Hans.

Fin had the man tucked under his arm as he swam back to the edge, Carrie close behind asking the same question.

'He's unconscious, I think,' Fin said as he stood and brought him closer to the edge. 'Oh shit, he reeks of alcohol.'

Ellen entered the water. 'He has a pulse but he's definitely unconscious.'

'Do you think he has mates up there or he was alone?' Hans asked.

'I'll run up and see,' said Carrie. She didn't bother with shoes and clothes, or even a hat.

And Ellen bet she hadn't put on sunscreen earlier. Sure enough there was a noticeable pink tinge to her shoulders already.

'Take your phone and call for help,' said Ellen. She might get better reception up top.

'He's going to need it,' said Fin. 'He could have broken his back. Do you think he hit the rocks underneath?'

Ellen stared at the face of the unconscious man, stubble on his chin, tattoos on his chest and neck. This was not how she pictured this day going.

14

Ellen

Back then

'ELLIE, CAN YOU PASS ME THAT THIN BRUSH?' CARRIE POINTED to the set of make-up brushes beside her on the table that were just out of reach. 'So is your dress emerald green?' she asked the young girl in her chair. 'I can match your make-up to it, just a hint. Do you trust me?'

The girl nodded. Her hair was in rollers and nearby her mum was snapping photos.

It was the annual school ball night and preparations were in full swing. Carrie's salon became a hive of activity. All her staff were on and every chair occupied with girls having curls or updo's before moving on to Carrie for their make-up.

The doorbell chimed again and Ellen silently groaned except it was Ingrid who walked in, turning her groan into a sigh of relief.

'Geez, is it always like this?' Ingi asked, arriving at Ellen's side after dodging hairdryers, ducking past curling wands, side-stepping hair straighteners and hairdresser elbows.

'Yes, thanks so much for coming.'

Ellen helped Carrie every year as it was a frantic time, and this year they'd convinced Ingi to join them.

'Can you guys sort Teegan out, please?' Carrie ordered, make-up brush in hand like she was Da Vinci and the girl in the chair was the Mona Lisa.

'To be honest, I'm a bit excited. I never got to my ball,' said Ingi as she followed Ellen to the till.

'Not at all?' Ellen was surprised. She processed Teegan's payment. 'Thank you, enjoy your night.'

Ellen ran Ingi through the till but she was a quick study, having used similar programs at the restaurant. 'Prices are here, for today. Carrie made it easy for us,' she explained. 'So, you never went to one ball? Did you finish school?' Ellen realised she'd never asked, just assumed.

'No. Not one ball. I graduated but wasn't at the ceremony.'

Right then, no one was coming or going. 'Let's go make a cuppa, while we have a moment.'

Some of the mums were in a state, pacing the room, eagerly waiting for their beautiful butterflies to break out of their cocoons. Ellen asked them if they'd like a drink – two said yes to coffee, so she led Ingi into the back room behind the curtain.

'Did you not want to go to your ball?' Ellen asked, picking up their previous conversation.

'I did. I was all dressed up, had my make-up and hair done, and I got as far as the car with Dad heading down York Street.

I didn't have a date because I didn't do after-school activities or sports. Besides, most people at school thought I was weird anyway. But I was determined to go.'

Ellen switched the kettle on, put out the cups and turned to Ingi and waited.

Ingi shifted her weight from leg to leg then leaned back on the bench in the tiny back room. This was hard for Ingi, Ellen suddenly realised.

'We were in the car, heading to the ball. I was so excited. I was in a gorgeous blue sparkly dress and the girl next door had done my make-up, so I felt like a million dollars. I'd never worn make-up or a pretty dress before and I almost didn't recognise myself. I couldn't wait to show everyone this new me. Mikey had been speechless, and that's when I knew I must have scrubbed up good. He'd laughed a little as if he couldn't really believe it was me.'

Ingi smiled briefly.

'But then on the way to the ball, Mum called. She'd been trying Dad, but he was driving and couldn't answer so she called me. I knew it was bad when the first thing she said was, "Where's your father?" Her voice was high-pitched and panicky.' Ingi let out a slow breath. 'You think I would have been used to it after all those years with my brother, but if anything, it put me more on edge.'

'What was wrong?' Ellen hated to ask, feeling this was not going to end well at all. She knew Mikey had passed away when Ingi was twenty-two and that it had been a disease, but she'd never felt it was her place to ask for details. It hadn't been something that had ever come up in conversation, until today.

'Mum was yelling down the phone that she'd called the ambulance because Mikey was having trouble breathing, and had gone lethargic and was turning blue. She was worried he was going to die. That's how most kids with DMD die.'

Ellen frowned, trying to remember what the acronym stood for.

'Duchenne muscular dystrophy,' Ingi said. 'I was four when he was diagnosed. At that age I could run better and faster than he could at six. Not that I remember. Growing up, Mikey was always struggling to walk and we were in and out of hospitals. Anyway, that night Dad spun the car around and we headed to the hospital. So I missed my ball by that much,' she said holding her fingers a centimetre apart.

'Oh Ingi, I'm so sorry. That must have been awful.'

'The part I remember the most was standing around in the hospital in my stupid ball dress, my feet aching from the heels, and having everyone stare at me. A tiny part of me was so angry that I'd missed the ball. I'd been dreaming about it for so long – I'd hook up with some nice guy and have that perfect night. Which was so selfish because Mikey had never been to any and he was the one stuck in a hospital fighting for his life. I was so scared for him. My make-up ended up smeared down my face, like the bride of Frankenstein. No wonder people kept staring.'

Ellen passed Ingi the coffee then rubbed her arm tenderly.

'He pulled through; Mum's quick thinking saved his life. She was full bottle on everything DMD. She was always watching him for signs. There's no cure for DMD and we'd been told he'd likely die in his twenties.' She took a sip from her cup. 'It's horrible, isn't it? A mother knowing her son wouldn't live long, never have a chance to get married, be a father or grow old.'

And a sister who knew her brother would die. Ellen was going to go home and google everything she could on DMD to try and understand. She wondered how much Bodhi knew?

'I feel so bad at having two healthy siblings when you lost the only one you had.' Ellen felt spoilt at her charmed life. Just how much had Ingi gone without? How much of her childhood had been spent caring for her brother? And here was Ellen fussing over a crush on her sister's boyfriend. It seemed so minuscule in comparison.

Ingi smiled. 'I'm glad you have two healthy siblings – well, one in particular,' she said with a wink.

'Ellen, Ingi, can you help serve, please?' came Carrie's urgent voice from the salon.

'The other one, not so much,' Ingi joked.

Ingi handed out the coffee while Ellen went to the till. The next time someone paid, Ingi had a go, and then completed the next few transactions under Ellen's watchful gaze.

'Nailed it,' she praised her.

The door opened again.

'It doesn't stop,' Ingi muttered as a young woman and her mother entered.

Ellen was about to say something when she saw Fin through the large glass windows heading their way.

'I'm just going to duck off to the toilet,' she told Ingi.

'Didn't you just go?'

'Must be last night's curry,' she mumbled throwing another glance his way.

His eyes found her just as he entered and she turned her back and escaped. It was almost unbearable to see Fin now, especially after the interaction at the pub a few weeks ago.

With Ingi's help, Ellen had decided that avoidance was best. Not seeing him would help her move on, she was certain of it.

Now she just had to figure out how long to wait outside next to the toilet block. Leaning against the cold wall, she hoped he was just dropping something off.

'What are you doing back here?'

Ellen jumped.

'Gee, nervous Nelly, anyone'd think you were trying to have a sneaky smoke or something.' Carrie squinted at her. 'Why are you out here when the salon is in chaos?'

'Just getting some fresh air – I was feeling a bit queasy. I think it's all the hairspray.' Well, it wasn't a lie.

Carrie pressed her lips into a thin line. 'Or is it because Fin came in? I know you all think I'm too dumb or busy to notice stuff, but you bailed from the coffee shop on Saturday when he turned up, and when I asked you to join us for lunch last week you said no and then I spotted you with Ingi and Bodhi.'

Okay, maybe her sister was more in tune than she thought. 'I'd already said yes to lunch with them,' she spluttered.

'You could have just said that – we would have joined you.'

That was why I didn't!

'While you've been trying to avoid us, I've been wanting to talk to you about something important.'

'Oh, you have?'

'Yeah. I'm thinking of moving in with Fin. I really wanted to know what you thought. Is it too soon?'

'*What?*'

Carrie leaned back at her outburst. 'Gee, it's not that surprising, is it? I thought you'd be excited for me.'

'No . . . it's . . . it's just that . . . well . . . you've never moved in with a bloke before,' she stammered, trying to regain some calm.

'Exactly. This is a first for me. A big step, but I think we're ready. And besides, I have to move out because Maddy's *boyfriend* is moving in.' She rolled her eyes at the inconvenience of it all. 'I told them they wouldn't even know I was there, but you know Maddy – she wants to play families. And besides, Fin has a great place.'

Ellen felt faint. *You've only been going out for a few months!* Was her sister that sure about Fin? 'I don't think it matters what I think,' she said, avoiding picking a side. 'It's how you feel, especially as it's only been a few months.'

'Actually, if you were ever around, you'd know it's over three months now, and we were casual even longer. He really is the best, Ellen.' Carrie smiled and took her hand. 'I'm thinking Christmas in his home would be amazing.'

Ellen already knew just how wonderful he was. But so did her little sister, and there was no way Ellen could break her heart. Christ, Carrie had taken four years to even leave home properly and yet now she was ready to move in with Fin. This was huge. She must really love him.

Now Ellen really had to try and rid Murray Finlay from her heart. But it felt like the more she tried to push him away, the more her brain fixated on him. It was so damn frustrating. She was spending so much time trying to avoid him it was wearing her down.

'It sounds to me like you've already made up your mind,' she replied when she realised Carrie was waiting for some sort of answer.

'Hmm, maybe. Anyway, come back inside please – it's utter madness. I wish you knew how to apply make-up,' she said with a sigh. 'Actually you do look a little pale.' Her hand went to Ellen's forehead. 'You sure you're not coming down with something? Want me to get you some Panadol?'

'I'm okay, thanks.'

'The flu is doing the rounds again, and being a nurse, you are at the epicentre of germs.' Carrie pulled a face.

'True,' she said, following her back inside, a little relieved that their conversation was over.

'Anika, you're next, my lovely. Jump in the chair,' said Carrie as she perused her collection of make-up colours.

Ellen went to stand at the till next to Ingi and kept her head down, deliberating over the appointment book.

'It's okay, he just left,' whispered Ingi.

'God, am I that obvious?'

'Only to me.'

'And Carrie,' she muttered. 'She's getting a little suss. I need to come up with better excuses about why I keep avoiding them.'

Ingi leaned on the reception desk, her head close to Ellen. 'Maybe we could make up a fake boyfriend?'

Ellen huffed. 'Just what I need – more lies and drama.'

'Maybe you could tell Fin the truth – that you're struggling and need time. Surely he'll give you some space then? Unless he's also a bit confused.'

Fin confused? She didn't think so. He didn't feel that way about her. She'd seen how he was with Carrie, watched them kiss. She was sure that all Fin had was some mixed-up emotions from one crazy night. If he really felt anything towards her then he would have broken up with Carrie. Maybe he realised it wasn't worth ruining her life for a 'what if?' There was too much at stake. Too many people who could be hurt.

Ellen was the only one whose feelings had bloomed into something more, but it was pointless and unreciprocated. It was just a matter of time and she could move past this, find a new man to set her sights on. Cutting Fin out of her life for now was the safest plan. At least that way the only one hurting was her.

She stood up and looked Ingi straight in the eyes. 'I'm fine . . .' Ingi's eyes narrowed. 'I . . . I will be.' Ellen couldn't lie to Ingi. 'I'll be trying bloody hard.'

'So, no fake boyfriend?' said Ingi.

'Ha, how about a real one? That would be nice.'

And wouldn't that solve a lot of problems.

15

Ingi

THE ALARM SCREECHED BY HER BED. GROANING, INGI TURNED it off and stared at the two mould spots on her ceiling, like eyes watching her every move. Was it God watching over her? Kids talked about God at school and how he saved people, yet he'd never answered any of Ingi's prayers. Was that because she didn't go to church? Was his plate full with all the other good Christians? Some days she flicked her middle finger at the ceiling, but other days she'd lie awake, hoping for a miracle.

Maybe those Disney movies she watched with Mike were giving her false hope? That shit didn't go down in the real world. There were no fairy godmothers, no magic, no 'love overcomes all'. Her family loved Mikey but it wasn't going to save him. He was dying. Wasting away before their eyes. There was no cure for Duchenne muscular dystrophy. Cancer had better survival rates.

Ingi threw her pink and blue Cinderella cover off and quickly got dressed into her black school pants and shirt. At fifteen, she had beyond outgrown her room, from the bedcover, to the dolls shoved on the corner shelf, to the bright pink walls. She'd grown tired of asking for new paint or a new cover. One day she'd try the op shop in the hope that someone might have given away a plain cover in anything but pink.

'Good, you're up. Let's get him ready.'

Her mum, Kath, paused by her door only long enough so Ingi could fall in behind. Everything was routine, like the running of a navy ship but less fun. Kath looked older than her mid-forties. Her wavy brown hair was riddled with greys and split ends, plus the old tracksuits she wore didn't help. She didn't wear much make-up but when she did it only highlighted her wrinkles. Ingi followed her white Target running shoes down the hallway. The carpet had been pulled up five years ago when Mikey started needing a wheelchair more often. The only carpet left in the house was in Ingi's bedroom but she'd happily take floorboards over the mottled pink, tan and pale green carpet that resembled spew. The only thing in its favour was its ability to hide stains, like when she'd dropped a can of Coke or spilt make-up she'd nicked from her mum's drawer.

Kath knocked on Mikey's door even though it was partially open. 'Good morning, sweetheart.'

She didn't wait for a response, but went straight in and kissed his forehead while removing his mask. Ingi turned off his BiPAP machine and started getting his clothes ready.

'Ingi, honey, can you take off the night splints then we'll help Mikey to the bathroom.'

Mikey sighed heavily as Kath threw back his blankets, revealing a tent in his pyjama bottoms.

'Did you have to wake me? I was having a great dream.' He shot a mischievous grin at Ingi. 'You might need to help me out to the lawn this morning,' he teased. 'My aim might be way off.'

'Mikey, you're a rascal,' Kath tutted and slapped his shoulder. 'You know I've been married to your father a long time – a morning glory is nothing new.'

'Oh, gross, Mum.' Ingi put her finger in her mouth and pretended to throw up, which made Mikey smile. *Yay.* It was always going to be a decent day if you could get him in a good mood early. To outsiders, their banter would probably sound icky, but when Mikey relied on their help for the most basic things, you had to make light of certain bodily functions. It couldn't be helped; Mickey didn't have the ability to control it and so they'd found ways to carry on without making him uncomfortable. If it was with laughs, so be it.

'You win, Mum. Please, no more horrible images of you and Dad,' said Mikey. He turned his head in her direction. 'No, Ingi, I want the Nike socks . . . yeah, the black ones.'

Ingi threw a pair of socks at his face and watched his nostrils flare. 'Put them on yourself,' she teased as she stretched his tendons in his feet.

'Don't make me come over there and sock slap you.'

Ingi laughed at the name they'd given to his weak punches. A while back they'd had a fight over something stupid and he'd tried to hit her but it had been soft. 'That was like a sock,' she'd said before they'd both burst out laughing, and from that moment on it had stuck. It was in those moments of laughter that they felt like other normal siblings, joshing and teasing.

'Settle, you two, I haven't taken my heart medication today. I can't take your sick banter just yet.'

Together they helped Mikey up and to the bathroom. Kath waited outside while Ingi went back and made his bed and put out his school clothes.

In a synchronised dance, perfected over years of practice, they had Mikey dressed and ready in no time. Ingi pulled his socks up his withered legs. His calves had once been like tree trunks but not anymore – the disease was wasting away his muscles at a rapid rate.

Next Ingi put on his black Air Jordans, a gift for his seventeenth birthday. It's what all the cool kids were wearing at school and Mikey had cried when he first saw his present. Well, they all had. 'I can't take them,' Mikey had said first, spluttering through his tears. 'I know how tight money is because of me.'

And yet he'd been unable to take his eyes off the shoes. He'd wanted them so bad.

'Yes, you will,' their dad had said. 'Seeing you happy makes us all happy.'

That day Mikey had done the most aided walking in ages, as if floating on clouds. Ingi had been happy for him, but also jealous. She'd dreamed of having things as well. Girls her age had iPods and phones, clothes from surf shops, Converse or Nike shoes and all the make-up in the world. She had to remind herself that she didn't need any of that anyway, she didn't have the time. It wasn't like she got to go to parties or hang out down York Street after school. It was hard to keep friends when you never had time for them, and they didn't like coming to her house because it was confronting.

'We've got your physio appointment this morning then I'll drop you at school,' Kath was saying. 'Ingrid, Uncle Peter will pick you up after school for work, so don't forget your change of clothes.'

'I know, Mum.'

Far out, anyone would think she'd forgotten that Ingi had been working at Uncle Pete's restaurant for the last two years.

'Bring me back some of that truffle pasta,' said Mikey as they settled him at the table.

They helped him walk to the kitchen every morning because it allowed his intestines to function better. A wheelchair sat in the corner of the seventies kitchen, its steel frame out of place against the green benches and walls. It was small and fit through the doorways easily, especially since their dad had removed all the doors. But for school, Mikey had a motorised wheelchair which they'd only got a few months ago after saving madly. It meant he had some independence and didn't have to be pushed around school all the time. Ingi could have half a life at school now too.

The motorised chair was where most of her over-inflated wage from Uncle Pete's had gone. It wasn't all bad, she got to keep a bit, which she saved, and Uncle Pete was always slipping her extra money here and there. 'To spend on yourself,' he would say. But Ingrid didn't have time for shopping or coffee dates, so she used it to go to the cinema with Mikey. It was one of their favourite outings. It also gave her parents about two hours to themselves.

'No pasta,' said Kath. 'We'll have a nice salad for dinner.'

'Mum,' Mikey groaned. 'Please, no more kale. My shit has been regular for ages.'

Kath pursed her lips at his language. 'Why do you think you're so regular? It's thanks to the kale and the salads. Now, take your pills and eat your high-fibre brekky so you can keep staying regular.'

He dropped his head onto the table. 'I hate my life,' he murmured. 'Can you sprinkle some poison over my muesli?'

Kath moved about the kitchen, sorting breakfast and pretending she hadn't heard him.

'Why won't you just help me die, it's going to happen anyway.'

Ingi headed out to the laundry on the back veranda to put a load on. The air seemed easier to breathe out here. She felt sick when Mikey talked like that; it made her stomach clench and the back of her neck go all clammy. She hated being reminded that he was dying and would be dead soon. Some days, when he was being a moody arsehole, she wished he would just die and save them all the trouble. But she never really meant it of course. Some days, like today, she was sure he never really meant it either.

Back in the kitchen, Mikey was eating alone and swallowing his collection of pills, or his 'candy', as he preferred to call his medication.

'You going to eat?' he asked.

'Yeah, in a minute, I'll just get my bag ready for tonight.'

Ingi headed back to her room, but she heard a noise that made her pause, ears straining. The sniffles were coming from the bathroom. Ingi pressed her hand against the door, trying to send her mum a hug of sorts. Mikey's words sometimes cut deep without warning. You'd think she'd have got used to them by now; then again, Ingi hadn't.

Feeling useless, she continued to her bedroom to pack her work clothes. Her mum would come out in a few minutes, all chirpy and complaining of her hayfever flaring up, but they all knew. Even Mikey. His puffy face – from the steroids – would flush pink whenever he spotted his mum's red eyes and blotchy skin, and for the rest of the day he'd be good – no more talk of death.

'I'll go get the car sorted. You two finish up here, please?' Kath said before heading outside to open the garage door.

Ingi glanced at Mikey as he nudged his bowl away.

'Don't you give me that look. I feel bad enough already,' he muttered.

'So you should,' Ingi said, feeling her own anger surge. 'Mum does a bloody lot for you to stay alive and you talking about dying is just throwing all that in her face. I hate seeing her upset. If you weren't already suffering, I'd punch you one.' She wanted to grab him by the shirt and shake him until his teeth rattled.

'No one understands how I feel. You all try, but you'll never know.' Spit flew from his lips with the last word. 'Do you think I like having to ask people for help? To have my mum and my sister look after me like I'm a baby? And I'm only going to get worse. I don't want to make any of your lives harder than they already are.'

Ingi's eyelashes fluttered as she blinked away tears. These days her emotions were all over the place. 'It's not your fault, Mike. You didn't ask for this disease. We love you and want to care for you. Besides, it could be worse, you could be some dero druggo living on the street stealing from your parents.

That would be way worse. You may need our help, but at least you're nice . . . some of the time,' she added before grinning.

He screwed up his face. 'I'm always nice. Well, actually that depends on what movie you pick.'

Ingi laughed as she cleaned up the dishes. 'I'm sure you told me you love rom-coms.'

'Like fuck I did,' he whispered, throwing a glance at the back door in case Kath was on her way back.

Ingi wheeled the chair to his side, pushed the table out of the way – which was lighter than a seventeen-year-old – and then tucked her arms under his armpits and lifted.

'You're sure, cos *Easy A* is on at the cinema . . .'

Before she even finished, he was shaking his head and moaning. 'Please no, *nooooo*.'

Ingi manoeuvred him into his wheelchair as Kath came back in.

'What's wrong now?'

'Ingi's trying to kill me with her shit taste in movies.'

Ingi ruffled his hair, which only pissed him off more. He tried to lift his skinny arm, attempting to fix his hair.

'Enough,' said Kath. 'Let's get you into the car and off to the physio, then school.'

'Don't forget your glasses, four eyes.'

Ingi let him have the last cheap shot, hiding her smile. They were back in safe territory. She could breathe easy.

Again they settled into their routine, one pushing Mikey to the front door, the other holding it open. Ingi carried their school bags after putting their lunches inside.

Sometimes school was hard, especially for Mikey, but other days it was nice to feel like a normal kid sitting in class listening to a teacher drone on. No responsibilities and no worries. She was just a fifteen-year-old learning. But by tonight she might be crying herself to sleep, lying awake, or dead to the world after a long night shift with Uncle Pete. She could never pick which one it would be. On those nights she couldn't sleep, when she was so overwhelmed and fell to bits, she wondered how her mum could have watched her own dad die this way and then go on to have her own kids and go through the same thing with her son? Ingi was never going to go through this again.

Never. Ever.

16

Carrie

Now

ONE MINUTE THEY WERE HAVING A RELAXING, TRANQUIL swim, the next it was like a scene from *Bondi Rescue*. A dark shadow had blotted out the sun, ever so briefly, and then chaos had descended as the huge splash rained water down on them.

'What kind of idiot jumps off a cliff not knowing what's below?' Carrie said, her heart racing as she arrived back with the others after calling for help. She may not be a smart qualified nurse like her sister, but she wanted to be helpful. If running up to the top in the searing heat to make a phone call was all she could do, then she'd do it again and again.

'A very drunk idiot. Do we get him out?' asked Hans. While Carrie had been gone, he'd entered the water and was holding the man, opposite Fin.

Fin shrugged and shook his head. 'I have no idea. If he's broken his back or other bones, maybe lifting him out wouldn't be so great. Ellen, what do you think?'

Ellen was checking the man's vitals with gentle hands, the same hands that had always helped Carrie up when she'd fallen over, or at night when she was scared. She never told her, yet somehow Ellen always knew when to reach across.

'His pulse is strong enough. His pupils are okay.' Ellen waded further into the water, her fingers working over his arms. 'Shit!' She slipped on the slimy rocks and crashed into Fin.

Crimson crept up her neck and face as Fin held her until she could get her footing. She didn't like needing to be rescued. Carrie had never understood that someone who helped so many, almost hated to ask for help herself. That whole Josh situation, for example. No one knew about the affair with his ex or the baby, not until Carrie visited Ellen and noticed all of Josh's stuff was gone from her house . . . then she'd made her spill the beans. 'I didn't want anyone to worry,' had been her excuse.

Clearing her throat, El continued with her inspection of the man, checking both legs and coming back around to the other side where Hans kept him afloat.

'Do you think he broke any ribs? Or swallowed a heap of water?' Hans asked.

Ellen didn't reply, just continued checking what she could. 'Did you have any luck, Carrie? That road is too rough for us to put him in my ute without the right gear.'

'Yep, help is on its way,' Carrie shouted even though she was at the water's edge. Her adrenaline was pumping. 'Will he be okay?'

'He's actually lucky it wasn't worse. I can't see any lacerations or bruising. His head seems okay, but there could be lots I can't see. He needs a hospital for that. We just have to wait.'

El continued to monitor the man, while the rest of them held him safe. The other people who'd been swimming had offered to wait at the top and direct the ambulance officers down when they arrived. Silence descended as they fell into their own thoughts.

Ellen was amazing to watch, so sure of herself, confident in her ability and knowledge. Carrie felt a weird mix of pride and jealousy. Having Ellen in the family relegated Carrie into the 'try-hard' section. Nothing she did would ever top what Ellen could do or all the special things she did for people. Carrie wanted to be more like her, only she'd never tell anyone. But it was true. Was that why her life felt so disjointed and empty? Was she too busy trying to measure up to what she thought people expected of her? Was she putting this pressure on herself? Was that why it was getting harder to be happy with Fin, especially knowing what direction he wanted to sail his boat while she was flailing around in the ocean looking for land. Was she being selfish holding onto him when she knew she couldn't make him happy? Maybe she was more than someone who needed rescuing from rough seas, maybe she was the anchor, embedded into the bottom of the ocean unwilling to budge.

Hell, she had no idea how to save herself. Carrie studied her sister, her boyfriend, their surroundings. She was physically here and yet she felt as if she was pretending, playing a part. Would this emptiness ever pass?

It felt like ages until the ambulance arrived from Tom Price; in truth it was more like forty-five minutes, but when you were standing in water holding an unconscious body, hoping he wasn't dying, those minutes felt like hours. The paramedics got an IV into the man and cuffed his neck then transferred him onto a portable stretcher. Fin was probably turning into a prune, but he never once complained. Carrie couldn't have done it. She wished she was more helpful – she wanted to be, she just didn't know how she could contribute.

'Here, let me take a turn at that,' said Carrie, taking the IV bag from one of the ambulance officers, who was starting to wince at having to hold her arm up for so long. After ten minutes Carrie was feeling her pain.

The narrow steep track made transferring him to the ambulance ten times harder. This was the sort of rescue that made the nightly news. Ellen collected everyone's towels and water bottles before heading up the cliff behind them.

'That was not how I expected the rest of our day to go,' she said.

'At least we'll never forget it. I just hope he'll be okay,' said Carrie, happy to pass the IV bag back. She hugged herself, even though there was sweat gathering in her pits and down her back. 'It's a bit unsettling,' she admitted.

Ellen put her hand on her arm, causing her skin to sting and suddenly feel hot. Damn, she was pink. They all stood nearby watching the man get loaded into the ambulance.

'Thanks, guys, for all your help. This bloke doesn't realise how lucky he is that you were there,' said the officer before closing the doors.

'Now what?' said Hans as the dust settled behind the ambulance after it drove away.

'Shall we head back? I'm starving,' said Carrie, heading over to the ute with Fin close behind. It was now well after lunchtime.

'You're glowing, Carrie,' he said. 'Might want some aloe vera on your face and shoulders.'

She winced. 'I know. I'm just waiting for El to say "I told you so". I didn't think we'd be stuck out in the sun helping some dude with a death wish.'

Carrie never listened to her big sister, even though she'd mostly been right over the years. But she was lucky to have her. El would drop everything for Carrie – help paint her salon, move house, organise parties for her. Carrie tried to be like her, but she was always late for events, forgot birthdays, but she often told her family how much she loved them and hoped that would be enough to make up for her shortcomings.

Why did everything come back to her? Was she so self-obsessed?

She didn't want to be.

17

Ingi

'WHAT ARE YOU THINKING ABOUT?' BODHI ASKED AS HE drove the van to their destination.

Ingi knew she'd been quiet, but she wasn't sure she could carry on a 'normal' conversation right now.

'Hmm, how I ruined the proposal,' she explained. Turning in her seat, she faced Bodhi. 'I wanted to wait until we were settled at the camp before we had our chat, but talking about anything else now seems . . . weird.'

He nodded. 'Yeah.'

She knew she'd scared him, and he'd no doubt found it hard to continue the celebrations with a smile when he was internalising their future 'talk'. Thank God the others gave them some space and didn't make a big song and dance over her abrupt ring return. Ingi was kicking herself for not making things so much clearer with Bodhi sooner, but she didn't think he'd propose – not yet at least. Or was she just deluding herself? Ignoring her concerns because she knew it could be a deal-breaker and she hadn't been ready to give him up. *Damn it, Ingrid.*

'I'm sorry I had to do . . . that,' Ingi couldn't bring herself to say it out loud, 'in front of your family, but I couldn't pretend everything was going to be fine when we don't know if it will be.'

'You're really worrying me, Ingi. Are you okay? Like . . . are you healthy?'

Bodhi's face was ashen and she winced as if she'd been punched.

'No. No, I'm fine.'

'Are you sure? I know you said you don't have DMD but you told me once you're a carrier.'

'Yes, I carry the gene. And in some rare cases females can have mild symptoms, but as yet I'm fine. So you don't have to worry about me.'

'That's good, I think,' he said, concern settling in the creases on his face.

The van slowed as they came into the camping area and Bodhi parked at the reception building. The cream tin structure was stained with red dust. Outside, cream sails shaded the picnic tables.

'If it's not that, then what? Ingi, you're worrying me,' said Bodhi as he leaned on the steering wheel facing her.

She twisted her hair around in her fingers, blue tips long gone, replaced with her natural brown. 'Bodhi, I love you. I want to spend the rest of my life with you.' She took a deep breath. 'But I thought I made it clear that I wasn't having children?'

He tilted his head, brows creased. 'Yeah, you mentioned not being ready for kids. I can wait.'

'No. I said I *wasn't having* kids. Not that I'm not ready for them.' Ingi stared into her lap, picking at the loose threads on her shorts. 'You only heard what you wanted to hear.' And to be fair, she may not have made the effort to explain it properly and make sure he knew *exactly* what she meant.

'I . . .' His mouth opened and closed. 'I'm in no rush. You might change your mind.'

'Bodhi,' she practically yelled. 'You're not listening. I am NOT having kids. End of story. If you want kids, then we can't get married.'

He stared at her blankly, frozen like a movie on pause.

The ring sparkled in the sunlight where it sat on the console like a loaded weapon between them.

'No, Ingi, you don't mean that. Look, let's talk about this.'

'Bodhi, do you want your own kids?' Again his mouth worked overtime. 'Yes, or no? It's a simple answer,' she pressed.

'Yes, of course I do, but I don't want to lose you over it.'

'And neither do I,' she replied. 'So you need to really think this through. My answer won't change. You will not have a child with me. And I can't have you resent me later because of it.'

Ingi got out. The afternoon heat was still bearing down, reflecting off the hard ground. She didn't head into the office, instead she followed a road that felt like it was leading to the middle of nowhere.

She didn't care. Bodhi needed time to think and she didn't want to sway him. She knew he loved her, would do anything to be with her, and yet it could still turn ugly. She'd seen parents leave because raising a disabled child was too hard and hadn't been the life they'd envisaged. Not that she thought Bodhi would do that, but the pressure on a family can change the dynamics. Bodhi might say he's okay with it now . . . but down the track, when all his mates had their own kids and he started to wish he had his own, the desire would build and start to cause tensions. The same when parents lose a child – it could tear them apart or bring them together . . . no one knows until it happens to them. She wanted to avoid the unknown.

Ingi knew firsthand about unwanted feelings that snuck up on you, days when she wished Mikey hadn't been born. God, how she hated herself for those thoughts, but it was the honest truth. She'd blamed him for her not being able to have a normal life like other kids. No matter how much she'd loved her brother, that resentment had surfaced, and it would for Bodhi too. Ingi would rather end it now while he had time to find a woman to have his children. She wanted the best for Bodhi, even if that meant him marrying someone else.

Glancing over her shoulder, only her footsteps remained. Bodhi hadn't followed. She kept walking the road as it went around in a big circle; fancy tents were set up at a good distance from each other. They looked out of place in the landscape, no matter how well they tried to make them blend in.

Feeling lightheaded she bent over, hands on her knees, as she felt the sky spin around her. She should have tried harder to make him understand her stance on children. Then again, she had mentioned it a few times. Did he just assume because she was a woman she'd eventually change her mind?

Ingi would compromise on most things to keep Bodhi, just not this.

18

Ellen

Back then

'ARE YOU OKAY?'

Tanya stopped at the nurses' station where Ellen was leaning against the wall in a matching blue uniform, right down to the ponytail and shoes. Some days they changed it up and wore matching scrunchies. Being December, their scrunchies were Christmas-themed and they'd put up a few decorations, like the gold tinsel Ellen was trying to hide behind.

'I'm just feeling off.' She rested her head on the wall and closed her eyes. She was hoping no one would notice her and she could rest a bit longer.

'You've been feeling off a lot lately – you sure you're not pregnant?'

Ellen gave her a dry humourless laugh. 'You're so funny. Got to have sex to get pregnant. Besides, I'm still having periods,' she added.

Tanya frowned. 'Didn't you say they were mucking around last month?'

Ellen had said that. They'd been light and a bit irregular. Hers had never been like clockwork so she hadn't over-analysed it.

'Maybe you should do a test and rule it out,' said Tanya.

'I told you. Sex makes a baby. The last time I had sex was . . .' Ellen did some rough calculations in her head. When was the concert? 'About three months ago.'

'Did you use protection?' Tanya asked. 'Why do I feel like I'm giving my teenage niece a sex talk?'

Ellen groaned like a kid getting said sex advice. 'I did use protection,' she said. 'The one I keep in my bag for emergencies.' One she also hadn't replaced. *Mental note: put new condom in bag.*

'And how long had it been in there for? Please don't say years! Did you check it in case it broke?'

Um, well, it had been in her bag a year, or maybe more. *Hell.* And it was pitch black and they were grappling around in the dark – no one had stopped to investigate if the condom had broken. Maybe they should have!

Holy shit! Surely not? Ellen felt the room start to spin.

'Before you panic, do a test,' said Tanya, taking her by the shoulders. 'I'd hate to be scaring you over nothing. There has been a bit of gastro going around.'

'Yes, you're right.'

'Come on, no time like the present.' Tanya shoved a jar into her hand and pushed her towards the toilet. 'Go pee.'

Lucky the maternity ward was quiet at the moment. An expectant mum was due in at four and the other two mums were resting with their newborns. But it was nearing Christmas and a full moon – an influx was imminent.

Tanya waved her into a spare examination room on her return.

'This is so embarrassing,' said Ellen, handing over her pee jar to Tanya who had her hand held out, fingers wiggling.

Snatching it up, she turned to test it. 'So who was the guy? You didn't go back to Josh, did you?'

'Hell no.' Ellen started pacing then made herself sit in a chair before Tanya told her off. 'I may have been stupid not to see through Josh's bullshit but I'm not stupid enough to go back to him. Please, I have some self-respect.'

Tanya laughed. 'I'm glad. Could you imagine if he got his ex pregnant and then his other ex pregnant.'

Ellen rested her head in her palm. 'This is not a romance novel, Tanya, this is my life.'

'Sorry. A little light humour to speed up the process.'

'Your bedside manner needs work,' she muttered but had to admit it was helping.

Ellen counted everything in the examination room. There were forty-six curtain clips. She counted twice just to be sure.

'Who's this guy then? Was he gorgeous? One-night stand? Affair?'

'Stop fishing for details.' Ellen threw her a dark look, trying to hide the nerves that were buzzing like a million bees. She couldn't think about the 'what if's'. 'But if you must know he was a hundred times better than Josh,' she added. 'No, a gazillion times better.'

'In bed or in looks?'

Ellen's mouth dropped open. Tanya was never backward in coming forward.

'Either way, that's good,' she continued, turning to face Ellen. "'Cos he's your baby daddy.'

'I hope you're fucking joking,' she said.

But there was no laughter on Tanya's lips. 'So, no congratulations then?'

Ellen shot up from the chair and snatched the test from her hands. The room faded to grey.

'Jesus, girl, sit down before you faint.' Tanya wrangled her back into the chair.

Ellen was sucking in deep breaths while darkness edged her vision. *No, no, no this couldn't be happening.* 'If that's right then I'm over three months along. Oh shit.' Her hand went to her belly. Suddenly all the bits started adding up. Funny how you could brush things aside when you thought it was impossible. Once she'd seen a woman in labour who didn't even realise she was pregnant.

That damn emergency condom hadn't done its bloody job!

Tanya crouched down beside the chair and brushed back the hair stuck to her face. 'So you don't want to keep it?' she asked softly.

A burst of laughter escaped at the same time tears welled and spilled down her cheeks. Was she losing her mind?

'I don't know. I need a bit more time to process this, Tan. For fuck's sake, I can't believe it.'

I'm pregnant. Bloody hell.

She'd always wanted children. But this baby, this was Fin's. *Far out. What the hell am I going to do?*

More tears flowed and Tanya fetched a tissue.

'Jesus. Was it with a married man?'

That only made Ellen cry harder. Tanya pulled her into her arms and held her while she sobbed, her mind whirling like a windmill in a tornado.

If she'd been six weeks or so, she'd have an abortion, but this far along, she always thought it was too much of a baby. At this stage it would be about the size of a lemon and moving its arms and legs and testing out its facial movements. A tiny baby, growing inside her. Her hand was pressed against her belly. No, she couldn't terminate this baby now.

But how could she keep her sister's boyfriend's baby! How the hell would she explain that? Tanya would say her life was a romance novel for sure.

Maybe Ellen could say it was someone else's? Maybe Fin wouldn't think it was his if she fudged the due date. But then she'd be a big fat liar, raising his child right in front of him. But if she told everyone . . . then what? Everything would come out and their family would fall apart. Could she destroy her sister's happiness for the sake of her own?

'Hey, hey, stop that,' said Tanya. 'Stop spiralling. You don't need to have the answers now. Just breathe. Nothing has to be decided today.'

She started rubbing her back and Ellen felt the warmth spread through her. She wiped at her face in frustration, the tissue all but a soggy scrunched mess.

'Oh Tanya, what the hell am I going to do!'

'Get up and finish this shift. Then tomorrow do it all again. Maybe go and have an ultrasound, start taking some folic acid and folate.'

'Yes, nurse,' she murmured. Ellen grabbed Tanya's hand. 'Thank you, for being here, for even suggesting it. Please, don't tell anyone. Not a soul.'

Tanya smiled. 'Your secret is safe with me.' She wrapped her arms around her tightly. 'It will be okay, El. I'm here for you in whatever way you need.'

'Thank you.'

A month later and Ellen was still clueless about what to do. For the moment it was a case of pretending nothing was happening. She went to work, went home, cleaned house, attended family dinners. Avoided Fin. The usual.

She'd endured Christmas with the family, which wasn't so bad as Fin was with his family and only came over for dinner. Yet he still managed to rattle her with a warm hug and a kiss on her cheek.

'Merry Christmas, El,' he'd said, holding her tightly.

If he'd noticed she was stiffer than one of Bodhi's surfboards, he didn't mention it. If anything, he seemed to go out of his way to engage with her. At one point, when she snuck off to the kitchen, he ended up in there too, getting drinks. She bailed as soon as she could, back to the safety of the others. But when he returned, he came and stood beside her. That's when he pulled a small wrapped box from his pocket and handed it to her. 'Merry Christmas, Ellen.'

That had been awkward, especially when he requested she open it in front of everyone! Even Carrie.

'But I didn't get you anything,' she admitted. Lorraine had got him something on behalf of the family.

'I saw this and had to get it.'

'He was like a dog with a bone, couldn't help himself, sis,' Carrie said.

Nervously she'd opened the cute box to find a silver necklace with a tiny bee hanging from it. It was all kinds of wrong and wonderful. She'd been lost for words. It was a heartfelt gift, one that reminded her of their night together, the very night she'd been trying so bloody hard to forget.

'You don't like it?' he'd said worriedly.

'No, I love it. It's so beautiful.' And she'd meant it. It took all her effort not to throw herself into his arms – her hormones no doubt playing a huge part in that. Automatically, she'd leaned over and kissed his cheek. 'Thanks, Fin.'

'Do you like it, sis? Want me to put it on you?' Carrie asked.

While Carrie helped her with the necklace, her parents told Fin the whole story of her bee saga, from Colin finding her sprawled out on the lawn to rushing her to hospital.

'It was God awful,' her mum explained. 'Nearly lost my baby girl.'

'Mum, I was twenty-two at the time.'

'It's so cute. Totally you.' Carrie beamed at Fin. 'Good job, babe.'

Ellen was now stuck with the awkward situation of having this constant reminder of Fin around her neck and close to her heart, or taking it off and dealing with the 'Where is your necklace?' questions from everyone. Maybe she could pretend she lost it? Talk about frustrating.

'How about wear it for a month, then take it off and say you lost it,' Ingi had suggested.

Turned out that the couple of weeks after Christmas she hadn't seen Fin or Carrie as she was busy with work and could have easily ditched the necklace. Should have. Even now she looked down at it in frustration. *You're already attached!* But the bee was super cute and something she would have bought herself. *Don't kid yourself, it's because Fin bought it for you.*

Damn it.

She tucked it under her shirt so no one would notice it as she headed into the White Pearl. Bodhi's thirtieth birthday was on tonight. Fin had booked out his bar, which was really nice except it meant Ellen had leaned heavily on Carrie and Ingi to sort most of the details with Fin. Carrie would hopefully be waiting inside and she wouldn't have to make small talk with Fin. Especially since the last time she'd been in his pub when she'd gone home so confused. If he'd noticed her very blatant step back from him he hadn't commented. Surely, he'd notice, because even Carrie had noticed. Maybe Fin understood why? Or maybe he didn't care?

'Sis, you're late! You're never late. Are you okay? You do look flushed,' said Carrie in rapid succession.

'It's the heat – my aircon is playing up again,' she said, thankful for her big floaty peasant dress. Her wardrobe was usually loose flowing dresses, so she was keeping with that – too scared to buy maternity jeans in case someone saw them on her washing line. For now she could easily get away with normal clothes. What was she was going to do at eight months? Live in a poncho? Never leave the house? Hopefully she'd have her story figured out by then.

'Come stand under the fan,' Fin said.

Ellen tried not to make eye contact. She was scared he'd know just by looking at her. Over Christmas it hadn't been so bad, but the last three weeks she'd felt the change in her shape. She loved the gentle mound of her belly but didn't relish the heartburn. And seeing Fin while carrying his baby was difficult. How did one behave? *Oh my God, is it written on my face?*

'Is everything ready? Cakes arrived?' she blurted, needing a distraction.

'Yes and yes. Stop stressing.' Carrie put her arm around Fin, who was standing by the entry to the bar. 'Fin has made sure everything is perfect. Haven't you, my love,' she said, kissing him.

Ellen pretended to straighten up the already perfect 'Happy Birthday' sign that was stuck to the bar. Carrie usually had to stand on tiptoes to kiss Fin, except the high-heeled boots she wore almost made her his height. She did look amazing in the mini skirt and fitted low-cut top. Made Ellen feel like a hippy frump.

Did it hurt to see them kissing, holding hands, smiling at each other? Every damn time.

Fin stepped away from Carrie then went to the bar. 'El, do you want a drink?'

'Ah, lemon lime and bitters, please,' she said.

'With vodka,' said Carrie.

Fin paused, glancing at El.

'NO vodka,' she replied firmly. 'Please.'

Carrie screwed up her nose. 'She wants vodka, it's her brother's thirtieth!'

'No, I don't,' she said sternly.

Maybe too sternly as they both paused and stared at her.

'Are you sure you're okay?' Carrie frowned.

'I had a big night last night, sick as a dog. I've decided I'm going dry for a while. And I will be sticking to it.' Carrie was no doubt thinking her declaration would be fun to break but not this time. 'I'll be your designated driver if you like.'

Carrie's face split into a grin. 'You're on. Cheers, sis.' She pulled out a stool and put it near the overhead fan then tapped the seat. 'You sit, I'll go get out the snacks.'

'Thanks.' Some days Carrie could blindside you with her thoughtfulness.

As she disappeared Fin arrived with her drink. 'Thank you.'

Lately she'd refrained from using his name where possible. It just seemed to save some of the awkwardness.

'So, how's work been? Tanya good?'

Ellen nodded. A little surprised he remembered Tanya's name. *Please don't bring up that night.* Meanwhile her pulse raced.

'How's living with Carrie going?' she asked, trying to put some walls between them.

Fin smiled. 'Interesting. We're getting into a routine of sorts.'

'I'm glad. You make her very happy.'

He nodded and she took a sip of her drink.

'Hey, Ellen . . .' He cleared his throat and glanced behind the bar. 'Are things ever going to be easy between us again?'

'What do you mean?' If Carrie thought she was flushed before she'd think she was a flare now. Her throat went dry so she gulped down more drink, wishing it could be vodka.

'The night at the concert, chatting to you was so easy. And afterwards. But not now. I miss that.'

It took everything she had to remain cold and aloof, to keep any warmth from her gaze. She shrugged. 'That was just a fun night where we got to be other people for a while. Now we're in the real world and life gets in the way.' She had no idea what she was saying. Baffle them with bullshit, came to mind. 'Work, and stuff, you know. It's not like we need to be best friends.'

His forehead creased at the same time her belly flopped. Only it wasn't gas.

The baby!

'Sorry, got to go.' Shoving her empty glass into his hand, she headed off to the bathroom. Once out of his sight she practically ran to the toilet and closed the door. Leaning against it she made herself relax and calm down while she held her belly. There it was again. A tiny swishing movement like wind shifting, only it wasn't wind.

My little baby. The cubicle swam through her tears. This wasn't at all how she pictured having a baby, but already she was in love with her or him.

My little munchkin.

One day she'd figure out what to do. Make up a fake one-night stand, or maybe just leave Albany altogether and have the child in secret. So many decisions, but she had time. Again, she pushed the hard choices from her mind and enjoyed this moment. Images of a newborn in her home, baby clothes on the line, nappies soaking in a bucket, faint cries through a baby monitor, rocking in a chair with a baby sleeping on her chest, that newborn smell. It was all the dreams she'd had for her future. She was missing the husband and doting dad, but being a mum – single or not – was still being a mum.

'El! Are you in here? El?'

Carrie came clip-clopping into the bathroom at a rapid rate.

'Yeah,' she replied, trying to dry her eyes.

'What the hell did you say to Fin?'

She wasn't expecting that. 'Nothing, why?'

'He seems to think you don't like him.'

Her voice came through the door as if she was leaning against it. Ellen thought about flushing, but the safety of the cubicle was more inviting than facing Carrie right now.

'Well, I didn't mean to give him that impression,' said Ellen. But if he wanted to believe that, then maybe it was a good thing.

'I don't see why you can't be nicer.'

'I am nice, I just don't want to hang out and be his mate. He's not my type.'

Liar. He's totally your type.

'He's everyone's type. Are you sure you're not just jealous?' Carrie grumbled.

Ellen thought long and hard about her reply. 'I'm happy for you both, really I am. He just rubs me the wrong way, you know. You didn't like Josh – did I give you curry about that?'

Carrie let out a big sigh. 'No, I guess not. But he was a jerk and I could see that. Fin isn't, otherwise Bodhi wouldn't like him. I want you guys to get on.'

'We do. I'll be nice, but I'm not going to be his best mate. I didn't ask you to be that to Josh.'

Her sister didn't reply.

'Carrie?'

'Yeah, I guess. I just hate seeing him upset. I love him.'

'I know. I'm so glad you've found someone.' Ellen could say the right things when her face wasn't in the firing line, giving away all her secrets. If only she could hide behind a toilet door for all the hard conversations.

'Thanks, sis. That means a lot. I love you heaps, you know that. I want you to be happy too.'

Ellen cradled her belly and smiled.

Carrie tapped her toilet door. 'Now hurry up, guests are starting to arrive.'

Her footsteps echoed as she went out of the bathroom and Ellen sighed in relief.

I am happy, she thought to herself. *I may not have a man, but I have someone to love unconditionally and I know they will love me back.*

19
Ellen

SOMEHOW ELLEN HAD MADE IT THROUGH BODHI'S PARTY, and through Christmas and New Year thanks to her volunteering for every available shift at the hospital. They all thought she was a workaholic and she'd fed them a bullshit line about going hard on paying off her mortgage. She'd also started hanging out with Tanya more than her family, though she always made time to see Ingi. Avoidance seemed easier than lying.

Except tonight couldn't be avoided. This was one of those 'suck it up' moments.

'Hi, El, thanks for the lift,' said Fin, climbing into the back of her ute with Carrie. 'You know I was happy to drive.'

'Yeah, sis. It's been a while since I've seen you let your hair down.'

Fin leaned forward between the seats, touching her shoulder. 'Hey you.'

He smelled like that night. Each time it was like a bucket of cold water in her face, and it wasn't like she could ask him to change it. *Please change your scent because I go weak at the knees every time and remember your lips on my body.* Yeah, that wouldn't go down well.

'Hi,' she blurted back. 'I'm happy to drive. I'm still sticking with my zero alcohol and I must admit, I'm feeling so good.' In a way, she could thank the baby for her new health kick.

'It must be working, you do look amazing,' said Fin.

She gave a nervous little laugh. 'Probably all the weight I've put on. With all the extra shifts I'm working I'm eating more,' she said, hoping that explained a few things.

Carrie scoffed. 'You make it sound like you're a whale, which you're not. You're gorgeous as always.' She paused. 'Are you really giving up alcohol?'

'Yeah. So far it's been liberating,' Ellen said.

'Wow, you've noticed that much of a change?' asked Fin. 'Not good for our bar takings,' he added with a smirk.

Ellen's lips curved. 'It has turned me into more of a stay-at-home person. Hard to socialise when you don't drink.'

'Well, I think it agrees with you,' he said.

'Babe, maybe we should try and go a month without alcohol?' Carrie said, reaching for his hand. 'Hell, who am I kidding? I love wine too much.' She laughed. 'You look so sexy tonight, babe.'

Carrie grabbed his face and kissed him. Ellen wished she hadn't picked that moment to look in the rear-view mirror. She was tempted to jam on the brakes. She felt like a mum driving around two horny teenagers. This was not what she signed up for.

'Did you put in for Ingi's graduation present?' she asked, as she drove down York Street to Ingi's uncle's restaurant. Ingi was working tonight – they were short-staffed as usual and she didn't like a fuss – so Bodhi had booked a table for them all, bringing the celebration to her. He thought he was such a genius.

'Yep, she's going to love it.'

'El, you won't believe it, but Carrie is wearing running shoes with her jeans,' said Fin.

'What?' She nearly drove into the car in front that had stopped at the roundabout. 'Are you for real?'

'It's just so I can help out Uncle Pete in the kitchen so Ingi can have a proper break. I want her to enjoy tonight.'

That warmed her heart. Ellen hadn't even thought about doing that, too preoccupied with what to wear that would hide her growing belly. So far no one had noticed anything, besides her not drinking. Hugs were always tricky, as her family were renowned huggers. At least she didn't have to worry about that with Fin. Hugs with him were avoided at all costs. Sometimes he caught her by surprise, wrapping an arm around her and she'd go rigid and forget to speak. Hopefully there'd be none of that tonight. It wasn't an event she could get out of, nor would she want to. This was a night to celebrate Ingi, and Ellen would be there with bells on if needed.

At the restaurant Bodhi had silver helium balloons with the number four floating above the table and a bunch of red roses in the middle.

'Does she know you're here?' Ellen asked her brother.

'No, she's been flat out. Sam said she'd get her out when we were ready,' he said, nodding to the waitress.

They only had to wait a few seconds before Ingi came out, black apron on and hair up in a tight bun.

'Congratulations!' they all chorused.

Uncle Pete popped his head out for a quick moment, eyes glistening and a proud smile taking up most of his face. The whole restaurant turned to watch the commotion.

Ingi put her hands on her hips. 'You guys!'

'Congrats on completing your Cert 4 in cooking, Ingi,' said Carrie. She got the first hug in. 'I'm going to help Uncle Pete so you can get a few moments here.'

Carrie ducked behind the kitchen doors, tying her hair up as she went and leaving behind a shocked Ingi.

'Is she for real?' she said as Ellen approached. 'Maybe Fin is rubbing off on her.'

El smiled but didn't like the image that popped into her mind. 'Congratulations, Ingi. I'm so proud of you.' Ingi lurched into her arms and hugged her tightly. Too tightly. Ellen pulled back quickly.

Her little munchkin was quite active now, especially at night when Ellen wanted to sleep. At least she still had Tanya to confide in. She had come to her ultrasound and it had been quite overwhelming, but Tanya, being Tanya, had kept her busy trying to guess the sex of the baby. Ellen didn't want to know. 'The first should be a surprise,' she'd told her. Tanya had also stopped asking Ellen what she planned to do. There was only so many times she could give the same answer: *I don't know.*

To this moment, she still didn't know. Take another job somewhere far away and have her baby? Adopt it out? *NO!* She'd already floated that idea and thrown it away. This was her baby and she was going to raise it. And if Carrie and Fin got married and had kids then she would take her secret to her grave. Or what if they couldn't have kids? What if they broke up? Would that change things? Ellen didn't want to leave her family but hurting them all with this wasn't easy to think about either. Carrie was happy and settled for the first time in her life. All she wanted was to see her baby sister happy, and learning that her boyfriend had slept with her sister, resulting in a baby, would smash that to smithereens. Maybe soon she'd have to start a story about a one-night stand with someone from work or something, in preparation for the baby news.

If she thought about it long enough, deep down she was scared that if Fin knew, he'd want to help raise the baby. That in itself would be hard, would hurt Carrie even more, plus the baby would be a constant reminder. Ellen didn't like lying to anyone but the truth would hurt everyone . . . at least this way the only one hurting was herself.

'You guys, I love them!' Ingi had tears in her eyes as she held out a white apron that said 'Licensed to Cook' and some other similarly corny t-shirts.

Ingi's parents arrived and that was their cue for the special gift.

The waterworks started properly when Bodhi gave Ingi her certificate, beautifully framed, which Uncle Pete then ceremoniously hung on the wall of the restaurant, next to his own.

Uncle Pete, whose wiry hair looked like he'd played with power sockets as a child, stood with his chest out beside the new wall hanging. 'I'm so proud of this woman. I've seen her grow up way before her time, endure things no child should have to, and yet she has worked so damn hard. Not just at home but here. Ingrid, you have a massive heart, and I am so blessed to spend so much time with you.' Pete wiped away his tears as Ingi threw her skinny arms around his big waist and hugged him tight.

'I love you too, Uncle Pete.'

'Mikey would be proud, nearly as much as we are, honey,' said Kath, scooping her daughter into her arms.

'So bloody proud of you, pumpkin,' said her dad.

Ellen was bawling like a baby. *Bloody hormones.* Fin held out a napkin and she seized it from him, patting her face as fast as the tears fell.

Bodhi popped a bottle of champagne. 'Let the celebration begin.'

Three hours later Ellen was ready to go home, thanks to a tired and achy body, but Carrie wasn't.

'I'm going to stay here and help Uncle Pete close up. Bodhi's going to take Ingi home early,' said Carrie. 'Uncle Pete said he'd drop me off. Can you take Fin home?'

Ah hell no! 'Sure.' What else could she say?

'Thanks, he's a bit drunk. Sorry, I kept giving him mine as I was too busy running in and out of the kitchen.'

Fin was indeed merry. His eyes shone and he wore a contented smile as he scratched at his beard. How could he still look so damn gorgeous?

'Love you.' Carrie kissed her cheek and disappeared into the kitchen, taking the garlic and tomato smell with her.

There was flour in her hair, but Ellen didn't have the heart to tell her.

Bodhi was watching Ingi chat with Fin, a goofy smile on his face. He'd had a few also but not as many as Fin. Besides, Ingi had the keys. Ellen wanted to hug her brother but didn't want to risk it so she sidled up to him and nudged his shoulder. 'Bodhi, can you help me get Fin to the car before you guys go?'

'No probs, sis.' He chuckled. 'Carrie stitched him up good.'

'She did.'

'So why won't you come surfing with me anymore?' he asked while trying to corral Fin from the restaurant.

'I told you, work's keeping me busy. We're so short on staff, and then my spare time has been taken up helping Tanya. Besides, aren't you busy teaching Fin to surf?' They headed outside and down the side street to her ute. Bodhi kept his arm on Fin, guiding him and half-holding him upright.

'That he is,' said Fin. 'And when I'm not scared shitless a shark's gonna eat me or a wave is gonna kill me . . . it's actually quite fun.' Fin burped and then chuckled to himself.

Bodhi and El shared a laugh as Ingi, who'd been busy with goodbyes, caught up. Fin managed to get into El's ute, only hitting his head once. So much for Bodhi helping.

'Night, guys. I love you both. You guys are so cool,' Fin said as Bodhi smiled and shut the ute door.

'Good luck, sis.' Bodhi winked and wrapped his arm around Ingi.

She mouthed 'Sorry' and looked genuinely concerned. Ellen gave her a wave and tried to reassure her it was okay.

'I'll call you tomorrow,' she told Ingi before climbing in.

'I really love those guys. I really love your whole family. They are the best,' mumbled Fin.

'I agree,' she said, pulling away from the kerb and driving through the quiet night. Streetlights lit up the dark and the ute felt warm and safe.

'I love you too, El, even if you don't like me. That's fine. I can handle it. But you look so pretty tonight.' His eyes shone as he stared at her.

'You are so drunk.' She chuckled, but nonetheless his words made her body heat up like a furnace. 'I think Ingi enjoyed tonight.'

'Me too. Bodhi's so lucky. She's a great cook.'

They talked all the way home about random stuff, mainly things Fin loved and more about his brewery. 'I thought of a name for it the other day and I couldn't tell anyone. The only person I wanted to tell was you,' he said.

Talking with a drunk Fin was easy and he'd probably not remember much of it. It was the first time she'd been alone with him, like really alone since the concert. It made all the hairs on her skin stand up. And for this one moment she allowed herself to chat to him with no reservations. It was tiring resisting the ease of talking to him, of being in his company. And she was tired. Worn down over the last months.

'Have you looked into it? Started planning?'

He had melted into the seat, arm along the window frame as the streetlights flickered over his face.

'What's the point? Dad's still onto me about stepping up and taking over the White Pearl.' He laughed dryly. 'And then there's Bodhi, who wants to grow your dad's sparky business and he won't let go of the reins. Good pair we are.'

Ellen pulled into his driveway but his words were circling. She didn't know that's how Bodhi felt. Her brother usually shared everything, nothing was off limits. Then again, she hadn't really been much of a sister lately. *It's not like you're sharing everything either!* So she couldn't get upset with Bodhi.

'Life is never easy,' she murmured, more to herself, but Fin agreed, right before he fell out of the car.

'Shit, are you okay?' she said after rushing around to the open passenger door and the crumpled mess beside it.

He was laughing and Ellen couldn't help but join in once she could see he was fine. He pushed himself up onto his knees but then grabbed onto Ellen as he wobbled again, holding her like a child clinging to a mother, his head nestled against her waist.

Ellen's hand remained on his shoulder, lost in his warmth, until everything came crashing back when his hand pressed against her belly, searching its roundness.

'Let's get you up and into bed,' she said, stepping out of his embrace and trying to pull him up onto his feet. 'Got the keys? I'll go unlock the door for you.'

His face was contorted, maybe trying to nut out what he'd just felt, but Ellen kept talking. Digging into his pocket in his snug jeans, he produced the keys and handed them over. She strode up to his front door and started trying the keys. The second one worked; she opened up and turned on the light.

He had a beautiful, tidy home. At every turn it was like the world was punishing her. In the beginning she'd told herself that they didn't really know each other and probably wouldn't be compatible; it had been a lie. Even then she knew he was a good fit. His home only confirmed this even more – the light wood furniture and bright white walls . . . and then the plants! There were plants in cute pots, monsteras in the corner that were thriving, and others trailing down shelves. Admittedly, he'd said his sister had helped with the decorating, but he maintained the home and all the plants were still alive.

But Carrie probably thought she and Fin were compatible too. Ellen tried hard to remember that.

Fin walked inside and turned to face her. 'Ellen . . .'

She knew that tone. That 'I have questions' tone.

'Night, Fin. Drink lots of water.'

Turning, she walked out and shut the front door and went back to her ute. But the vision of him standing in his living room with the soft light behind him never left her mind.

20

Carrie

Now

IT WAS THE MOST PAINFUL RIDE BACK TO THE CAMPGROUND. The adrenaline of the accident had worn off and they were all feeling deflated. Carrie was hot, the aircon not doing anything for the sting of her sunburn. She was drinking water, trying to rehydrate, but it was a bit late with a headache already coming on. The need for the toilet didn't help either.

'How much longer?' she asked, moving to cross her legs, then hissing as the angry red skin behind her knees bit back in protest.

'Nearly there, just passing the airstrip now,' said Ellen.

'These bumps do not help my bladder,' Carrie protested. 'Can you stop at the loo?' she added as they started on the one-way road around the camping area.

Ellen pulled up outside the long-drops and Carrie bolted. She yanked open the tin door and threw her hand against her nose. The day's heat had really permeated – it was no eau de toilette.

By the time she got back to camp, Fin had the chairs set up in the shade of the campervan with water and some moisturiser at the ready.

'Thanks, babe,' she said as she sat in the chair. She threw back the Panadol he offered and took a gulp of the cold water. 'What would I do without you?'

'You'd survive,' he said as he started to smear the moisturiser onto her sunburn.

The relief was instant; hopefully her headache would be gone soon too. 'What are El and Hans doing?' she asked.

'She's gone to get organised to do the Dale's Gorge walk and Hans . . . I don't know. He went back to his van, I suppose.'

Carrie closed her eyes, enjoying the shade. She didn't feel like moving. That whole kamikaze-man rescue had taken it out of her. How Ellen dealt with all that drama she didn't know. Carrie would be too scared she'd injure someone more or crack under the pressure. As a midwife and nurse, Ellen often held a person's life in her hands. Her sister could be a know-it-all but Carrie still thought she was amazing, always calm and level-headed.

She'd always thought El had her life sorted and was happy, but this sudden move to Challa Station and giving up nursing had confused the hell out of her. Even their mum and Bodhi couldn't understand the need for such a dramatic change. But then again, she could also understand El's need for something different, a complete change of scenery. Was that what Carrie should do too? Would that help her find out what she wanted from life? If only she was as brave as her sister to uproot everything. Carrie had built her salon into a thriving business – could she just walk away? Or was she using that as an excuse? *Oh, these thoughts are too heavy while you have a thumping headache.*

A crunching of footsteps came their way. 'You guys ready?' said El.

She had on her hat, walking shoes and a small backpack, and had changed into fresh cotton shorts and a t-shirt. Carrie recognised the shirt as the one Bodhi got her for Christmas a few years ago. It was white with a black print of a scene from Point Break and the words 'Bodhi's Surf Shop'. Carrie bet Ellen's backpack had water and a snake kit. Probably snacks too. She would make a good mum. She'd always been someone Carrie could go to with her secrets knowing El would never tell – she was a vault. Their mum still didn't know about the time Ellen caught her smoking, and nobody knew about the boy in Year Seven who helped himself to her privates behind the school toilets. It was easy to confide when you knew it stopped with El. She wasn't into idle gossip and wasn't on social media. Such strength of character, it was endearing. *And annoying.*

'We have to go now before it gets too late. The walk takes a good two hours.'

Carrie put her hand on her forehead. 'I don't think I can do it.' She really didn't want to go anywhere right now.

Fin frowned. 'We don't have to walk fast, and the heat is dying down already.'

Carrie knew he'd been keen to go and she didn't want to hold him back. Besides, it might be good for him and Ellen to spend some time together and try to work out their differences. She should have locked them in a room together ages ago and told them not to come out until they were besties.

'I'm fine here by myself. You go with El – I know you really wanted to do the walk.'

'I don't mind going alone,' El added quickly.

'You are not going alone. What if you fall or get bitten by a snake? There's no way I'm letting you go by yourself. Fin?'

Carrie saw Fin's 'knight in shining armour' button activated and knew he wouldn't let her go alone either.

'Yep. No one goes solo.' He jumped up and grabbed his water bottle and hat. He handed Carrie the cream. 'Keep putting that on and drink lots of water.'

'Don't put yourself out on my account,' El said.

'I'm not. As Carrie said, I really wanted to go.'

Defeated, her sister nodded. 'Righto. We should be back before it's too dark.'

'I'll be here,' Carrie said, waving as they left.

The crunching of gravel faded away and soon there was only the faint sound of bugs and movement from other camps. Someone must be travelling with small kids as she could hear a baby crying. Carrie thought they must be nuts. Who'd want to travel with a baby? In this heat with no reception or help nearby? To be honest, babies scared her. Such tiny fragile things. Older kids were much better – at least she could talk to them and they could take themselves to the bathroom.

'Hello?'

Carrie squinted up. 'Hey, Hans.'

'Where is everyone?'

She wondered if he meant her sister in particular. She'd been trying to work out if there was some chemistry between them. Jury was still out.

'Fin and El have gone to do the walk. Pull up a chair,' she said, hoping he'd stay and keep her company. She nearly told him that he could catch up with them but decided his company would be very welcome, plus she'd love to learn more about him and where he was from. And the fact that he had a gorgeous smile and sexy hair didn't influence her decision . . . much.

Hans sat in the spare camping chair and took his hat off then wiped the sweat from his brow. 'Wow, today was something else. Being around El is entertaining, that's for sure. Flat tyres, tears, engagements and death-defying acts.'

Carrie was nodding along, until she clocked one of the words. 'Tears?'

'After the flat tyre, I found her pulled over again further along, except this time she was crying.'

'Crying? What about?'

'I don't know. She said she'd been through a trauma. She was a mess. Did something bad happen to her?' he asked carefully.

Carrie sucked at her bottom lip while her mind raced. 'I don't know. She had a job she loved . . . well, we assumed she did, and then suddenly she just up and left to go and work on the station.'

'No clue why?'

She shrugged. 'We all thought it was strange, but she just kept saying she needed a change and her friend's parents needed a worker, and she wanted to go exploring before she got too old. We just thought maybe work got too much, you know? But working as a midwife had always been her dream.'

'Oh.' The gaze of Hans' vibrant blue eyes dropped to his lap. 'Maybe she has other dreams? She strikes me as someone with a big heart.'

'She does. She's the best. Miss Perfect.' Never does anything careless, reckless or wrong.

'That must be hard to uphold.'

Carrie frowned. She'd never thought of it like that. Did El find her life hard work too? That keeping up a certain persona was tiring? 'I've never thought of it like that. El is someone who seems like she has her life sorted.'

'So many people "seem" like they do, but in my experience nobody actually does.'

Huh. Now there was food for thought.

Carrie still felt like shit, and the water wasn't quenching her thirst at all. At least the shade and cream were helping, along with the company. 'Do you want a beer?' Maybe it would absorb better than the water.

'Sure, that would be great. Thank you.' He rubbed his hands together.

'So tell me more about yourself, Hans. How long have you been in Australia?'

'Which time? I was here for a holiday about five years ago and fell in love with this big country. I came back three years ago and I've been on a working visa.'

Carrie handed him a beer and settled back into her chair, her sunburn protesting with each movement. 'Oh, cool. What work have you been doing?'

'Farm work mostly, some station work. Gives me a chance to get around in between and see the country. I'm on my way to Port Hedland to work at the Homeless Breakfast Program for a bit, then I'm helping out a group in Roebourne.'

'Wow, you seem to know your way around.' Carrie was impressed and a little embarrassed. She lived in this country and had never been to the top of the state. As for volunteering, sure, she'd helped out at her mum's art centre and at the restaurant, but nothing like what Hans was describing. It sounded so . . . meaningful and life-changing.

'I love meeting new people,' he said, 'learning their stories. Such a huge land, so different from my home. Our family is originally from Wäldi in Switzerland, near the German border.'

Carrie noticed they'd both finished their beers, usually a coldie would hit the spot in the heat. Except she didn't feel any better. In fact she felt ill.

'Do you want another beer?' she said, standing up and swaying. Hans shot up and caught her, helping her back into her chair.

'I'll get them.'

Carrie didn't feel much like drinking, but took the one he held out. He continued talking about his travels and work and Carrie felt herself fading in and out.

'Carrie? Carrie?'

She blinked, realising Hans was talking to her. 'Oh, sorry.'

'I was just asking if you feel okay? You don't look so good and you're glowing red.'

'Yeah, I feel like shit. I'm burning up.'

'I'll help you to bed.'

'Thanks.' Trying to stand was hard, so Hans took her hands and heaved her up then guided her to the van.

'It's like I'm on fire.' She couldn't decide if she wanted to be sick or just sleep forever.

She lay down face-first on the bed and felt relief shoot up her legs. 'Ohh, that's better.'

Hans was smearing the aloe vera over her legs and arms. He was even kind enough to dot some over her face, but at some point she fell asleep and didn't even hear him leave.

21

Ingi

Back then

IT HAD STARTED OFF AS ANOTHER BEAUTIFUL MORNING IN
Albany – clear skies over green rolling hills that reflected off
the coastal waters – but it soon became a day that Ingi would
never forget. It was early morning, and she'd just come back
from the beach with Bodhi. She was supposed to be meeting
Ellen for a coffee as she was rostered off and Ingi didn't start
at the restaurant until the afternoon. Ingi loved starting her
day like this – with Bodhi at the beach and then El, who'd
become more than just Bodhi's sister over the years. Plus she'd
been dying to find out about her ride home with Fin last week.

When Ingi reached home at seven thirty, she sent a text.
Running on time. See you there.

At eight, she sent another one. *I'm here. I'll order your
cappuccino.*

At eight fifteen, she called and got Ellen's voice message.

By eight twenty, she was back in her car heading to Ellen's place, a little concerned. It was unlike her not to reply or answer her phone. Hell, it was unlike El to *ever* be late.

El's front door was locked but not the screen door, as if she'd been in a rush maybe? Her little old home sat perched on a hillside and from this spot you could see Middleton Beach. The beautiful view was worth the land alone, but El had been working on her little home over the years, transforming it into a warm, inviting space. Only today, no one was home, and yet Ingi could see the lounge room light had been left on. Strange.

The lean-to off the side of the house was empty – her ute was gone. Maybe she'd been called into work? Except she'd said she wasn't on call. Ingi had nothing else to do until work so she drove to the hospital, trying not to freak out. What had happened that would make Ellen forget their coffee date? Especially when she'd sent a text yesterday morning saying, *See you tomz at eight for coffee. Love you.*

At the hospital, her ute wasn't in the staff parking area. 'Ellen, where are you?' she muttered as she slowly drove around the hospital. She finally spotted her ute out the front of the hospital, in the general parking. *What is it doing there?*

Had Ellen got sick? Was the staff parking full? Maybe someone had taken ill and she'd been put back on roster? Ingi found an empty parking spot and walked into the hospital and down to maternity. She knew she wouldn't rest easy until she saw El. Her gut was telling her something was amiss and after years of learning to trust herself with Mikey, she wasn't about to ignore it.

The set of doors to the ward opened and as a man walked out, Ingi scooted in. No one was at the desk; she kept going, past a room where a new mum was bathing her newborn and towards the sound of a woman giving birth. Ingi didn't want to pry or intrude, she just needed to see that El was okay and then she'd leave her to it. Just a glimpse to put her worry to rest.

Ingi stepped past the doorway slowly, trying to sneak a look inside, but the door was closed. All she could hear were the sounds of a woman in pain and murmured whispers of an encouraging nurse. Did that sound like El? Ingi strained her ears before glancing around. The rest of the ward was quiet – were all the nurses in this room? Was it a risky birth? She was about to go see if she could find somebody else when the door beside her whooshed open and someone collided into her.

'Oh, sorry . . .'

Tanya's words fell away when she realised it was Ingi. Her eyes bulged.

'What are you doing here?' she demanded.

Ingi frowned. 'I'm looking for El. We were supposed to meet.' Her eyes darted to the room. 'Is she in there?'

Tanya's mouth worked overtime but no words came. The paleness of her face and the nervous twitching sent alarm bells through Ingi's head.

'What is it?'

'I think you should come with me. Prepare yourself.'

Tanya latched onto her arm and dragged her down to the next room. Ingi thought she was about to see El at the side of the bed, rubbing some woman's back, but what confronted her was completely unexpected. El was in the bed, her body hunched over as she looked down at something in her hands.

'What the . . .' Ingi's brain couldn't work out what her eyes were seeing.

'Don't just stand there gaping, go help the poor girl,' said Tanya giving her a nudge from behind.

She stumbled towards the bed when Ellen glanced up. The moment she recognised Ingi, her face folded in on itself. Tears flowed down her cheeks, like an ocean of nonstop waves.

'Oh Ingi,' she sobbed.

Hearing the despair in her voice made her knees give out. Ingi fell into the chair beside her bed. 'El, hey, what's going on?'

'My baby,' she cried, lips twisted and teeth exposed like a wounded animal.

Until that moment, Ingi still hadn't realised what was really going on. It hadn't clicked. *My baby*. Ellen was pregnant! Her mind was spinning trying to figure it all out. None of it made sense. How was this possible? When did it happen? With who? How did she not know any of this?

And that's when she paid more attention to the knitted bundle El was holding.

El's words were soft like a hum on the gentle breeze. 'I had a baby.'

Mouth open, Ingi glanced at Tanya who nodded sadly. Inside her mind was screaming. *What the fuck is going on!* 'You have a baby? El?'

Ellen, lips wobbling. 'I'm sorry I didn't tell you. I couldn't. I couldn't tell anyone.'

Tanya silently moved to the end of the bed. Ellen was still sobbing, staring at the tiny bundle in her hands.

'I don't understand,' Ingi shot to Tanya.

The worry lines were deep around her eyes and she kept glancing nervously at Ellen. 'Look, all I know is some guy got her pregnant and she wouldn't tell anyone. But recently she noticed something was wrong.' Tanya paused and moved to El's side, brushing her damp hair back from her face. 'You have such good instincts, El.'

'I can't believe none of us even realised. How is this possible?'

Ingi could see Ellen's soft belly bump. To have a belly that round meant she had been months along. Did that mean . . . 'Is it Fin's?'

El's head snapped her way. 'You can't tell anyone, Ingi. Promise me,' she said through gritted teeth. 'Promise me.' Her voice was deep and demanding.

'I promise. But if it's Fin's baby then you must have been . . .' She tried to do the numbers in her head. 'Like, around eighteen weeks pregnant.' Which would mean this baby wasn't ready to be born.

El nodded and rocked through her pain.

'Oh my God.' Ingi's hand flew to her mouth. The tiny bundle El was holding was her baby, she now realised. Her head hurt, spinning to keep up with all the information pouring in. So much to comprehend. 'You had a miscarriage? Oh El, honey, I'm so sorry.' A lump choked off her air as the room began to shrink. How was any of this possible?

Tanya's expression was grim. 'I'm glad you came, Ingi. Ellen's going to need you. She came in yesterday, concerned, and we couldn't find a heartbeat. So we had to induce.' Tanya's voice was soft and tender. 'Sometimes it can take days for the baby to come but this little one was quick.' Her voice was edged with relief.

Ingi nodded as more tears ran down her cheeks, but she swiped them away. Ellen needed her strong, not a mess.

'Do you want to see my baby girl?' she asked through her

tears. 'I understand if you don't – it's quite confronting. But she does look like a baby, in case you're worried.'

Ingi was uncertain at first but felt Ellen needed to share this. She nodded, and Ellen opened the little blanket. Like a tiny deep pink doll, the baby was silent and still. Skin shiny. You could tell she needed more growing time but she had all her fingers and toes, skinny arms and legs.

'A little girl,' El murmured as she stared down at her baby.

Her shoulders began to shake with silent sobs. Tanya caressed her shoulder, standing strong by her side.

The pain taking hold of El's body now must be a million times worse than what she'd just been through with the birth. Even though she gazed down at her baby with love, there was a darkness behind it, a deep wound that would probably never heal. It made the lump in Ingi's throat feel like it was starving her of oxygen and it took so much effort to push it down and be strong for Ellen.

She tried to think of something to say. 'Have you thought of a name?'

'There was this one I'd been thinking of if it was a girl – Celeste. It means "heavenly",' said Ellen.

'That is a lovely name,' murmured Tanya.

'It suits her perfectly,' said Ingi. 'A little angel.'

'Can I get you anything, El?' asked Tanya.

Ellen shook her head. Her sobs had subsided somewhat, instead she was transfixed by her baby. Ingi handed her a few tissues. She cleaned up her face and left the soggy pile on the bed.

'I'll go get some water and be right back.' Ingi headed for the door, immediately followed by Tanya.

'Are you okay?' she asked Ingi once they were outside.

'I don't know. How do I help her, Tan? I feel so helpless. What happens now? Do you know why the baby died?'

'Not yet. Ellen was spotting blood yesterday and came straight in, only to learn her baby had already passed away.' She leaned in, her tone soothing. 'I know it's hard to watch her in such pain, but honestly, just sitting beside her so she's not going through this alone will do more than you'll ever know.'

'My God, this has all happened so fast. I feel like I'm still trying to catch up.' Ingi glanced back at the door, her anxiety rising. 'How do you . . . ?'

'You just do the best you can. Okay? We have a specialist coming to chat with her but nothing beats the support of a loved one. I know this is a lot for you to take in and I know you must have questions, but El must come first.'

It all sounded so awful. 'Does this happen a lot?'

'Not usually with second-trimester babies, but it does happen. Sometimes it's obvious why and other times we can't find a reason.'

Tanya gave her a hug. 'Go and get a coffee, a strong one, and then come back and be the strength that she needs to say goodbye to her baby.'

Her words were firm and wise, but behind them was a tremor in her voice and sad, glistening eyes. This day would not be forgotten by either of them.

Ingi wondered what was worse, losing a child you never got to know or watching one slowly suffer and die. Either way, she knew she'd never have her own children. It was a promise she'd made to herself the day she tested positive for the carrier gene.

And it was one promise she intended to keep.

22

Ingi

Now

THE SETTING SUN STAINED THE TRUNKS ON THE GHOST GUMS a champagne colour while their shadows danced along the scorched earth.

'Wanna go for a walk?'

Ingi spun around to see Bodhi and her heart leapt. He still took her breath away. She held out her hand and he slipped his in and together they ambled up the road.

'I've signed in and parked at our tent. It's pretty cool.' His voice was upbeat, a little too upbeat.

He was trying so hard and she didn't want to shut him out.

'Look, Ingi, I don't want to fight.'

'Neither do I.' She stopped and squeezed his hand. 'I love you, Bodhi. I want you to be happy. I also want you to understand what I'm saying.' *Please understand.*

'That you don't want kids?'

'I like kids, I love kids. I just won't be having any of my own.'

Bodhi scratched at his chin for a moment. 'Does that mean you're open to adoption?' He raised his brows, hopeful.

'Of course I am. But will you be?' She put up her hand to stop the 'yes' she could see forming on his lips. 'I know what you're going to say, but have you really thought it through? You are the only Sutton son, the only one to carry on the family name. Are you saying you'd be happy to end it with you? To not hold your own flesh and blood, to see your own eyes or chin on their little faces?'

His mouth opened, formed an O and then closed. He sighed. 'I honestly haven't given it any thought.'

They continued walking, a lizard scurried across the path and Ingi noticed a slither track through the dust that looked like it was made by a snake. She inched closer to Bodhi.

'Can't we still get married?' he asked worriedly. 'I don't want to live my life without you, Ingi. Are you really going to let this break us apart?'

'I don't want it to,' she said truthfully. 'But I don't want this to come back and ruin us down the track. I'd rather end it now before we go too far.'

Bodhi halted, blinking rapidly as he stared off into the distance. After a moment, he whispered, 'It's already too far for me, Ingi.'

'I feel that way too, but believe me, resentment can grow like a cancer in the most beautiful of relationships. Let's sort this out now and be on the same page.'

Bodhi turned to her. 'I know you said you're a carrier for DMD, but that doesn't guarantee our child will have it too. Do you know the statistics?'

'Yes, but even a ten per cent chance is too much for me. Even if we have a healthy girl, I can pass it on to her and then she'll have the issues I'm facing now. I don't want that for my children. I don't want anyone to go through what my family went through.'

'But still, you wouldn't have given your brother away after all that?'

'Of course not, I loved him,' she said angrily. 'But if he was never born he wouldn't have had to live such a restricted life. I want to stop it before it gets to a point where my child wants to harm himself because he hates being stuck in a chair while the other kids play.' Ingi could feel herself getting worked up, could feel the pressure building from years of bottling her emotions. 'Mikey tried to take his life once and I found him. Do you know what that's like?' she demanded.

Bodhi was like a deer in the headlights. Stunned, he shook his head.

'You cannot understand when you haven't walked in my shoes.'

He grabbed her by the shoulders and waited for her to take a deep settling breath. 'Then tell me,' he said calmly.

So Ingi did. They walked and she talked. She told Bodhi the frustration Mikey had watching other kids and even his sister do things he couldn't.

'I could run around the backyard before he could and he's two years older. By ten he was needing a wheelchair. Going anywhere became a mission. He didn't have many friends, let alone girlfriends. He had to rely on Mum, Dad and me to do so much. Mum had already watched her dad die and then she had to watch her son die. And I had front row seats to the destruction of her heart.

'I loved my brother but there were days, I'm ashamed to say it, that I hated him and I hated his disorder. I hate myself for having those thoughts. My teenage years were hard, resenting him because I didn't have a life. I had no spare time to play, I was always helping Mikey, or else doing housework because Mum was helping Mikey. I was dragged around to all his medical appointments and treatments. The only escape I had was working for Uncle Peter at night. That was my saving grace. And yet Mikey didn't even have that. He had no escape and I had no right to feel sorry for myself while he was suffering much worse.

'I don't want that life for my child. I made a promise to myself, Bodhi, that I would not pass this gene on.'

'I can't begin to imagine what you've been through, Ingi,' he said, pausing to brush a finger across her chin.

'And it's not just about me and Mikey – Mum and Dad's lives were hard. If we had a DMD child, not only would our lives change, but your whole family would feel the need to take some of the strain. And my parents, who've been through this twice before. I can't ask that of them, but we wouldn't be able to manage on our own. Do you understand why I feel this way?'

'I think I do. You're trying to protect everyone. But are you sure there's not a way to have a child and test it beforehand?'

'I think they can test at about fifteen weeks, but if it comes up positive that means I would not go through with the pregnancy.' Ingi stared at him hard. 'Do you really want me playing Russian roulette with every pregnancy, to go through that every time? How many abortions before we get a good one? I've seen a miscarriage firsthand, it's heart-wrenching.' God, she'd seen what Ellen went through. She nearly blurted that out to Bodhi there and then but managed to clamp her lips shut. *You promised her.*

He squirmed and rubbed at the back of his neck. 'No, no, Ingi, I don't want to see you hurting, ever.'

'And I feel the same way about you, Bodhi. That's why I'm doing this. I'm happy to adopt, I'm happy to get a donor egg and your sperm so you'd still have your own child, it just won't be from me.'

Hazel eyes drank her in and his lips creased at the corners. 'I would have loved to have a little girl the spitting image of her mother. It's a weird feeling – I already feel like I've lost a child.'

He drew her in against his chest and Ingi hugged him tight. 'I know. Believe me, I've thought of all that, many times. But I just can't do it, Bodhi. I want to have children with you, I really do, but we can't use my eggs. I don't need an answer right away, I really want you to think on this.'

'I already want to say that I'm okay with that, but I know you want me to be a hundred per cent sure, so I'll take the time.'

His lips pressed against the top of her head, and she closed her eyes and listened to the rhythmic beats of his heart. His shirt was warm and smelled like his deodorant and sweat. He felt like home.

That night after a wonderful meal they sat drinking champagne outside their tent as the sky simmered red then dulled to black and showcased the stars. All the tents around them glowed like lanterns floating out over a still lake. They talked about work, Karijini, Mikey, and then got ready for bed.

Skin on skin they cuddled, Bodhi's fingers trailing up and down the length of her arm, making her feel loved up and sleepy.

'You know when you gave the ring back, I had all sorts of bad thoughts, like maybe you were sick. I don't know, I couldn't figure it out. I know you love me. But it all makes sense now. I wish you'd told me more about your life with Mikey – all of it, not just the good stuff.'

'I know, I'm sorry. I feel like I'm betraying his memory by mentioning the hard stuff. And showing my horrible side, the dark parts that admitted how hard life was because of him. I hate that girl.'

'It's only normal to feel resentment, Ingi, especially as a teenager. I'd be no different. You have the most generous heart of anyone I know.' Bodhi's fingers paused. 'Hey, what did you mean before when you said you've seen a miscarriage firsthand? Has that happened to you? With us?'

'No!' Ingi sat up, the sheet falling away and pooling at her waist. 'It wasn't me.'

'Oh that's a relief. I can't bear the thought of you going through something like that. You would tell me, wouldn't you?'

'I would.' Especially now that they'd talked about children and he understood where she was coming from.

'I've never known anyone who's been through that.' He frowned at Ingi. 'Was it someone I know?'

Her heart rate jumped. 'I . . . I was promised to secrecy.'

'We're about to get married, Ingi. I hoped there'd be no secrets.'

Ingi felt like a rabbit about to step on a trap. Was there any escape? Maybe there were times when family had to look out for family. 'I really think someone in her immediate family needs to know. I worry about her.'

His eyes bulged. 'Jesus, are you talking about Carrie or Ellen?'

She could tell his thoughts were spiralling out of control.

'I don't want to keep secrets from you, Bodhi, but I also feel like breaking a promise is just as bad.'

'But I'm your life partner, no lies, no secrets – please, babe?'

She touched his hand, trying to reassure him, her mind made up. 'It was Ellen,' she whispered. 'But you have to promise not to tell anyone.'

'What!' His eyebrows shot up. 'Are you saying Ellen had a miscarriage? When was this?'

Ingi nodded. A sense of betrayal washed over her, yet she hoped Ellen would understand her reasoning. There was no room for secrets in her relationship. Ingi should have told Bodhi sooner. Family were supposed to support you and help you through times of need. Ellen was such a stubborn, suffer in silence kind of person. The kind who kicks her toe and says she's fine then later finds out it's broken. The kind who's in love with her sister's boyfriend, even has his baby, and doesn't tell a soul.

'I'm not sure if I should tell you any more,' she stammered, suddenly guilty. There was so much more to this bombshell.

'Come on, Ingi, just tell me the whole story. Is this why Ellen left Albany? Why she's changed?'

Ingi blinked.

'Yeah, I'm not blind. I know something happened, but I figured she'd tell me when she was ready. Will she ever be ready?' he asked.

'I honestly don't know. It's much more complicated than you can imagine.' She sighed.

'Honey, spit it out. Maybe if I know the whole story, together we can help her. She normally tells me everything. I just don't understand.'

Ingi caressed his face. 'Babe, it's not you. She didn't even tell me, I found out by accident.' His concern and disappointment made her open her mouth and blurt it all out. 'Back in September, Ellen met Murray at the John Butler concert, they had a one-night stand and didn't see each other again until your parents' anniversary lunch.'

'Say what now? Are you talking about Fin? Fin and Ellen?' Ingi nodded slowly.

Bodhi stared in disbelief. 'For real? Is that why there's always been a weird vibe between them?' Bodhi shook his head. 'I can't believe Fin cheated on Carrie, that's not who I thought he was.'

Ingi gritted her teeth. 'He didn't. Fin and Carrie were just casual before then and only decided to have a relationship after he told Carrie he'd slept with someone. So they got serious and then weeks later Fin comes to the family dinner and sees Ellen and . . . boom.'

'Wow. How did they not know?'

'Ellen slept with a bloke called Murray. Carrie never calls Fin by his first name. Have you ever heard her call him Murray?'

Bodhi pulled a face. 'No.'

'And due to Josh swanning around town with his new baby, Carrie kept their relationship low-key because she didn't want El to feel bad.'

'And then they meet up at the lunch,' said Bodhi. 'Oh my God, no wonder she had a headache.' His face reacted to each thought as he remembered back to the lunch, moments falling into place. 'This is unreal. I can't believe they never said anything.'

'You know El, she doesn't want to hurt anyone. But,' Ingi said with a sigh. 'That's not the worst of it.'

'A baby,' he said suddenly.

'Yep, El ended up pregnant. She used her emergency condom.'

'No way, that thing's been in her bag since . . . like, forever,' he said, gobsmacked.

'Hence why it didn't do its job properly. Anyway, she was so confused about what to do – she didn't want to hurt Carrie, so she kept it a secret. But at eighteen weeks she knew something was wrong, and they couldn't find the heartbeat. She had a miscarriage. A little girl . . .'

'Eighteen weeks?' Bodhi exclaimed. 'That's . . . that's like four months. How did I not notice?'

Ingi held his hand while his brain was trying to catch up.

'She wore loose clothes, and she kept her distance.'

'That's why she wouldn't go surfing with me. No wonder she was AWOL so much.' He shook his head. 'I can't believe it. She had a baby girl. Fin's baby?'

'Yeah, it was so sad.'

'How did you find out?' he asked incredulously.

Ingi went on to explain that day. It poured out of her in a rush of relief. Those feelings had been locked away in secret, festering like a bad wound. Tears ran down her face as she told him every detail. Bodhi cried alongside her, sharing her pain, sharing his sister's pain.

'El and I have shared everything, I can't . . .' His words died. 'I hate that she was so alone through all of that but I'm angry that she didn't come to me. It hurts that she didn't want my help.' His fingers tugged through his hair.

'Me too.' Ingi nodded. 'Look, she didn't know how to deal with it and thought the best way to protect everyone was to tell no one. Don't worry, I felt angry and upset that she didn't come to me either. It kills me that she went through most of it alone. I am grateful that I managed to find her and be there ... at the end. It was the most devastating thing I've ever experienced, and I've been through a lot.'

'What happened to the baby?' Bodhi whispered as he tucked Ingi back into his arms.

There was a chill to his skin and their combined body heat didn't seem to shift it.

'She was cremated. Ellen still has her ashes. Her name was Celeste.'

23

Ingi

Back then

IT WAS A NORMAL TUESDAY AFTER SCHOOL. HER DAD WAS at work and her mum was at the part-time cleaning job she did on the days Ingi didn't go to Uncle Peter's. She'd just dropped them home and headed off and Ingi had just finished unpacking their lunch boxes.

'You didn't eat much today.' Ingi put Mikey's barely touched sandwich in the bin. It was no good now that the tomato had made it all soggy. He hadn't even eaten his banana.

'I wasn't hungry, and Mr Jones kept me back to sort out some homework for me.'

'Oh. Need any help?' She meant to set up his computer or put in a USB, not actually do his maths homework – that was way over her head. Mikey was so much smarter – he had to help Ingi with her homework more often than not. He had the

219

brains to be anything he wanted, except he wouldn't live long enough to do it.

'You wanna watch a movie? I'll let you pick,' she said.

His dark hair was hanging over the side of his face, nearly in his eyes. He was staring into his lap.

'I'll make popcorn?' she added.

Mikey shook his head then looked up. 'Nah, you watch what you want. Can you take me to my room, please?'

Ingi jumped up. 'Sure, okay. Well, if you change your mind just yell.'

'I usually do.'

She smiled as she pushed him down the passageway to his room. He had his own TV – it wasn't big, but they'd tried to put things in his room that would make him more comfortable. He used to have an old PlayStation but it was getting harder for him to play. Ingi wondered if she should take it away so it wasn't a reminder of what he couldn't do. They used to spend hours playing Star Wars LEGO and Batman LEGO. They used to play a lot more games too, like Monopoly and cards. Now movies were their thing.

Picking up the TV remote, she put it within reach on the table beside his bed, which also doubled as his work desk, and had drawers full of all the bits he needed – night splints, braces and spare masks.

Mikey touched his head, squeezing his eyes closed.

'You okay, bud?'

He shook his head. 'Nup. Ingi, can you bring me some Panadol or whatever Mum has? I've got a bad headache and I've run out.'

'Oh, of course. Why didn't you say sooner?'

In her mum's bedroom, with the yucky yellow floral bedcover from her nana, she pulled open the medicine drawer in the bedside table and got out the Panadol. She tossed them to Mikey on her way past. 'I'll get some water.'

He had his head in his hands when she returned. 'Don't choke,' she said, dropping the full glass beside him. When he didn't smirk or pull the piss back she frowned. 'Hey, do you want a cold flannel or something? Want help getting into bed?'

'Nah, I'm fine here. I'll take these then I might watch something.'

'Righto. Ring the bell if you need to pee, just in case I don't hear you yelling.'

The bell was their dad's idea. Dennis had one at work on the front desk at the funeral place owned by his father. Byrne & Byrne was Albany's longest running funeral directors and was also where her parents met. It wasn't the most romantic meet-cute but Dennis helped Kath when her dad died. They hit it off and the rest was history. Ingi often wondered why death surrounded their family.

She put a bag of popcorn in the microwave and made herself a hot chocolate while bopping to the sounds of popping corn as if it was an actual song. Then she set up the lounge, putting the old beanbag directly in front of the TV along with the throw rug. The beanbag was Ingi's special seat but it had to stay on top of the couch when not in use so Mike could get around.

Shoving a handful of popcorn in her mouth, she smiled and chewed as the opening credits rolled. The beans rattled around her as she snuggled herself in until she was satisfied she had the best position to last the duration of the movie. Movies were her escape – she'd totally immerse herself in them and always got excited, even with ones she'd watched a million times over.

Sometimes she wished Ava would come over and watch movies with her, but Ava always had excuses. They were good friends at school but out of school Ava was too busy meeting friends downtown and with her sport. She'd been to their house a few times, but the visits had been short. Kath said people found things they didn't understand scary and most didn't like 'different'. By different she meant Mikey.

Last time Ava visited, Mikey had needed help to the toilet.

'You don't have to help him do *it*?' Ave had asked warily.

'No, of course not. Mum does all that stuff,' Ingi replied flippantly.

Ava hadn't seemed comfortable after that, glancing towards the door and leaving quickly. No one ever stayed for sleepovers, as if hanging around longer meant they might catch Mikey's disease.

Just as the movie was getting to the good bit, there was a knock at the door.

'Argh, bugger,' she muttered, wiping the last of the butter onto her pants and finding the remote to pause the movie. She climbed her way out of the beanbag and stomped to the door. *It better not be someone wanting to preach to me!*

On opening the door, she found a tall gangly teenager and her cheeks grew warm. This boy could preach to her about anything and she'd hang off every word.

'Hey, Aaron,' she said.

He was from her brother's year, and was one of the nice ones – probably the best friend Mikey had since David moved away three years ago. He had some online mates and ones that he met up at muscular dystrophy camps. Aaron sometimes dropped in to see Mikey but he was usually busy as he played just about every sport and also helped at his family's strawberry farm.

'You here to see Mike?' Ingi asked.

'Kind of. How is he?' Aaron scratched the back of his neck.

'Fine, why?' At least she thought so, but Aaron's sheepish face was making her think otherwise.

'Something happened at school,' he said, dropping his voice.

'Oh?'

Ingi stepped out onto the front porch, closing the door a little. Aaron took a step back. He was so much bigger than her, she could have fitted under his arm. Black hairs randomly sprouted from his chin and sideburns and he had the kindest dark eyes. She wasn't the only one at school who thought he was cute. Plus he was friendly, but he never seemed interested in Ingi, who was a short thin plain girl. She was still waiting for her boobs to arrive. Girls with boobs were always getting asked out and they always had heaps of girlfriends too.

'Well . . . um . . . you know how he likes Casey, yeah?'

Another girl with boobs who needed a decent bra, fancy that. Ingi nodded. 'Yep, had a thing for her for the last two years. He said they've become good friends lately.'

Aaron looked down at his feet. 'Um . . . well . . . that's because she actually wanted to get to know me, so it turns out. I didn't know until she asked me out, right in front of him.'

Shit. 'Oh, how did he take that?' Ingi had seen Casey's name doodled in his books. Only it was getting harder and harder to read.

'He sounded okay, but then after school he saw us . . . ah . . . kissing. I just . . . I like her too, you know?'

'Yeah.' That explained why she was watching a movie alone and he was in his room with a headache. 'Thanks for checking up on him, Aaron. I'll go see how he is . . . He might not want to see you just yet.' Ingi splayed her palms up in an apology.

'No, I get it. I feel shitty. He's a good guy . . . it's just . . .'

He's a guy in a wheelchair who's gonna die and will never get the girl. No matter how good a bloke he is.

'I know.' She moved back inside, suddenly keen to see Mikey. 'Thanks, but I better go. Bye, Aaron.'

'See you tomorrow, Ingi.'

She waved him off, locking the door.

The TV was still frozen on Jennifer Lopez on a runaway horse and would remain so until she got back.

'Hey, Mikey,' she called out as she headed to his room. He didn't answer. Probably asleep as usually he'd holler something smart-arsey back.

'How's the headache?' she asked as she stepped inside and saw him in his chair, watching the TV through his eyelids. Silver blister packs caught her eye, lots of them, empty and twisted on the table. *All* the blister packs of Panadol were out and empty. The box Ingi had given him was empty, but he must have found more, probably in his drawer. She stepped closer and rifled through them. Numbers flashed through her mind, trying to count. Why would he take so many?

Casey and Aaron! Had they really made him that depressed? Was he really trying to kill himself right now?

Grabbing his shirt, she started shaking him. 'Wake up, Mikey.' Her chest was heaving, heart pounding. 'How many did you take? Is this a joke?' Please let it be some sick joke of his and there were pills hidden somewhere.

His eyelids fluttered. 'What,' he whined.

'Mikey, how many did you take?' Her voice rumbled with anger and shook with fear.

His lips twitched. 'Hopefully enough.'

She froze. *Oh shit.*

She wanted her mum. Where was her mum?

'Shit. Shit.' *What do I do?* Ingi ran to the kitchen and grabbed the phone and rang her mum's mobile.

'No, you can't eat the leftover cake,' Kath said on answering.

'Mum,' she cried. 'I think Mikey's overdosed – he's taken all the Panadol.'

'What?'

Ingi had to repeat it again in more detail.

'That's a lot! Ingi, call triple zero now,' she yelled. 'I'm coming straight home. Call now.'

The line went dead and with shaky fingers, Ingi dialled for help, explaining how many pills he'd taken and about his DMD. Then she ran back to his room to stay by his side.

'Help's coming, Mikey,' she told him, holding his hand.

'I don't want help, Ingi,' he muttered, trying to pull out of her grip. 'I just want to be rid of this life. It's pointless. I can't get a girlfriend, I don't have many friends. I won't get a job or get married. What's the point of living this fucked-up life?' he said angrily. Tears filled his eyes.

Ingi's teeth mashed together as she fought the awful thoughts racing through her mind. 'I don't want you to die, Mike. I love you. You're my brother.'

'Your life will be better without me, sis. You'll have friends and free time,' he said with a weak smile. 'I want you to have all that. Instead, you're here babysitting me. You know I'm only going to get worse. I'll have to have a tractotomy soon, I heard Mum talking about it with Dad. It's going to make my life last longer, but I don't want to be in this body anymore.'

Listening to her brother was churning her up, making her feel sick. He was going to die one day, but not like this. 'This is the coward's way out,' Ingi spat, trying to make him see sense. 'You think Mum and Dad are going to be happy? No fucking way. I don't want you to go, Mikey,' she sobbed and fell to the floor trying to hug him as he sat in his wheelchair. 'I love you, you stupid arsehole.'

His hands rested on her shoulders, and they sat like that for a long time, crying. Ingi was too scared to look up in case he was already dead. Frozen in fear she clung to him, hoping it was enough to keep him here.

'Ingi!' Kath ran into the room, hair frizzy like she'd been electrocuted and her face red like she was about to explode. 'Michael Richard Byrne, you're lucky I don't kill you myself for doing such a stupid thing.'

'Sorry, Mum.'

Ingi could tell in that moment, from Mike's voice, that he truly was sorry to upset his mum. She sat up, relieved to hear he could still talk as sirens wailed outside.

'I'll bring the officers in. Ingi stay with him.'

How could her mum be so level-headed at a time like this? Ingi couldn't get herself off the floor, let alone think about what else she could be doing.

'He's in here. He has Duchenne muscular dystrophy. I'll get his medication list for you,' she said, bringing the ambulance officers into Mikey's room.

'Ingi, go call your dad and tell him to meet us at the hospital.'

It was confronting to see new people in his room and it spiked her anxiety as they started their checks. Ingi left the room to call her dad.

It seemed like seconds later she was sitting at the emergency department, waiting for her dad to arrive while her mum had gone in with Mike. It wasn't a great place to sit and wait, though no areas in hospitals were exactly fun. They needed to have better chairs and more pictures to look at, maybe a slushy machine in the corner. Ingi might write a letter and recommend they make it more homely somehow.

'Ingi? Is he okay?'

Dennis Byrne strode towards her, his brow creased and his tie askew.

'Dad!' She jumped up and hugged him. 'I'm still waiting to hear.'

He hugged her for a long time, to the point she started to cry again. She was so relieved her dad was here, it sucked waiting by herself with no clue what was happening. He hugged her until her tears finally dried up and they took a seat side by side.

After about five very long minutes, her dad shot up like something had bitten his butt. 'Here's your mum,' he said, as Kath walked towards them. 'How is he?'

Today was one of those days where her mum looked as old as her nana. But who could blame her? Her eyes were red and puffy, lips dry and tight but her eyes, as tired as she looked, were bright.

'He'll be fine. We got to him super early, so the tablets didn't have much time to be digested, and his liver will be okay.' She turned to Ingi and brushed her fringe from her face. 'You saved his life, sweetheart.'

Her parents pulled her into a hug but all Ingi could think about was that she'd nearly killed him. She'd been the one to leave the pills there. What if Aaron hadn't come by?

'He's going to be just fine,' Kath murmured again, rubbing her back.

Ingi felt the strength leave her legs and sagged against her dad. He sat on the chair with her on his knee, tucking her against his chest as if she was a little girl as she began to shake with silent sobs. How was it possible that she had more tears to shed? Wasn't she a dry desert lake by now? Yet the tears and cries would not be held at bay, as they carved their way up and out her throat. So many emotions threatened to drown her but the gentle rocking and strong arms of her dad helped.

'He's going to be fine, love. It's okay,' he whispered into her hair.

This time he was fine. One day soon he would not be.

24

Ellen

TANYA WAS A GODSEND. SHE WAS A ROCK OF STRENGTH AND a guiding light through the darkness. Because that's all life was at the moment – a big black tar pit in the dark that dragged on her legs with each step and hindered her ability to see anything.

The first week at home, she couldn't even remember much besides the emptiness and the pain. Physical and emotional. It didn't help that her jiggly belly felt hollow and her breasts were sore. Reminders she did not need.

Ingi and Tanya visited daily – Ingi with meals and Tanya with stories from work. Without the two of them, she wasn't sure she'd have survived.

'Morning!'

Ellen opened her eyes and saw a fuzzy Ingi standing by her bedroom door.

'Am I hallucinating?' she asked.

'No, I used your spare key when you didn't answer the door. I was worried.' Ingi came into the room and sat on the side of her bed, the sea-blue tips of her hair swishing like waves.

'Was that what I heard? I just assumed it was the pounding in my head.'

'Have you got a headache?'

Ellen didn't want Ingi to be concerned, it made her feel like a burden. She didn't want to be that to anyone. 'It's only from crying and not drinking enough water.' And being in this bed, this house, these walls, which were no different to her head, her skull, her mind. Both a prison.

'It's been over a week – Tanya said your pains should have stopped by now.'

She squeezed her eyes as if it could make Ingi and the world disappear. 'I am a nurse, Ingi. I'm well aware.'

Being a bitch didn't make Ellen feel any better, but she couldn't stop the anger. And if it wasn't anger, it was tears and they were messy. Anger was easier and less wet.

'I'll go make us a cup of tea. Go and have a shower and it'll be ready when you're done. I'm going to take you on a little drive.'

Ellen threw her blankets back. 'Fine, I'll have a shower,' she grumbled. 'I think I'll hide that key somewhere else,' she muttered on her way to the bathroom.

Under the hot water her anger subsided, only to be replaced by a horrible realisation. She prided herself on always being fair and polite, she had to apologise to Ingi for being so rude. She knew she was only trying to help.

'You look much better,' said Ingi, who was sitting at the kitchen table with two hot cups of tea and a container of melting moments.

Damn, her favourites.

'I feel better,' she said plonking down beside her. 'Ingi, I'm sorry I –'

Ingi held up her hand and shook her head. 'You don't need to apologise, El. I had a moody, suicidal teenage brother. I get it. You're allowed to be angry and mad. Life has been cruel to you. I'd be pissed too.'

Her understanding made Ellen's eyes smart. 'But still, I'm not happy with my behaviour. It's not me and I hate it. I just can't seem to get a grip on my emotions.'

'Oh El, I hate that you have to go through this alone.'

She sighed deeply enough to ripple the air around her, like a rock dropped into a lake. 'I'm not alone. I have you and Tanya. You two have been amazing. Thank you.'

'I wish I could do more.'

'Hey, I appreciate the food so much. I just haven't had the motivation to cook.' Ellen reached for a melting moment, one big bite and she did feel a little better. The shortbread crumbled in her mouth, mixing with the creamy centre. 'What did you tell Bodhi this time?' she asked.

Ingi's lips pressed into a thin line. 'Well I was going to say you were sick and I was coming to look after you, but then I knew he'd tell your mum and next minute they'd all be calling or wanting to drop by and feed you chicken soup.' Ingi rolled her eyes. 'So, I said I was going shopping.'

'Yeah, good option.'

Ingi was right, her family would be all over her like a rash. And that was why no one else could know. It was bad enough Ingi knew, except deep down Ellen was relieved she had someone to confide in, someone who knew Celeste was real, someone to share the awful, lost and so, so empty feeling.

Ellen reached out and held her hand. 'Thank you for being here.'

'You're my best friend, El. And I love you to bits, but it's time to get you out of the house. So I'm going to take you somewhere.'

With their empty cups left on the sink, they headed outside and got in Ingi's car. Neither spoke as Ingi drove them out of Albany and eventually came to a stop by the Kalgan River.

She grabbed a bag from the back of her car. 'Come on, down here.'

On a grassy bank, overlooking the almost still waters of the river, Ingi took a seat and gestured to Ellen to do the same. They sat listening to the bubbling river, the water birds, and the breeze tickling the leaves of the tall trees.

'It's pretty here. Leaving the house was a good idea,' said Ellen, a sad smile all she could muster. 'And yet I still feel so sick inside. Will I ever stop feeling like this?' Some days she felt so cold and hard, just watching the world go by in a haze of nothing. And other days, she felt *everything*! Couldn't even make a cup of tea without bawling.

Ingi made sympathetic sounds as she reached for her hand. 'My heart breaks for you, El.'

Ellen's eyes filled with tears. She didn't wipe them away, she hardly noticed them anymore. 'You know, I can't stop feeling like I killed her,' she whispered, staring at the grass so she couldn't see Ingi's reaction. 'I wonder, did all the worry about everyone finding out about Celeste put too much strain on her? Did she give up to save me?' Ellen rubbed at her eyes. 'I talked to her every night, telling her how much I wanted her and loved her, Ingi – I was ready to be a mum. I was so excited even though I didn't know what I was going to do. I did want her.'

'Celeste would have known your love, heard it in your voice when you talked to her. You didn't do anything wrong. Listen to what Tanya's been telling you. You're a nurse, you know. This isn't your fault.'

Ellen didn't want to cry anymore but Ingi's words were beautiful. 'You know the worst part is that I really want to have a child now. It's like my womb aches because it's been abandoned. My body is mourning as much as I am.'

Ingi started taking things out of the bag as she spoke. 'You can still have children, and there will be more, I know it. You will be such an amazing mum.'

'Do you really think so?'

'Of course I do. You have so much love to give, El. You're a natural mother.'

'So are you, Ingi. I've seen you with babies and kids at the restaurant.'

Ingi didn't reply, just focused on the matches and tea lights she was pulling out of her bag.

'You and Bodhi will make such beautiful babies. Have you guys talked about having any?'

Ingi's sigh was so deep and heavy that Ellen thought maybe she'd hit a nerve. 'Ingi?'

She shrugged. 'I'll never have my own children.'

Ellen opened her mouth, 'I'm so sorry . . .'

But Ingi continued, cutting her off. 'I *can* have them, but I won't, it's too risky. I need to stop the cycle of DMD so I've made myself a promise not to have my own children.'

'Oh,' said Ellen, startled by this new information.

'It's okay. I didn't make this choice lightly. I still wish I could see what my own children with Bodhi would look like.' She let out a sigh. 'But I made a promise and it's one I intend to keep. Besides there are so many kids out there who need loving parents.'

'So you'll adopt? What does Bodhi say?'

'I don't know. I haven't really talked to Bodhi about it. I'm kinda scared. What if he really wants his own children? But I can't go through it again, El. Mikey was hard enough. I think about him every day. And I'm sure you will think about Celeste every day. Soooo,' she drew out the word. 'I thought we could honour them both by sending off some lanterns.'

The matches and the tea lights made sense now. Ingi pulled out two paper lanterns from the bag and then a texta.

'I want you to write on it. Anything. A message to Celeste maybe?'

'Oh Ingi, what a thoughtful gesture. That's so sweet, I love it.'

Ingi picked up hers and wrote, *Mikey, I miss you every day. Hugs, your li'l sis.*

Then she placed the candle inside, lit it and walked to the water's edge.

Ellen held up the texta and was swamped by emotions, though instead of tears she felt a faint smile. A real one.

To my darling Celeste, you will always be loved.

Together they pushed the flickering lanterns out onto the water and watched the gentle current take them slowly downstream. Ellen put her arm around Ingi and together they stood watching them until they disappeared out of sight.

A few days later Ellen returned to work, feeling not quite ready but she'd already had two weeks off. The bleeding had all but stopped and worst of all her energy was coming back, which somehow felt like a betrayal to her baby. Soon her stomach and boobs would be back to normal and there would be no reminders that Celeste had been there at all. It was devastating.

'Hey, there you are.' Tanya strutted down the corridor and gave her a hug. 'What a shitshow you've walked into. Are you sure you're ready to be back at work?'

Ellen heard what she wasn't saying: *Are you ready to be back in a maternity ward?*

'I tried to roster on to general but apparently there's a full moon or something and we're short-staffed in maternity.'

'Yeah, that sucks. I'm here if you need me, at any time, okay?' When Ellen nodded Tanya continued. 'Righto, let's do this. We have a new mum and bub in rooms two and three, plus three who've called to say they've gone into labour, and I've got one now who's starting to push.'

'Right back into it. Crazy. Okay, who's been working with you?'

'Kerry's between the other rooms and had been helping here but she's off in ten minutes. No doubt she'll be looking for you to do handover.'

'I'll go find her then I'll be back.'

By the time Ellen was caught up to speed, Tanya was with a woman in a pink nightie who was at the business end of her labour.

Ellen didn't bother to announce herself to the woman who wriggled in her upright bed. Sweaty brow, red face and eyes wide in fear. Her partner stood close by, same look just minus the nightie. He was struggling with his wife's agony but every time he went to rub her shoulder or hold her hand she flung him away.

'Get this baby out now,' she wailed.

Ellen's instincts kicked in and she helped Tanya prepare, even taking a quick check herself. Seeing the head crowning always brought a smile – new life was on its way.

Tanya flicked her a grin, glad to see she was going okay. Ellen was surprised herself. She could do this.

'Another deep breath and push,' she coaxed the woman.

A long low growl escaped and her baby slipped its way out into the doctor's hands.

All was quiet.

There was an echoing thud throbbing through her body as Ellen watched the still lifeless baby. *No, no, no! Make it stop*, she wanted to scream. The room started to spin and blur from her tears. She saw herself on the bed, tiny bundle in her hands, her heart being ripped from her chest. Was this the same room? All that pain with no reward.

A splutter, then a cry. 'Congratulations, a little boy,' Tanya was saying to the couple. 'El, do you want to do the checks?' she began to say and then paused. 'Oh honey. I've got it, you go take a moment.'

Somehow Ellen found the door and an empty chair in the hallway. She hunched into a ball, almost rocking as she stared into space, trying to collect her thoughts. How long would this grief go on? How long would this ache last and the feeling she was missing something? Her hand went to her belly and it felt so empty. Across from her, through the door she saw another mum, sitting in her bed holding her newborn, singing softly.

Jealousy hit her so hard she almost couldn't breathe. How come that mum got to keep her baby while Ellen's had died?

Because you didn't want yours enough.

The thought had appeared so rapidly that Ellen almost physically choked. Again the same questions washed over her. Did Celeste know how confused she was? How tormented with what to do? Had she wished her away?

Don't be silly, Ellen. You wanted your baby.

Her future path had been undecided but she did want her baby. But had her fears and stress been too much? Was it also karma? For sleeping with a man who could never be hers? For deceiving everyone?

'Hey, El, you okay?'

Tanya was squatting beside her chair, eyes filled with worry. Her head shook even though her mind was still racing.

'Maybe you need more time?'

How much time? A month? A year? Five years? Never? Would she ever be the old Ellen? It seemed impossible, as if the old Ellen had already died, replaced by a jaded ghost of a person who didn't belong anywhere. Nowhere felt comfortable, not the hospital she'd once loved, not her perfectly organised home, not the bustling streets of Albany. All of it was alien, as if she was walking around in someone else's skin.

'I think you're right, Tan. I don't think I can work here.' She couldn't work as a midwife, or even in this hospital. She couldn't face her family with all her lies, she couldn't face Fin.

'I need a real break.'

If she didn't take one, there might be no pieces of her left to put back together.

'You really think so?' Tanya asked. 'What are you going to do? Where will you go?'

'I don't know. Maybe look for a job in Perth, maybe just go drive around the state on a holiday.' But as she said that she remembered a phone call with her friend from uni about a month ago, saying her parents had been trying to find some workers on their station up north, near Mount Magnet. About a thousand kilometres away.

Far enough away that no one would visit. On a station with cows and red dirt. No babies in sight. No mums, no interrogating family. No Fin. No reminders.

'I'm going to see the nurse manager and find out what my options are.' Ellen stood and wiped her face, more determined than she'd felt in a long time.

'Whatever you need, I'll support you. Are you going to tell your family? Or Ingi?'

Ellen shrugged. 'I feel bad enough that she has to lie for me. But she deserves to know. As for the family, I think it might be easier to leave first.'

Fifty million questions as to why she was leaving nursing and Albany would pepper her until they got a satisfactory answer. At least up north she could just ignore her phone.

Was she doing the right thing? Would this be running away from her demons? Was she a coward?

Maybe.

25

Ellen

Now

'WE'LL HAVE TO WALK FAST SO WE DON'T GET STUCK IN THE dark,' Ellen threw over her shoulder to Fin. 'That could be dangerous,' she added. She didn't want him to realise it was him she wanted to avoid in the dark.

'I think we'll have enough time. I have the light on my phone if it comes to that,' he added happily.

He jogged to catch up and walk by her side. Ellen forced herself to unclench her hands.

The path led to Circular Pool lookout where they stopped to take photos before following the rim of the gorge, past white-barked snappy gums and more pale green grasses that covered the ground like a shag-pile rug.

'It's just so stunning. I'm so glad we came,' he said.

Ellen remained silent, preferring to enjoy nature's silence. Not to be rude . . . well, maybe a little. It just felt as though every time she talked to Fin she lost more of herself to him. Soon she'd have nothing left.

The path weaved along the rim and ended where the three points of the gorges met. A rusty viewing platform hung scarily close to the edge as they both drank in the view and took some photos.

Ellen turned just as Fin took her photo. 'Hey.'

He smirked. 'It can go with the other one I have.'

Ellen turned back to the view, not sure how to take what he'd said. 'It's so breathtaking. Can you see where the path leads down?'

'Over here.'

Fin had walked around and found the little coloured dots that marked the path.

'Jesus, that's it? Looks like a goat track.' Ellen felt a little giddy as she glanced down the rocky steps. No fancy iron staircase here, just the natural version.

'Wow, I saw a family with kids here yesterday,' he said. 'Mind you, kids could probably handle this better than adults. More nimble.' He began to step carefully downward.

Ellen followed behind, each step taken with care. The path was easy enough to follow as it was worn from use, so there was no chance you could end up going the wrong way. At times she pressed a hand against the rockface to steady herself, and keep her body away from the sheer drop on the other side of the track. One wrong foot and she could tumble down like a pebble, rolling over and over.

Fin made it down a big step between two rocks and turned, holding out his hand.

'I got it,' she said, ignoring his help. There was no way her heart could handle holding his hand. No way in hell.

'Okay, be careful.'

He continued down while Ellen stumbled, giving herself a heart attack and wishing she could have just taken his damn hand. Thankfully he hadn't noticed her near fall to death.

'I wonder how many people have fallen off this track?' she asked and then cursed herself for making conversation.

Fin turned to her with a huge smile. 'That's not something I want to discuss until I've actually reached the bottom safely.'

Ellen couldn't help but return his grin. *Damn it, Sutton, stop going all googly eyed.* 'Fair call.'

It was hard on her thighs, taking the brunt of each steep footstep down, made even harder by the haphazard rocks, some providing only half a foot to balance on. And yet it was exhilarating, and the view was magnificent.

Yellow dots were their guides. Down they stepped, around tree roots, jagged rock faces, down a steep metal ladder, and eventually they found the bottom.

'I love how tranquil it is. I thought there'd be heaps more people here,' said Fin as they stopped for a drink and a rest.

'Must be the time of the year. Too hot for most I guess, but at least the water is beautiful to swim in.'

'Oh, it's perfect. I'm hoping to end the walk with a quick dip. I can imagine at peak time this place would be crawling with people. I'm glad we're here now.'

It was intimate, too intimate. Ellen shoved her water back into her backpack and started along the gorge floor, following the yellow markers and putting distance between her and the man who could turn her legs to jelly with one dimpled smile.

One minute the floor would be smooth like hard marble and the next they were crawling over jagged chunks like a Flake chocolate bar. All those layers and layers.

'The rock formations are fascinating,' said Fin as he fell in step behind her.

It wasn't a track you could walk shoulder to shoulder, only in some sections when it opened out into flat treeless areas. They reached a section where the gorge was wide, and water pooled across the area with many little waterfalls tricking down tiers of rocks.

'This is just . . . wow,' she had to admit. 'I feel like I could sit here all day and drink it in.' Ellen hopped across dry rocks to explore the area. The tinkling of running water was the only sound in the valley. It was a really romantic spot. *Don't go there, El!*

'Penny for your thoughts?' Fin asked. His hat was tilted back and he'd removed his sunglasses, allowing those brown eyes to swirl with hints of gold in the dying sunlight.

'My thoughts aren't worth it,' she muttered and tried to out-step him.

If Fin's shoulders got too close, Ellen would stop and pretend to look at something or move faster to capture a certain rock feature with her camera. Keeping a distance from him was getting tiring. She thought she was doing a great job until Fin called her out on it.

'El, do you really hate me that much?'

'No, what makes you think that?' Her pulse thudded in her neck and she couldn't bring herself to face him.

'I'm not stupid – the fact that you avoid me at any cost.' He chuckled but there was no humour to it. 'I must have imagined that whole concert night. I actually thought we had a great time and got on so well.'

Ellen's mouth went dry, as if she'd left her tongue out on one of the rocks all day, but she didn't dare stop to get her water out. Already she was feeling the flustery heat work its way up her neck. Her mind raced for a reply.

'I just wish you'd had the decency to come out and tell me straight instead of dodging me all this time. Carrie said you didn't really like me. What is it you don't like?'

His hand was suddenly on her wrist holding her. 'El, talk to me?'

'Fin, I can't. I can't do this with you.'

She broke free of his grip and tried to march on with heavy legs.

'Why not?' he pushed.

The hairs on the back of her neck rose, sensing his nearness.

'What is it about me that repulses you so much? I just don't get it. Around everyone else you're the most kind, gracious, sweet person I've ever known and yet you can't even look me in the eye. At first it was fine, but then you just pulled further and further away.'

Ellen stopped so suddenly he stumbled into her. They stood there for a moment, sharing the same large slab of smooth rock. Breathing heavily. The air was thick with electricity, her body was zinging. It was taking everything she had to try to push it back into its box, when all she wanted to do was kiss him.

'Damn you, Murray,' she grumbled. She went to walk off, but he reached out and pulled her back against him.

'Careful using that name,' he whispered near her ear.

It was a warning. And truth be told she knew using his real name sparked something in him and had tried hard to avoid it.

'Ellen, what have I done wrong?' he almost begged. 'I care about you, so much. I need to know.'

His words ripped through her and she pulled away from him angrily. 'You've done nothing wrong,' she shouted, stomping her way up the next rocky outcrop. 'How could you? You're passionate, loyal, and one of the most amazing men I've ever known, and I can't stand to be near you.'

'None of that makes sense,' he shouted back, jogging to try to catch up with her. 'Is this because of what I said at the pub that night? I saw your face – it was like I'd slapped you, and since then you've built a Great fucking Wall of China between us. You should have told me I'd overstepped the mark.'

Ellen was wondering what he'd actually said that night. She hadn't heard the last bit and had imagined all sorts of things. Only now she wasn't game to ask him. God, he was infuriating. Couldn't he just let her be?

'You just don't get it,' she spat back. 'I'm *trying* to put distance between us. I need a fucking big wall because I don't want to be in love with you, I can't be in love with you. It's all just so fucking confusing. I can't even think straight when you're near me, I can't breathe.' Ellen was puffing as she forced each word out and for some stupid reason she was jogging through the obstacles like she was on *Ninja Warrior*. Until her foot slipped into a crevice while the force of her body continued. Her ankle was like a car striking a tree, her body the passenger flying through the window.

'Ah, shit,' she cried out in agony. She went down like a sack of bricks, skinning her knees. A sound filled the air, like a twig snapping. It was either her leg breaking or she'd cracked off some rock, but by the pain that instantly shot up her leg she was thinking the former.

'El, El, are you okay?'

Fin skidded to a halt beside her.

'Don't touch me,' she cried out. 'I think I broke my leg.'

Tears pressed against her eyelids as she worked hard to keep them in. *Deep breaths, Ellen.* She tried to control the pain, to get a moment of calm so she could think through what to do next.

'Can you tell?' he asked.

Gingerly she sat up and reached down towards her ankle. Fingers feeling around carefully.

'Shit, it hurts. Thank God it's not a compound fracture. It's just above my ankle. Bloody hell what a mess.' Ellen put her hand over her face, feeling stupid as tears leaked from her eyes.

Fin handed her his bottle of water. 'What can I do to help? Can I take you to the shade over there? Should we splint it?'

Ellen had been ready to wallow in her self-pity but Fin's calm voice brought her back. 'Yes, yes, good thinking. Maybe we should try and splint it before I move.' She shrugged out of her backpack. 'I've got a small first-aid kit in here, we can use the bandage to help hold some sticks in place.' Focusing on what to do was taking her mind, ever so slightly, off the pain.

She sipped his water while he went off to find a couple of straight sticks.

'Will these do?'

'Perfect.' Of course he'd managed to find straight ones and had made them roughly the same length.

Together they did the best they could to immobilise her leg.

'Have you got any Panadol in your bag? I think you'll need it,' he asked worriedly.

'I'll be fine,' she said. After all, she'd been through much worse pain, this should be a walk in the park. Only she couldn't tell Fin about that pain, both physically and emotionally.

'You're a tough nut. Here, put your arms around my neck and I'll take you to that shade.'

He motioned to a ledge nearby that was under a canopy of river gums.

With a sigh she did as she was told, lifting her arms and holding onto him as he pulled her up against his chest. She rested her head on his shoulder, taking comfort in his scent and strength as she clenched her jaw against the wave of hurt.

Fin sat on the ledge, keeping her in his arms. 'How are we going to get you out of here?'

There was no way she could navigate this track with just Fin's help, and he couldn't carry her while trying to negotiate those rocks in the fading light.

'Maybe you should just leave me here and go get help? I don't think anyone else is going to come along.' The sun was dropping, casting a shadow across the gorge. She was glad she hadn't done the walk alone. Then again she probably wouldn't have broken her leg if she'd been alone. The words she'd yelled at Fin came back to her in wave after wave, like the pain that was shooting up her leg. Hopefully he'd forgotten them.

'I'm not leaving you down here alone, El. By the time I got up and then back down you'd be here for nearly three hours on your own. What if a snake slithered by?'

El shivered and was a little relieved.

'I'm staying right here with you. Maybe the ranger will come by?'

'Maybe,' she whispered. The area above her ankle was throbbing. 'I need to get this elevated and preferably iced.' She gritted her teeth. 'Not sure how that's going to happen.'

'Leave it to me.'

Fin got up and laid her down on the ledge, using her backpack as a pillow, and found a few rocks to elevate her leg. Then he pulled off his shirt and walked off.

As pain meds went, his shirtless torso rated pretty high. When he came back, his shirt was wet and he laid it gently over her swollen leg. The coolness of it hurt but it would at least help with the swelling.

'Thanks, doc,' she said gratefully, trying not to ogle his bare chest against the glowing gorge backdrop. She'd had sex with this man and yet she'd never seen him naked.

'You're welcome. It's nice to be able to do something for you,' said Fin, sitting beside her on the ledge. 'You never hang around long enough.'

'Well, I'm not going anywhere now,' she said reluctantly, wishing his shirt could have remained on. Okay, maybe not. The heat had eased a little with the setting sun but Ellen felt like she was burning up. Would the shock hit soon and send her into a cold chill? Would he keep her warm?

'Good,' said Fin. 'I'm glad you can't run away – pun intended – because we need to discuss what you yelled at me just before you fell.'

Oh shit.

26

Ellen

'I DON'T RECALL,' SHE SAID, FLOPPING HER ARM OVER HER face, hoping he'd drop the subject. But Fin had his intense eyes focused on her and she was stuck like a sheep up to its neck in a dry dam.

'Is it true?'

'Does it matter?' she replied.

'It matters to me.'

Ellen peered at him from beneath her arm. 'Why?'

Why would he care? Her heart was racing. Stupid heart. Ellen didn't want to be having this honest conversation with Fin. Except deep down, a desperate girl wanted to know if he felt anything beyond that night.

'Jesus, Ellen. I wish I'd known sooner.'

Eyes wide, she stared.

'I still think about that night. Don't you?'

Not trusting her words she locked her lips together and nodded.

'I was fine at leaving it as a one-night stand. I was happy with Carrie, and then you showed up.'

'Actually, it was you who showed up.'

'Ha, funny.'

Only it wasn't.

Ellen moved and regretted it as pain shot up her leg. She closed her eyes and breathed through it, hoping Fin didn't notice.

He rubbed the back of his neck. 'You know, as time went on and the more time I spent with you the more I liked you, the more that amazing night came back to the front of my mind, blending with all the wonderful new things I was learning about you. But I was with Carrie and you seemed to dislike me.'

His words were like thick honey, slowly drizzling over her body, coating her in a warm sugary coma.

'When I saw you at the pub that night with Tanya, it was the first time I wondered if I'd made a mistake. I thought I'd felt something between us growing. I wanted to know if . . . God, I don't know,' he said, yanking his hat off and pushing his hand through his hair as if he wanted to rip it from his head. 'Who in their right mind falls for their girlfriend's sister? On what planet was that ever going to work out?' he huffed. 'Anyway, you didn't seem impressed, if anything you grew so distant, practically ran from me.'

Fin started picking at the rock edge where he sat. 'I didn't know if you were pushing me away on purpose, and then Carrie said you just didn't like me. So then I'm thinking I'd been imagining the static between us, that maybe I'd made it all up? Maybe you'd realised I wasn't the bloke you liked at the concert.'

'I'm sorry,' she whispered, trying to think over the ache in her leg. 'You didn't imagine it. I felt that damn pull every damn time. I couldn't handle being around you, I didn't trust myself. And you seemed happy with Carrie, and she told me that you might be the one, and then you moved in together. Carrie has never been that committed to anyone before. I couldn't get between that. I love my sister. Like you said, who in their right mind falls for their sister's boyfriend?'

Fin stood and paced back and forth, glancing up and down the gorge. He was like a caged animal, pacing the perimeter, looking for a way out.

Ellen had no idea what he must be thinking now. Missed opportunities, mistaken feelings, confusion. El had all that and a broken leg to contemplate.

'I don't think anyone is coming. We might be here a while,' Fin muttered before glancing up at the sky.

As the seconds passed, the sky was growing darker. Ellen looked at her watch. Carrie wouldn't be expecting them for maybe another hour yet before she'd start to get worried.

'Will we be here all night?' Ellen tried to sit up and winced.

'Hey, don't move. Rest. I'll be back.'

He disappeared up the track and she wondered if he'd finally gone for help. Ellen would be okay here. Sure, the rock wasn't as comfy as a swag but beggars can't be choosers.

When Fin returned, he had armfuls of grass. 'I know it's not much, but it might be more comfortable. Especially if we do end up here for a while.'

She liked how he didn't say 'all night'.

By the time he'd finished collecting enough grass to make some sort of bush mattress it was almost too dark to be walking around, and she'd been worried he might disturb a snake in all that long grass.

He took his shirt off her ankle. 'I'll go wet this again.'

'No, stay here. I don't want you getting hurt too.' Hopefully the panic wasn't noticeable but now it was dark, being on her own was a scary thought. 'I'm already too cold.'

Fin touched her forehead, then her arm. 'You've got goose-bumps. Is it a bit of shock?'

In seconds he'd joined her on the ledge bed, shifting closer to her body.

Ellen wanted to protest but his skin was warm and she moved in closer. 'Thanks.'

It wasn't cold and it didn't feel like it would get cold at all tonight. Maybe early morning might bring a drop in temperature. At least she didn't have to worry about freezing to death.

'Do you think they'll come for us?' she asked as she pressed her back against his chest for more warmth. It was hard with her leg. Damn leg.

'Unlikely. It's unsafe at the best of times, let alone in the dark. They should come at first light,' he said reassuringly.

A trickling of water was the only sound other than their breathing. And she could see the stars. It would be magical if she didn't feel like someone was stabbing her in the leg with a knife. She'd probably wake up thinking a dingo was chewing on her leg. Did dingoes get down into the gorges? Would snakes slither over them during the night or curl up next to them for warmth? She shuddered at the thought.

'You know I asked Carrie if we should break up yesterday.'

Ellen rolled onto her back so she could face Fin, she could see his outline but not his features. Her hand itched to reach out and touch him so she could read his expression.

'What?' This was news. Had they been having issues? She hadn't heard anything. Then again it wasn't like she called home much after she bolted up here. And she kept most of her calls to short conversations.

Hi, Mum, yes I'm fine, having a great time up here. She found if she could get in first she'd tell them all about station life and then 'have to go' and hang up before they could interrogate her. Didn't stop them from trying. Ingi was the one she avoided the most and she felt bad about it, but Ingi knew her secrets. Every time Ingi would ask how she was coping, Ellen would find an excuse to hang up. She was trying to escape all those memories. It just felt easier being at the station, working and pretending none of that had happened.

Fin cleared his throat. 'I haven't felt happy with Carrie for a while. You know, I think I've been deluding myself for some time now. It wasn't until you left Albany that things suddenly felt different, as if the sun had vanished and the days were always cloudy. It was then that I realised just how deep my feelings for you were. I'd been pushing them aside, avoiding it, and when you left, it hit me. I started to see my relationship with Carrie differently. How she never really seemed herself around me and I'd never pushed to find the real Carrie. I don't know if that makes sense, but it felt a bit empty. Carrie and I just don't want the same things.'

'Oh wow, I'm sorry. I didn't know.' How could she?

He sighed, deep and long. 'We started off great with so much possibility, but I don't think we are "rest of our lives" suited. Our relationship was starting to feel casual, like I'm Carrie's safety blanket more than any kind of great romance.'

'Sorry.'

He shrugged. 'Don't be. It happens. How could I love Carrie when I'm not sure who she is, and I'm not sure she even knows that herself. She's successful, fun, has a big heart she doesn't let many see, and yet I can tell she's unhappy, but she won't admit it to me or change anything.'

His fingers found her face, sending ripples of pleasure through her body, drowning out the stabbing pain. 'But I feel like I know you, Ellen. I know the curve of your face, the depth of your eyes. I know how genuine and heartfelt you are and how you go out of your way to protect others. I know all your smiles. There's even one just for me, well, I like to think so. I've only seen it a few times. The concert and the pub.'

Ellen smiled.

'That's it there.' He grinned. 'You wear your heart on your sleeve and you have so much compassion. A natural nurturer. I can't believe it took me this long to realise just how much you mean to me.'

'Wow. That I did not expect.'

'Even when you were pushing me away, I was still just happy to be in the same room as you, Ellen. To see you smile, the way you doted on your family. Sometimes I thought my feelings were that strong because you were so similar to Carrie – I was getting good at believing my own bullshit, my own reasoning as to why I liked being around you. God, I wish I knew how you felt ages ago.'

Ellen was wide-eyed, as if her pupils were trying to suck any bits of light from the night to see him. 'I thought I was the only one feeling that way. I couldn't tell you, I shouldn't have told you now. I don't want to hurt my sister,' she said.

'I care for Carrie, I do. But I don't see a future for us. I want to be with someone who makes the sun shine on a cloudy day. Who wants to have a family and who makes my body hum on a deep connected level.'

Her mind was spinning. She'd dreamed of hearing words like this from him. Was the pain making her delusional? *Somebody pinch me!*

'Stop thinking so hard. I can hear your cogs turning,' he said with a faint chuckle.

'Murray, I just don't know what to say. I'm gobsmacked.'

His throat rumbled, almost like a purr. 'God, I love hearing you say my name. It's like you see me, all of me, and accept me for who I am. I finally told Carrie about my brewery dream, and she said, "Why would you want to do that when you've got the White Pearl?" Seriously, she didn't get it.'

'You need to do something for you, not your father,' said Ellen. 'The brewery is your dream. I do see all of you. I tried hard not to fall in love but it was no use. I've never been so jealous of Carrie before, wanting what she had.'

'And yet you put her happiness above yours,' he said. 'Still showed up at every family event and endured being there with me. You're amazing.' His eyes dropped to her lips and then he pressed his against them.

Soft and sensuous, she was drawn back to that moment in the trees. His short stubble tickled as she kissed him back. Her body felt like it was levitating as they deepened the kiss. It had been a long wait to do this, and now that it was happening she couldn't believe it, couldn't believe how amazing it was to taste him again. Murray Finlay was her drug of choice. It was as if her nerve endings were implanted with his DNA and only came alive at his touch. Her tongue brushed against his and he groaned into her mouth, causing a fresh wave of electricity.

'Damn, tell me you didn't feel that?' he said between huffed breaths.

Ellen pressed her palm against his cheek. Her heart had swelled to twice its size and her chest felt too small for it. 'Was that real?' she asked.

'I better make sure.'

He kissed her again and it was sweeter than the first.

Fin nuzzled her neck, his lips dancing across her skin as he spoke. 'I wish I'd followed my instincts earlier. Even though I thought you didn't feel the same.'

'I thought I was doing what was right for you and Carrie.'

'Stop doing what you think is right and start doing what your heart wants. What does it want, Ellen?'

His lips brushed her cheek and her toes curled causing immense pain with the pleasure. 'I want my leg to stop hurting.'

'Shit, sorry. I wish I could help with that.'

'You are,' she replied and moved her hand into his hair and pulled him closer. 'My heart wants you, Murray. Since that night in the pub, it's wanted nothing else. I love you.'

His body trembled against her skin. It was the most amazing sensation.

'I love you too, Ellen. I feel like I've been denying it for so long. I'm tired of fighting it. I just want to be with you.'

Ellen was riding high on his words, soaking them in like rain on the dry red dirt. Voices in her head tried to say *What about Carrie?* and *What about your secret baby?* but she pushed them away.

In the dark under the stars, with the trickling of water in the background, was a world away from reality, and right now she just wanted him all to herself.

His taste, scent and touch were all she wanted to think about right now. The rest could wait.

27

Carrie

Back then

SUNLIGHT PEEKED IN BETWEEN THE GUNMETAL GREY CURTAINS that dropped to the floor, thick-backed to keep the light out, and yet Fin left them open about a foot in the middle, apparently because he liked waking up with the sun. Carrie woke up to her screeching alarm, having picked the most annoying sound she could to wake the dead.

Grey covers were thrown back on Fin's side, the bed empty. The smell of coffee floated into the bedroom and the hiss of frothing milk. Fin was ever reliable. The first one up, he'd always have a coffee made and brought to her in bed. She would sit up and sip it while scrolling through Facebook, Instagram and TikTok, before it was time to get ready for work. At this point, Fin was already dressed and had finished in the bathroom. He liked to have another coffee sitting on the back veranda in the sunshine and read the local paper. Every morning he did the same; most normal people just read the news on social media. But not Fin – a traditionalist dedicated to his routine. He just needed a pair of round glasses, an old man's body, and he'd be like her grandad.

'Good morning.'

Fin entered, coffee in hand, wearing low-fitting black track-pants. Golden skin, carved muscles, that sexy sleeve tattoo and his hipster beard were all a recipe for desire, old man tendencies aside. He had a big heart, more manners than her whole family put together and always took care of her, sick or hormonal, or just pissed off after a long day at work. Carrie knew he was amazing ... and yet ... there was a hole in her chest, and she didn't know how to fill it. Life felt bland. All the things she'd strived for, she'd accomplished. She owned her own hair salon, was a qualified beautician, had heaps of friends and a wonderful family, had a great guy ... tick, tick, tick. So why did she feel like there were still boxes left unticked?

'Careful, it might be hot, I overdid the milk,' he said, putting the cup down beside her.

Normally he left the room then, but this time he sat on the edge of the bed. Carrie's jaw tightened and she pressed her lips together. *What now.* Again, she couldn't help the nasty edge of annoyance.

'Hey, is there a family funeral soon?'

Carrie sat up and reached for the coffee. She wasn't expecting that. 'No, not that I know of. Why do you ask?'

'I was at Bodhi's yesterday. We were out the back having a drink and making up some more fishing rigs for when we head out to the salmon holes.'

Carrie waved her hand, hoping he'd hurry up and get to the point.

'So I had to duck inside to get something, and that's when I overheard Ingi and El talking about a funeral.'

'Oh.' Carrie tapped her finger on her lower lip. 'What else did they say?'

Fin looked uncomfortable, as if he didn't want to be spreading gossip.

'Come on, spit it out.'

'I just heard Ingi ask when the memorial was on and say that she was going to be there for her – for Ellen. It sounded serious . . . really heavy. I got the impression it was someone El cared about. Hence why I thought it might have been family.'

'Not that I know of. She does have her own friends and ex-boyfriends. Maybe it's someone from her schooldays – an old teacher? Her first boyfriend? Someone from work? I wouldn't worry about it, Fin, sounds like Ingi's making sure she has support. El would have told me if it was serious. There's never been secrets between us.'

Fin nodded slowly as he got up. 'Ah, okay. Yes, you're right, I'm sure she would have said something to you or Bodhi. Well, I better get ready for work.'

He rushed from the room and finally Carrie had some quiet time to herself. Was that what she needed? Quiet time? Surely not – every time it got too quiet at home she'd go visit a friend or head to the shops. Or was that the point? *Maybe I need to learn how to be on my own more?* Or at least she needed to enjoy being by herself. Was she scared to be alone? Was that why she'd moved in with Fin so quickly? Wasn't that what you were supposed to do when you found a great guy? Next was marriage and kids.

Carrie's stomach flipped at the thought. *Marry Fin?* Sure, she liked hanging with him, he was a great lover and he had a nice home – except she wasn't keen on all the plants. Her thumbs were not green, and she was scared they'd all die on her watch.

With her cup empty, she got out of bed and headed to the kitchen to put it in the sink. The bed would probably be made by the time she got back. Sometimes living with Fin was like living with her mum; well, before she chucked a hissy fit and refused to do any more cleaning up after her youngest.

'How anyone who takes so much pride in how they look can live like such a slob is beyond me,' her mum once said. And she was right. Carrie didn't mind dirt and mess, she'd grown up outside with all their pets, sleeping on the dogs' bed or barefoot in the chook pen with poo squishing between her toes. Even now coming home from a night out, she'd quite happily just crash on the bed or couch or floor and sleep in her jeans, face still caked in make-up.

Fin, bless his soft heart, might remind her that the bathroom towel goes back on the rail, not on their bedroom floor, but he'd never got super angry over it.

Except last night he'd been a big gruff, asking if she could please put her make-up stuff away when she was done with it.

'Every time I try to turn the tap on, something falls in the sink, sometimes the hairdryer. I'll fry myself one day, Carrie. One of your powders fell off yesterday and shit went every-where, took ages to clean.'

It was the most worked up she'd seen him. Truth be told, she felt like he was pulling away. He used to make an effort to eat together or watch TV together, now they seemed to be at opposite ends of the house most of the time.

'Oh, I'm sorry. I was running late and didn't have time to put it all way.'

'Can't you do your make-up at work?'

'The mirrors are shit there. You need a bigger cupboard,' she'd said, and realised that wasn't the answer he'd been waiting for.

Carrie headed back to the bedroom now when her phone pinged. 'Hey, Bodhi just sent me a text.' She paused, reading. 'He said El is leaving Albany.' She whirled around to Fin. 'Did you know?'

He went rigid. He touched his throat and moved his neck like something was stuck.

'No. I've heard nothing. What did he say? Where's she going?' He reached for her phone and read the message.

Ellen just told me she's leaving Albany. Did you know?

'What the heck is she up to?' Carrie stared at him, as if hoping he had all the answers. Which he wouldn't. 'I'm going to call her.'

Carrie rang her sister while she stared up at Fin. 'This has to be a joke? Bodhi must be messing with me.' It wasn't a very funny joke.

'Carrie? What's up?' Ellen's voice was a monotone. Maybe she'd just woken up.

'Shit, sorry. Did you have a late shift?' Damn, she didn't even think about her work hours.

'No, no, it's fine, I've been awake a while,' she said with a sigh. 'What's up?'

'Um, you tell me. Are you leaving?'

'Gee, news travels fast. Don't say anything to Mum and Dad just yet, please? I want to tell them in person before I leave.'

'Bloody hell,' she said, pacing the length of the bedroom. Fin was stationary but watching her as if he was at a tennis match. He was mouthing words but she couldn't focus on him, not when El was leaving. 'Where are you going? Why didn't you tell me?'

'Just calm down. My friend needs a worker on their station up north. I've always wanted to go mustering, so I've taken time off work and I'm going on a working holiday of sorts,' she said.

Fin was waving his hands, wanting to know what was going on, but Carrie shooshed him with her palm and turned her back.

'When are you going? For how long? This is so sudden.' She didn't want her sister to go anywhere. None of them had really left Albany. Did she say she was going mustering? *What the fuck!*

'I was going to call you today. I can't believe Bodhi said something before I could call. I've only just told him.'

Carrie squirmed. El was her only sister and yet she called Bodhi first. That ticked her off.

'Do you have to go right away?'

'Yeah, they need someone now so I'm off tomorrow. Won't be for long, just enough for me to get my cow fix and then I'll be back.'

Her words sounded promising, but her tone didn't. Something about her expression made it feel permanent.

'You okay, sis? I know I haven't checked in for a while, but you'd tell me if there was something up, wouldn't you?'

The phone was silent for a beat and then El's soft voice replied, 'I'm fine. It'll be a good break from the hospital, you know?'

Carrie did know. She'd celebrated with El after her first shift and consoled her after her first horrific crash victim. They were a lot closer before they ended up with boyfriends and jobs. It just seemed harder to find time for catch-ups. 'I'm sorry I haven't been around much. Can I see you before you go?'

There was so much more she needed to say in person. So many more questions. Like exactly how far away was this station?

'I'll come see you at the salon and bring coffee.'

'Oh shit, the salon. Fuck, I'll be late.'

'You're always late.' El chuckled.

That made her smile. There was her beautiful happy sister. 'Yeah, true. Okay, I'll see you soon. Love you.'

'Love you too, Carrie.'

She hung up and turned around to find Fin a mere foot away, staring at her, eyes wide.

'Well, what's going on?'

He sounded panicked. Probably because he was now late for work too and Fin hated being late. He set all the clocks in the house, his car and his watch, ten minutes fast. Talk about anal. But she had to admit it did get her to work on time.

'Is she really leaving?' he asked.

'Yep. Tomorrow.'

'What! Why?'

Carrie shrugged. 'She's off on a holiday to muster cows.'

'What?' Fin scratched his head and then checked his watch. 'Fuck. I gotta go but tell me more when you know something. Is she going to come say goodbye?'

'Yeah, she's coming in to see me at the salon.'

His lips twitched as he stared at his phone. 'How long is she going for?' he said softly.

Carrie went and rested her head against his chest, needing some comfort. He put a hand on her shoulder. There was that distance thing again. It only made her heart feel heavier.

'She didn't really say. I miss her already.'

Fin murmured then stepped back. 'I really have to get to work, the truck is due in any second. Sorry.'

He strode out of the room and Carrie felt like she'd been sucker-punched. By Fin and El.

Would life get any better? Would this strange emptiness ever leave?

What did Carrie have to do to make things better, to feel fulfilled and happy?

'Where's a damn fortune cookie when you need one.'

Reluctantly she got ready for work. She didn't hurry. She knew she had ten minutes extra.

28

Carrie

Now

FOOTSTEPS IN THE GRAVEL WOKE HER UP WHILE THE THICK curtains in the van kept most of the light out. *Oh my head!*

So much for getting rid of her headache yesterday afternoon. Her skin felt brittle and even frowning made her forehead sting. Damn sunburn.

For a moment she couldn't think straight, couldn't figure out what was going on. Last night she'd been drinking with Hans . . . then somehow ended up in bed. That's right – she'd felt like shit and Hans had helped her.

'Carrie, are you up?'

Speak of the devil. 'I am now,' she muttered.

'Sorry,' Hans said, opening the van door. 'I thought I better come see how you are. You were really wiped out last night.'

'Yeah, thanks for helping.'

'You still look burnt,' he said.

'I still feel burnt.'

She scanned the van, feeling like something was missing but she couldn't think what in her groggy morning state.

'I'm heading off soon and just wanted to check in on you before I say goodbye to everyone.'

'Oh bugger. That time already,' she said, moving to the edge of the bed and patting her out of control hair as she went. She saw one of Fin's hats and thought about jamming that on her head to hide her hair. Suddenly she knew what was missing.

'Have you seen Fin?' she asked Hans.

He squinted into the dark van. 'I thought he'd be in here with you.'

He must have gone to the loo. She looked over the bed – she'd laid diagonally across it all night, even in sleep her sunburn had stopped her from moving. There would have been no room for Fin. Weird. Had he slept outside because she'd hogged the bed? There was nowhere else for him to go, besides in El's ute.

She rubbed at her eyes and drank some water, bracing herself to head out into the morning light.

It was nice outside, cool but not cold, and there wasn't a fly about. Empty chairs were lined up against the van, but there was no Fin.

'Maybe he's in the toilet. Did you notice if Ellen was up?' she asked Hans. For a strange moment she wondered if they were together. Had they sorted out their problems? Got roaring drunk together?

Carrie walked up to the next camp bay, Hans beside her, feet shuffling noisily against the gravel. El's ute came into view, her swag on the back. It was flat, unused. Her ute was also empty.

'That's weird.' Carrie put her hand up to shield her eyes from the morning light and glanced around. 'Where the hell is everyone?'

Surely they both weren't in the toilet? Carrie put her hand in the swag, it was cold. 'What is going on?' Her fingers pressed against her head as she willed her brain to think.

'They should have been back from the walk before it got dark but I crashed out and never heard anything.' She glanced up at Hans in hope.

'I put you to bed and then went to my van. I didn't see them. Sorry.'

'Did that mean they didn't get back from the walk?' *Fuck.* What if something happened? 'Oh shit. What if they're hurt? I need to find them.'

Carrie ran back to the van, unsure what she needed to be doing first. She felt suddenly out of her depth. Ellen was the best one in an emergency. Not Carrie.

'Do you really think so?' Hans' eyes bulged. 'What are you going to do?'

'I don't know. I can't think of any other explanation. Fin and Ellen didn't sleep here last night, so where are they?' she said, raising her hands. 'We need to pack some water and get down there. Shit, I hope they're okay.'

Carrie started rushing around in circles, trying to think of what to take. 'I wish Bodhi was here. I wish I could bloody call him. Stupid no signal. What's he going to think when he arrives and no one's here?'

'Maybe write them a note?'

'Oh, good idea.' Carrie stepped into the van and churned through the drawers looking for a pen and paper. Thank God

Hans was here. She'd hate to be doing this alone. She was trying not to panic but the mind could be a dark, unhelpful place when it wanted.

Fin and El didn't come back from Dale's Gorge walk. Gone to find them.

'What else should I say?'

Hans squinted, still adjusting to the morning light. 'Um, say to start from Fortescue Falls end, because if we need to get them out it will have to be up that staircase. Safest option. Also, if Fin and El do turn up, then they'll know where we are. Hopefully we'll cross paths.'

Nodding, Carrie added that to her note then placed it on the ground by the van door and held it down with rocks.

'Let's take El's ute.'

They set a brisk pace to her ute and in true trustworthy El style, her keys were still in it. Carrie hardly let the ute tick over before reversing out.

'I feel so awful. I didn't think anything would go wrong.'

'Don't be too hard on yourself. By the time you would have realised they weren't back, it would have been too dark to go find them without putting yourself at risk too.'

Hans was right, and yet Carrie still felt sick with an anxious dread. *Please let El be okay.*

'I wonder what's happened?' said Hans. 'Is Fin hurt or El? Or someone else? Maybe they got lost?'

Carrie hadn't even thought about Fin, she was too worried about her sister. Gee, what did that say about her? If she had to choose between Fin and El, it would be her sister every time. *Sorry, Fin!*

'I know. I can't help thinking someone has slipped, fallen down the side of the gorge. And snakes ... thank God El's a nurse. Maybe she had to stop and help someone?' After that bloke cliff-diving yesterday, she wouldn't be surprised if El had stayed to help a person in need. *Please let it be that.*

Carrie sped through the camp, hitting all the speed humps with a bang. They almost hit the roof every time but she wasn't slowing down for anything.

The car park at the entry to the falls was empty so she stopped nearly on top of the track to the lookout and jumped out of the car, running down towards the platform and stairs.

Bile threatened to rise as she descended the steps too fast and had to slow herself down. *You're no good to your sister wrecked.* Hans was two steps behind her, he never faltered.

'You must be pretty fit,' she said when they reached the bottom, pausing for a quick drink while her legs trembled. 'I feel like my legs are going to give way any second.'

Hans shook his head slowly. 'Me too. I walk lots but I'm not this kind of match fit.' He grinned weakly.

After a beat she said, 'Thanks for coming, I ...' Her words caught in her throat. She couldn't imagine doing this on her own, what she might find. His help could be handy, and his company was reassuring.

Hans put his hand on her arm. 'Let's go find them. Try not to think the worst.'

How could she not?

At first they had trouble trying to figure out where the track started and had to scoot along the rock edge around the pool at the bottom of Fortescue Falls then across where the pool overflowed and headed down the gorge. The stones were small and some were underwater, so Carrie's shoes ended up soaked.

'They needed a wash,' she said with black humour as Hans held out his hand to help her up a big rock on the other side of the pool.

'Look, this is the way.' He pointed to a sign. 'Follow the yellow dots. Let's go.'

Carrie had to step over rocks, balance on tiny ones sitting in water, hop like a frog between others, and was starting to worry how rescue teams saved anyone from down here.

'You know, maybe she's just stopped to help someone else who's injured, she is a nurse after all,' she said, more to herself but Hans mumbled an agreement. He'd grown quiet. She glanced back and saw the sheen of sweat along his forehead, his hair swept up high on his head. His water bottle was half-empty already.

'You okay?' she asked.

'If I'd known we'd be needed on a rescue I wouldn't have over-indulged last night. I had a few quiet ones in my van after I'd popped you off to bed.'

'Oh bugger.' Carrie pulled a face and hoped he wasn't suffering too badly.

Large white trunks grew out from cracks in the rocks, their roots like twisted fingers. Yellow straw from dead grasses covered rocks and dirt along with dead leaves. New green shoots pushed through the dead litter in sections until it spread into big clumps of green grasses. They added colour to the ochre landscape. The rocks retracted, and Carrie's feet found a dark chocolate-brown earth.

'This is not how I imagined taking this walk but circumstances aside, it's still so amazing,' said Hans. 'I'm in awe of this landscape. Australia is so beautiful and rugged.'

'I know. Seems a shame to run through it so fast.' Her anxiety was so high she felt like she was rushing through a mirror maze, trying to get to the end, to her sister, and trying not to panic.

God, if you can hear me, I'll be a better sister, I promise. Please just let Ellen be okay!

It felt like they'd been running – or the best they could manage through the twisty, uneven, sometimes tricky path – for ages.

'How long have we taken?' she asked, hoping Hans had a watch.

'Over half an hour at least. Do you think they're near the start?'

I hope not, she prayed again. Carrie saw movement up ahead and strained to see through the tall grasses as she manoeuvred around more rocks that were scattered about like giant LEGO blocks.

'El!' she yelled out, feeling a sudden urge to call out. It had to be her. *Oh, please let it be her.*

'I think that's Fin,' she shouted back to Hans and picked up her pace.

'Take it easy, you'll break something,' Hans yelled.

Carrie was past caring about herself, she just needed to know her sister was okay. Fin appeared around a large slab of rock – El's arms around his neck and legs around his waist.

'Careful,' Fin warned.

Carrie stopped just short of them, catching her breath and drinking in the sight of her sister, perched on Fin's back.

He backed up to a nearby rock and sat El down on it and then stretched his arms over his head.

'Oh my God, you're okay! I was so worried.' Carrie went to Ellen, who didn't look so great. Sweat dripped along her hair-line and her face was as white as the ghost gums nearby. She spotted the makeshift splint on her leg. 'Shit, what happened?'

'I broke it,' said Ellen. 'I'm glad you finally came.'

Carrie put her arm around her and kissed her head. 'I'm so sorry I didn't get here sooner. I passed out from dehydration last night and didn't know until this morning that you hadn't got back. I was freaking out.' Ellen gave her a weak smile. 'Do you need some more water?' Carrie handed over her water bottle.

'Here, Fin, looks like you're all out too.' Hans handed him his bottle.

'Thanks. Trying to carry El through here is hard work,' he said before throwing a wink at Ellen. 'But we're getting there.'

'I don't know how you're going to walk tomorrow,' El said. 'He's been nonstop trying to get me back. It hasn't been easy.'

She glanced at Fin and Carrie saw something she'd never seen before – awe, admiration, appreciation, affection? Had she finally worked it out with Fin? Maybe a scary night alone in a gorge in a remote area was enough to make anyone bond.

Fin's gaze was reflecting the same, but she'd always known he liked her sister. He spoke of her as highly as he did of Bodhi.

'You look like shit, Hans,' said Fin, passing his water back.

'Hmm, I've been better. Just glad we found you. What happened?'

Fin and El shared a glance. Fin opened his mouth, but El got in first.

'I was charging along like an idiot and my foot slipped into a hole and snap, down I went. Simple as that.' Ellen glanced at her lower leg. 'It was too dangerous to try and get out last night, but since first light we've made some progress. Well, Fin has – he's doing all the work.'

Ellen blushed and Carrie knew that having to use Fin as a pack horse would be killing her. She went above and beyond for others yet wasn't very good at taking it in return.

'I'm not the one coping with a broken leg and no painkillers.' Fin stood up straighter and stepped towards her. 'On that note, let's keep going. The sooner we get you to hospital the better.'

'It's okay, it's not that bad,' Ellen said.

Carrie wanted to call bullshit but decided that maybe Ellen was trying to convince herself more than she was them.

Fin sat back in front of her sister and Ellen wrapped her arms around his neck. Seeing them so intimate was strangely confronting.

'Carrie, can you lift my leg for me, please?'

'Got it.' She helped Ellen raise it up so Fin could put his arms around her legs to hold her in place. Her strapped leg shot out straight and made it look like Fin was a soldier with a big gun on his hip about to shoot down anything in his path.

'Do you want me to take the next shift?' asked Hans.

'Sure. But now could you walk in front of me so I can lean on you in the tricky spots? It's hard to keep my balance and hang on to El at the same time.'

Carrie walked along beside them, staring at her sister as she rode on her boyfriend's back.

'I'm so sorry I wasn't here sooner, El,' she said softly. 'I feel awful that you had to spend the night out here in pain.' Just imagining it gave Carrie the chills.

'You couldn't have done anything anyway, but I'm glad you insisted Fin come with me. I wouldn't have liked to do that alone.'

Carrie reached up and squeezed her arm affectionately. 'I love you so much. I'm so relieved you're okay.'

'I love you too, Care Bear,' she replied with a half-smile.

Fin stumbled and she clung to him tighter, his shirt bunching under her. Ellen's eyes were sad and she looked exhausted.

'I'm going to take care of you,' promised Carrie.

I will be a better sister. God delivered and so will I.

29

Ingi

INGI WOKE TO THE SUN AND BODHI'S HAIRY CHEST TICKLING her nose. His body was warm and the rhythmic thud of his heart against her ear was luring her back to sleep.

'Hey, gorgeous.' Bodhi's hand moved to her head as he gently massaged her scalp.

'Oh that's so good,' she groaned. 'I never want to leave.'

Waking up with Bodhi for the rest of her life would be a gift. As much as she didn't want to push him about the baby issue, she longed to know his answer. It felt like she had to hold her heart back from loving him so hard, but that would be like trying to stop a tsunami with your hand. She couldn't *not* love him, which was why she was prepared to walk away to give him the life he deserved. Even if he might not see it like that. Ingi just wanted him to be fulfilled and happy.

'But we should get back to the others,' said Bodhi. 'I feel bad dragging you away from El. Who knows when we'll see her again?'

His words were heavy and Ingi felt the emotional shift. 'I know. I feel the same. I loved our night together but I'm also ready to get back to her. I can tell she's not over Fin or the baby and I hate leaving her alone with the others.'

'I still can't wrap my head around all that. It's almost too crazy to believe. Ellen is the last person I'd pick to be going through this – Carrie maybe, but not Ellen.'

Ingi sat up. 'Your sister is still human, Bodhi. She has wants and desires like the rest of us, and can make mistakes like the rest of us. I know you're upset she didn't confide in you, but I don't think she's ever dealt with something of this magnitude before.'

'And Ellen being Ellen, she's trying to deal with it herself so no one else gets hurt,' said Bodhi. 'I'm just so worried about her. I want to smack some sense into her and yet hug her at the same time.' His dark eyebrows drew together, his forehead wrinkled. 'I'm worried about her. Moving up here, it's a huge change. I'm not sure running away is the answer.'

'It's not. It might give her breathing space but at some point she has to face it . . . when she's ready. That's why I don't want us to run away from our problems. I want us to always face our issues together, to share our burdens and work through all situations.'

Bodhi cupped her chin. 'I will honestly try my hardest.' He kissed her lips. 'I want kids with you, Ingi. Sure I'd love to have our own child but I understand where you're coming from and I respect your wishes.'

'Good, I'm glad you've been paying attention. Now, can we go spend time with El?' Ingi pressed her lips to his and he wrapped her up in his arms, dragging her down to him.

'Hmm, in a few minutes,' he mumbled.

When they finally returned to Dale's Gorge, Ellen's ute was gone.

'They wouldn't have gone to the other gorges without us, would they?' Ingi said, frowning.

'No, we would have passed them. Maybe they had to drive to Tom Price for supplies?'

But then they found the note.

'Shit, Bodhi, how did this happen?' Ingi's hands shook as she read and re-read the note.

'Let's go.' Bodhi was ready to run there now but Ingi latched onto his arm.

'Wait, let's take supplies. They might need water.'

Bodhi nodded. 'Oh yeah, good idea. Quickly.'

Ingi shoved water bottles into her backpack while Bodhi drove the van to the car park.

'Ingi, look, El's ute.' Bodhi parked two cars down from it. 'Doesn't look like anyone's back yet. That's not a good sign,' he said.

Piling out of the van, Bodhi took Ingi's hand, and they set off running to the stairs. His grip was helping ease the frantic concern rattling around in her head.

'Sorry, excuse us, emergency,' Bodhi huffed as they squeezed past a family with two small boys carrying floaties while their parents lugged the water and towels down the steps.

How they made it down so quickly without falling or hyper-ventilating, Ingi would never know. They stopped for a two-second breather before sussing out the way to the Dale's Gorge walk.

Scooting around the edge of the pool then across the bottom of the gorge they found the start of the walk and headed off at a pace. They'd been at it for fifteen minutes when Hans appeared around a corner.

'Did you find her?' Bodhi called out.

Hans smiled and sidestepped, revealing Fin behind with Ellen on his back.

'Oh sweet Jesus, you're okay! What the heck happened?' exclaimed Bodhi, as he and Ingi rushed towards them.

Ellen's face lit up when she saw Ingi. 'I got my foot stuck in between some rocks and I'm pretty sure I've broken something. So good to see you guys.'

'Right back at you,' said Ingi, giving her a hug after Fin gently put her down.

He staggered two steps and then sank to the ground himself.

'Why didn't you call the emergency number?' Bodhi asked.

'No,' said Ellen. 'I'm not calling people all the way from Tom Price for a broken bone. I'll drive to the hospital.'

Carrie rolled her eyes. 'She means, we'll drive her there and be her pack horses. But she has a point.'

'We are able. We got you, sis.' Bodhi gave her a wink.

'You turn up when all the hard work is done,' Fin scoffed.

'Fin will be dead on his feet – he carried me most of the way until Hans came along,' said El.

Ingi wondered how El was really feeling about it all. Having to cling to the man she loved while her sister walked beside them . . . Jesus. Poor girl.

While the water was passed around, they got caught up on the situation.

'So you spent the whole night down here? With a broken leg? Fark, sis, I feel so bad. I'm glad you were here, Fin,' said

Bodhi, giving him a clap on the back. 'Why didn't you go?' he directed to Carrie.

She blushed and kicked at a small rock. 'I had a headache and was really sunburnt after the incident yesterday.' She went on in great detail about the drunk-diving bloke. 'Then when we got back, Ellen was going to go on the walk on her own but I made Fin go too,' she muttered.

'Good call,' said Bodhi.

Ellen looked tired and had been quiet. It could be the pain, but she wasn't making eye contact with anyone. Fin wasn't overly talkative either and he was keeping a close watch on Ellen. Ingi was picking up a weird vibe – she couldn't put her finger on it but there was definitely an undercurrent.

Not surprising if Ellen and Fin had spent a whole night together. *Oh Ellen, you poor girl.*

Ingi moved to sit on the rock beside Ellen. 'How are you? *Really?*' she whispered.

She pressed her lips together and shrugged. 'Where do I start?'

Her eyes were huge, maybe from the pain, or maybe from a whole shitstorm of things she couldn't mention. Ingi wished they were alone so she could hear it all. The others were focused on working out a game plan to get Ellen the rest of the way back to the ute – it gave Ingi a small window of opportunity. 'Was it hard?'

Ellen shook her head. 'At the start it was. But then . . .' She sighed. 'He knows the truth,' she whispered.

Ingi's eyes bulged but she dipped her hat so no one would notice. 'Wow,' she mouthed.

That would explain Fin's reserved behaviour. Poor bloke was probably trying to internalise all the information.

'Let's keep going,' said Fin, standing.

He made his way to Ellen, his eyes only for her.

'You ready?' he asked tenderly.

Ingi felt the energy between them like static electricity and the hairs on her arms tickled. *Oh boy!* She was dying to know everything that had happened. She was excited for them, and yet she knew it would mean pain all over again.

'Nope,' said Bodhi. 'I've got this. Fin, you look like you've already lugged an elephant ten blocks.' He stepped in front of Ellen and gave her a goofy grin. 'Just like when we were kids, piggybacking you around the place like your own personal horse,' he teased. He turned his back to her and Ellen slipped her arms over his shoulders as he crouched down.

'I'm coming,' said Carrie, rushing to her side and helping to ease her leg up into Bodhi's arm. 'We've got a good system going,' she added.

Fin watched carefully, giving Bodhi tips. 'Yeah, hold her leg higher, saves it bouncing on your hip.'

Ingi wondered if Carrie had noticed the different vibe between El and Fin, or was she too preoccupied with her sister's wellbeing? Or did Ingi just have insider knowledge that made it easier for her to detect it? But the way Fin's eyes had melted when she took his hand . . . It was a lover's touch. *He knows.* And if he knew then he must feel the same way as El? God, she had so many questions.

'We're right behind you,' said Fin. 'Yell out when she turns into an elephant and I'll take over.'

As it turned out, Bodhi lasted ten minutes at a slow gruelling pace under her weight and the tricky terrain. Ingi didn't know how he could step up rocks with the extra weight, no wonder it had worn him out. How had Fin coped for so long?

'I think I better put you down here. I'll need a rest before tackling the pool crossing,' he said.

'Thanks, Bodhi. I feel so bad that you guys are having to lug me.'

'Don't sweat it, sis. This is great exercise. People pay money for these intense workouts,' he said, bending at the waist to catch his breath like he'd just run a marathon.

'The next bit will be a bit tricky,' said Fin. 'Carrie and Hans, you help guide us so we don't slip,' he added as he loaded El onto his back.

'Yep, on it,' said Carrie.

Ingi reached out and grabbed Bodhi's hand, stopping him from following.

'Here, have a rest and a drink of water,' she said.

Bodhi leaned against a rock and sucked hard at the water bottle. Ingi waited until the others were out of earshot, then stood on tiptoes, clutching onto his shirt to bring her close. 'Fin knows everything,' she whispered.

'What, how do you know?' he whispered back.

'El just told me.'

'What did he say about it?'

Ingi dropped back onto her heels and shrugged. 'I don't know. That's all she had time to say. He knows the truth.'

'Wow, sounds like they had an interesting night.'

'Didn't you notice the vibe between them?'

'Nup,' he said, face blank.

'You boys can be so blind. Anyway, this is a breakthrough. Hopefully together they can heal,' she said. 'Come on, we better catch up before they wonder what we're up to.'

His eyes sparkled. 'I don't mind what they think we're doing.'

Ingi slapped his arm playfully and marched ahead of him. The relief of finding them alive and okay had eased the tension from her bones. She even felt a flutter of hope. She was happy for Ellen. To have spent the night with Fin, being able to talk about it all, must have been a huge turning point. Maybe now she could come home?

Hopping across the rocks like a child, Ingi smiled as she pictured their usual morning coffee catch-ups and family dinners.

This trip had really turned out to be so much more than she'd expected.

Ellen would be coming home.

30

Ellen

'I'M SORRY YOU HAVE TO CARRY ME.' HER VOICE WAS LOW
as her lips brushed against Fin's ears, causing him to miss a step.

'Don't be,' he replied. 'I like it.' As if to prove his point,
he gave her good leg a gentle squeeze. 'I didn't really need the
others. I would have got you home safe.'

She laughed. 'Even if you won't be able to move tomorrow.'

'Totally worth every ache.'

It was hard to stop her heart from racing hearing him talk
like that. It was even harder to be clinging to his back and
not kiss his neck and nuzzle into him like she had last night.

They'd kissed long into the night, between talking about
the sky, work, the gorges, her leg. And then Carrie.

'I need to tell Carrie how I feel . . .' Fin paused. 'And then
I'd like to be with you, Ellen. I don't know if we should have
a grace period, or if that would just make things worse, but I
want to be honest with Carrie and tell her how I feel about you.'

'I know what you mean. And as scared as I am, Carrie deserves the truth from both of us.'

They'd grown quiet then, both playing out various scenarios in their heads, no doubt. How would Carrie react? How would the rest of the family react? Ellen hadn't set out to steal her sister's boyfriend, but would Carrie see it that way? Would she hate her? Maybe they should have a grace period? Fin had floated the idea of just breaking up with Carrie and then getting together with El later, but neither of them could live with the lies. At least for El it would be one less secret to keep.

'I think Carrie knows that we're at the end of our relationship,' Fin had said, 'but she's clinging on for dear life. I don't want you to worry. Carrie loves you more than me, she will come around.'

Ellen had drifted in and out of sleep, praying he was right.

—

'This bit will be tricky,' Carrie called out.

She'd taken it upon herself to be the scout, warning those coming down the track to move aside, and pointing out all the awkward spots up ahead. She was now directing the last section like a major in the army.

'That's what you said about the last bit,' said Hans.

When Fin had stepped into the water, Ingi had her hands on El's back and Fin was holding onto Bodhi's shoulders, while Carrie and Hans flanked them on either side like a protective cocoon. Together, they'd kept them both upright and slip-free.

'I can't believe we've almost made it,' said Carrie gazing up at the staircase.

The last hurdle.

Bodhi shot Ellen and Fin a glance. 'Anyone would think she'd carried you herself,' he muttered. 'Good job, Carrie.' Bodhi slapped her on the shoulder making her cry out.

'Hey, my sunburn.'

'I could probably get up the stairs by myself. I can hop,' Ellen said, keen to get this over with. The pain was constant and wearing her down – she just wanted to lie down and rest. Riding on Fin's and Bodhi's backs had worked well, but the jolting hurt and her legs and arms ached from hanging on. It was like she'd ridden a horse all day for the first time.

'The steps might be wide enough for the three of us if we take a shoulder each,' said Fin.

'On it,' said Bodhi, getting into position on her left side.

Fin took the right, and together they took most of her weight and she was able to hop on her good leg.

'Just try not to hit my bad leg,' she begged. 'I might pass out.'

'We'll be careful,' Fin promised.

It was a slow steady climb to the top and they stopped at the benches along the way for breaks.

'What are you going to do now, sis?' said Carrie. 'You won't be any good at the station with a broken leg. Maybe you should come home with us?'

'I don't know, Carrie. I can't think about it at the moment, I'm in too much pain.'

Ellen didn't know if she was ready to go back to Albany just yet. She might have told Fin her feelings but that didn't mean that all her problems were solved. She still had a big, big secret.

Carrie persisted. 'You said yourself that mustering was over. Surely they don't need you anymore. You can always go back to nursing.'

'I'm not sure I'm ready for that,' she said honestly. The pain was making her feel like she had the flu – her head was thick with fog and it was hard to keep focused. Thank God there were only two more steps and they'd be at the top.

'You guys get Ellen to the hospital, Carrie and I will follow,' Fin said, shooting Ellen a look that held the weight of a thousand bricks.

Her chest constricted. What was he going to say? Hope and fear surged through her.

'I'll take over,' said Hans, as he slipped under Ellen's arm and together he and Bodhi headed to the car park.

'Thanks,' said Fin.

Ellen knew Carrie had no idea what Fin was about to say. It made her stomach twist and that sick feeling returned, along with a thumping headache.

Bodhi finally announced, 'Nearly there, thank God.' He shot her a grin. 'I mean for your sake.'

'Sure you did,' she said, giving him a half-hearted grin back.

Ingi opened the door of the ute. 'You can take the back – you should be able to stretch out sideways.' Suddenly Ingi's eyes doubled in size. 'Oh shit,' she muttered.

Ellen heard the hard stomping steps behind her, followed by huffed breathing.

'Have you been having an affair behind my back?' Carrie screamed.

Ellen turned as her stomach dropped to the ground. Carrie's face was neon red, her hands fisted at her side.

'No, we haven't.' Ellen's heart stopped as Carrie's eyes fell on her. 'I promise you. But it's complicated.'

Carrie planted herself in front of her while Fin skidded in beside them, ready to throw himself into the ring if arms started swinging.

'It's complicated?' Carrie spat. 'What the fuck is that supposed to mean?'

'Carrie, this is about you and me, not Ellen. Let's go somewhere to talk now, please?' Fin begged.

But this did include her. It was all very complicated and confusing and Ellen's heart went out to her sister. How did she explain meeting Fin and the concert and then every moment since, trying not to fall in love with him? Right now, her sister didn't want to hear it. Her eyes were brimming with betrayal and hurt. Nothing would penetrate them.

'Carrie.' Fin tried to take her arm and move her away but she shook him off violently.

'Carrie,' El tried again. 'Fin and I never had a relationship. We met at the John Butler concert and slept together and that was it. A one-night stand. I promise. I didn't even know who he was until the day you brought him to Mum and Dad's,' Ellen tried to placate her sister.

Ingi was silently crying, Bodhi stood open-mouthed beside her, Hans was hiding behind him, and Fin looked pale and in shock. Carrie was still red with rage. They must have looked a spectacle, but Ellen had forgotten where she was or even that she'd broken her leg. The pain in her sister's eyes was overwhelming.

'You bastard,' Carrie yelled at Fin and slapped his face. It echoed across the gorge like a whip crack. 'You never said it was El who you slept with at the concert. Liar!'

'I didn't know who she was then. Carrie! I wanted to be with you.'

'I don't want to hear it, *Murray*,' she spat. 'I can't believe you. I trusted you both. How could you both do this to me?' The fight had gone from her voice, replaced by disbelief.

'It's complicated,' Ellen said through quivering lips.

'Fucken complicated, my arse. Just open your mouth and tell me the truth.'

Ellen never wanted any of this to happen. Why couldn't she have just kept her big mouth shut last night? Hell, she never thought Fin would tell her he loved her back. She'd lost all sense, had started dreaming of 'what if' and forgotten all about why she'd remained quiet in the first place – to stop this very moment. Had it all been for nothing?

'Ellen, tell her about the baby. She needs to know,' stammered Bodhi.

Someone gasped.

It was Ellen. A wail as her life unravelled.

She shot Ingi a 'what the fuck' look. 'You told him?'

Ingi's eyes welled with fresh tears. 'I thought you said Fin knew the truth . . . about all of it?'

Ellen shook her head.

'Wait, what do you mean, "baby"?' asked Fin.

Carrie's eyebrows shot up. 'What?' She stared at Ellen's belly. 'You don't look pregnant. What the hell is going on, El?'

'I lost her . . . at eighteen weeks.' Her eyes went to Fin, pleading, begging. 'I'm so sorry.'

'It was mine? Ours? How . . . how could you not tell me?' said Fin.

'How could I say anything? I thought you and Carrie were happy.'

'I can't believe you didn't tell me this! Our child? You had all last night to say something,' said Fin, the hurt in his voice tearing her heart into pieces.

Carrie's eyes narrowed. 'Who are you?' Shaking her head, she took a few steps backwards then turned and ran off between the parked cars.

Silent tears fell down Ellen's face as Fin stepped away from her too, his eyes mirroring Carrie's hurt and disbelief. The disappointment. All the things she'd tried to prevent.

'I'll go after her.' Fin gave a nod to Bodhi and jogged after Carrie.

Would he ever forgive her? Ellen didn't know if she could even forgive herself so she wouldn't hold it against him.

'Let's get you in the ute and off to hospital,' said Bodhi.

Hans nodded and helped manoeuvre Ellen into the back. She was so numb she'd forgotten about her leg. What was a broken leg after all this? Hearts were breaking everywhere – bones were much easier to fix.

'Yes, let's go,' said Ingi as she held the door open.

Ellen couldn't face Ingi just yet – she didn't feel very forgiving at the moment. The betrayal that Ingi had shared her secret, the one she promised not to tell, cut to the core.

It was like a hand grenade had been thrown with Fin and Bodhi's words. Relationships had been torn apart and it was hard to know if any of them would heal. 'I'll drive, you follow in the van,' Bodhi said to Ingi.

'Take care,' said Hans, sticking his head into the back of the ute. 'If I don't see you again, it was lovely to meet you, El. I hope things work out for you.'

All she could manage was a sharp nod and a half-smile before he shut the door and banged the top of the roof.

Ellen dropped her head back and closed her eyes. Her legs stretched out along the back seat with her back against the door. On the outside she might have looked like she was sleeping, but inside she was screaming, smashing things, pulling her hair out, sobbing and rocking and more screaming. She wanted to scream and scream until her lungs were raw. But what would it change? What would any of it do? What was done, was done.

It had all been for nothing.

31

Carrie

'CARRIE, WAIT UP.'

His voice was growing closer but she didn't want to slow down. Slowing down meant thinking over all the things that had been said. She wanted to stay angry, pissed off, stomping like an ogre because it felt easier, easier than confronting . . . well, all that.

'You okay?'

Shoulder to shoulder, Fin settled in beside her, matching her stride.

'Do you think I should be?' she snapped. 'I don't want to talk to you right now.'

'Look, wait, please?' He touched her arm and she stopped suddenly.

She let out a grunt. *May as well get this over with.*

'What?' she snapped.

He bent so his eyes were level with hers. 'I need you to know that I've always been honest. I told you I slept with a girl at

291

the concert, and we moved past that and went all in on our relationship. When I found out that girl was actually your sister . . . well, I was shocked and so was she, but neither of us wanted to hurt you. It was just a one-night stand and we both agreed to forget it ever happened. You and I were happy together. El was happy for you too.'

Carrie couldn't handle his raw and honest gaze. She dropped hers to the ground, trying to digest his words. 'I thought we were. Happy, that is.'

'Well, I know I was. But if I'm honest, that was in the early months. Then you moved in and it was still great . . . for a while, then it changed. I know you felt it too. We became bland, stuck in this routine, and I felt like I never really got to know you, Carrie. You wouldn't open up to me, you had this wall around yourself. And somewhere in all that I was falling for Ellen. I didn't plan it, I didn't seek her out. She was just her open, honest, caring self and I couldn't help it.'

Carrie tilted her head, open-mouthed. She didn't want to believe it or say it, but he was maybe a little bit right. A smidge. She had been closed off, but not on purpose.

'It was hard to give you my whole self,' she spluttered, standing straight, shoulders back, 'when I didn't even know who I was.' There, the truth was out. She'd finally admitted it out loud. 'But it's not like I pushed you away, or fell in love with anyone else. I can't just get over this . . .' She waved her hand at him. 'Whether you think we were nearly over or not.'

She turned around in a circle, hands on her head, pulse throbbing at her temples from angry crying. 'My head is spinning. I need time to process.'

After a few deep breaths she felt some control come back. She flung her hands down and went toe to toe with Fin. 'I still feel betrayed and lied to, no matter which way you spin it.' She squinted at him. 'My *sister,* Fin. My fucking sister.'

How would that make family dinners now? What would her friends think?

The sun was leaching the fight from her, it all seemed too hard now. Too hard to stay angry, too hard to think straight, too bloody hard full stop. 'I need time.'

'I understand. I never wanted to hurt you, Carrie. I still care for you a lot. I just couldn't help who I ended up falling in love with and I wanted to be honest with you.'

God she hated him for being so honest and understanding. His words had rung true about them being at the end of their relationship, only she didn't want to admit it. He was the one in the wrong, she wanted him to suffer a little more at least.

'You have broken my family, Fin. I don't know if I can ever forgive either of you.' Straightening her shoulders, she headed towards camp. 'Don't follow me.' The ten-minute walk would fry her further but it beat facing anyone at the moment.

It was a few minutes later when she heard fast footsteps behind her. She spun around, ready to let loose at Fin.

Hans' steps faltered, and she could see he was thinking about bolting like a scared mouse.

'I'm sorry. I thought you were Fin.' She tried to paste on a smile and hoped it didn't look like a snarl.

'He headed back to the gorge,' said Hans. 'Something about a swim to clear his head. I just wanted to see if you were okay?'

'It's all just a bit much at the moment.' *That was the fucking understatement of the year!*

'What are you going to do? Did you want to head to the hospital?' he asked.

'Hell no. I want to get far away from them all.' And how the hell was she going to do that when her only way home was in a campervan with Fin? Go with Bodhi and Ingi, those two traitors? Both of them seemed to know everything. Everyone knew everything . . . except Carrie. That's what stung the most. She was the last to know. Bodhi would always tell Ellen stuff but never Carrie. Being the youngest, she was always left out.

The only person she could handle being around right now was Hans. He hadn't lied to her.

'When are you heading off?' she asked, studying him.

'Um, well, I was going to pack up soon and take off.' He frowned. 'Why?'

Carrie was thinking fast, trying to find a way out of her situation. 'What are your thoughts on a travel companion?'

His eyebrows shot up. 'I'd never say no. Are you for real? Do you think that's the right thing to do?'

'I don't fucking care what's right at the moment.' Carrie shrugged. Running was what her sister had done. 'I don't want to go home, not with any of them. I just . . . I just . . .' She didn't know what else to do. 'Could I just catch a ride with you until I figure something out?'

'Really? You'd just ditch all this and come north with me?'

'Why the hell not? That's if you don't mind me tagging along, and if we get sick of each other I can just catch a flight home. Or get a lift with a truckie.'

The more she thought about it, the easier it seemed. The perfect solution. Besides, she doubted Fin would care what she did right now. He was probably off to the hospital to see El.

'You can come with me if you promise not to slap me?' said Hans, shooting her a smile.

She wanted to smile at his joke but there was nothing left inside but a twisted ball of rose thorns. So she nodded instead.

Carrie loved her family. The Suttons were the best family you could ask for. Well, she used to think so. It was like someone exploded the Sutton balloon and it could never be how it was, ever again. Did her parents know too? Had they *all* lied to her? God, she felt so stupid.

'I can get my stuff together real quick,' she said as they entered the road to their campsite. 'Thanks, Hans. You're a lifesaver. Beats hitching a ride with tourists.'

True to her word, it took five minutes to shove all her clothes and bits into two bags. She even took Fin's straw hat and his aviator sunglasses from the front dashboard. And because she wasn't a completely heartless arsehole, she left him a note.

Catching a ride with Hans. I'll find my own way home. Will let you know more when I get phone signal.

If he ended up in Tom Price with El then he'd have a signal there, and maybe by then Carrie would have figured out what she was going to do. With her bags in hand, she headed over to Hans' site.

'That was quick. Here, I made some room for your things. Sorry, it's not very big but this little van has everything I need.'

He pushed open the sliding door to reveal a bed behind tied-up curtains. The van was tidy enough. Could she stay in here for a day or two, maybe a week or more with Hans? Share his double bed? *Time will tell.*

Right now, the only plan was to get the hell out of here.

'Did you get to see much of Karijini? I hope I'm not cutting your trip short.'

Hans smiled as he climbed into the driver's side. 'No, this is my second visit, and why wouldn't you – it's magic. Besides you never know when you might meet cool people.'

Carrie snorted. 'Ha, I'm not sure my family fits the "cool" category. More like crazy.' Crazy was how she felt at the moment. One minute she was laughing, the next her lower lip was wobbling and tears threatened.

She sank down in the front seat of the old van. It smelled a little funky. There was probably no aircon and her window handle was broken. Yet as Hans steered through the campsite to the exit, Carrie didn't mind one bit. If anything, she felt like someone had taken their foot off her chest.

Scanning the landscape she didn't spot one person – probably all out sightseeing and swimming. Was Fin still swimming like he didn't have a care in the world? Was his conscience lighter now he'd spilled his guts, while Carrie was feeling chewed up and spat out? Were the others halfway to the hospital by now?

A wave of shame hit her. Tears fell down her face. It felt wrong not to support her sister, even though it was just a broken bone. Ellen had been with her for both her hospital visits – after she fell out of the tree, and when she broke her ankle in those heels. But that was before Ellen became a backstabbing sister.

'It seems I'm good at helping girls in distress.' Hans held out a tissue box that had been beside his seat. 'It makes more sense seeing Ellen upset when I found her on the side of the road. I wonder if she'd been thinking about the baby then?'

Carrie ripped out a tissue and blotted her face. *The baby.* 'I can't believe I heard that right. A baby?'

'Hmm. Bit sad. A miscarriage is very traumatic. My sister – she's ten years older than me – she lost three babies that way. Each one took a piece of her heart.'

Hans' words were soft but heavy, like a weighted blanket. They made her think.

Images of Ellen losing her baby flooded her mind as she stared blankly out the windscreen. How was it even possible? Ellen hadn't even looked pregnant. And to be – Carrie tried to count on her fingers from the concert – four months! She had all these questions but no answers. There was no way she was calling anyone to ask either. It might look like she gave a damn.

'I'm trying to think back . . . I don't remember seeing a bump,' she said, rubbing her head. 'Do people show at four months?'

'My sister didn't show much with her first but by the second she was huge. Ellen probably carried it well. Did she wear loose-fitting clothes? Dresses or big jackets and tops?'

Carrie thought back to Bodhi's party and Ingi's celebration night. 'You know what, she did. Shit, how blind were we?'

He shrugged. 'It's easy not to see something when you don't expect it.'

'I can't understand why she didn't tell me.'

'She didn't tell Fin either,' said Hans. 'It blew him away. He was so shocked.'

'Oh really?' She hadn't noticed, too busy being angry at him and El that it had clouded her vision. So El hadn't told him about the baby. Why not? What was she going to do when it was born? Pretend it wasn't his? Ever? Why would she do that? Why wouldn't she tell anyone that she was even pregnant?

God her head hurt. None of this made sense.

When Carrie thought of Ellen having a miscarriage by herself, it just . . . it hurt to think that she preferred to do that alone than confide in her own sister. Carrie would get over the Fin thing, but being pushed away by her only sister . . . that would take time to understand. It made El feel like a stranger, which made Carrie feel more confused about her own self.

Who was she now? A discarded sister and partner. Without those titles she felt even more adrift in life, no compass, no bearings.

Maybe it was time to find her own feet and figure out what it was that she really wanted in life. Hairdressing wasn't it. The apprenticeship had come up after Year Ten through one of her mum's friends, so she'd taken it without much thought if it was what she wanted, more excited to be getting out of school. Doing make-up wasn't it, either. None of those things made her happy. They were just jobs of chance, not choice.

Glancing at Hans, she wondered if this was the trip she needed to take. Sure, she wasn't alone, but Hans didn't know the old Carrie so it gave her room to search inside herself for her true self.

As the spinifex and gum trees flashed past over the rise and fall of red mounds, Carrie breathed in a deep breath and leaned her head back against the seat.

Today was a new beginning. A search for meaning and fulfilment. No looking back, no worrying about the future.

32

Ingi

INGI PARKED THE VAN OUTSIDE THE SMALL HOSPITAL AT TOM Price. She'd detoured to pick up some coffee, breakfast wraps and snacks, knowing they all might be starving. It had nothing to do with the fact she was nervous about seeing Ellen again. Okay, maybe it was, but who wouldn't be scared to see such disappointment aimed at you from your best friend. Ingi didn't have many friends, true friends that would rock up at a moment's notice to see if she was okay. That was Ellen. Just her.

The tiny hospital sat on the outskirts of town surrounded by bushland and there was only one other car in the car park. Ingi sighed. By now Bodhi would have Ellen safe inside and getting treatment, and was probably wondering where Ingi had got to.

'Just go,' she muttered before climbing out of the van.

She found Bodhi sitting in a chair in the waiting area.

'Oh, there you are. I was starting to worry,' he said, jumping up.

He bent to kiss her, his stubble tickling her skin. Ingi leaned into him, needing his comfort.

'How is she?'

'You can go see her,' he said as he took a coffee and gestured to his seat.

Ingi sat beside him, shaking her head. 'I don't think she wants to see me.' Her throat constricted as she said the words, her emotions on the cusp of flowing over.

Bodhi took a sip of his coffee and moaned. 'You are amazing. I needed that, thanks.' Then he dug through the bag she held out and found a wrap. 'You think of everything.'

'I got some fruit too,' said Ingi. 'Thought El might be starving. Depends if they put her on a drip or if she needs surgery. Do you know anything yet?'

'Nah, I left her to the docs and came to find you.'

'Did she say much on the drive over?'

He shook his head. 'No, I think the pain and everything got to her. She slept, well I think she did – she didn't reply to my questions.' Bodhi put his hand on Ingi's leg, giving it a gentle squeeze. 'She will get over it, Ingi. You didn't do anything wrong.'

Why do I feel so bad then?

'I broke a promise, Bodhi. You should have seen the way she looked at me.' Ingi would never forget it. Her eyes were on fire and could have cut her into two like Superman's X-ray vision.

She sipped her coffee and hoped the caffeine would help her feel better. Her foot tapped erratically on the floor as she stared at the five empty chairs and the usual pamphlets and posters.

'It's okay,' Bodhi said. 'You two are best friends and I know neither of you will let something like this come between you. Besides, she couldn't expect to keep something like that from her close family and Fin – he has a right to know he has a baby . . . had a baby.' Bodhi winced. 'I still can't fathom it.'

'You know she was just trying to protect everyone. If she'd told Fin, do you think he would have stayed with Carrie? Do you think Carrie and Fin would have survived that news?'

He rubbed at his eyes as he sighed. 'I don't know . . . but still, she found out she was pregnant, carried it and lost it with no family to support her. You wouldn't have known either if you hadn't stumbled across her that day.' His hands fisted. 'How did she manage all that alone?'

It was heartbreaking. 'She had Tanya. But I know what you mean.' Ingi sighed. 'I'm glad it's out in the open, less suffering in silence. Things usually get worse before they can get better.' Or at least she hoped so.

Bodhi was about to reply as a woman walked in with a small crying child in her arms, her blue eyes frantically searching the room.

'Have you guys been seen?' she asked breathlessly.

'Yes, we're fine,' Ingi replied and her heart melted watching this poor stressed woman as she rocked the child in her arms, muttering to him as she dropped kisses on his wiry black curls.

'Are you okay? Do you want me to go find someone?' she offered.

'Seb's had a bad earache and now his temp's up.'

Her white arms were stark against Seb's dark skin as she held his skinny legs and arms against her. Seb had tears streaming down his face and his cries were a steady moan, but his eyes were glued to the woman.

A nurse appeared. 'Julie, what are you doing here?' Her eyes dropped to the child. 'Oh, poor Seb. What's up, mate?'

'I'm really worried about him – his temp is up and the Panadol isn't relieving his pain,' she said, dropping a kiss on his forehead.

Someone burst into the waiting room, dressed in yellow hi-vis, his pale face red and sweaty. 'Julie, I'm here.'

She turned so he could see Seb in her arms. 'Oh hey, little man. Ear didn't get any better?'

'Come into the exam room and I'll take a closer look,' said the nurse.

The couple followed her down the corridor, Seb no longer crying.

'Poor little guy,' said Bodhi. His nose wrinkled as he tilted his head to the side. Ingi knew that thinking face well.

'I guess we'll be here for a while,' she said.

'I guess so. She may have to stay here overnight.'

Ingi stood up. 'Right. It's time we go and find out what the verdict is and sort out what to do from here.'

She strutted down the corridor, riding a wave of determination. Bodhi pointed out her room and Ingi hovered by the doorway. Ellen was in bed and a nurse by her side waved them in.

'I'm just about to take her for an X-ray, now the swelling has gone down enough. But I'll give you a few minutes.'

When the nurse left, Ingi dropped into a plastic chair.

'Hi,' said Ellen, avoiding her gaze as she picked at her shirt.

Ingi waited for her best friend to face her but Ellen didn't budge.

'Look, I know you're angry with me, you have every right. I just don't know how you're coping on your own, Ellen. I needed to share it with Bodhi because it was churning me up inside and it didn't even happen to me. It was tearing me apart. Keeping that secret was hurting you and I hated seeing you suffer.'

A tear rolled down Ellen's cheek, but her gaze never lifted. Ingi found her resolve fading. *Just look at me, dammit!* She wanted to scream. Shake some sense into her, but nothing she said now would register. Ellen had to find her own way out of her pain. Ingi might as well be shouting at a deaf person.

'I love you. And I'll always be here for you.'

Ellen lifted her eyes, blinked away more tears and murmured, 'I love you too. It's just a lot to take in. I tried so hard to avoid this from happening. It's all a bit of a shock.'

'Yeah, I'm sorry, sis, for opening my big mouth,' said Bodhi who was leaning against the door.

They both turned to him – he was red-faced and sheepish. Ingi turned back to El and knew she'd already forgiven her idiot big brother.

'How was Fin? Did you see him before you left?' Ellen croaked, glancing between the two of them.

Ingi wished she had a better answer. 'We didn't see him after he walked off after Carrie. I don't know how he's going, sorry.'

It wouldn't help Ellen to say that Fin looked as if his heart had been dug out by a fork. Carrie had been angry, but Fin – he was the one who'd really been hurt in the end. But there was no way Ingi was going to say that out loud.

Ellen pulled at the hem of her shirt. 'That's okay, I don't expect him to forgive me. I had plenty of time to tell him last night . . . but I couldn't. He'd only just told me he cared for me. I needed that, if just for a moment, you know? It's been hell, and to have those few hours where I felt normal . . . I know it's selfish but I didn't know if it would even work out. He might have got back to Carrie and changed his mind. What if it was just the ambience, the romance of Karijini?' She sighed heavily. 'I don't know. I've spent so much time guessing how people will react or what they'll think that I'm so confused and unsure.'

'You just think about yourself for once,' said Bodhi as he stepped closer.

His hands came to rest on Ingi's shoulders, bringing a shot of strength with them.

'Yep. Just worry about yourself for now. You're going to get this leg sorted and come home with us,' Ingi added.

Ellen sighed, as if the thought alone was tiring. She had been putting herself first – that's why she left Albany – but she hadn't been putting her mental health first. Locking stuff away wasn't moving forward, and Ingi hoped that now her friend could finally grieve, sort and process.

'I know. But we're not going home until you two have worn yourselves out exploring the gorges.' Her lips curled up but her smile was half-hearted. 'A ride home would be nice. We will have to stop in at Challa to collect all my stuff though.'

The nurse came back in, ready to take Ellen to X-ray.

Ingi stood up. 'Don't worry about all that, we have time. We're in no rush to head home.'

'Give us a text when you're back out or know what's happening, sis.'

Ellen glanced at her phone by the bed and nodded. All their phones were probably going crazy with messages and social media updates now that they had a signal.

Ingi took Bodhi's hand and they headed outside into the heat.

'See, I told you it would all work out. El could never hate you. She doesn't have it in her to hate anyone, even Josh,' said Bodhi, nudging her with his shoulder.

'Yeah, that's true.'

Bodhi scratched his head and glanced around. 'Shall we go for an explore around town while we wait?'

'Yes, let's walk.' She just needed to be doing something, anything to release the tension of the morning.

Neither spoke as they headed away from the hospital. Lost in their own thoughts, trying to process everything. Ingi was wondering what they'd find back at camp. Were Carrie and Fin even talking? What were they going to do?

'You know I thought my family was everything,' said Bodhi suddenly.

Ingi frowned. 'They are. I love your family.' Where was this coming from?

'Yeah, I do too. But I mean my life doesn't have to revolve around them. My happiness is you. You are my new family and that's all that matters.'

'Aw, Bodhi, that's beautiful. I feel the same way.'

'It got me thinking, you know? Especially seeing that foster family earlier. I know I could love any child – yours, mine, someone else's, it wouldn't matter. Families are what you make them. And I'm happy to make our own family, whatever that may be.'

Ingi nodded and wondered where Bodhi was going with this. Did he want to adopt? Foster?

He wiped his hands on his shorts before turning to face her. 'I want the kids, the dog, the home – I want all that with you in any form it comes. Adoption, surrogacy, donor egg, fostering

... whatever path we go down it doesn't matter because I know that you and I will love whatever child comes home with us. Maybe my swimmers are useless, maybe we only have pets. I don't care, I just know that together we can do anything.'

Bodhi reached over and wiped away her tears.

'What do you think? Will you marry me and make a little family? Or a big one – I'm open to ideas.' He frowned. 'But like, cap it at five maybe?'

Ingi laughed through her tears. Taking his face in her hands she kissed him. 'That sounds so beautiful. I want that too. Let's make our own family. And yes, I'll bloody marry you, Bodhi Sutton.'

'Woohoo,' he whooped. 'For real?'

'Yes, for real,' she said, pushing her glasses onto her head so she could wipe her face properly. 'I love you so much, Bodhi.'

To hell with everyone else. All she needed was him. His words were full of honesty and she believed that he truly would be happy no matter how their family grew.

'I love you too, babe. Can we be engaged now? I really want you off the market,' he added with a cheeky grin.

Ingi ran her fingers over his stubbly chin and into his short hair. His hazel eyes were brimming with tears and smouldering with heat.

She couldn't love him any more if she tried.

33

Ellen

SHE WAS LUCKY THAT BODHI AND INGI WERE TAKING HER home, broken leg and all. She'd stayed the first night in hospital, mainly because she was dehydrated, and they had to set her leg. Then she'd organised some accommodation in Tom Price, while Ingi and Bodhi could explore and make the most of their holiday.

'I'll be fine here until you're ready to leave,' she'd informed them.

'Are you sure?' Ingi had protested. 'What if you need help or –'

'I can order food to my door. I won't starve, Ingi, and if I do fall I can call the motel staff to help. Satisfied?'

Ellen had lain on the bed for days and spent most of that time watching crappy TV, sleeping, and deliberating about what to text Fin and Carrie. She knew nothing about their whereabouts and had no idea if either of them was back in signal range. She couldn't even contact Ingi to see if she'd seen them at Karijini – again, no signal. She'd had to wait until Ingi and Bodhi returned to her motel room.

Having the truth exposed had released the weight but it had been replaced by the loneliness of having lost both Fin and Carrie. Ellen knew there was no apology that would repair the fracture, not instantly. This would take time and many attempts. And what would she say? Would they even listen? They would need time, but how much?

Ellen decided to send them both texts with the same words. *I'm so sorry.*

Maybe one day they'd forgive her but for now it was a waiting game.

⟿

The moment she opened the door to Bodhi and Ingi, Ellen asked her burning question. 'Did you see them at all?'

'Gee, sis, no "'Hi, how were the gorges? Great to see you?",' Bodhi said sarcastically.

'Sorry. I do want to hear all about it. Come in and let's talk.'

They put her out of her misery first.

'Yes, we saw Fin. He was leaving, said he didn't feel like hanging around and was going back to Perth for a bit. And Carrie left with Hans.'

'What?' Ellen stared at Ingi. 'Carrie went with Hans? Where?'

Ingi shrugged. 'We don't know. She just left a short note for Fin and her stuff was gone.'

'Oh my God.'

'She'll be fine, sis. You know Carrie – she's like a cat, she always lands on her feet,' said Bodhi.

Ellen felt as if the earth had shifted on its axis. The world wasn't going to be the same anymore. It was hard not to worry about her little sister, jumping in with a random backpacker and heading off to uncharted territory. They hardly knew Hans – he seemed okay, but Ellen had seen enough scary movies to know it was the unsuspected one who did all the killing. *Now you really are being dramatic. Carrie is a grown woman and can take care of herself.* Ellen sighed and remembered Ingi's words from the hospital. 'Just worry about yourself for now.'

Straightening her shoulders and trying to look stronger than she felt, she said, 'It's time to go home.'

—

Challa Station was their first stop on the way home. Debbie gave them a tour, giving Ellen time to pack and finally tackle some important calls. Time to be a better person, to rebuild what she'd broken, and that meant putting her heart out there and facing the hard stuff. Hiding away wouldn't solve anything.

So she started with a phone call to her mum.

'Ellen, honey? Is it really you? What is going on with my family! Do you know how inconvenient it's been having no phone signal? Carrie's phone still goes straight to message bank, and so I went and saw the girls in the salon and they tell me she's taking a few weeks off. What are you guys doing up there? At least Bodhi called to tell me they got engaged.'

Ellen chose to ignore the Carrie bits and focus on the positive. 'It's so exciting. It was perfect, Mum. I have lots of photos to show you when I get home.'

'Home? You're coming home?' Her voice rose, clearly delighted.

'Yes. I have lots to sort out and lots to tell you, Mum. I don't really want to do it over the phone but it might be easier, and I'd rather you hear everything from me.'

And so she started from the very beginning – the concert with Murray aka Fin.

Lorraine was patient, letting her speak without interruption – well, besides a few gasps and groans.

'Oh Ellen, I can't believe all this happened. To lose your own child like that. All alone. I'm so glad you're coming home. I need to hug you,' her mum said through her sniffles.

'I know, Mum. I'll be home soon. I miss you.' And it was the truth.

Saying those words had caused a rush of warmth. *Home.* It felt so good knowing she was going home, and even though she was apprehensive, there was nothing to hide, nothing left to fear. Well, except Fin and Carrie not talking to her ever again. But she couldn't think about that at the moment. All her focus was on getting home and healing – her leg and her heart.

'Now I know why Carrie isn't answering her phone,' said Lorraine. 'She's one for sulking, but I'm sure she'll reach out when she's ready. I might send her a text and let her know I'm here to talk.'

'Thanks, Mum. I think she'd appreciate that.'

Next, Ellen tried to call Carrie but her phone went to message bank. *Of course.* So, she typed out the longest text in history. Hopefully Carrie would take the time to read it and understand just how hard she'd tried to put her first.

To be pregnant and not have you by my side to share it with was so hard. Then when I lost Celeste, all I wanted was you – but how could I expect that after what I'd done? I don't want to lose you over a guy. You're my sister and I love you. I'm so sorry I fell in love with Fin. I tried hard to fight it. To stay away.

Ellen kept adding to the message until she'd said everything she wanted and then pressed send. It had been nearly two weeks and Carrie still hadn't made contact. Bodhi hadn't heard anything either, but then he got an emoji about four days ago – it was the hand pulling a middle finger. At least they knew she was okay.

Fin's had been the toughest. Ellen decided a letter would be the best way as he might not take her call, and besides, talking with him would be too hard. As it was, writing her feelings down on paper was tricky enough. And letters were personal and heartfelt.

Dear Murray, I love you so much. I'm sorry I didn't tell you about our child and I'm sorry I couldn't keep her. I lost our baby. I wished her away.

Ellen scribbled out the last sentence and stared at the page before screwing it up and starting again.

Dear Murray, that night at the concert and every meeting with you after that just cemented my love for you, no matter how hard I tried to fight it. But I had to for my sister as her happiness was more important than mine.

He knew most of this. She'd said as much when she was stuck in the gorge with him, but it seemed fitting to explain it again.

I still love you, very much. I understand if you don't feel that way after I kept our baby a secret. I was so torn about what to do. Tell everyone and ruin our family, or keep it a secret and leave you both to be happy. I was going to leave Albany and raise her by myself, but I knew there'd be questions and more lying needed. I was so conflicted, and I fear that's why she died. I feel responsible for her death, as if she could sense my uncertainty and gave me an option that solved all of it. But it didn't, because by then I was already in love with her, and I lost a piece of my heart when she died. I don't know if I'll ever be whole again.

It was so hard to face everyone after that. So much guilt. So I ran away, but it didn't solve anything. I'm glad it's all out in the open now, even if I've lost everyone I love because of it. If only I'd just expressed my feelings to you early on then all this might have happened differently. It's weird how we do these hurtful things to protect the ones we love because we think it's the best option at the time. Regret is a horrible thing. I regret the hurt I've caused but I can't say I regret the concert, and I don't regret carrying our baby girl as I'll never forget those magical moments.

Ellen had to pause to mop her eyes so she could see to finish off the letter.

I'm so sorry, I hope one day you can forgive me. Love always, Ellen.

There were teardrops smudging the pen in spots, but it would have to do. She could rewrite this letter a hundred times and never get it perfect. This would be a start.

Ellen folded it up and slipped it into an envelope. She would post it in Mount Magnet on the way home.

Finally righting her wrongs was helping her mentally. Each breath seemed to chip off more bits of the battered and bruised Ellen, revealing a new strong woman ready to take back her life.

34

Carrie

CARRIE SAT ON THE GRASS IN THE WARMTH, ARMS LOCKED around her knees as she stared at the flat blue ocean visible between palm trees that seemed as though they'd been dropped on the lawn like bowling pins. Some were straight, others leaned this way and that, crisscrossing through her view.

The Dampier coastline was silent and still, so peaceful. It was such a world away from Albany. Even her skin had turned caramel over the last month.

Her phone sat on the grass beside her, but she didn't feel the urgency to pick it up and scroll like she used to. Most of that was thanks to Hans and his backpacking ways. Carrie never thought she'd find herself volunteering at the Juluwarlu Art Group in Roebourne, helping to preserve Yindjibarndi knowledge and history. Hans had opened her eyes to a whole new world. The thing she'd loved the most was spending time with the children. She loved the brightness and freedom that exuded from their gorgeous faces. Just a few days ago a skinny

FIONA PALMER

boy with long dark lashes and the biggest chocolate eyes said, 'Hey miss, you take my photo!' and he'd smiled a big cheesy grin while the other kids laughed and jostled to be next. They loved to hold her hand and show her things. 'Miss, miss, see 'ere. Goanna been 'ere.'

Who would have thought following tracks in the sand would be so much fun? The kids seemed to take great delight in teaching her what they'd learned from the elders. And without knowing it, they'd taught her the importance of family and culture and beliefs.

Time had flown by so quickly – before that they'd been up at Port Hedland. Now she was sitting in Dampier, home of Red Dog, and she'd never felt so contented, so fulfilled. That weird sensation that had left a hole for years had been filled, and she wasn't entirely sure why. Maybe no pressures from her business, no keeping up appearances and doing what she thought was expected of her? Maybe it was just having time by herself, to sit, breathe, find out what gave her energy and fulfilment. Certainly living this carefree, unstructured life suited her.

'Another glorious day.'

Hans dropped down beside her, his hair up and his body a golden brown. Carrie smiled, feeling a kindred spirit to this man. Her hair was out, unbrushed and wild. Thongs were her footwear of choice these days and shorts and singlets what she lived in. Carrie had donated her make-up to a young Aboriginal woman she'd met in Port Hedland while Hans had been searching out information on the flatback turtle monitoring program he'd heard about. The girl had asked if she was lost, because Carrie had been standing in the street just soaking everything in.

'I'm not lost . . . well, I don't think so. What's good to see here?' she'd asked her, and the girl had given her a list of things to see while they walked together.

'Where are you headed?' Carrie had asked eventually and found out she was applying for a job as receptionist at a real estate agency. So Carrie asked if she could help do her hair and create a good first impression. Next thing they were back at the van and Carrie was doing the girl's hair and make-up, showing her how to apply it. 'Here, you keep these. If you get the job then you can look ready for work every morning. You'll need them.'

'For real?'

Carrie remembered the feeling that came with making someone's day. 'Here, take it all. Maybe you have friends who could use it.'

Carrie didn't want it anymore. It was so much easier living without feeling like she had to be perfect all the time. Like an actress always ready for someone to shout 'action' at any moment.

'I like Dampier,' she said to Hans now. 'It's so pretty.'

'So are you. You look gorgeous when you're content,' he said with a grin. 'Better than the Carrie I first met at Karijini.'

She laughed. 'Who'd have thought the backpacking, volunteering life would suit me?'

'So you're not planning on heading home anytime soon?'

Carrie glanced at her phone and sighed. 'I think I need to. I have commitments, staff, things to sort out. I keep reading Ellen's text and I feel like a shitty sister. I didn't even love Fin the way I think she does so I can't help feeling awful for punishing her.' Carrie rested her chin on her knees. 'But once I've sorted out the family drama and my other life, I want to get back to doing more of this.' She opened her arms and breathed. 'Just being me.'

'Sometimes when we strip back all the expectations and material things and just live for what's important, it can reveal a deeper self-worth and acceptance.'

Carrie nodded. 'Totally. I feel good in my own skin finally. I want to go home and make up with Ellen, and then I want to sell my salon and do more photography – maybe teaching the local kids skills like we have here. I've never done anything that felt so worthwhile and rewarding.'

'Now you see why I love doing what I do.'

He put his arm around her, and they sat there admiring the view, drinking in the perfection of it all.

'Ingi and Bodhi tried calling a few times and left messages to call them back.'

'Sounds serious,' Hans replied. 'Did you call back?'

Carrie nodded. 'They're having an engagement party and want us to be there. You did say you wanted to see Albany?' She gave him her best tour guide smile. 'Want to come with me?'

Hans squinted at her. 'Is this because you need my van to get you there?'

Carrie rolled her eyes and he chuckled.

'When is it?' he asked.

'In a few weeks. What do you think? Is the van up for a long trip south?'

'Considering I've heard so much about this place and the white sandy beaches, I think I'd better. I was also looking at doing a harvest down in the Wheatbelt. I've heard they're short of workers – maybe I could suss out some work prospects.'

'Awesome, sounds like a plan.' And it would be nice to have his company, not that she wasn't ready to face everyone – she was. It was more that it would be good to have someone who had her back for the fifty million questions that were sure to be coming from her family.

Carrie picked up her phone and texted Ingi back.

Hans and I will be there. See you then xx

Carrie thought about texting Ellen, or even calling, but turned off her phone instead.

Some things were just better done in person.

35

Ellen

DIPPING HER TOES BACK IN ALBANY HAD BEEN STRANGE. FOR one, the weather was a little on the cold side – her fingers had frozen and her nose glowed as red as Rudolf's for those first two weeks. Yet the sound of the waves crashing at Middleton Beach while she sipped her cappuccino had soothed her soul. It brought back memories of Mr Whippy ice-creams there as a kid. Of seeing the whales out off the point and dolphins surfing the waves. Of the huge ANZAC dawn service that their dad always made them get up for every year. Of driving down Bridges Street with all its twists and turns. It was hard to leave a place that was ingrained in every memory.

The past few days, finally moving out of her mum's place and back to her own, had been therapeutic. With her house being rented, she'd moved in with her parents, and given her leg the time it needed to heal. Ingi and Bodhi had offered a bed at their place but she'd knocked them back.

'I think I should spend some time with my folks and let you and Bodhi enjoy this time together. It's special,' Ellen had replied, gesturing to the ring that hadn't left Ingi's finger since the day after 'the explosion'. That's what Ellen had been calling it in her mind because that's what it was – hearts had been torn apart and minds shattered.

Being back in her family home had been so good. It helped her find her footing – well, one foot – and her connection to her old self. Even better was the news that Carrie and Hans were coming to the engagement party, which would make it nearly two months since 'the explosion'. It was the longest time she'd ever gone without seeing Carrie. She was excited, but also apprehensive. Carrie had sent a text over a week ago that just said, *We'll talk when I get home*. So ominous.

⌁

The night of the engagement party seemed to arrive quickly – maybe it was the build-up of seeing her sister or the excitement of a celebration, or maybe the prospect of running into Murray, she wasn't sure. One good thing – her cast had come off and she was back on her land legs.

'I'm so glad Carrie's coming,' said Ingi as they set up the extra chairs in their backyard. 'I hope it means she's moved on a bit.'

Ellen had loved helping Ingi decorate. There was plenty of room for all the guests in their large backyard. It was funny how both Bodhi and Ellen had found places with lots of space. Growing up with a large paddock to play in had obviously rubbed off.

Bodhi walked out the back door, clean shaven and looking handsome in a crisp white shirt and tan pants. But there was a grim expression on his face.

'Um, Ellen um . . . can you take a seat for a moment?'

'Oh dear, did I go overboard with the decorations? Too many balloons? Not enough fairy lights maybe?' she said, teasing him. It had been his catchcry the whole day, 'Not more balloons?'

'You're not funny,' he said seriously.

Bodhi sighed heavily and she frowned. 'Just spit it out, bro.'

He winced. 'I asked Fin to come tonight. He's still my best mate and I really wanted him to be here for this. I hope you don't mind?'

Ellen hadn't been expecting that. Sure, she'd wondered if she might bump into Fin at the shops or at Bodhi's, but it hadn't happened. Either he was unaware she was back, or he knew and was in hiding. She wasn't about to chase him down – he knew where she was when he was ready, that's if he'd ever be ready. Maybe he was done with her for good.

Oh, that thought made her suddenly nauseous. Would he totally ignore her tonight? Could she handle that? Was it what she deserved? Probably.

'How do you think he'll react to seeing me?' said Ellen.

Bodhi's face tinged pink as he took a nearby seat. 'I've been in regular contact with him, making sure he's okay. I'm sorry, sis, I didn't know how to tell you so I just kept it to myself. He's been in Perth for a while but he's come back for tonight.'

'Oh.' What was he doing in Perth? How long had he been there? 'How did he take it?'

'Better than I thought. He's such a genuine guy, El. His heart is so big – I think that's why your news hurt him so much. I know how much he's wanted to start a family.'

Shame threatened to claw its way through her and instigate a panic attack, but she breathed deeply and tried to let it go. *You can't change the past, remember. Look forward, not back.*

'You okay?' Ingi asked as she touched her shoulder.

'I am. I won't lie and say it'll be easy, seeing him again. He probably hasn't read my letter if he's been in Perth.'

Oh no, what if he hadn't? Would she have to say all that again? Well, maybe face to face was the right way to do it. She was stronger now, she thought, as she tried to stop her hands from shaking before anyone noticed.

'Is this dress okay?' she asked suddenly, glancing down and realising it was the same one she'd worn to the concert when she first met Murray. *Oh.*

'You look stunning. I've always loved that dress on you,' said Ingi.

'Should have done something about your monobrow though,' Bodhi teased, poking her between the eyes before darting away with a chuckle.

'Whatever,' she yelled after him. But he'd put a smile on her face, if just for a few seconds.

'He's such a child,' said Ingi, yet the adoration on her face implied otherwise. 'Let's finish setting up. I think all the parents will be turning up any minute.' She nervously ran her hands down the white strap dress overlaid with lace that resembled daisies. She'd topped it off with a pale blue knitted cardigan that was her favourite.

'I love your dress, where did you get it?' Ellen never saw Ingi in dresses – ever practical, she preferred jeans and hoodies.

Ingi looked self-conscious. 'Your mum bought it for me. We had some bonding time on Monday – in other words, shopping and coffee. God, I'm such a pushover. Next time I'm only shopping with you.'

'No, don't be like that. Mum did good. She's an artist, remember – she knows how to put things together and that dress is perfect.'

Ingi blushed. 'Your brother thought so too. It nearly came off not long after I put it on.'

Ellen stuck her fingers in her ears. 'La la la la,' she cried.

'We have guests,' Bodhi bellowed from the back door.

They quickly finished putting out the last of the chairs around the gas heaters, which were on full bore. Ellen gave the backyard a once-over. The huge patio was strung with lights, as was the large lilac tree in the back corner, which made the yard feel romantic. Balloons hung in bunches around the place and a table against the wall of the house was covered with a white tablecloth and laden with meats, cheeses, nuts, dried fruit, dips and crackers of every sort. Beside that sat a smaller table with another white cloth, holding a two-tiered cake in white topped with blue hydrangeas, Ingi's favourite. She had a thing for blue, maybe from her love of the ocean – who knew?

As the guests started filling up the backyard, Ellen was kept busy opening bottles of champagne and wine, pouring glasses, and making sure the guests were looked after. Ingi's parents and uncle had arrived, along with her cousins and Ellen's parents and their cousins. No Carrie or Fin yet – she'd been watching the door nervously.

'Relax,' Ingi muttered to her as the sun started to disappear.

'I'm trying. My anxiety is growing with each passing second.'

A weird sensation prickled along her skin and Ellen glanced across to the back door, past the heads of the milling guests. Sure enough, there was Fin hugging Bodhi and chatting away happily. God, he looked good.

'Breathe, Ellen, breathe,' Ingi hissed.

Ellen sucked in a breath and turned away, her heart racing from the rush of love that consumed her. She'd tried so hard to move on from him, but time and time again it had proved futile. He was the flame, and she was a mere moth.

'Hello, stranger.'

Ellen glanced up, shocked at the voice she recognised. 'Oh my God, Hans. It's so good to see you.' She threw her arms around him then jumped back scanning around him for Carrie.

'She's here,' he said, gesturing to the woman standing by the gas heater rubbing her arms. 'Go catch up, we can chat later.'

'Thanks, Hans. I'll hold you to that.'

Ellen had to blink, unsure of who she was seeing. It was Carrie, the same long dark mane but wilder and she had a natural glow. Ellen took tentative steps towards her, drinking in the simple yellow dress and make-up-free face.

'You're wearing thongs?' That was not what she expected to be the first words out of her mouth upon finally seeing her sister.

Carrie laughed. 'Hey, sis. I missed you too.'

They stood staring at each other, so much said and no words uttered.

'I'm so sorry,' Ellen said eventually as the well of tears began to build.

Carrie shook her head as she reached out and pulled Ellen into her embrace. 'Don't be. You're my sister and I love you. Nothing will ever change that.'

Carrie's arms were so tight around her and yet Ellen felt like a bird soaring in the sky. They hugged for a long time, before they pulled apart, holding hands and studying each other with glassy eyes.

'You're so brown. And . . . different?' Ellen couldn't put her finger on it but Carrie just seemed so relaxed. Normally she'd be running around taking photos and trying to talk to everyone at once.

'I'm frozen. I forgot how cold Albany is, or maybe I'm just used to the northern heat now.'

They fell silent and then Carrie dragged her over to a quiet corner of the patio.

'I have so much I want to tell you,' she said in a rush.

'Me too. I want to explain everything.'

Carrie shook her head. 'No need, I read your text, quite a few times actually. I'm just so devastated I wasn't there for you. I know I can be a selfish cow.'

Ellen's mouth dropped open. She hadn't been expecting that. 'Who are you?' she said, squinting at this other Carrie.

Her sister smiled. 'I think going north with Hans was the best thing I could have done. I haven't been happy, El, not for a long time, and I couldn't work out what was missing. I didn't know who I was, and there was this emptiness in here,' she said, touching her heart.

'I thought you'd still be angry.'

'You did me a favour, seriously. Sure, I was angry at first – who wouldn't be? But as I had time to find out who I was and what I wanted in life, I began to understand what was more important. And the truth is that I was never "in love" with Fin. He was my security blanket of sorts. I felt safe with him and I thought he'd give me the life I was supposed to have, even though it didn't feel right for me. So please don't worry about me anymore. I'm honestly the happiest I've been in such a long time. If Karijini didn't happen, I'd still be that sad and lost girl.'

'Wow, I had no idea you felt like that, Carrie. I feel like a bad sister for not realising.'

'Well, can we call it even then? 'Cos I feel bad for not being there for you in what should have been a magical time. I know how much you want kids, sis. I'm so sorry. I've been meaning to say all this for a while but it's way better in person than over shitty reception.'

Ellen couldn't stop staring at this person before her – eyes bright with life, relaxed smile on her tanned face. Yet it was still her baby sister, with that smattering of freckles and the little nose scrunch she did when she was thinking. 'I'm so glad you're here. I've missed you.'

'Me too. I have so much I want to tell you . . . and Fin. Is he here?' Carrie surveyed the area before grinning at Ellen. 'We must have lunch tomorrow so you can catch me up on everything.'

Ellen grimaced, realising what Carrie was implying.

Carrie tilted her head in surprise. 'What? Are you two not together? I just assumed . . .'

'Fin's been away in Perth, Bodhi said. I've not spoken to him since . . . then. I'm pretty sure I'm the last person he wants to see.'

'Oh no.' Carrie frowned and pulled Ellen into her arms again. 'I'm sorry. Do you still love him?' she whispered.

Ellen could only nod. 'I wish I didn't. Life would be much easier, but my heart refuses to give him up.' Even now just talking about him had her pulse thumping like a stampede.

'Oh, I see him. Still hot as ever. Well, he's here, that's something. He's not the type to ever hold a grudge, El. I'm sure of it.'

'I hope you're right, sis.' Ellen really wanted a glass of wine she could scull and drown the butterflies going crazy in her stomach right now. 'It's so good to see Hans again,' she said, changing the subject. 'You both seem really happy.'

Carrie threw her head back and laughed. 'Oh my God, sis. We're not together.'

'What? Really?' Ellen squinted as if that would help her see what she'd been missing.

'Oh believe me, I did try to go there. I kissed him not long after we left and it was a disaster.'

Ellen screwed up her face. 'What happened?'

Carrie rubbed at her arms. 'Well, for one, he said he wasn't going to be anyone's rebound. And two, he much preferred our brother.'

Say what now? Ellen's mouth dropped. 'Really?' She spun around and sought out Hans, who was indeed standing next to Bodhi and Fin with a sparkle in his eye. 'How did I not see that before?'

'I know, right? I didn't either. Anyway, once we cleared that up we just became the best of mates. Who knew I'd find what I needed from a gay backpacker in the Pilbara.'

Ellen was gobsmacked. When she'd envisioned her reunion with Carrie, this was not how it went down. Her sister seemed so grounded and happy and forgiving. She was really looking forward to some quality sister time with her. It had been too long.

Carrie's cold fingers brushed her arm. 'Hey, are you going to go speak to Fin?'

'I hope to try,' she said honestly. *That's if he'll let me*, she thought.

At that moment their eyes met and the whole world slowed down. Scenes from their time together played out in her mind like a drama on Netflix – the kisses, the touches, the lingering looks. Only now Ellen couldn't read him, or was she too scared to try?

The moment was broken by the sound of someone clinking glass with a knife.

'Can I get everyone's attention?' said her father.

Colin moved to the front of the area where a big blackboard stood with the words in chalk: 'Welcome to our engagement.'

'I just want to say how happy we are to be here tonight and welcome you all to celebrate with our wonderful son and his beautiful bride-to-be. Ingi, you're already like a daughter to us – for the happiness you bring Bodhi, the devotion and love, and not to mention how close you are to Carrie and Ellen. You really are a perfect fit to our family.'

Lorraine moved to the blackboard.

'Bodhi and Ingi, up you come,' said Colin and the crowd watched as the couple made their way to his side. 'I'd like to be the first to congratulate you on your engagement and welcome Ingi to the Sutton family.'

Suddenly gasps from the crowd had everyone standing on tiptoes and craning their heads to see what those at the front had seen. When she caught sight of the blackboard, Ellen also gasped.

Lorraine had wiped off the word 'engagement' and written 'wedding'.

'What the hell!' She turned to Carrie. 'Did you know?'

36

Ellen

'THAT'S RIGHT, FOLKS, WELCOME TO BODHI AND INGI'S wedding,' Colin yelled over the crowd.

Carrie's mouth hung open. 'Bloody hell. They kept that a surprise.'

'Carrie and Ellen, can you come forward? And Fin and Tom.'

Colin had the best booming voice for the MC job.

Ellen and Carrie made their way through the crowd to where Lorraine had rearranged the area, and Fin and Tom brought in an arch covered with flowers. Where had that been hidden?

Ingi grinned sheepishly as they approached. 'Will you two be my bridesmaids?'

'Of course,' said Ellen, still trying to take it all in.

Everything was moving quickly. They were shuffled into position beside Ingi, while Tom – Bodhi's mate from school – and Fin were moved to his side. Then a woman appeared with a microphone and speakers. Ingi shrugged off her cardigan and gave it to Lorraine in exchange for a bouquet of blue hydrangeas.

'Welcome to the wedding of Bodhi Jay Sutton to Ingrid Shanae Byrne. My name is Alyse Carmen, I'm the celebrant who will unite this beautiful couple.'

Ellen stood proudly beside Carrie and Ingi as she watched her brother marry the love of his life. Tears pooled in their parents' eyes and smiles lit up the faces of every guest, making it hard not to get emotional. Ellen snuck a glance at Fin, who was watching them with a grin from ear to ear. Maybe there was hope that they could be friends or at least get to speaking terms, or was that too much to ask? Ellen felt over-whelmed with gratitude at already getting her sister back and felt as if things might just be okay. Was adding Fin to that list being too optimistic?

In that instant, Fin's eyes rested upon her and it took her a moment to glance away, face heating, her nerves rattled.

'You may now kiss your bride,' said Alyse and the crowd cheered as coloured rose petals rained down.

Both parents from both sides were throwing them, which meant they were all in on the surprise marriage. It was so like Bodhi and Ingi not to want a big wedding, but Ellen had thought they would want it on the beach.

'Time to cut the cake,' Tom cheered at the newlyweds who were still kissing.

As if they were all alone, Ingi and Bodhi gazed at each other with such devotion and passion that Ellen felt like bursting into tears she was so happy for them.

'We need to talk.'

Hairs on her neck prickled at the sound of Fin's voice. He stood by her side, his muscled arms crossed and his aftershave encompassing her like the scent of rain in a downpour.

'I know. I'll answer all your questions,' she said quickly. He must have a million of them.

He leaned in closer. 'I'll meet you down by the lilac tree in a minute.'

He walked off the edge of the patio, the darkness licking at him until it eventually swallowed him whole.

Ellen finally got to the newly married couple, hugging them both.

'Cheeky buggers. I hate surprises, but I must admit this one was pretty cool. I'm so happy for you both.'

'Thanks, El,' said Ingi. 'You don't know what it means to both of us to have you here. I'm so glad you're home.' She hugged Ellen tighter.

Ellen headed into the night across the long stretch of lawn, using the fairy lights to guide her to the lilac tree. Strand upon strand of tiny twinkling lights zig-zagged back and forth around the tree and nearby shrubs and Bodhi's shed. It was a little hidden oasis away from the party.

'Ellen?'

She stood up straighter, his voice alone turning her to jelly.

'Hey,' she said nervously as Fin stepped out from the shed and sat beside her on the garden wall

Her mind went blank just looking at him. *Stop drooling and think, Ellen.* 'I . . . um . . . wrote you a letter but I didn't realise you weren't in Albany,' she blurted.

Fin seemed calm and collected, while Ellen felt like she had a million ants crawling over her skin.

'I've been studying in Perth. I finally took the plunge.'

'Studying what?' Ellen was confused.

'My local brewery idea. After . . . you know . . . I just felt like I needed to focus on what I wanted. So, I finally told my dad about the brewery and I've been working towards it ever since. I'm taking some courses in micro and craft brewing , and Dad's helped me look for some land just out of Albany. We've found one property that's promising with an awesome view. We're sorting out an offer. It's all coming together so quickly. Some days I can't believe it's finally happening.'

'Wow, that's amazing, Fin. I know you'll make it successful.'

'Thanks, Ellen. You really gave me hope that it would happen one day.'

She was delighted for him, but her chest remained crushed with the weight of her apology. If she didn't get the words out soon she just might die from lack of oxygen. 'Look, I know you probably never want anything to do with me again.' Hey, it was a miracle he was even speaking to her now. 'But at the time I thought I was doing the right thing. I didn't mean to hurt anyone, especially you.' Ellen dropped her eyes, watching the fabric of her dress twist in her fingers.

'I know. I got your letter.'

She jerked her head up. 'You did?'

'Yeah. When my sister said it was from you, I had her express post it to me.'

'Oh.' That meant he'd read all her outpouring of love and sorrow. Heat crept up her neck to her face.

Fin's hands moved to hers, covering them in warmth as he drew closer. 'It was a shock, and I took a while to calm down and realise it had hurt you way more than it had me.

You were the one who suffered alone. I wasn't sure if you'd even want to see *me* again. I wasn't sure if that would bring back too much pain, or where I even stood anymore. But it was learning about ... *our baby* that made me realise that tomorrow is not a given. We need to live our dreams today. Hence the step towards the brewery.'

'That's so good to hear,' she said with relief.

'Ellen?'

His voice was soft, his hands still on hers. He gave them a squeeze before returning them to his lap.

'Can you tell me more about her? Please?'

Her eyebrows rose. 'Celeste?'

'That's what you named her?' His voice was hoarse.

'Yeah, it means heavenly.'

His eyes remained closed for a moment. 'That's perfect. Celeste,' he murmured before opening his glassy eyes that shimmered in the fairy lights.

'I'd lie awake, trying to feel her move. Most nights I'd sing, hoping she'd hear me.'

'What did you sing?' he asked gently.

'A few John Butler favourites,' she said, unable to stop her grin.

'What did ... where ... Um, sorry, I don't want to push you if you're not ready.'

She knew what he wanted to know.

'It's been hard. I stopped nursing because that's where it happened, and I couldn't handle seeing happy mums ... I felt so lost, and like it was all my fault.' Her voice faded away. 'But I've done a lot of work to move forward and I want to remember Celeste and talk about her. I have her ashes at home.

Ingi wanted to hold a little memorial, but I couldn't part with them, and I was hardly functioning so I haven't done it yet. Also, it wouldn't feel right without you there.'

Fin sat quietly for a moment, his breaths even. 'Thank you, I'd like to be there when you do decide to spread her ashes.' He smoothed out his beard with one stroke before asking, 'Ellen, could we catch up for a coffee sometime?'

'If . . . if you're sure?'

His Adam's apple bounced as he swallowed slowly. 'Did you mean what you said in your letter?'

She frowned, wondering what part he meant. 'I meant all of it, Murray.' Surely, he could tell how much she still loved him, how she seemed to drown in his eyes and melt at his touch? 'I still do.'

His eyes dropped to her lips as he reached for her hands again. 'I was hoping you'd say that. I knew the moment I got your letter that I was still in love with you, and to see you tonight in that dress . . . I knew for certain there's no one else for me. It's like I'm magnetised to you. I think about you all the time, and when I see you, I just want to be near you and listen to you talk, watch the way your body moves, your expressions. I can't get enough of you. Even after all we've been through, I can't give up on us.'

She had no words. Her mind was filled with images of his face as his softly spoken words 'I can't give up on us' echoed on repeat in her mind.

His hand cupped her cheek and she closed her eyes. Would she wake up any minute and find this was all a fantasy?

The tickle of beard then his lips against hers had her hands reaching for him. He pulled her close and their lips parted as they clung together in a tight embrace, her head resting on his shoulder as she breathed him in.

'I love you, Ellen. Please don't leave again.'

She gripped his shirt as if clinging on for dear life. She was the one who should be begging him to stay. And for his forgiveness.

Her heart raced against his but she pulled away so she could see his eyes, so he knew she was making him a promise she intended to keep. Her fingers stroked his beard, before sliding behind his neck. 'I'm not going anywhere. I'm home for good.' She kissed him, and it was deep and sensual, and it felt like some of the broken pieces of her heart had clicked back into place.

Murray was right. Tomorrow was unknown, right now was all that mattered.

Epilogue

'HELLO, MY BABY GIRL,' WHISPERED ELLEN AS SHE GAZED down at the little silver urn. *Your wings were ready but my heart was not,* engraved on the front.

Fin put his arm around her and tucked her in tight to his side.

He glanced down at Ellen as she tried unsuccessfully to hold back tears. Her hands rested on her belly, the familiar slight bump felt so beautiful. This time round she wasn't taking anything for granted and cherished every moment. Deep down she knew this baby would not leave her. Maybe it was the constant reassurance from Fin and her family, but she truly did believe it.

'Aunty Carrie sends her love from Broome.' Carrie had made her promise to say something on her behalf when they got off the phone yesterday.

'I wish I could be there with you,' Carrie had said. Hans had returned to his homeland after hearing his dad was sick, with no idea of a return date. But Carrie was contented travelling solo these days. Mingling with children from all walks of life and volunteering where she could, selling her photos online and living like a nomad chasing that perfect shot.

'I can't believe how much her photos have taken off.'

'She always had a great eye. Mum is so delighted. She knew someone would take after her. Of course it's all thanks to her that Carrie's work is being recognised.'

'Jealous?' he asked, giving her a nudge.

Ellen smiled. 'Not at all. I think we all have what we've always wanted. Love, fulfilment and purpose.'

She glanced back down at the water's edge, waves lapping at their feet. 'I can't believe it's been over two years. Some days it feels like yesterday I felt her moving around. I guess it's easy to think that now this one has started to move.'

Her mum was going to use the little silver urn to make a keepsake for them, a memorial they could put at their new home. It was being built out near Fin's boutique brewery where they had acres of space for pet sheep and cows, plus chickens and dogs. El couldn't be happier, giving her future kids the freedom she'd had growing up.

Life had been ticking along, and the brewery was in full swing. Fin's dad was even selling his beer at the White Pearl, which was helping build its name. Finlay Ridge Brewing – a combination of the farm Fair Ridge, where the grain was sourced, and of course Fin's last name. Ellen had loved collaborating on the logo and design for the brewery and outdoor beer garden. They had planned for growth, anticipating a full restaurant in the future and live concerts. One day they might even host John Butler Trio.

'It's a perfect day,' said Lorraine.

Their family stood beside them, her mum and dad one side and Bodhi and Ingi with her hand on her belly. She wasn't showing yet and it was still early days, but far enough along that the family all knew.

Ingi and Bodhi had approached her cousin Sam from her dad's side, and asked if she'd be an egg donor for them. She'd said yes, and things had gone pretty smoothly, despite a busy schedule of tests and treatments and lots of waiting around in doctors' rooms. But Ingi had taken it all in her stride like a pro. Bodhi had also taken on the running of the family sparky business – he'd finally plucked up the courage to ask his dad. Much to his disbelief, Colin had been delighted, something about wanting to play more bowls instead of doing paperwork.

Ellen had taken a while to get back to nursing – it had been a gradual toe in the water until she could walk the corridor without the lingering memories. She was more in a part-time role now, dividing her time between the brewery and nursing. She'd also been taking courses on management and hospitality, and Ingi had been talking her through running a restaurant and what kind of meals they would eventually serve at Finlay Ridge Brewing. All preparation for the future. She'd need to have all of this under her belt before their child arrived because, as her mum reminded her often, *You won't have time to scratch yourself once the baby's born.*

'Are you ready?' asked Fin, squeezing her closer to his side. Ellen nodded. *Yes, it was time.*

Fin opened the lid of the urn, giving it a gentle shake as the ashes caught on the breeze and drifted out across the waves, dropping lower and lower until they'd been sucked into the ocean.

Ellen leaned her head on Fin's shoulder. She closed her eyes, remembering the day Celeste was born. It wasn't as painful now, but she'd never be pain-free. Sometimes bad things happened, but that didn't have to mean the end of the journey. There was always new growth after a fire.

Thanks to Celeste, they were all trying to live each day the best they could.

Acknowledgements

LAST YEAR OUR FAMILY STOPPED AT KARIJINI AND CHALLA Station on our way to Karratha. Such amazing places to experience and I knew straight away that I *needed* to write both places into a story. The next step was coming up with the plot, and eventually the Sutton family was born.

Firstly, I must thank Ashley and Debbie Dowden for their wonderful hospitality at Challa, the sunsets, tours and allowing me to write you guys into the book. Amazing people, and I'm so glad I got to meet Debbie through the RRR Network. Our daughter also spent time at Challa mustering when she was seventeen: a special memory that will stay with her forever. (Hopefully one day I will be back for mustering. I can just see myself in one of those buggies!)

To Lyn Tranter, my agent from the beginning, thank you for everything you have done for me over the last ten or so years. Usually handling the hard stuff so I can just worry about the easy bits.

Hachette publisher extraordinaire, Rebecca Saunders, for believing in me, especially on those days I don't believe in myself. Thank you. There is a wonderful team at Hachette – thank you to all who have worked their magic on this book, especially Senior Editor Karen Ward, Campaign Manager Kirstin Corcoran, Publicist Ailie Springall, Rights Manager Emma Dorph, and also Dianne Blacklock for the copy edits which always challenge me to look at my work with new eyes.

My writing buddies Rachael Johns and Anthea Hodgson who are my lifeline in this writing caper: you guys are the best. You listen, offer superb advice, and keep me entertained and laughing, even on down days. (Also Possum and Addy, who deserve honourable mentions.)

To my dearest friends, new and old, some who only hear from me in a blue moon as life just seems so busy. Thank you for always being there and picking up where we left off. Life only seems to get busier and fly by faster, which means absences, but it doesn't mean I love you any less.

Booksellers and readers, a huge thank you for all your support. Receiving personal messages from readers is the highlight during the long days of writing, as well as seeing my book on a beautiful display in a store.

Also, my apologies if this story was triggering for some. I hope Ellen's journey helps others understand just how painful and heart-wrenching it is to lose a baby. I send you my biggest embrace and love. A massive, massive thanks to a very dear friend who let me ask questions so I could better understand. Thank you for sharing. I love you lots and will not forget.

Lastly, to my family. Their love and support make writing books easier. If my son hadn't been racing in the speedway state title in Karratha, I never would have seen Karijini so soon. I plan to go back and explore more as there just wasn't enough time. I love writing books about the places I've seen, highlighting some amazing towns and sights in our state. And I hope my readers love it too. It's been about fifteen years since I first put pen to paper . . . for those who have been with me from the start, THANK YOU!

hachette
AUSTRALIA

If you would like to find out more about Hachette Australia, our authors, upcoming events and new releases, you can visit our website or our social media channels:

hachette.com.au

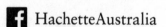 HachetteAustralia

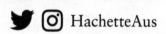 HachetteAus

Before becoming an author, **Fiona Palmer** was a speedway driver for seven years and now spends her days writing both women's and young adult fiction, working as a farmhand and caring for her two children in the tiny rural community of Pingaring, 350km from Perth. The books Fiona's passionate readers know and love contain engaging storylines, emotions and hearty characters. Her novels are consistently Top 10 national bestsellers.

fionapalmer.com  fiona_palmer
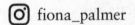 fiona_palmer  FionaPalmerAuthor

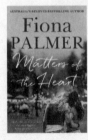 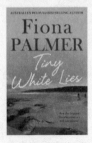